SIPHON

A CAYDEN MARCH THRILLER

P.G. KASSEL

Storyteller Works

ISBN: 978-0-9967919-5-3

Library of Congress Control Number: 2023912334

Storyteller Works

Los Angeles, CA

Cover Design by Stuart Bache

ACKNOWLEDGEMENT

Many thanks to my friend, and former Special Operator, who will remain nameless here for obvious reasons. His guidance, patience, and invaluable information made this book possible.

PROLOGUE

The commotion jarred Alan Fenland's attention away from the mostly eaten cheeseburger sitting on his desk. Nobody ever ran in the Powell-Booth Laboratory building, so the sound of rapid footsteps echoing in from the hallway came across as downright clamorous. And then there was the slamming door, like a gunshot. Alan nudged the burger into the trash can beside his desk and climbed out of his chair. The computer lab scheduling office sat between two hallways, with doors providing access from either. The doorway leading into the east hall was open, so he headed for it.

He stepped into the hallway, swiveling his head in both directions. A couple of students chatted as they entered a room down the corridor. There was no sign of what had caused the racket. He saw nothing out of the ordinary at all. More footsteps sounded, not running this time, but moving fast. Alan hurried down the hall to the adjoining corridor and looked around the corner. Nothing to see there, either. He waited a few moments to see if the culprit would run by again, but the only sound was the quiet clacking of fingers against keyboards. With a shrug, he headed back to his office, deciding to take the west hallway to see if the disturbance might be coming from there.

It took him less than a minute to reach his office again, and his mind lamented the burger he'd chucked as he stepped to the door. So, when the door burst open, it startled the heck out of him. A man he didn't recognize hurried out, almost bowling him over. There was something about the guy that felt off, but Alan couldn't quite put his finger on what. He was a late thirty-something with dark hair, and he wore a casual sport coat and khakis. Nothing about him stood out except a small egg-shaped birthmark just above his left eyebrow.

Most people on the Caltech campus were easy to label. Students, professors, researchers, even office staff—most of them projected a subtle sense of comfortable familiarity. But not this guy. Alan thought he looked very out of place. Without saying a word, the man pushed past him and sprinted toward the exit at the end of the hall. Weird.

Frowning, Alan walked back into the office and took a careful look around. He had no idea why some random guy would be in his office. He was just a graduate student, one of six part-time people who helped students and professors schedule computer time. There was nothing valuable to steal in the room, and there was no sensitive research stored here.

He found nothing out of place, and the east door was still open. Alan walked across the office, stepped into the hallway for a final look, and stopped in his tracks.

Hurrying toward him at a brisk pace was another man in his thirties with dark hair and an olive complexion. He moved with confidence, like a panther tracking prey. The man with the birth-mark had been running. Maybe this guy was chasing him. Panther guy paused the moment he saw Alan. His brown lambskin leather jacket looked pretty slick over his designer jeans and dark paisley shirt. The man made no attempt at a greeting, and he offered no smile. His unwavering gaze made Alan feel as if he was a pig in a pen, and the farmer was trying to decide if he'd be the next slab of bacon.

He didn't appear like he belonged on campus any more than

the trespasser with the birthmark. Without a word, the man pivoted and hurried down the hallway toward the lobby. Alan watched until the stranger disappeared. The entire encounter had taken a matter of seconds, and left Alan wondering, *"What the hell?"* With no answers forthcoming, he stepped back into his office.

The clock on the office wall showed 3:00 p.m. and that meant quitting time. Ingrid, the girl who followed his shift, hadn't arrived yet. It didn't matter. She'd be along soon enough, and if anybody needed help, they'd wait for her. Alan gathered up his backpack, stuffed his books and lab notes inside, and headed out into the chilly December afternoon.

His place was walking distance from campus, and during the stroll home, he reflected on a day that had not been one of his greatest. His only class that morning could have been best described as a total embarrassment. The professor, one of Caltech's finest, had found Alan's approach to solving this week's quantum conundrum to be less than brilliant. The old academic had taken his time, painfully picking apart his methodology.

Alan's meeting with his graduate advisor turned out to be a major ball-buster as well. The man found what he described as an "irregularity in logic" in the most recently completed section of Alan's dissertation. What on Earth did that mean?

Sometimes it felt like he'd never see the sheepskin. The plan was to complete the master's in science program, get into the quantum optics program, and begin work on his doctorate. His goal was to get his PhD before his twenty-eighth birthday, but he was already behind his self-imposed schedule.

Oh well. His little bungalow was now in view, and he looked forward to kicking back with a little TV before dinner. One of his premium channels was streaming *Suicide Squad*. He loved Margot Robbie, and there was no doubt in his mind that Margot would be attracted to a guy with a PhD. Less than ten minutes after walking through his door and kicking off his shoes, he sprawled out on his old but comfortable sofa with a Corona and a bag of Fritos.

About two hours after he landed on the couch, his tonally challenged doorbell announced someone at the door. A quick glance at his watch told him it was 5:30, too darn late to deal with a cable salesman trying to convince him to change his service. He glanced toward the door, but ignored it. He just wanted to relax. Maybe they'd go away.

After the doorbell repeated its discordant clang for the fourth time, Alan groaned in frustration. The visitor didn't seem inclined to leave him in peace. He picked up the remote and thumbed down the volume, reducing the explosions and screams of the bad guys to a whisper. Tossing the remote back on the cushions, he trudged to the door and wrenched it open, prepared to launch a verbal attack that would send whoever was on the other side packing.

Except no sound came out of his mouth. He just stood there like a fish, his eyes open wide, his mouth opening and closing, wondering why the universe had placed such a pleasant surprise on his doorstep.

She looked to be in her late twenties, one or two inches shy of six feet. Her brushed denim skirt was as short as her legs were long; her breasts were a perfect fit for the rest of her. Her hair fell just below her ears with an attractive shagginess, multi-colored in reddish and orange tones. A purse dangled from a strap draped over her shoulder. Alan would have sworn her gray eyes twinkled as her full lips formed a charming smile. "Hi. Sorry to bug you. Hoping you can help me."

What the heck, Alan thought. Margot could wait.

T he Fenland guy lived in a little California-style bungalow on one of Pasadena's wooded streets less than a mile from the California Institute of Technology campus. Danny had gotten out of the car a half-block away, and Cyn proceeded on her own, parking in front of Fenland's house. A little quiver of excitement washed over her. This was going to be fun.

His expression as he opened the door amused her. She was used to that look, especially with this type of guy, but she still got a kick out of it. He wore the unofficial uniform of the geek: worn jeans and a long-sleeve pullover shirt with a graphic from one of the *Avenger* flicks screened onto the front. He appreciated her legs, fighting to keep his eyes focused up where they should be.

"What's up?" he asked with genuine warmth.

"Sorry to bother you. My car, it won't start, and my cell isn't working. Could I use your phone?"

He looked over her shoulder at the Chevy compact parked at the curb.

"I've got zero signal here," she embellished.

"I'm not much of a mechanic, but I can take a look for you," he said, his eyes heading south again.

"No, that's okay. If I can just call the rental company, they'll take care of it."

"Oh, okay."

"So, can I use your phone?"

He must have realized he was still staring. "Sure. Of course. Come on in."

He pulled the door open so she could enter. She paused just inside, closing the door behind her as he walked toward his cell phone sitting on a side table at the far end of the couch.

"Alan," she called to him.

He turned around as she caught up to him, his face masked with confusion, wondering how she knew his name. This was her favorite part. The part where he'd go from thinking he might get lucky to realizing that he never had a chance. She smiled in anticipation, and she could see him relax again as he fixated on it. Before he even knew what was happening, she lunged forward with a quick jab, striking him in the larynx with her middle knuckle.

His hands grasped at his throat as he dropped to the floor and rolled onto his side, a harsh gurgling sound escaping his bluing lips as he struggled to take in air.

Pulling on a pair of latex gloves from her purse, Cyn stepped back to the front door and locked it. She then strolled into the kitchen and unlocked the back door. Danny, the name he was using for this job, stood waiting. Already gloved, he slipped into the room, still looking hot in his jacket, jeans, and Nat Nash paisley shirt. He closed the door, locking it behind him.

Cyn always marveled at Danny's instincts and efficiency. Back at the Caltech campus he had told her where to wait, promising to chase the CIA guy straight to her. And as sure as people bleed when you cut them, mister CIA ran right into her arms. Technically, he ran into her fist as she stepped into his path. It knocked him out cold without a struggle.

When Danny had caught up, they carried the guy to their car and zip-cuffed him to the grab handle built into the door. Nobody appeared to notice them on the way. After injecting him with a little cocktail to loosen him up, Cyn questioned the man, judiciously using her knife to help things along. Once she knew he wasn't about to give her a thing, they drove him to a spot near the Rose Bowl, killed him, and dumped his body in the foliage.

During the campus pursuit, Danny had spotted this Fenland guy stepping out of an office. Based on the kid's behavior, he thought it possible mister CIA had been in there. Danny hurried back to Fenland's office. He didn't find the flash drive, but he did find the kid's name and address on a posted work contact sheet. So, here they were.

"Where is he?" Danny asked.

"Front room." She rubbed up against him, giving him a firm kiss.

"I'll get started," he said, breaking away from her and walking out of the room.

She began opening the kitchen drawers. The third drawer she tried yielded an item that would do just fine, a metal barbecue skewer about a foot long with a wooden grip. It still had a few specks of charred grease on it.

Danny was searching the living room when she ambled back in. He opened every drawer, every cabinet, moving systematically through the room, conducting the search just the way he'd taught her.

Alan, now lying on his back, his hands still grasped to his throat, did his painful best to draw in some oxygen. She straddled him, standing over him while she ran her fingers up and down the barbecue skewer.

"Being a leg man, how's this angle working for you, Alan?"

His eyes stared up at her, clouded with confusion and fear.

Danny breathed an audible sigh, laced with annoyance.

She smiled down at the grad student. "I know you were looking before."

Alan managed a feeble shake of his head.

"Did I remember to put on a thong today, Alan?"

"Cyn," Danny hissed, his tone reproving. "Come on."

She looked down at Alan, feigning a pout. "Really, I can't remember."

Danny swung around toward her. "Stop screwing around and get on with it."

She dropped to her knees, the skirt riding up her thighs.

"Don't mind him, Alan. He can be a real buzzkill sometimes."

She dropped the skewer to the carpet next to her and pried his hands away from his throat, pinning his arms beneath her knees. "Okay, here's your question," she said, retrieving the skewer. "A man gave you a little flash drive this afternoon. Where is it?"

He looked confused, again shaking his head.

"We already went through your office. It's not there. So, it's gotta be with you, hon," she continued.

"No," he gasped.

"No, what?"

"I don't have anything," Alan gasped.

She stroked her fingers over the barbecue skewer one more

time, then positioned it with the pointed end centered over his left eye. He began struggling, jerking his head from side to side.

"Uncomfortable?" she asked, not caring about his answer. "Here."

She adjusted her position, moving forward so her knees locked around his head, preventing him from turning it. Her skirt covered his face, and she had to bunch it up around her waist to get it out of the way.

She lowered the point of the skewer a couple of inches closer to his eye. "Where is it?"

"Don't know what you're talking about," he panted, his voice rising in pitch.

"No man? No flash drive?"

He closed his eyes tight as she lowered the skewer. She let the point rest against his eyelid for a few seconds before pulling it back an inch or two.

"Some guy ran through my office this afternoon, but I never saw him before."

"The man gave you something," she pushed. "He won't mind if you tell me. He's dead."

"I don't know what you're talking about." Alan forced the words out in a desperate gasp.

Cyn felt confident that she'd gotten at least part of what she needed. Through his fear, the truth was there. She had become very good at this kind of thing, and she could tell when somebody was feeding her a line of crap.

"I don't think he has it," she reported to Danny.

He paused in the bedroom doorway, glancing across the room at her. "All right," was all he had to say, stepping through the doorway.

She sighed. "Well, hon, guess we're done here."

She lowered the skewer again. Alan shut his eyes tight, as if expecting armored protection from the closed lids, and began thrashing beneath her. As the point met the center of the eyelid, a scream began deep in his chest. Her hand clamped across his mouth as she jammed the skewer downward with substantial force. It penetrated the lid and continued down through the eye into the brain. She placed both hands over the skewer's wooden handle and pushed down until the point reached the back of his skull.

His body bucked under her. It was taking too long, so she moved the skewer around a little, as if stirring a thick stew. He grew quiet, and the thrashing gradually subsided. His body twitched beneath her for almost a minute before it was still. She stood up and straightened out her skirt.

"For God's sake, Cynthia." Danny walked in from the bedroom, looking down at the body. Blood pooled in the eye socket and oozed down the cheek.

She shrugged. "I like to try new things."

"Give me a hand with the rest of the place. Just to make certain."

"Sure." She stepped over the body. "But it's not here."

CHAPTER ONE

They finished the first chorus of "Take It Easy" and were moving into the second verse when Cayden March saw the trouble begin. He was sitting in, playing rhythm guitar and singing back vocals with one of the cover bands that often played the Bicycle Bell Saloon. From his position on stage, he had a good view of the rustic, brick-walled room. He spotted the two grinning guys, both in their late twenties, approaching a girl with long, sandy-blonde hair perched on a stool at the old mahogany bar. Each had a bottle of beer in hand, and they walked as if they'd been tossing them back for a while.

The girl, Kate James, was a friend of his. The two guys didn't concern him. Kate could handle herself. But all the same, he monitored the situation. He always looked out for her. She looked especially pretty tonight in bell-bottom jeans, as usual, a cream-colored shirt, and moccasin boots. Her suede, fringed coat lay across the bar stool next to her. Kate wasn't one to follow current fashion; her tastes aligned more with sixties hippie styles more than anything else.

The two guys were now standing next to her. Friendly by nature, she chatted with them. Cayden knew the guys were bound for disappointment. His friend never picked up men at bars, especially drunk men. As the lead guitarist transitioned into a solo, one of the guys moved a little closer to Kate and put an arm around her shoulder. Kate said something to him, and he withdrew his arm.

They continued talking, but now Kate's body language spoke caution. The two guys seemed fine with keeping their distance. It all stayed cool as Cayden leaned into the microphone to sing a tenor harmony in the final chorus. But by the time he began the tag, the handsy guy invaded Kate's space again. This time, he pushed his body against her and leaned down to kiss her cheek.

With impressive swiftness, Kate slipped off the bar stool, stomping down hard on the cheek kisser's foot. He emitted a painful cry that no man in his right mind would want heard around other men. His friend looked surprised as Kate backed away from them. Cayden knew Kate intended her foot stomp to be the end of it. But now, anger showed all over the kissy guy's face, and he moved toward her.

As he closed in, Kate launched a snap kick that landed center on his solar plexus. Doubled over and gasping for breath, he stumbled backward, losing his balance and going down. Cayden couldn't help grinning. Kate's three years of kick boxing lessons, and all that sparring time with him was paying off.

The second guy on Team Stupid saw his friend go down, and began yelling at Kate, shaking his fist in her face.

On the last chord of the song, Cayden muted his guitar and placed it on its stand. The house bouncer was making his way toward the commotion, but he was still across the busy room. Cayden was closer. He stepped down to the floor and hurried toward the bar. With the band no longer playing, and the patrons stopping conversation to see what the commotion was all about, the room quieted.

As he reached the bar, Kate took a step away from the cheek-kisser's friend. "Why don't we call it even?" she tried to reason with him.

The drunk's response was to make a fist and draw his arm

back for a punch. Cayden shook his head in disbelief; this guy intended to strike a woman in the face. Before he could swing, Cayden gripped the drunk's wrist in both hands, then stepped back while twisting downward. He let go when gravity took over and the guy hit the floor screaming, landing just a few feet from his friend.

Cayden looked up to see Kate glaring at him. With the adrenaline still flowing, her breathing was fast and deep. The house bouncer, a big muscular guy in his late twenties, stepped in beside Cayden.

"I couldn't have done that any better," he said, pointing at the two guys on the floor.

"If anything's broken, I'll pay for it. It's well worth it," Kate said, retrieving her coat from the stool.

"If anything's broken, these two idiots will pay for it." The bouncer took the cheek-kisser by the forearm and pulled him over beside his friend. "Time to leave," he told them, dragging them to their feet and escorting them as they limped toward the exit.

Cayden offered Kate his most charming smile. "First bar fight?"

"You could tell?" she asked, her voice a little shaky.

The noise level in the room returned to normal as he ushered her toward an empty table at the side of the room. "You had that first bar fight glow."

Kate hung her coat over the back of the chair, and they sat down. The Bicycle Bell had become a comfortable hangout for them. Cayden discovered it first, drawn to the room's good-sized stage and excellent PA system. The saloon also featured an open mic night each Monday. Once the management had become familiar with him and his musicianship, he was welcome to use the stage whenever he liked. He'd spent many hours there, jamming with other musically inclined friends.

Kate fixed a stony gaze on him. "I didn't need any help."

"Maybe not, but that guy was about to punch you in the face. Very unchivalrous."

"They were just drunk."

"Yep. But what would your PhD committee say if they found out one of their top candidates took part in a bar brawl?"

She rolled her eyes, but Cayden caught the hint of a smile on her lips. At a university overflowing with exceptional, bright people, Kate James was a supernova. No stranger to accelerated programs throughout her youth, she graduated from high school at sixteen and Caltech was happy to accept her into their undergraduate program. She earned her master's in mechanical engineering and then got bored and switched to computer science. The change made perfect sense; she was a gifted hacker. Now, at age twenty-six, Kate James was in the middle of her doctorate program.

The familiar awkwardness surfaced in him as he sat across from her. Kate was his type, but she was also his best friend's little sister. Besides, she never displayed that kind of interest in him.

Kate sighed. "You don't have to keep an eye on me all the time."

"Okay. But I—"

"Yeah, yeah," Kate interrupted. "You promised Rob."

Cayden turned his gaze across the room to the band on stage, preparing for their next set. The mention of Rob James always triggered melancholy in him.

"Cayden," Kate said, drawing his attention back to her. "My brother didn't expect you to take that promise to heart like you have."

She didn't know just how seriously he had taken the promise. After leaving the military, he'd returned to Pasadena. The first thing he did was look her up. Their first conversation was hard for him. She was still grieving the loss of her brother. He explained how he'd met Rob when they were both stationed in Stuttgart, Germany. He described how they'd grown to be best friends. And then he told her how he had died.

"You going to say anything?" Kate sounded annoyed.

"Rob was your last surviving relative. Your parents are gone. It can't hurt to have somebody looking after you."

Kate gazed at him for several seconds and then leaned closer to him, her elbows on the table. "You didn't kill my brother, Cay."

His body tensed, and now he wanted to be anywhere else but at this table, talking to Kate about her brother. "I didn't pull the trigger, but—"

"And you weren't responsible for it, either," she interrupted.

Cayden felt his palms become slick with sweat, and he rubbed them against his jeans. "He was under my command. Nobody else put him in harm's way. I did. He shouldn't have been there."

"He volunteered to go with you." Kate sounded exasperated.

"I shouldn't have allowed it."

Kate slumped back in her chair, looking at him with sad eyes. "Cayden."

Taking advantage of the conversation lull, he looked at his watch. "It's getting late, and I have to work tomorrow. I'll walk you to your car."

"Okay, but you don't have to be my guardian angel."

The morning following Kate's bar skirmish, Cayden maintained an easy running pace as he turned onto his narrow, shady street. At an inch over six feet, his long legs covered a fair amount of ground with each stride. As often as possible, he ran in the morning before getting ready for work. His running clothes kept him warm against the atypical chilly December air. California weather was normally mild during the holiday season, but this year had been wet and cold. Cayden slowed to a walk as his house came into view.

It rested in a ravine at the edge of the Arroyo Seco, a 1923 Frank Lloyd Wright creation on a heavily treed crescent. An exotic melding of textile concrete block, rich wood, and ironwork, the house was reminiscent of a weathered Mayan temple set in a jungle of eucalyptus and sycamore. He loved the house. It had belonged to his grandparents and was full of good memories.

When he was ten years old, Cayden's mother had died in a car accident. His grandparents missed and grieved their daughter, and they seemed to find comfort in having Cayden spend as much time with them as possible. And he found comfort in being with them. His father loved him but was always busy, and not the warmest of men. Only a superficial connection existed between them. Cayden welcomed any opportunity to stay with his grandparents.

His grandmother passed away a few months after he returned home from the service. His grandfather became ill only a few months later, so Cayden gave up his studio apartment and moved into the spacious house to better care for him. They'd always shared a special bond, and during this period, that bond grew stronger than before. Five months after becoming ill, his grandfather caught pneumonia, dying a week later.

His grandfather left the house to him, and in the trust, expressed wishes he keep the property in the family. Cayden took those wishes seriously.

He stopped by the mailbox at the edge of his driveway to retrieve yesterday's mail, sorting through it as he strolled to the front door. Buried between the real estate agent advertisements and coupon cards was a green envelope. A Christmas card. He knew who the sender was even before tearing open the envelope. As always, the card was expensive and tasteful, bearing a politically correct *Happy Holidays* greeting. The signature inside read, *Dad*. Cayden recognized the handwriting. It showed progress; his secretary didn't sign it this year.

He'd thought of calling his father with the idea that they would get together for Christmas. The thought occurred to him every year, but he never acted on it. It was supposed to be a time for families to gather, but theirs wasn't a simple relationship, and it had been several years since they'd seen each other.

Cayden was about to toss the mail on the side table near the door when he spotted another envelope. The return address read County of Los Angeles. He felt a sinking feeling just looking at it. Separating it from the pile, he dropped the rest of the mail on the table and opened it. It was what he thought it was, his property tax bill. The last property assessment valued the house at $4.5 million. The annual property taxes on that came to over $30,000. Along with the house, his grandfather had left him some cash to help pay the taxes and cover any required repairs or refurbishments. The money helped at first, but so much of it went to necessary repairs it became more challenging to pay the taxes with each passing year.

This year, Cayden was short by a little more than half. As he stared at the bill his mind began looking for solutions, but none were coming. There was nothing he could do about it now. He had to get to work.

CHAPTER TWO

The lighted paths and area lights gave the Caltech campus a soft glow. Students and faculty headed toward night classes or laboratories, keeping the walkways busy. Cayden emerged from the locker room, joining the rest of the Caltech folks on the path. He always changed out of his uniform at the end of his shift, preferring to wear his own clothes when he left campus.

He worked as a security officer for the university. *Security Officer* was the official title, but he was just a security guard. Well, he was a little more than just a security guard. The Chief of Security, Raymond Chalmers, had promoted him to second-in-command of the security force less than a year after Cayden started the job. And he was one of only three guards on the force, including Raymond, certified and licensed to carry a weapon. His Beretta 92 Elite LLT Compact was holstered on his belt, concealed under his coat.

He glanced at his watch as he walked back to the security office. It was almost 5:30 p.m. He was right on time. He'd clock out and head home. As he walked, Cayden mulled over his property tax problem. It was his own fault, partly. He could have taken a job with one of the elite security firms protecting political dignitaries, celebrities, or visiting royalty. He'd had offers. And then there were the independent military contractors that provided high-end security in hot spots around the world. Either of those options would pay him five times what he was earning at Caltech. But with those jobs, he would be responsible for people's lives again. He didn't want to do that anymore. He couldn't do that anymore.

Cayden was certain of what he didn't want to do, but figuring out what he should do was a greater challenge. After leaving the military, he felt lost when he returned to Pasadena. He didn't have plans; he didn't feel like doing anything. When the security job opened up at Caltech, it provided a simple solution. There would be no life or death situations at the university, and Rob's sister took classes and worked on campus. It made his decision to take the job easy. He'd be close enough to Kate to ensure she was doing okay.

His cell phone began ringing. Pulling it from his pants pocket, he saw Ray Chalmers' grumpy photo on the caller ID.

"Where are you?" Raymond's voice crackled from the cell, bristling with irritation.

"Hey, Raymond. What's up?" He always answered his boss's indignant greetings with an upbeat response. Most of the time it diffused Ray, at least a little.

"What's up? Where in blazes are you?"

"I'm a half block from the security office. What do you need?"

"I didn't ask how far away you are," Raymond barked. "One of our part-time guys was making the rounds and saw police activity on a campus property on Oakdale. A lot of activity."

"And you want me to check it out." Cayden had a friend who lived on Oakdale and wondered if the activity was near his house.

"Of course I want you to check it out. They wouldn't tell our guy a thing."

"I'm supposed to clock out in two minutes."

"You can clock out for good if you don't get your butt over there right now," Raymond said.

"You have an address?" Cayden asked.

"No, I don't have an address. Just look for the house with all the police cars. And call me once you know something. Now get going and pick up some overtime."

He would've gone anyway, but overtime was definitely something he could use.

"On my way."

The connection went dead.

CHAPTER THREE

Cayden spotted the red and blue flashing lights two blocks away. The police had blocked off most of the street to traffic. Not a good sign. He parked his Toyota 4Runner around the corner and hurried back to Oakdale Street. He was keen to see if the police activity was anywhere near his friend's house.

Most of the houses on the block were decked out with their Christmas finest. The damp mist hovering in the air created a soft halo around the multi-colored lights strung along their perimeters. Nearing the police vehicles, a knot tightened in his gut. The police weren't near his friend's house; they were in his driveway and on his front lawn. He quickened his pace, hoping that Alan wasn't in any trouble.

The part-time security guard who called it in was nowhere to be seen as Cayden neared the property, but plenty of neighborhood residents had gathered near the barricades. Others watched from their front lawns or porches.

Cayden reached the barricade just as a city ambulance pulled up. He already knew by the overwhelming police presence that this was more than a break-in, but the ambulance arrived with no siren. No siren, no need to rush. The knot in his stomach tightened even more. A rugged looking policewoman dragged the end of the barricade, opening a space for the ambulance to pull through before moving it back into position.

She kept a watchful eye on the crowd from the front of her patrol car, and Cayden offered a friendly smile as he approached her. "Evening, officer. I'm Cayden March. I'm a security officer at Caltech."

The policewoman glanced at his identification with an impressive amount of indifference, but didn't bother with a reply.

He waited for a response, a smile, anything, but only got a blank stare. "Caltech owns this house," he continued. "Can you tell me what's going on?"

"We've got a crime scene and an investigation underway."

"Somebody hurt?" Cayden pointed toward the ambulance.

"There's nothing I can tell you, sir. Have your office call the department later tonight. Maybe they can help you then."

Sometimes people who insisted on doing their job could be a real pain in the ass. He was about to try a different approach when an olive-complexioned man wearing a well cut blue suit emerged from Alan's front door. Cayden recognized him. Detective Anthony Mandala had conducted a couple of informal crime prevention seminars for Caltech, a cooperative effort between the security office and the Pasadena Police Department to ensure student safety on campus.

"Detective," Cayden called out, lifting a hand in the air to draw Mandala's attention to him.

The detective's face registered a flicker of recognition and headed toward the barricade. From the few times Cayden had met him, he knew Mandala was friendly enough, but all business when it came to his job.

"Detective Mandala," Cayden offered a handshake and then his ID. "I'm with Caltech security. We met the last couple of times you were on campus."

"Sure," Mandala said. "You're Ray Chalmers's guy."

Cayden nodded toward Alan's house. "Caltech owns this property. Can you tell me what's going on?"

Mandala kept his eyes on Cayden, but didn't offer a reply. After an endless moment, he gestured to the policewoman. She treated Cayden with a thin smile and stepped back, creating a passage between the patrol car and the barricade.

Mandala watched him closely. "Did Ray send you?"

"He did. And the guy who rents this house is a friend of mine."

"How good a friend?" the detective asked.

"Very good." Cayden wondered if his growing anxiety was leaching into his voice. "If he's hurt, I'd appreciate knowing."

Mandala drew in a breath, then released it slowly. "The man inside is dead. We found a wallet on the end table next to the sofa. It belongs to an Alan Fenland. Is that your friend?"

Cayden's throat went dry. "Yes."

"We've got his driver's license photo, but would you be willing to take a look?"

"Yeah, okay."

He fell into step with Mandala, who was already walking up the lawn to the front steps.

The detective stopped on the front porch, placing a restraining hand on Cayden's arm. "Before we go inside, your friend was murdered. Are you up for that?"

Ice formed in Cayden's veins. "Murdered? Who'd want to kill Alan? He was one of the nicest people I know." Cayden realized he'd just blurted out a question Mandala couldn't answer. The apprehension he'd felt when first seeing Alan's house surrounded by police grew by leaps and bounds.

"I'm sorry," the detective responded. "Ready to go inside?"

Cayden nodded.

"Don't touch anything and watch where you step."

"Understood."

Mandala led the way into the bungalow, maneuvering past members of the Pasadena Police Department's CSI team. A lab photographer was clicking away with a digital camera, recording every inch of the murder room. The medical examiner stood beside the body, a clipboard in his hand, jotting down notes on a form.

Cayden had seen more than his share of death. He had seen friends cut down by automatic weapons fire. He had seen comrades blown into plasma by bombs rigged in the most insidious ways. But looking down at Alan's corpse, a knot of anger formed in his gut. This was twisted in a way he'd never seen. A barbecue skewer jutted obscenely from his friend's eye socket. Dry blood streaked across his pale skin. His mouth was frozen in a grimace of pain, and there was an ugly, swollen bruise just above the base of the throat.

"Forensics set time of death sometime yesterday afternoon or early evening," Mandala said, his voice soft.

The detective's words sounded muffled and distant, as though they were spoken under water. Cayden recognized his reaction. Shock. Alan was one of the sweetest, funniest guys he had ever come across. He never hesitated to do a kindness for someone, friend or no friend. Cayden'd spent some of his best times in Alan's company.

Whoever had done this to him took pleasure in it.

"Is that Alan Fenland?" Mandala asked.

"Yes." Cayden's mouth set in a grim line as he shook away the shock and sadness he felt before looking over Alan's body again. He didn't like the signs he was seeing, and his eyes scanned the rest of the room to cement his theory. With a sigh, he said, "This won't help you much, but professionals did this."

"Why do you say that?"

"It's not a robbery." Cayden pointed at the percussion kit in a corner. "Just that conga set there and that djembe are worth a few hundred a piece. His laptop's still on the desk. Flatscreen's not too big to walk out of here, and there's that Bose Bluetooth speaker over there in the corner."

"But whoever was here tossed the place." Mandala pointed to the open drawers in the small media center.

"Yes, but it was systematic as searches go. The place is still neat. They didn't throw stuff all over the place. Nothing's knocked over or torn apart. The drawers are open, but the contents are still inside or stacked on the buffet. They were looking for something specific."

"Any idea what that might be?"

"No."

Mandala looked at him with interest. "You said *they*."

"Two of them," Cayden replied. "I might be wrong, but my gut tells me two."

Mandala gazed at him for a long moment before speaking. "You have some kind of background in law enforcement, Mr. March?"

"Cayden is fine, and no."

Mandala gestured toward the door. "Let's step out."

Cayden took a last look at his friend and then followed the detective out of the bungalow. Now he had one less person in his life and another lasting nightmare image to add to his collection.

Mandala stopped in the middle of the front lawn, turning to face him. "I'm sorry about your friend."

"Yeah… thanks."

"Was he involved in anything questionable?"

"He was a grad student working toward his PhD. He held down a part-time job on campus in the computer lab scheduling office."

"Not what I asked you," Mandala said.

Cayden's mind filled with questions. Could his friend have been into something criminal? Drugs? Cyber crime? Blackmail? Did he know the people who killed him? It was just too hard to believe any of that.

Cayden shook his head. "No, at least I never saw signs of it. He was just a genuine, hard-working guy. A good friend."

"The people who did this, were they looking for drugs?" Mandala continued.

"I have no idea."

"Describe your relationship with Mr. Fenland," Mandala said.

"We were close. We were both musicians; that's how we met. Both of us are amateurs. We'd work on songs together. Some of them we recorded. Sometimes we played live together. You develop a bond sharing something you love," Cayden explained.

Mandala nodded. "Music was the extent of your relationship?"

Raising an eyebrow, Cayden said, "If you're asking if we were a couple, the answer is no."

"No, no. I was wondering if you shared some other interest. Something that might get us closer to understanding what happened here," Mandala said.

Cayden shook his head in frustration. "No, nothing."

"Was there somebody pissed off at him, holding something against him?"

"No, at least nobody I knew about. He never talked about anything like that."

Mandala looked over at the flashing lights. "You know where I was yesterday about this time? Another murder scene."

At that, Cayden's interest piqued. There had to be a reason the detective was mentioning another murder. "Where?" Cayden asked.

"Near the Rose Bowl."

"Who?"

"Can't say."

It was possible the detective actually didn't know, but Cayden suspected he did, and someone or something else prevented him from answering.

Mandala continued. "Forensics placed the time of death an hour, to an hour-and-a-half before the time of death of Mr. Fenland. Two murders within twenty-four hours of one another, less than four miles apart. It's less than a twenty-minute drive."

Cayden nodded. "You got assigned to this one, too, because someone doesn't think it's a coincidence."

"I don't think it's a coincidence," Mandala said

"I get that. But who else doesn't think so?"

"The FBI."

Miroslav Dragović did not appreciate losing a good man. There was the matter of time, money, and training invested in each of his personnel. And then there was the need to fill the vacant position. He found it all more than vexing. In fact, he was furious.

Bojan Simic, Dragović's head of security and his personal bodyguard, guided the car down a French country lane near the Rambouillet forest, about fifteen miles north of Chartres. He viewed his security team as an unfortunate necessity. As a global arms dealer, and in his occasional collaborations with terrorist organizations, he was frequently in the company of dangerous people. Some of them were fanatics, most had critical agendas, and some of them were sociopaths. Bojan did a marvelous job of making certain that his business transactions ran as planned. He did an even better job of keeping him alive. They had worked together for many years, and Bojan was as close to him as a brother.

"The other surviving member of the security team said Abanda copied the software to a flash drive the moment the CIA team approached the house," Bojan reported.

"Yes, and then he wiped the laptop's drive clean. It explains the Americans leaving it behind," Dragović grumbled.

The car slowed and turned onto a rain-soaked gravel drive that curved through the dense stand of trees. A quarter mile later, they emerged into a clearing, stopping in front of the decent-sized farmhouse, surrounded by thick forest, save for the driveway. The nearest neighbor was at least a mile away, so there was no need for concern regarding any noise they might make here.

As Bojan hurried around to open the rear passenger door, Dragović reached into his overcoat pocket and pulled out his Walther CCP M2. Walther had promoted the weapon as the "ultimate" concealed carry pistol. Perhaps it was, perhaps it wasn't, but the pistol was very easy to hide. Racking the slide, he chambered a round as he walked toward the house. One of Bojan's men opened the door for them.

Two more of Bojan's team stood guard in the main room of the house. The personnel problem in question, Fuad Ghanem, sat in a wooden chair, duct tape wrapped around his upper torso, pinning his arms to his sides. Unexpected was the second man, also restrained, in the chair next to him.

Dragović stared down at the terrified Ghanem, growing more angry now that the man was in front of him. "You've caused me a great trouble. And you cost Mr. Abanda his life."

"This is wrong," hissed the man in the chair next to Ghanem. "He did everything he could."

"Who's this?" Dragović inquired to no one in particular.

One of Bojan's men gestured with his handgun. "His brother. Visiting when we got here."

"I don't appreciate your perspective," Dragović responded to the brother, and then raised the Walther and pulled the trigger.

The man's head jerked back as the 9mm slug hammered into the bridge of his nose. The bullet exploded through the back of his skull, carrying bone and brain with it, imbedding itself in the wall beside the fireplace.

Ghanem's face went white with shock and horror.

Dragović noticed Bojan's disapproval, but ignored it. "Where were we?"

"Please. I'm loyal. You know I'm loyal," Ghanem pleaded, sweat pouring down his face.

"Loyalty is good, failure is not."

Ghanem squirmed in his chair. "They were on us too fast. We did what we could with the time we had."

"If you'd done all you could, Mr. Abanda would still be alive, and my weapon would still be in my possession."

"It happened so fast," Ghanem whined.

"Your failure can have catastrophic consequences for me." Dragović's voice raised, along with his anger. "I invested a great deal of money in Mr. Abanda while he developed the software. A one-of-a-kind cyber weapon. Now it's gone."

Ghanem opened his mouth to reply, but Dragović didn't give him the chance. "And the people who paid me millions for this weapon, and even more millions to deploy it on their behalf—you think they'll be understanding of your mistake?"

Ghanem tried to speak again, but Dragović raised the gun and fired two rounds into his chest. The man's body jerked backward and then was still.

Dragović sighed as he slipped the pistol back into his coat pocket. No, he did not appreciate losing a good man, and he felt no better now than he did when he first arrived.

Two minutes later he was back in the car. He noticed Bojan glance at him in the rearview mirror.

"You acted out of anger, Miro. Ghanem did everything possible," Bojan commented.

"Our people will be less likely to make mistakes when they learn how I responded to Ghanem's failure."

"But still."

"He and his men allowed a CIA team to get past. They got Abanda killed, an irreplaceable genius," Dragović ranted. "With Abanda alive, at least he could've produced a replacement. But now, the only copy of the weapon is in the wind, and its designer is dead."

"You always find a solution," Bojan commented.

"What matters now is getting that flash drive back before Kazimi learns it is missing," Dragović snapped.

"You're not worried about him?" Bojan asked. "You're too important to him, to his organization," Bojan said. "He'd attempt nothing."

Bojan's assessment amused Dragović. "Kazimi is a fanatic who is less tolerant of those who fail him than I am. The man is ruthless, and he's paid a great deal of money for the weapon, and for us. I'm nothing more than subcontract labor to him. Kazimi expects what I promised and nothing less. If we don't deliver, he won't hesitate to seek vengeance."

"As you say…"

They drove on in silence for several miles. Wishing to leave the unpleasantness at the farmhouse behind him, Dragović felt a strong desire to speak with his daughter. Her sweet voice always cheered him. Besides, he needed to tell his wife he was heading home. He was reaching for the phone to make the call when it began chiming.

"Yes."

"We followed the case officer to California." Daniel Russo's voice crackled through the speaker.

"California?"

"Yes. We caught up to him in the city of Pasadena. I'm certain he went there to meet someone at the California Institute of Technology."

"The place is known for its science and research," Dragović said. "It's possible the CIA had someone at the university who could help them get past the software's encryption."

"I thought the same," Russo said. "But I haven't yet determined who. At any rate, the CIA man unloaded the drive somewhere before we got to him."

"So you don't have it."

"Not yet."

"A poor answer," Dragović said, his voice like iron.

"We tracked him close. We'll get it back."

"Do it fast."

"Of course," Russo replied.

Dragović punched the 'end call' button and immediately dialed his daughter. He needed her brightness more than ever.

CHAPTER FOUR

Detective Mandala gave Cayden a few minutes to report in to Raymond, after which he spent another hour interviewing him. The last question was predictable. Mandala asked him to account for his last twenty-four hours. Cayden did, providing Kate's name, Raymond, and the security office's timekeeping records. Mandala assured him he'd check on all of them. The police were doing what they do, and Detective Mandala was a sharp guy, but Cayden knew it was unlikely they would ever find the professionals who killed Alan.

Cayden didn't mention it to Mandala, but Raymond had instructed him to get over to Alan's office on campus and look around. Some of the projects at Caltech could be sensitive, and even though Alan Fenland wasn't involved in any of them, Raymond wanted to play it safe. Cayden wanted to see the office before the police or FBI disturbed it.

On the short ride back to campus, Cayden navigated a troubling path of thoughts and emotions. He knew loss well, but being familiar with it didn't make this any more tolerable. He struggled, unable to comprehend why anyone would do something so brutal to a guy like Alan. Cayden was familiar with several strikes that would incapacitate or kill a man if expertly delivered. They'd leave the same kind of bruise he'd seen on Alan's throat. Then there was the house. The search had been thorough, professional. The room he had seen showed signs of it. He was certain the other rooms did as well.

Cayden turned onto Holliston Avenue and parked next to the path leading to the Powell-Booth building where Alan had worked. Several students were still on campus; most of them coming out of an evening class or on their way to a lab session or study group.

Cayden mounted the six steps to the wide landing and entered through the double glass doors. Housing the computational science department, the place was always busy. Caltech, being one of the leading schools of science and engineering in the world, had more than its share of students, professors, and researchers vying for computer time.

Administrative offices occupied most of the ground floor, with the computer labs filling the upper levels of the building. A small group of students moved through the lobby, but the ground floor was empty. He glanced up at the security camera mounted in the upper corner of the lobby. There were more like it positioned along the hallways.

Cayden crossed the lobby, entering the administrative wing through the inner lobby doorway. He hurried down the hallway leading toward the scheduling office, glancing at his watch. Haste was essential if he wanted to investigate without interruption. It was only a matter of time before Detective Mandala found his way here.

Cayden opened the door of the scheduling office and switched on the lights. His gut knotted seeing his friend's belongings on the desk. He fought it, determined to focus on the task at hand. From the look of it, whoever killed Alan had also been here. The only difference between Alan's bungalow and his office was that the search here was much sloppier. Whoever it was didn't have the time to be as thorough here.

He stood in the doorway for a moment, taking the scene in. The emptiness of the office struck him. Alan would never be here again. Unable to contain the anger and hopelessness building in him, he slammed his fist down on the desk with an unrestrained yell, rattling the desk and everything on its surface. The outburst did little to ease his anger. After staring at the desk for several seconds, he gathered himself and got back to business.

Cayden pulled a sheet of Kleenex tissue from a box on the corner of the desk and began a cursory examination of the office. He started with the bookshelves and filing cabinets, using the tissue on any object he had to touch or move.

Finding nothing that piqued his interest, he stepped over to Alan's desk. The first drawer Cayden opened was a muddle of paperclips, pens, pencils, a PEZ candy dispenser, sticky note pads in a variety of sizes, and a small calculator. Working through the rest of the drawers produced the same results. Something about the desk struck him as being a little off, but he couldn't put his finger on anything specific.

Cayden switched off the lights, closed the door behind him, and continued down the hall toward the equipment room. He swiped his ID card through the scanner to unlock the door and entered. He sat down at the workstation next to the rack of security camera hard drives, woke up the computer, and entered his password. He wasn't worried about his fingerprints on the keyboard. He used this system frequently, and he was certain the police would find no prints that didn't belong here.

The large display populated with time-stamped images from each of the building's security cameras. A few keystrokes brought up images from the exterior cameras. A few more keystrokes and he'd isolated all the camera feeds from each side of the building. He started with the building's main entrance, running the footage back to 12:00 noon, and then played it forward at triple speed.

Nothing unusual jumped out at him as the images sped by. There was the normal foot traffic and the occasional electric utility cart passing by. One-by-one, he viewed footage from the remaining three sides of the building. Again, nothing.

Cayden closed out the exterior cameras and brought up the interior building feeds. He isolated the first floor east and west hallway cameras, and narrowed it down to only the angles capturing the scheduling office entrances. Students and faculty navigated the hallways. A custodian pushed a cleaning cart past the camera and disappeared from view. Cayden leaned forward as Alan appeared on camera, leaving the scheduling office. He glanced at the timestamp, 12:20 p.m. He reappeared holding a food bag from the commons, twenty-two minutes later.

Alan didn't leave his office again. The footage continued forward, displaying nothing out of the ordinary. Suddenly, the east and west hallway images disappeared, replaced by a field of dark blue. Cayden stopped playback and rewound to where the camera image had disappeared. The time-stamp displayed 2:23 p.m. Whoever wiped the drive had serious hacking skills, and the experience of getting the door to the equipment room open without damaging it.

Resuming playback, he sped forward. The blue field disappeared at 3:42 p.m., replaced by a normal video feed. Whoever had wiped the drives wanted to hide whatever had taken place after 2:23.

Cayden pulled Mandala's business card from his shirt pocket and punched in the number on his phone.

"Mandala," the detective answered.

"It's Cayden March."

"What's up?"

"I checked our surveillance system in the building where Alan Fenland worked. Somebody wiped out the video recorded between two-thirty and three-thirty this afternoon."

"You didn't touch anything in Fenland's office, did you?" There was no mistaking the irritation in Mandala's voice.

"I stuck my head through the door for a look. That's it," Cayden fibbed. "Just so I can tell my boss I did what he told me."

"Chalmers told you to go to Mr. Fenland's office?"

"He did."

After an uncomfortable, long pause, Mandala's voice sounded through the phone. "I'll want to see that surveillance footage. I'm going to be tied up here until late, but you tell Ray Chalmers I'll be in his office first thing in the morning, eight o'clock."

"Sure, but I can meet you."

"I don't want you anywhere near that footage. Just do what I asked."

"Of course."

Mandala broke off the call.

Cayden logged out, locked the equipment room, and headed back to Alan's office. Something was still out of place there, and the little voice in his head told him to take one more look.

Once back inside, he left the door ajar. He crossed the office and opened the opposite door several inches. It was very possible whoever had searched the office earlier might return. He'd prefer to hear them coming.

Cayden switched the lights back on and searched the office again, hoping that he might spot something he'd missed before. He was only a few minutes into his search when the dull metallic sound of the foyer door mechanism echoed down the empty hallway. He switched off the lights and moved behind the door. His training and experience resurfaced; the adrenaline was pumping through him, but at his core he felt calm and prepared.

The footsteps drew closer, one person treading toward the office from the east hallway. Whoever it was, it wasn't the people who killed Alan. They'd be much more difficult to hear.

The footsteps slowed and stopped outside the door. Cayden tensed as the door opened wider. He adjusted his balance for an offensive.

"Cayden?"

CHAPTER FIVE

"**K**ate," he answered with genuine surprise.

The girl gasped, whirling around to face him, almost jumping out of her tennis shoes.

"What do you think you're doing?" she asked, angry at being frightened.

He raised his finger to his lips. "Keep it down," Cayden advised, his voice low.

With impressive swiftness, she moved forward and delivered a punch to his shoulder. The punch was solid, but Cayden knew she'd held back.

"What are you doing?" she repeated. "Hiding in the dark? You almost made me pee in my pants."

"Been training?" He rubbed his shoulder.

"The news about Alan is all over campus. I've been trying to get hold of you," Kate blurted. "Why do you have a cell phone if you never bother to answer it?"

Cayden pulled out his phone and looked at the list of incoming calls. "Yeah, there you are. Sorry. It's been a bad day."

"No kidding. Our friend is dead. I called the security office and your boss told me he'd sent you over here," she continued. "Oh, and he said to tell you if you want to keep your job, you'd better call him with a report tonight."

Cayden switched the lights back on. He felt good that Kate was here. Considering the circumstances, he felt better in her company.

"Alan was murdered?" Kate asked, her sadness unmistakable.

"Yes, but let's talk about it later."

"I adored him. He was the nicest guy, so fun."

"We've only got a few minutes here."

"We?" she responded, the irritation still edged in her voice.

"Keep an eye on the hallway. I'll just be another minute," he said, walking around the office.

"What am I keeping an eye on the hallway for?"

"Just let me know if anyone comes this way." There was no reason to let her know professional killers might come back to the office; it would only upset her.

"This sounds shady. I assume you'll take care of any legal costs I may incur," she said, pushing a wisp of hair from the side of her face.

"That implies a negative outcome."

His eyes moved across the office, but his gaze kept going back to the desk.

"What are you looking for?" Kate asked.

"I'm not sure." Cayden returned to the desk. He examined the desk surface, cluttered with the typical office paraphernalia and remnants of Alan's daily duties. He pulled two new sheets of Kleenex from the box and picked up one of Alan's personal lab books. The mathematics and notes meant nothing to him, so he showed it to Kate.

"Notes from his optical engineering lab," she explained. "Nothing important."

He pulled open the top drawer of the desk, seeing the same hodgepodge of office supplies he'd seen before. It was the same thing with the other drawers.

"All right, let's go," he said.

Kate pushed open the door, and Cayden ushered her out. He

switched off the light, but a misty image resting in his memory made him pause. Switching the light back on, he went back to the desk.

Kate leaned against the doorjamb. "What now?" she asked.

Cayden used the tissue to pull open the top desk drawer and studied the contents. His eyes moved to the PEZ dispenser. It sported the head of Darth Vader from the *Star Wars* movie franchise. The black bubble eyes recessed in the ominous helmet stared up at him from among the office supply rubble. Cayden picked it up in the tissue, placed it in his jacket pocket, and closed the drawer.

Kate moaned. "You're stealing candy from our dead friend's office?"

"Sometimes you just can't deny the sweet tooth." He gestured her out of the office, switched off the lights, and shut the door behind them.

CHAPTER SIX

The drive from Caltech to Cayden's home took fifteen minutes. On the way, Cayden made his requisite call to Raymond. Aside from conveying Mandala's intention of a morning visit to view the security footage, he had little to report.

Kate parked her 2016 Nissan Rogue beside his car in front of the double garage. Cayden led her through the main entrance to a small vestibule on the second floor of the house. A light burned in the living room, activated at nightfall by a Lutron switch. He saw the property tax envelope on the side table as they entered, and once again felt a knot tightening in his stomach.

"How's the fixing up work going?" Kate asked.

Her question triggered thoughts of house repair costs added to the property tax bill, and the knot tightened even more. "Fine. It seems like there'll never be an end to it."

"Well, the place looks great." She shivered and pushed her hands into her coat pockets.

Cayden crossed the living room and switched on the thermostat. "I've got tea."

"Tea would be great."

They descended to the kitchen and dining room on the bottom floor of the house. Kate leaned against the kitchen counter while he put the kettle on and began rummaging through the cupboards. He placed a box of Earl Grey tea, a plastic honey bottle, and a half-empty bottle of Old Forester 1920 Prohibition Style Bourbon on the counter. Another cupboard produced a large mug and a whiskey glass.

"So, what's bothering you?" Kate asked.

The question caught him off guard. "Sorry, what?"

"It looked like you stressed when you saw that envelope on the table upstairs."

"You don't miss much, do you?"

"Now and then, but not tonight. What's going on?" Kate pressed, as the kettle began whistling. She took the mug he passed to her, dropped a tea bag in, and filled it from the steaming kettle.

Cayden poured a double shot of bourbon into his glass, unsure if he wanted to share his financial issues with her. "It's no big thing."

"You know I'm just gonna keep asking," Kate said, stirring a spoonful of honey into her tea.

He took a sip of bourbon, buying a little time while he thought about it.

"Well?"

"Property taxes."

"What about them?"

"It's a hefty bill. I have about half what I need," Cayden replied.

"How big a problem is that?" Kate asked.

"Worst-case scenario, I could end up having to sell the house if I can't come up with the money."

"You don't want to do that."

"I pretty much grew up here," he said, taking another sip from his glass. "I promised my grandfather I'd keep the place in the family. It's a promise I don't want to break."

"My saving account is pretty healthy these days," Kate said. "I can front you some cash."

"Great. You have about $15,000 handy?"

Her eyes widened. "Holy crap. How much do you owe?"

He shrugged. "Like I said, a lot."

Kate gave the matter some thought. "Could you ask your father for it?"

It had already occurred to him that his father could help, but he knew from experience asking his father for anything would end up with them at opposing sides all over again. "That would be difficult," Cayden said.

"But he could help."

"Yes."

After a long minute of silence, Kate looked up from her mug. "You remember the last time I was here?"

"Sure. Alan and I were laying down tracks for that country-rock song we wrote. You were hanging out with us. And you kept us eating pretty well that afternoon, if I recall."

"I had a great time that day."

Cayden headed for the wooden-framed glass doors that opened out to the patio and garden. "Bring your tea," he said.

They crossed the patio in the light spilling from the house. Cayden unlocked the hand-carved redwood door leading into the studio and switched on the lights, then ushered Kate inside.

"What are we doing?" Kate asked.

"If we're going to remember good times with Alan, let's do it where most of it happened."

Cayden loved this space and spent a fair amount of time here. The building, just over 1,800 square feet, was built as a pottery studio by the original owners. His grandparents used it as a storage space. It took him several weekends to clean the place out, but once the work was done, he had a blast converting it to a recording studio. There was a small kitchen and bathroom down the short hallway on the main floor. Stairs led up to the loft where he kept a bed and a desk. He sometimes crashed up there when he was too lazy or too tired to return to his bedroom in the main house.

"Cay, can we have a fire?" Kate asked, shivering again.

Cayden set his glass on the mantle and went to work getting a fire started in the small hearth as Kate took a seat on the sofa. When the flames began licking at the logs, he reclaimed his glass of Old Forester. He pulled the PEZ dispenser from his pocket and dropped it on the coffee table in front of the sofa as he sat down beside her. The black plastic shell reflected the firelight. *What was Alan doing with this thing? And did it have anything to do with his death?*

"Alan loved spending time here." Kate looked into the growing flames. "I think he considered you his best friend."

"Yeah? I wasn't aware."

Kate regarded him thoughtfully. "You going to tell me why you were sneaking around Alan's office?"

"I wasn't sneaking. Raymond sent me there to check it out."

"Did you find anything?"

His eyes went back to the PEZ dispenser. "Anything like what?"

"Anything that might help."

"What do you mean, help?"

"Help the police. And stop being an ass." Kate glared at him over her mug while taking a sip of tea. "You're answering my questions with questions. It's like gathering information one word at a time with a pair of tweezers."

"I told the police what I found, but it wasn't much," Cayden said. "I gave them my opinion."

"Which was?"

"Whoever killed Alan was looking for something."

"Ahh, the special ops thing is kicking in," Kate said.

He took a healthy swig from his glass. No one on campus knew the details of his military background—not even Raymond. "No need to talk about that."

"I only mentioned it to you," Kate said, rolling her eyes. "So, what're you thinking?"

"I think pros did the job. And whatever they were looking for, they didn't find it."

"How can you be so sure?"

"My gut."

"Well, as long as it's something concrete." Kate quipped.

Cayden didn't bother with a response. He understood her frustration over losing a good friend and feeling helpless to do anything about it. The anger inside him became almost tangible. He had a strong desire to hunt down Alan's killers. But how was that going to work? The police would never tolerate him investigating independently of them.

Kate's voice pulled him from his thoughts. "Cay. You still with me?"

"Yeah, sorry," he mumbled, his eyes fixed on Darth Vader. It seemed almost as though the plastic villain was taunting him.

Kate followed his gaze, leaned forward and picked up the candy dispenser.

"So, what's with this thing?" she asked.

"It's Darth Vader. Dark Lord of the Sith."

"Funny," Kate replied. "You lifted it from your dead friend's desk."

It suddenly came to him why the dispenser looked out of place among Alan's possessions. He held out his hand, and Kate dropped the PEZ dispenser into his palm.

"Alan didn't eat candy," Cayden said, setting his glass down on the table. "He'd eat a chocolate donut, pie, stuff like that, but he never cared for candy."

Kate's brow wrinkled. "He might have bought the PEZ for some kid. You know, a little brother or sister, nephew."

"Maybe." He thumbed the dispenser mechanism. Darth Vader's head tilted back on its plastic hinge and a pink piece of candy dropped into his hand. It was just a piece of candy — nothing else. Cayden worked the dispenser mechanism again. Another piece of candy, and then another.

"How many pieces are these things supposed to hold?" Cayden asked, weighing it in his hand.

Kate shrugged. "No idea. I was twelve the last time I had one of those things."

Switching on a floor lamp beside the sofa, Cayden held the PEZ dispenser under the light and, using his fingertips, began applying pressure at the seams.

"It's a candy gadget, Cay, not an anti-matter weapon," Kate said.

He reached into his pocket and produced a Swiss Army knife. After opening the smallest blade, he began working the steel into the bottom seam of the dispenser. He carefully probed around the four sides of the plastic casing. With the soft snap of a relenting plastic tab, the flat bottom of the dispenser pulled away from the casing. Attached to it was another plastic casing, about two inches long and only slightly smaller than the surrounding enclosure. Protruding from its end was a USB connector.

"A flash drive," Kate said with surprise.

"I'm gonna say Alan didn't buy this for a kid," Cayden murmured.

CHAPTER SEVEN

Daniel Russo watched the Caltech security guard and the girl walk from the main house to the outbuilding. He had an unobstructed view through the ornate iron gate at the back of March's property. The gate was set in an eight-foot wall covered with tangled ivy and secured with a heavy chain and padlock. The lock was of little concern; he'd pick it or go over the wall. Cyn was positioned at the front of the house, parked down the block in their rented midnight blue Cherokee, with instructions to keep her butt in the car.

The property spanned from its front entrance to the street running along the back of the large lot. As far as the layout went, the whole place was convenient. Heavy lines of trees on either side of the affluent street lessened the chance of him being spotted by any passing vehicles. Across the street, a high wall protected a large estate, its driveway visible through the shadows well down the block. It was unlikely anybody would spot him from there; you couldn't even see the house from the street. In fact, most of the houses on the block were set back from the street. Farther up the block, the glow of Christmas lights from the few homes closer to the street cast a colorful glow in the darkness.

Earlier in the evening, he and Cyn had returned to the Powell-

Booth computer lab, intending to give Fenland's office a more thorough search. There hadn't been enough time to be thorough earlier. They'd taken their time at the kid's bungalow, so he knew it wasn't there, and it wasn't on the CIA officer's body. The officer got rid of it somewhere, and the last place before they'd caught him was Fenland's office.

They'd no sooner entered the Caltech campus when they saw March and the girl leaving the Powell-Booth building. Cyn, as usual, voted to kill them both before they could leave the campus, just in case they had it with them. He vetoed the idea; the campus was still busy. Besides, he recognized something in March's body language that made him cautious. The efficiency in the way the man moved, swift and direct; the casual way he absorbed every detail of his surroundings. There was no big trick in recognizing one of your own. There would be more fruitful results calling on March at his home. Russo already had the address, finding it on the internet in public records.

Once March and the girl had cleared the building, he and Cyn entered Fenland's office and conducted a more thorough search. They found nothing. It was then he decided to visit March's residence. And here they'd been for more than an hour, waiting and watching.

A tone sounded in Russo's earpiece, and then came Cyn's voice. "What've you got there, babe?"

"They just went into an outbuilding behind the main house. Sit tight," he answered, keeping his voice low.

She was amazingly capable, showing a natural and unfailing efficiency at killing, but he didn't want her trying to take on the security guard alone. Russo knew Cyn's greatest weakness; she enjoyed their profession a little too much.

He'd found her on a street in Houston one night nine years ago. He was in town for a job, a corrupt judge who had made the mistake of cheating someone much more powerful than he. Cyn was a runaway from home and was about to get raped when he first spotted her.

He'd visited a club to listen to a little music before looking up the judge at his home in Cinco Ranch. He was walking to his rental car when he saw this scrawny teenage girl in an alley with a couple of twenty-something punks all over her. One of them held her from behind, his hand clamped over her mouth, while his buddy struggled to pull the underwear off her kicking, twisting legs.

Any other night, he would have just kept moving without even a glance back. This kind of street stuff happened all the time, and this little ruckus was none of his business. But something about the way the girl was fighting caught his attention. Instead of showing fear, she was fighting back with a smoldering, determined rage. She wasn't going to give it up easy.

Russo moved into the alley, and the punks spotted him at the same time. The underwear hound let go of the girl's panties and turned to face him. A six-inch knife flashed in his hand, causing his buddy to give a whoop of approval.

Seconds later Russo had broken the underwear hound's arm, shattered his kneecap, taken the would-be rapist's six-inch knife, and slit the guy's throat with his own blade.

The guy holding the girl let her go before his friend hit the pavement, running from the alley as fast as he could move. Russo wasn't too worried about the guy going to the police or identifying him if he did.

While the girl pulled up her panties, he wiped down the knife and looked over the area, making certain there was no evidence of his presence. A few minutes later, they were in his car on Memorial Drive, heading for the Westheimer Parkway. She'd eyed him with suspicion at first, answering all his questions with a single word.

It had still been a little early to deal with the judge, so he found a diner off the highway and got some food in her. The meal warmed her stomach and loosened her tongue enough to free her name, Cynthia Murray. He was certain she made up the last name as a precaution; she didn't want anybody delivering her back home.

Much later, before they became lovers, he learned there was good reason for that caution. Her stepfather had been going at her since she was thirteen. The punks in the alley didn't frighten her because what they might have done to her couldn't compare to the depravity her mother's third husband had already inflicted. Cyn was inured to the most twisted nature of man.

After reaching Cinco Ranch, Cyn waited in the car three blocks from the judge's house while he helped hasten the wayward judge's demise by what the coroner would conclude to be cardiac arrest. When he returned to the car, she seemed to know what he'd been doing, and it fascinated her.

At first, he avoided her questions. Then he began fielding them. When it became apparent that they weren't about to stop, he trained her.

She was athletic and in three years' time was more than proficient in the fighting technique he practiced, a lethal combination of Krav Maga and Dim Mak. Dedicated to improving and with several opportunities for practical application over the years, Cyn was now very much an expert in these martial arts. She absorbed everything he taught her about human psychology, tactical planning, firearms and cutting weapons, as well as the use of death inducing pharmaceuticals and exotic poisons.

But it was one thing training to kill; it was something else to do it, especially for a civilian. So he created a test for her, one that pleased him greatly. It possessed some humor, a lot of irony and, best of all, a healthy quantity of revenge.

He let her handle the entire thing. The preliminary surveillance, noting the subject's movements and daily patterns, determining the best time and location. Cyn did it all herself. And when it was time for the task itself, Cyn's big, balding, stubble-chinned, tattooed stepfather died very slowly. The slowness was not because of any ineptness on Cyn's part.

Russo's earpiece beeped again. "Hey, babe. Anything new?" Cyn's voice whispered.

"Nothing."

"I'm so bored. How much longer do you think?"

"As long as it takes. We'll get ourselves breakfast and sleep in when we're through."

"That sounds nice. It doesn't have to be all sleep, does it?" she inquired.

"It never is."

"Love you, babe."

"Love you, too."

CHAPTER EIGHT

With Cayden looking over her shoulder, Kate used a USB to USB4 adaptor to connect the flash drive to his Mac Studio. An unlabeled drive icon appeared on the desktop, displayed on the forty-two inch monitor mounted on the wall above the recording desk.

"Let's look at the volume properties before we do anything else," Kate said.

The creation and modification dates, format information, and volume capacity appeared on the screen.

"The last modification date was six days ago," Cayden observed.

"A 500 gigabyte drive, 101.3 gigabytes available. Whatever's on this thing is taking up a lot of space," Kate said.

She closed the properties window, then double-clicked the drive icon. The computer hummed, and the screen went black.

"Is this thing going to destroy my computer?" Cayden asked.

"We're about to find out," Kate answered.

An object about the size of a tennis ball emerged from the blackness. Precise, deep blue luminous lines outlined the object and created patterns within the outer borders. It rotated slowly clockwise on the screen.

"An octagon," Kate observed. She leaned in closer to the display. "Sixteen cells around eight cells, around a concentric octagon. See, it's three dimensional."

"Did you see the cursor blinking in the center before it rotated out of sight? An entry field?" he asked.

"I'd say so." Kate positioned the mouse and clicked on several cells in the octagon. Nothing changed on the screen; and in a few seconds, the blinking cursor rotated back into view. She quickly clicked on the field and typed a variety of characters. Aside from the first character appearing in the center field, the octagon remained the same. In another couple of seconds, the field containing the character disappeared from view again.

Kate leaned back in the chair. "I've never seen anything like it. It's encrypted up the wazoo, and you can't enter a code manually."

"Why is that?" Cayden asked.

"No other cells activated when I clicked in them, and the cell with the cursor accepted only one character. I'm thinking a correct character entered in the first field unlocks the next field, and correct entries in subsequent fields do the same. The rotating octagon is all for show; whoever wrote the code must be into science fiction."

"It serves no function?" he asked.

"Possibly, but I doubt it."

"Does it take an additional program running to decrypt the file?"

"I can't say for sure, but it's a good guess," Kate answered.

"Okay, so to access whatever's on the drive, it has to be in the computer port, and then a second drive with the decryption program has to be plugged in as well?"

"There could be a laptop already containing the decryption software, activated when the drive's plugged into the port," Kate said. "It could even be a cell phone with a pre-programmed chip installed."

"Cell phones don't have USB ports. You'd need an adapter setup to connect," Cayden said.

"Sure, but that's no big deal. You can get what you need right off the shelf."

Cayden stared at the glowing octagon. There was no way to know what was on the drive, but he knew Alan. He was certain his friend wasn't involved in anything shady or criminal. He didn't believe the drive belonged to Alan, but this flash drive had to be connected to his murder.

"We need to find out what's on this thing," Cayden said. "It might help explain what happened to Alan."

"I was thinking the same," Kate said with a nod.

"You want to take a whack at it?"

Leaning closer to the screen, she said, "I'd love to find out how this thing ticks. But I'm not sure if I—"

"You've got over-the-top hacking skills," Cayden interrupted. "My money's on you."

"Yeah, but let me give this some thought before you place your bet." Kate pursed her lips and continued staring at the display. They sat in silence for a couple of minutes. Shadows from the crackling fire crept up the walls and across the ceiling.

"Okay," Kate said, breaking the silence. "I know somebody who's a downright genius when it comes to hacking. We're not really close, but she might help."

"You really need help?" he asked. Kate was one of the most talented people he knew at Caltech, and that was saying something.

"Yes, I'm a genius, too," Kate grinned. "But nothing like Mariana. I can crack this thing, but it'll take time. With the two of us combining our efforts, our chances of getting in are better, and we should be able to do it faster."

"You're talking about Mariana Vasquez," Cayden said.

Kate looked surprised. "You know Mariana?"

"We busted her for hacking into the JPL astrophysics server. Well, kind of busted her."

A delighted smile lit Kate's face. "So that story's true?"

Cayden couldn't help laughing at her awe. "Not that we could prove she did it. Somebody at JPL picked up on the security breach. Their people traced it back to our network system and then tossed it in our lap. When we narrowed it down, Raymond had me bring her in for a chat."

"But you couldn't bust her for it?"

"No. But I guarantee you she did it."

"What about JPL?" Kate asked.

"They didn't pursue it. We made it clear the whole thing was just another Caltech stunt and guaranteed we'd take action against the person responsible. We banned her from the school mainframes for sixty days and issued our best intimidating warnings. She thought it was all pretty amusing."

Kate laughed at the story. "So, do we call her?"

Cayden wondered if getting someone else involved with the flash drive was such a good idea. But Kate's confidence about decrypting the drive with Mariana's help gave him a spark of hope. If they pulled it off, the contents might lead to Alan's killers.

"Yeah, I'm not so sure we should," his voice trailed off.

"You think it's dangerous?" Kate asked. "It could make Mariana a target?"

"It's dangerous." He pointed to the drive in the USB port. "Eject it, please."

Kate took hold of the mouse and disengaged the flash drive from the Mac, then pulled it from the computer and handed it to him.

"I want you to stay here tonight."

Kate smiled mischievously. "You didn't even buy me dinner."

She always enjoyed teasing him like that. It made him wonder if she was trying to tell him something, or if she was just having fun messing with his head. Maybe a little of both. At any rate, he was never sure how to respond.

"It's safer if you stay. Just until we figure out what we're dealing with."

Kate frowned. "Crap. I'm toast because I've been looking at this thing?" She gestured toward the drive as Cayden slipped it back into the PEZ casing and secured the cover.

"I won't let anything happen to you," he assured her, slipping the drive into the PEZ casing. "But whoever's looking for this, they murdered Alan just because they guessed he might have it. At some point, they might want to find out if you or I have it."

She let out a frustrated breath. "Well, okay, I guess. But I'm not prepared."

"I'm sure I have anything you might need."

"All right."

Surprising himself, he gave Kate a taste of her own medicine. "I can throw in a movie with that dinner."

She looked astonished, and he immediately regretted making the remark.

But then Kate replaced her expression of shock with a sweet smile. "Very generous. Now, where will you be sleeping?"

CHAPTER NINE

After getting Kate settled in the second floor guest bedroom of the main house, Cayden returned to the studio to lock up. After dropping the PEZ dispenser on his desk, he ended up stretching out on the single bed in the loft office without bothering to undress. Many nights he fell asleep on this bed, nights when it was too much effort to make it across the footbridge to the house.

Cayden's body slept, but his mind churned through an ever changing collage of images. First there was Alan, stretched out on the floor of his living room, the barbecue skewer jutting cruelly from the coagulated puddle of blood that was once his eye. The image assaulted him from every perspective. His muscles tensed and his breathing rate increased as his slumbering subconscious mind registered an intense hatred toward whoever had done this terrible thing to his friend.

Alan's lifeless body faded into the shadows, replaced by a moonless night and the scarred white walls of the desert compound. The dim, glowing lights of the compound pushed through the darkness, slowly illuminating the face of Rob James, his M4. muzzle flashes slicing through the night. Cayden saw the spurt of blood as a bullet struck his friend's side after getting through a small opening in his vest. The sharp cracks of gunfire echoed around him as Rob's face contorted in pain.

Cayden awoke with the echo of a formless sound fading into the blackness. He was lying on his side, facing the stairway that reached up to the loft from the studio's main floor. Motionless, he listened, waiting for some sense of what might have woken him.

A sharp pop suddenly cut through the silence as a pocket of sap within the embers of the dying fire exploded in the hearth downstairs. And there was something else, something of experience and instinct. A spike of adrenaline jolted through him in the same moment he saw the shadowy figure of a man coming at him from the darkness.

Cayden rolled swiftly from the bed, hit the floor, and kicked with his right leg. His foot struck the intruder's tibia, but not hard enough. The guy stumbled, tripping over the corner of the bed, but didn't go down.

Cayden got to his feet in time to see the ambient light spark off the edge of a blade. The guy held the knife in a reverse grip with the dull edge of the blade aligned parallel to his forearm, the cutting edge facing out.

A chill numbed him as he thought of Kate, alone in the guest bedroom. He hoped this man and his knife hadn't already been in the main house.

The guy lunged forward. Cayden feinted to the side and crowded in close, forcing the guy's knife arm down and back with his left hand as he slammed his right elbow into his attacker's jaw. He reversed the strike, dropped his elbow, and slammed the back of his fist into the man's nose. He heard a grunt as the intruder twisted away, regained his balance, and moved forward again without hesitation.

Cayden knew he survived the initial attack only by instinct and a lot of luck. This had to be one of the killers who murdered Alan. This intruder couldn't be a coincidence, not with the PEZ dispenser lying on the desk only feet away. The realization energized Cayden with a firm determination to kick this guy's ass into another dimension. He quickly rallied, drawing on his extensive military training and experience.

The loft had little space to maneuver, and it seemed even smaller with the knife in the room. Cayden retreated backward toward his desk as the killer advanced. The blade thrust forward; he blocked it, barely managing a strike to the attacker's forearm. He felt the edge of the desk against the back of his thigh.

Cayden planted his hand on the desk to steady himself, and brushed against something cold and hard; the three pound Civil War cannon ball he used as a paperweight. Somebody had welded a stem on it from which protruded a fake fuse, so the thing looked like one of those classic cartoon bombs.

Cayden grabbed the ball and rolled to the side, spinning around and landing a kick to the guy's kidney. The man flew back, jamming his knife hand down on the desktop to catch his balance. Cayden rushed toward him. He locked his right arm over the killer's knife arm and used the forward momentum to hurl him down on the desk. A lamp clattered to the floor as Cayden swung the iron ball, striking the guy's knife hand just behind the wrist.

The assailant yelped and released the knife, but quickly squirmed into an efficient recovery position. Cayden swung the ball toward his head, but a vicious upward block numbed his arm and sent the cannon shot thudding into the hardwood floor.

With every move he made, Cayden's breaths became more labored. He still had extensive skills, but they'd dulled with lack of use and careless late nights. His opponent came at him with a torrent of strikes and kicks that had him on the defensive, unable to launch a strike of his own. For the first time in a long while, he felt fear mounting within him. It was very possible he was about to die.

With every blow his opponent got through, tendrils of nauseating panic spread through his gut. He was getting winded and sluggish. His timing was failing. The guy delivered an unexpected strike to his solar plexus that sent a wave of dull pain through him and almost took him down. In the next instant, another kick propelled him backward.

Cayden reached behind him, grasping for anything to keep him upright, but there was nothing. His balance gone, he continued downward, but the floor wasn't where it should be and he kept falling. There was nothing but jarring pain as he tumbled backward down the stairs. He had a brief glimpse of the ground floor before slamming to rest on his back, the breath forced out of him.

He attempted to rise, but nausea rippled through him, and he was overwhelmed with dizziness. The killer appeared at the top of the stairs, heading down toward him, the knife now gripped in his left hand. It had been dark in the loft and everything moved too fast for Cayden to get a good look at the guy. Now his blurred vision prevented him from clearly seeing anything. He fought the urge to vomit. The last thing he saw before the darkness overwhelmed him was the light flickering off the blade of the knife.

CHAPTER TEN

Miroslav Dragović always enjoyed the drive along the Aurelia. A scenic array of vineyards, olive orchards, and tomato crops bordered the road, increasing the farther one traveled from Rome. In the spring, vibrant colored wildflower fields covered the landscape. Under the gathering clouds and dull gray sky of December, the area was more subdued in its beauty, but he still found it pleasing.

He had chosen Northern Italy as his home because of this beauty and because of the climate. The coastal area was delightful, especially through the warm months with its pristine beaches and soothing sun. Dragović didn't remember the sun of his childhood in Serbia being something to enjoy. It was there, of course, but obscured by the smoke of whatever battle his country was fighting at the time.

They reached the Monte Argentario promontory and Bojan turned off the main highway, maneuvering the town car along the narrow road that twisted along the coast to Porto Ercole. White-hulled boats docked in double ranks and the sienna hued buildings against the deep green hills created an ideal postcard photo.

In a few minutes, they were climbing the hill above the harbor, passing the spacious villas that spotted the slopes. As the car reached the peak, the entrance to his private drive came into view. An electric surge of anxiety coursed through Dragović, and he quickly drew his pistol. He instructed his household to keep the front gates shut and locked. But now they were open. Bojan guided the car up the drive, his hand resting on his gun in the center console.

A late model silver Mercedes was parked on the cobblestones in front of the house. Its driver, a fit young Afghan man who looked capable of doing more than driving, stood on the passenger side of the limo, his arms folded across his chest.

Dragović recognized the driver and knew immediately who his visitor was. But knowing the visitor did nothing to ease his concern. He was out of the car before it came to a full stop, slipping his pistol back into his coat pocket as he headed for the house. Bojan caught up to him before he reached the porch. The driver appeared unconcerned, but his eyes never left them until they were through the front door.

Assad Kazimi, dressed in woolen slacks, a linen shirt, and a casual sport coat, sat on the custom-made ten-foot damask sofa, facing the front door. He was a slender, rough-looking man with jet black hair, a bit on the long side but well groomed. His skin, darkened and tightened by the desert sun, made his age difficult to determine. Kazimi's personal bodyguard stood a few feet away from him, an older, more experienced version of the man standing post outside.

Dragović's wife, Melina, sat on the matching sofa opposite Kazimi. Next to her sat their beautiful daughter, Elissa, keeping busy with a bright blue learning game console on her lap. A cartoonish gong sounded from the video game. "That's wrong," Elissa giggled to herself.

"Ah, Miro," Kazimi greeted him.

Doing little to disguise his displeasure, Dragović walked around the end of the sofa. "Assad," he said, extending his hand. "You honor us. Why do you come?"

Kazimi grasped Dragović's hand in both of his. "We have a matter to discuss, you and I."

Elissa's video game gonged again, and as she shifted her position to show her mother the screen, the console slipped from her hands, dropping to the carpeted floor. The bodyguard stepped over, picked up the game console, and handed it to Elissa. Smiling, he moved a strand of hair out of her eyes with his finger. The gesture infuriated Dragović, but he returned his daughter's smile when she looked up at him.

"We'll talk out on the terrace." Dragović moved toward the French doors at the back of the room.

Kazimi rose from the sofa and followed him. "My man will remain inside with your permission, of course, Mrs. Dragović."

Melina formed a thin smile, though her eyes showed steel. "Of course."

Dragović knew she was a remarkable woman, strong and capable. He had met Melina, Greek by birth, fifteen years ago in Rome where she was on holiday. She knew what he did for a living and expressed neither approval nor disapproval. Any apprehension she felt now was not for herself, but for their daughter.

With a gesture from Dragović, Bojan took a position closer to Melina.

Dragović ushered Kazimi out to the terrace, closing the doors behind them.

Kazimi leaned back against the broad marble balustrade that ran the length of the patio. Far below, the picturesque harbor rested lazily in the embrace of the Tyrrhenian Sea.

"You do not come to my home for business," Dragović said. "You do not bring your business before my family."

"Why did I have to learn from my own staff our weapon is no longer in your possession?" Kazimi responded, his voice losing its previous charm.

Dragović masked his surprise Kazimi had found out so soon. "A temporary situation."

Kazimi gazed at him a long moment before saying, "You didn't think it necessary to tell me," Kazimi continued.

"I don't consider it a serious problem. Why trouble you?" Dragović said.

"I don't understand your petulance, Miro." Kazimi frowned. "The last day of December is approaching. Five years since American forces murdered your father and brothers. You, not I, chose that same day to take revenge. How can you—"

"The schedule is important and I intend to keep it," Dragović interrupted, unable to disguise his anger.

Kazimi folded his arms. "Yes, you want your revenge, and the money. And I wish to strike a powerful blow against the American infidels. Still, keeping to schedule would seem more practical if you had the weapon in your possession."

"We'll have it soon," Dragović responded. "I have reliable people on it."

"We've paid you millions for it. And advanced a sizable deposit for you to oversee using it. I will not risk losing millions from my cause, or have my honor stripped from me for your failure," Kazimi bellowed.

They both fell silent, each sizing up the other. Dragović trusted no one, but his mistrust of Kazimi now intensified. He knew Kazimi felt the same about him. Their relationship had just grown more dangerous.

"Enough bickering," Kazimi said. "The software is now in the United States, yes?"

Dragović nodded. "California."

"You're certain it's the only copy?"

"The late Mr. Abanda wiped his laptop the moment his security team spotted the CIA team. After copying the weapon to the flash drive," Dragović explained.

"You can't just rewrite the program? There must be someone."

"At some point, we might find someone with Mr. Abanda's genius and skills. But such people are rare, and who can say how long it might take?"

Kazimi shook his head, his irritation almost tangible. "And you didn't keep a single copy."

"We discussed it and you agreed," Dragović replied. "No copies as a security measure."

"To be clear, the missing drive contains the weapon?" Kazimi said.

"Yes. But it requires a complex decryption code to launch it."

"Which you have?"

Dragović nodded. "Abanda prepared a smartphone with the decryption software pre-programmed on a chip of his own design. If something occurred preventing the use of his laptop, we'd have the phone to decrypt the drive and trigger the weapon. Easy to transport, portable access to the internet, and no one looks twice at a cellular telephone."

"Still, the weapon is in the United States," Kazimi said, pacing. "We intended to launch the attack from my country."

"That is still best," Dragović said. "But if the retrieval doesn't go as I believe it will, I'm prepared to launch from the United States."

Kazimi's brow furrowed. "That would increase the risk. There'd be no interference at home, but in America the FBI is a serious threat to our purpose."

"We may not have a choice."

"And you're certain we can use the software without Abanda?" Kazimi asked.

Dragović nodded. "Once the decryption program on the phone unlocks the software on the drive, the weapon is triggered. The rest is automatic. It aggregates all the data needed to breach the target accounts, and then siphons the money into our new accounts in Switzerland, the Caymans, and Hong Kong."

Kazimi's expression relaxed for the first time since stepping onto the terrace. "The thought is exhilarating, is it not? Billions flowing into our hands within only minutes. Funds to finance our cause without limits."

"More your cause than mine," Dragović thought. But as long as

he was paid—and the United States suffered—he didn't care how the rest of the funds were used. "It will happen, and on schedule."

"You will keep me informed of every development."

"Of course."

Kazimi gazed at him for an uncomfortable amount of time, and then turned, strolling back toward the house. "I must go."

"As you say." Dragović followed him.

Kazimi took hold of the door lever, then paused, looking back at him. "See that you get it back, or you'll have no need of money."

Outwardly, he held his smile, but the threat angered Dragović. He resented it, and now he'd have to deal with it.

CHAPTER ELEVEN

The emergency room at Huntington Memorial Hospital was quiet when Cayden came to. He was flat on his back, looking up at the too-bright lights recessed in the ceiling. The voices of medical staff calling out information to one another made their way through the partially open sliding glass door of his room. Taking stock of himself, he noted a warm blanket covered him and he was wearing only his boxer shorts.

The first question that formed through the throbbing waves rolling in his head was, *Why am I still alive?* He followed it up with, *I wonder what's broken and how fast can it heal?* And then he remembered Kate, and a sickening fear pulled at him.

"Good, you're back with us," said a slender white-coated Indian man with dark, short-cropped hair standing over him. "I thought it best to just let you sleep."

"Kate." Cayden tried to sit up from the examination table.

The doctor stopped him with little effort, aided by the sharp stab of pain emanating from his chest. "You have three bruised ribs," the doctor explained. "If you're asking about the young woman who was staying at your home, she's in the waiting room with the gentlemen from the FBI."

Cayden relaxed back against the bed, relieved beyond measure that Kate hadn't been attacked. He looked up at the doctor. "FBI?"

The doctor nodded. "I'm told they called the ambulance and came in with you. Since you're not in handcuffs, I'm assuming you aren't on their ten most wanted list."

Cayden managed a slight laugh at the comment and received another stab of pain for his sense of humor. The FBI presence might explain why he was still alive. And it meant that the flash drive masquerading as a PEZ dispenser was an item of interest. He wondered if his attacker had found it. He wondered just what Kate might have told the agents.

"What time is it?" Cayden asked.

"Six-thirty-two in the morning," the doctor answered as he adjusted the surgical lamp, positioned Cayden's head and peered into his eyes. "I assume you have a headache," he speculated.

"Now that you mention it."

"How about any ringing in your ears?"

"No," Cayden answered.

"Good." The doctor gazed at him analytically. "Okay, let's see how you do upright."

A middle-aged Hispanic nurse with a professionally measured display of cheer suddenly stepped into his field of view, moving to the side of the bed.

"This is going to cause you some pain," the doctor warned Cayden.

The doctor took one arm while the nurse took another, and together they eased him into a sitting position on the edge of the bed. Another burst of pain from his ribs hit him, but then soon transformed into a deep, dull ache.

"You'll have some discomfort for quite a while," the doctor said. "You're lucky the ribs didn't fracture. Any dizziness?"

"No."

"You have a mild concussion to go along with the ribs," the doctor reported. "There's some bruising on your face, chest, and arms. Nothing requiring stitches. Considering you fell down a flight of stairs and took a decent beating, it could be worse."

"Appreciate the encouragement," Cayden said.

"You can go home, but take it easy for a few days," the doctor said as he retrieved a prescription pad and begin scribbling. "Those ribs are going to bother you for quite a while. I'm going to prescribe hydrocodone to help with the pain. If nothing else, it'll help you get some sleep. Four days' worth should be more than enough."

The nurse retrieved his clothes from the rack under the bed and handed them to him. She placed the shoes beside a chair against the wall and retrieved a coat from a nearby shelf. "Your girlfriend out there brought this along for you," she said, draping it across the end of the bed. "I'll be right back with a wheelchair," she announced.

"No, thanks," Cayden said. "I'll be fine."

The nurse paused, looking at the doctor for guidance.

The doctor shrugged, then nodded.

They exited the room, leaving him to get dressed, the nurse drawing privacy curtains across the glass door. It took him longer than normal to get dressed thanks to the pain in his ribs. The nurse's timing was excellent because Cayden had no sooner tied his shoes when there was a tap on the glass and the door slid open a few inches.

"How are you doing?" the nurse asked.

"Ready to go." Cayden stood from the chair under his own steam as the nurse slid the door open and pushed back the curtains. It relieved him that he felt relatively normal as his legs took on the support of his weight.

"I'm good," he assured her.

She eyed him skeptically. "Yeah? So what's the other guy look like?"

"I'm guessing a lot better than I do."

She laughed. "I'll show you the way out."

The nurse stayed at his side as they walked down the hallway.

Pain from the ribs radiated in his chest with every step, reminding him that one of Alan's killers had broken into his house and tried to kill him. The implications of the attack angered him. There was no question the assassins wanted the flash drive and would murder anyone in their way to get it. But they'd made a big mistake when they tried to murder him. The night before, he wondered how he could conduct his own investigation without bringing the police down on him. Now he was determined to find the killers, no matter what the police or FBI thought about it. He'd worry about them when and if it became necessary.

They reached a set of automatic double doors.

"Here we are. These open to the waiting area," the nurse announced.

"Thanks," Cayden said. "And thanks for patching me up."

"Merry Christmas," the nurse smiled, turning away and heading back along the hallway.

"Same to you." Cayden stepped toward the doorway.

The automatic doors hissed open, and as the emergency room became part of Cayden's past, the FBI loomed large in his immediate future.

The waiting room contained only a couple of people. An elderly couple seated in plastic chairs appeared tired and anxious. A college-aged man leaned on the counter at the check-in station, speaking with the duty nurse. He held a washcloth stained with blood against the side of his head. Kate sat in a chair at the far end of the room near the main entrance. Aside from signs of fatigue, she looked none the worse for wear. Leaning against a column near her stood Detective Mandala. Next to Mandala stood two men.

Cayden gauged the blonde guy to be in the six-foot-plus range. He had the build of somebody who'd played ball in high school or university, and was holding a thick manila folder. As Cayden moved closer, he noticed the folder bore a United States Secret Service stamp. The other man was shorter, and with a darker complexion. Both wore suits, starched white shirts, and sported conservative regulation FBI haircuts.

Both also looked haggard. Kate wasn't the only one who had been up all night. Cayden knew he was heading into a potential minefield. He had found the flash drive and neglected to turn it in. If they found cause, the police and FBI could charge him with obstructing an investigation. It was likely the FBI had already questioned Kate, and he had no way of knowing what she had told them or if she had given them the drive. He didn't believe in worrying about things he couldn't control. He'd just see how things progressed.

Kate, her face creased with lack of sleep, hurried to him as soon as she saw him. She wrapped her arms around him in a relieved hug.

"Easy." He winced. "Ribs."

"Sorry," she said, releasing him. "What the heck happened?"

"Later," he said, his eyes taking in the rest of her. "You all right?"

"Yeah, but don't count on me anytime soon for any more sleep-overs at your place."

"Party pooper."

"I didn't even know anything was going down until it was all over," Kate explained.

Cayden watched the FBI agents over Kate's shoulder, both of them waiting with respectful impatience. Detective Mandala appeared content to observe.

The blonde FBI man seemed to decide they had waited long enough. He stepped forward, reaching into his coat and producing his identification. "Mr. March, I'm Special Agent Patrick Langford, FBI." Agent Langford cocked his head toward his partner. "This is Special Agent Denbo."

Special Agent Denbo produced his identification as if it were a necessary inconvenience.

"Your doctor filled us in on your injuries," Langford continued. "How are you feeling now?"

"Like somebody beat the crap out of me and kicked me down a flight of stairs."

"You seemed to hold your own pretty well," Agent Denbo remarked.

Cayden didn't bother responding.

"Our business is time sensitive, I'm afraid, and we need to speak with you. Mind taking a ride with us?" Agent Langford asked.

"As long as you're taking me out to breakfast," Cayden answered. "I could really use some food." It was true. His stomach was churning.

"I had more of Pasadena Police headquarters more in mind," Langford replied. "Detective Mandala has arranged a place for us to talk."

"We can probably find you something to chew on," Mandala said.

"I assume I'm not under arrest," Cayden said.

"Should you be?" Agent Denbo responded, his tone brusque.

Denbo's remark irritated Langford. "Nobody's under arrest. You can understand why we have some questions. And we'd like to show you something that might help."

Cayden gazed at Langford, wondering what on earth the FBI wanted to show him. Questioning by the authorities was inevitable. He'd expected it, and there was no reason to put it off. Besides, he might learn something that would help him find Alan's killers.

"I know you've had a tough night." Langford let the sentence hang.

"No problem," Cayden said. "I'll help you however I can."

"Let's go then," Agent Langford said, gesturing toward the exit.

"Ms. James, we'll have someone drop you at home," Mandala told her.

"I'd like her to stay with me," Cayden blurted. "She was in my house last night. I'm concerned about her safety."

Mandala looked to Langford for a ruling.

Langford thought about it. "Okay, fine."

As they made their way to the hospital's parking structure, Cayden took the lead in his conversation with the FBI agents. "The nurse told me you guys brought me in. How'd that happen?"

"We were watching your house," Agent Langford answered.

"Were you now?" Cayden asked, hiding his surprise.

"Our surveillance team suspected someone breaking in," Denbo added.

"Suspected." Cayden glanced over at Mandala, but the detective's expression gave nothing away.

Denbo continued. "They saw movement at the back of your property. Somebody heading toward the house. Our guys moved in for a closer look."

Cayden thought it amazing they'd spotted the professional assassin at all.

"You didn't ask why the FBI was at your house," Mandala said.

Cayden's eyes went to the detective again. "It's not all that much of a stretch."

"Our guys heard the ruckus coming from inside," Agent Langford continued. "They broke in and found you at the bottom of the stairs, out cold."

"What about the guy?" Cayden asked.

"Gone by the time our team got inside." Agent Denbo shrugged. "Had to hear us coming."

"Looks like you guys have a good sense of timing," Cayden said. "Thanks."

"Glad we were there," Special Agent Langford said.

Cayden looked over at Kate, who was managing the entire misadventure as if it were something she went through every day. "I assume you've met Special Agents Langford and Denbo? Oh, and Detective Mandala?"

"I did." Her gaze moved between the agents, and without missing a beat, she said, "They had quite a few questions."

Good, Cayden thought. She understood he was interested in what she'd told the FBI.

They reached the parking structure, and Denbo punched the elevator call button. An elevator reached the ground floor, the doors slid open, and they all boarded.

Kate rummaged in her handbag. Her hand emerged, holding the Darth Vader PEZ dispenser. She thumbed the black helmet head and a piece of candy dropped into her palm. She popped it into her mouth. "PEZ?" she offered Cayden, extending the dispenser to him.

"Thanks," he answered, extending his hand. That answered the most important question. The candy dispenser meant nothing to the FBI.

Kate worked the mechanism, and a candy tablet fell into Cayden's palm. As he put the candy in his mouth, Kate held the toy up to the lawmen. "Guys?"

"No, thanks," Agent Langford answered.

Denbo just shook his head.

"Why not?" Detective Mandala accepted.

Kate handed him the PEZ dispenser. Mandala pulled back the Darth Vader head, caught the candy, tossed it into his mouth, and handed the toy back to Kate.

"I'd like another one, if you don't mind?" Cayden asked her.

Kate handed him the dispenser. "Keep it."

"Yeah? Thanks."

"No problem."

CHAPTER TWELVE

The morning was overcast and cold, with slivers of sunlight piercing through the clouds. Uneven patterns of shadows stretched across the blend of late nineteenth century brick and the more modern buildings typical to Pasadena. The older buildings helped preserve the city's small town feel.

Cayden rode with Kate on the way to police headquarters. They caravanned behind Mandala in his department issued unmarked Dodge Charger. The FBI agents took up the rear, driving a black Suburban. It took only ten minutes to reach Pasadena Police Department.

Mandala led them into the building and up to a lackluster meeting room on the second floor. Coffee in insulated paper cups and a box of assorted donuts waited for them on the large table in the center of the room. Mandala must have called ahead. Despite the institutional gray walls and utilitarian furniture, Cayden was grateful, for Kate's sake, it wasn't a formal interrogation room.

Special Agent Langford opened the Secret Service manila envelope he'd been carrying and pulled out a file folder. Everyone waited in silence while he scanned through the contents.

"Describe your relationship with Alan Fenland?" Langford began.

"We were friends," Cayden answered, pulling a cup of coffee closer and reaching for a chocolate glazed donut. "Good friends."

"Was he having any money problems?"

"Not that he ever mentioned," Cayden said. "I'm assuming you know Detective Mandala already asked these questions, and I already answered them."

Mandala took a sip of coffee but remained silent.

"Now you're answering them for us," Denbo said, an edge in his tone.

Kate glanced at Denbo, her eyebrows raised.

"Did Alan Fenland give you anything to hold for him?" Langford continued.

"No," Cayden said, taking a bite of his donut. It was true; Alan hadn't given him a thing.

"Had he visited your home recently?" Langford asked.

"Maybe a month ago."

"Purpose of his visit?"

"We recorded some music."

"You have any idea why somebody would want to break into your house, do you harm?" Denbo asked, a hint of accusation in his tone.

"I didn't know the guy, if that's what you're asking." Cayden's patience all but disappeared. He studied Denbo, wondering what the agent's problem was. Perhaps just being a suspect was enough to shorten the agent's temper.

"Can you identify him?" Denbo asked.

"I doubt it." Cayden kept his answers brief. If he wanted to mine any information, it was best to let the FBI do the talking.

"His face was covered?" Langford asked.

"No. He seemed confident I wouldn't be alive to ID him."

"You got a look at him, then?" Denbo pushed.

"No. It was dark, and I was busy trying to make sure he didn't cut my throat," Cayden replied.

"Yeah," Denbo muttered.

Cayden fixed his eyes on the FBI man. "You have some kind of problem with me, Special Agent Denbo?"

"If anybody has a problem, it's you," Denbo responded. "I think you're in this up to your elbows."

"Enough," Langford said, his voice edgy.

Whatever Denbo's problem, Cayden was tired of being on the receiving end of it. "Why don't you tell me who it was?" Cayden flung the question.

It caught Denbo off guard. "What?"

"I think you know."

Denbo's expression showed that he didn't much like a suspect thinking so clearly.

Kate had been observing the proceedings as if it was a scientific experiment that fascinated her. "This is my first interrogation. It's great."

No one in the room acknowledged the comment with anything more than a momentary glance at Kate. But Cayden couldn't help smile at her irreverence.

"We looked at the security footage from the Powell-Booth building," Langford took over. "Why were you in Mr. Fenland's office last evening?"

"As soon as we learned there was police activity at the house Alan rented from the school, my boss sent me over to find out what the problem was. He told me to check out the scheduling office as well. I went over there after Detective Mandala finished asking me his questions."

"You were there in an official capacity? That's what you're saying?" Denbo asked.

"Why else would I be there?"

"You didn't mention you going to the office when we talked," Mandala said, moving out of his corner.

"Like I already explained, my boss asked me to."

"Can you account for the hour of wiped surveillance footage?" Langford asked.

"How could I?" So far, neither FBI agent was impressing Cayden much.

"Have we confirmed Mr. March's whereabouts on the day of Fenland's murder?" Denbo asked Mandala.

"We checked his office's timekeeping software, and interviewed Raymond Chalmers, March's boss. On campus all day. Worked his normal shift," Mandala explained.

"And the day Mr. Fenland's body was discovered?" Denbo asked.

"The same," Mandala answered. "And Mr. Chalmers confirmed he'd instructed Mr. March to check out the Fenland residence."

"What was Ms. James doing with you at the scheduling office?" Langford asked Cayden.

"You viewed the security footage. You know she didn't come with me. She arrived after I did."

"Answer the question," Denbo insisted.

"I already told you, we were all friends," Kate said, finishing a donut and reaching for a second. "I hunted down Cayden to find out what happened to Alan."

"Why did Ms. James return home with you?" Langford took over again, ignoring his partner.

"I invited her." Cayden didn't bother to hide his impatience. "It was late. Our friend was dead. We were both upset about it. It seemed like a good idea to have her over."

Langford gazed unwaveringly at Cayden, processing what he had heard. Cayden stared back, wondering if he had pulled off getting to the other side of the minefield. He realized he was on uncertain ground. The drive in the PEZ dispenser was important enough to kill for. He didn't know what was on it. And he didn't know if he could trust anyone with the knowledge it was in his possession. Even the FBI.

"We're certain these murders are linked to a matter of national security," Langford said. "You all understand that everything discussed here stays in the room?"

Everyone voiced their understanding.

"Detective Mandala told you your friend wasn't the only one murdered that day," Langford said to Cayden, pulling a thin stack of 8 x 10 color photos from the folder in front of him. He pushed them across the table to Cayden. "Do you recognize this man?"

The man in the photo was dead, laying on his back with his arms stretched out above his head. An ugly gash stretched across his throat and blood had pooled in the dirt around his neck and head. He was an average-looking guy except for a small egg-shaped birthmark on his forehead. Cayden sifted through a half dozen other photos, each showing a different perspective of the crime scene. He recognized the landscape of the Arroyo Seco, the old eucalyptus trees and wild foliage growing on the hillside and alongside the paved road that ran around the Rose Bowl.

"I don't recognize him," Cayden said.

"His name is Donald Lincoln," Langford responded. "He was working out of the US embassy in Paris."

"He was a diplomat?" Kate asked.

Kate's assumption was logical, but Cayden knew diplomats were unlikely to be targeted by killers. The murdered man had to be a spook, using the embassy as a cover.

"He was CIA," Cayden answered for the FBI agents.

Neither Langford nor Denbo contended his statement.

Kate sat up a little straighter. "No way. Really?"

"A jogger found Lincoln's body the same afternoon your friend was murdered. Pasadena police responded, and that led to Detective Mandala getting involved," Langford explained. "We don't think it's a coincidence."

Cayden looked at Mandala. The detective told him someone else didn't think the two murders were a coincidence. Now Cayden knew who. But he still believed Alan was not involved in any wrongdoing. "Alan had nothing to do with your spook community."

"As far as you know," Denbo said.

Cayden didn't appreciate the remark.

"The CIA informed us that Lincoln had a contact at Caltech." Langford looked through his file. "A Dr. Franklin Zhandry."

"Everybody knows Dr. Zhandry. I mean at Caltech," Kate said. "He's a leading expert in quantum computing, quantum information processing, and decryption."

"Lincoln had consulted Zhandry in the past," Denbo explained. "He had more faith in Zhandry than our people at Langley."

The CIA case officer's presence at Caltech made sense to Cayden, especially since the flash drive ended up in Alan's desk drawer somehow.

"We think Lincoln needed Dr. Zhandry's help to decrypt something he was carrying," Langford said. "The trouble is, Zhandry was out of the country, lecturing in Great Britain. Lincoln didn't know that."

Now he knew why Lincoln brought the flash drive to Caltech. Cayden frowned. "Any reason you're sharing all this information with us?" Cayden asked.

"The same question occurred to me," Mandala added. "It sounds like this all should be classified."

"Well, Mr. March is no stranger to classified material," Langford said. "Isn't that right, Mr. March?"

Langford's tone made Cayden realize he was about to be backed into a corner. He eyed the Special Agent warily, wondering how much he knew.

L angford pulled two more folders from the manila envelope. He dropped them on the table, opening one. "It turns out you're a pretty interesting guy, Mr. March."

Cayden didn't respond. Langford's remark meant the FBI had run a background check on him. And being a federal agency, they had access to a lot of information. He didn't like his personal and professional life examined, especially in this environment.

"Entered UC Santa Barbara at age seventeen. Dropped out after four quarters with no declared major," Langford read from the file. "Enlisted in the United States Army, basic training at Fort Benning, Georgia. Deployed to Iraq where you drove convoys for a year."

"Uh oh," Kate muttered, just above a whisper.

"PCS to Stuttgart, Germany," Langford continued. "With letters of recommendation from your commanding officers you fast-tracked into the Army Rangers, and then the Green Berets."

Mandala leaned forward with rapt attention.

"You leave the Green Berets after two years, and then, and this is where it gets interesting," Langford said, looking up from the folder. "There's not much in your file after that except you had another change of station to Fort Bragg, North Carolina."

Mandala sat up straighter. "No kidding. Special ops?"

"And here we go." Kate slumped in her chair, crossing her arms in front of her.

Cayden knew what Kate meant. She'd experienced it with her late brother. When most civilians met someone in the military, they generally reacted by thanking them for their service. But with someone from special operations it was different. It meant a barrage of uncomfortable, or unanswerable questions. He knew those questions were about to come his way.

"JSOC CAG," Langford said.

"Delta Force," Mandala said, stunned and impressed.

"Your file has a lot of redactions, Mr. March," Langford said.

Cayden leaned back in his chair. "I'm a pretty boring guy. Somebody probably crossed out all the boring stuff."

Langford frowned. "I was so disappointed in your file that I put in a call to a Major Steven Dorn at Fort Bragg," Langford said. "He's assigned to Waste Management Operations at the base."

Everyone but Cayden and Kate chuckled at the command description.

"Major Dorn wouldn't answer a single question about you. Not one. He only acknowledged knowing you to assure me you're a man to trust in matters such as these. He implied we'd be wise to enlist your help. Unofficially, of course."

"Thanks anyway," Denbo muttered.

Kate leaned forward. "Cayden's got a major vouching for him. But nobody is vouching for me. What qualifies me being here?"

"Not a thing," Langford answered. "But we can prosecute you should you repeat anything discussed outside this room. We trust you're smart enough to avoid ten years in a federal prison."

"I'm also smart enough not to appreciate being threatened," Kate answered.

"You wanted to see if I'd show any sign of recognizing your CIA man," Cayden said, redirecting their attention to him. "I didn't. Now, if that's all, I had a rough night. I'd like to get home, get some rest."

"You want us to get the people who murdered your friend?" Langford asked.

"That's your job, isn't it?" Cayden answered.

Langford pulled more photographs from the folder. He spread them out on the table, pushing one across the table to Cayden.

The photo featured a couple walking shoulder-to-shoulder from a busy airport departure gate. It was of only moderate quality, taken from an airport security camera. The man appeared to be in his thirties, with an olive complexion and dark hair. The hair was longish but neatly combed, and he wore a short, trimmed beard. Large aviator sunglasses obscured his eyes. The girl was in her late twenties, also wearing sunglasses. She was tall and shapely. Her hair was light brown with some kind of color streaking or highlights.

Langford placed a finger on the print. "Robert Mendez and Terese Morrison, Mr. and Mrs. Boris Zeitlin, Ari Renaldi and Karen Switzer, Mr. and Mrs. William Metz."

"Just pick a name you like because we don't have a clue what their real ones are," Denbo interjected.

"This photo came from LAX security. They arrived four days ago from Paris using the names Daniel Russo and Cynthia Craven," Langford said, pushing a second photo forward.

This photo was taken from an elevated vantage point through

a high-quality telephoto lens. The same couple stood out among a throng of dark-skinned pedestrians as they strolled down a dingy retail street. In this photo, the man was clean shaven and wore a baseball cap. His muscular arms bulged from a short-sleeved bush shirt. The girl wore jeans and a linen blouse. She wore a wide-brimmed shade hat, and long brown hair cascaded down past her shoulders. As in the first photo, sunglasses covered their eyes.

"We know nothing about the girl. But judging by his looks and body language, we're guessing the man has military training. From what military, who knows?" Denbo said.

Cayden agreed. His assailant had displayed recognizable techniques and movements, and a level of expertise maybe better than his own.

"As far as nationality, that would be a guess, too," Denbo continued. "These are the only two photographs we have of them. The second one there was taken two years ago in Monrovia, Liberia."

"While they were there, a Liberian cabinet member named Garmuyu Quire ended up dead. Quire opposed the terms of a government deal that would enable the Genocorp steel conglomerate to establish a massive operation in the country. Somebody didn't agree with his position," Langford remarked.

"Professional assassins?" Mandala stared at the photos.

"And then some," Denbo responded.

Cayden leaned forward to get a better look at the photographs before him. "Okay, these people killed Alan and the CIA case officer. But why?"

"Now they're working for a man named Miroslav Dragović," Langford said.

"Who's that?" Mandala asked.

"An international arms dealer with strong terrorist connections," Cayden answered. One of Dragović's weapon shipments was the target of his special ops unit early in his career. The attack on the building housing the arms did not go as planned. Several civilians ended up dead. Members of Dragović's family died as well.

"You're well informed," Langford commented. "Dragović is more interested in profit than he is in fanatical terrorist causes. But it's his love of money that makes him willing to take part in terrorist activity."

"So, he provides guns to the terrorists?" Kate asked.

"There's some evidence that he's done more than just that," Denbo said.

"You believe this all has something to do with a potential terrorist attack? In this country?" Mandala asked.

"We do," Langford answered.

Cayden's thoughts shifted gears. If Alan's murder was linked to terrorist activity, it changed the situation. He'd kept his possession of the flash drive a secret because he believed its contents might reveal who killed Alan, and why. If the flash drive was connected with a terrorist plot, keeping it from the FBI could prove harmful to the United States. But he still wasn't sure he trusted them.

Langford continued. "We know Lincoln took something that belonged to Dragović, and whatever it is, it's the key to this mess. Dragović sent these two after him to get it back."

"How long have you known about these people?" Mandala asked, picking up a photo.

"The CIA passed us the information late last night," Denbo answered. "We're not withholding anything from you, detective."

"They're still looking for what Dragović sent them after?" Mandala asked.

"Yes, it may be why Fenland is dead."

"How's that?" Kate asked.

"Lincoln was on campus. If he somehow ended up in Alan's office, Russo and Craven probably knew about it," Cayden explained. "When they didn't find what they were looking for on Lincoln, they retraced their steps. The deleted security footage says it's a good bet these killers were in the building, and in Alan's office."

"But how was Fenland involved?" Denbo asked. "Did he have a background in decryption, too?"

Kate shook her head. "He was in a different field of study."

"So, Lincoln was in Fenland's office, but we don't have any logical answer why," Langford said, his voice hinting frustration.

"It's possible Lincoln didn't have a good reason to be in Alan's office," Cayden said. "If Russo and Craven were on his tail, the office might have been a convenient place to hide."

The words were barely out of his mouth when he realized Lincoln wasn't in the office to hide. He was in the office to ditch the flash drive. Cayden studied the photographs of Russo and Craven. These animals had killed his friend. He felt the desire for vengeance growing stronger.

Denbo tapped a finger on the photos. "Look, March, these people broke into your house last night. The only conclusion that makes sense is they think you have what they want."

Cayden did have what they wanted. If only Kate had been able to access what was on the drive, he would have a better sense of what to do with it. If the contents of the flash drive really were a threat to national security, then holding on to it was a dangerous thing to do. He no longer needed the drive to identify Alan's killers; the FBI had done that for him.

"So what about it, Mr. March?" Langdon pressed. "Do you have what Dragović's hired guns are after?"

CHAPTER THIRTEEN

Cayden felt every pair of eyes in the room focused on him. A part of him didn't like giving up control, but he was certain of the right course of action. Kate reacted with surprise as he reached into his pocket and placed the PEZ dispenser on the table in front of him. He found the puzzled expressions from Mandala and the FBI agents both satisfying and amusing. "Anybody have a pocketknife?"

Mandala produced one and handed it over to Cayden. He opened the smallest blade, found the seam in the dispenser's plastic, and pried it open. The flash drive popped from the casing and fell onto the tabletop. "This was in Alan's office."

"You should've handed it over to us the minute you found it," Denbo said. "Expect an obstruction charge coming your way."

Denbo never failed to confirm he was a contentious pain in the butt. Cayden wondered if the agent's animosity stemmed from the frustration of being unable to recover the drive himself, or if he was just a tool. "Knock yourself out," Cayden responded. "I found something you guys couldn't find. I didn't know its significance, and once you told me what it was, I gave it to you."

"Did you access the drive?" Denbo sounded pissed.

"Kate and I clicked into the drive at my place last night, but that's all we did."

"Whatever it is, it's protected by a sophisticated encryption program. I've seen nothing like it," Kate said.

Denbo began a reply, but Langford interrupted him. "I'd like to know how you came by this."

Cayden related the facts about how he found the PEZ dispenser in Alan's desk and why he found it unusual to be there.

When he'd finished, Langford gestured to Denbo. "Call the Director. Let him know we have it."

Denbo nodded, pulling out his phone as he stepped from the room.

Langford leaned toward Cayden. "Why do you think your friend hid this in his desk?"

"I don't think Alan hid anything in his desk," Cayden answered. "I believe your CIA guy dropped the PEZ dispenser in the drawer because Dragović's people were closing in on him."

"Lincoln was out of time," Langford agreed.

"It's the most logical explanation."

Mandala strolled around the table. "So, the killers went to Mr. Fenland's home when they didn't find the drive on Lincoln. They found nothing when they searched his home, and Fenland couldn't tell them anything because he didn't know what they were talking about. That would've pissed them off, which might explain the way they killed him."

"Getting pissed off had nothing to do with it," Cayden said. "Whichever of the two killed him enjoyed doing it. Alan ended up dead because they don't leave people alive to identify them."

Denbo hurried back into the room. "The Director wants us to find someone here who can decrypt the drive."

"What?" Langford responded, shocked. "The Quantico lab is much better equipped."

"No arguments here. The Director's concerned about security while the drive's in transit. He's also concerned with the time element. Enlisting someone here is safer and more efficient."

"That may not be so easy," Mandala said. "We know Dr. Zhandry is out of the country. If he's the leading expert in his field, who can step in for him?"

"He's not the only person at Caltech with the capabilities," Denbo said, glancing at Langford.

Langford tapped his fingers on the file folder in front of him. "True. Ms. James is a gifted hacker."

"No." Cayden smacked his fist down on the tabletop.

Kate straightened in her chair. "Well, I was thinking—"

"Kate," Cayden interrupted. Her mouth closed, a look of surprise on her face.

"What's your problem, March?" Denbo said.

"At least two people are dead because of this thing," Cayden said, unable to keep the growl from his voice. "Kate is already at risk because she was at my house last night. You're not painting a bigger target on her back. Find somebody else."

"What were you going to say, Ms. James?" Langford asked.

"Nothing." Kate kept her eyes on Cayden. "I had a thought, but it got away from me."

"If you think this is the time to jerk us around, you're way off the mark," Denbo said, more impatient than ever.

Cayden fixed an icy stare on Denbo. "Mind your manners, Special Agent."

Kate shifted in her chair, her eyes moving to the FBI agents and then back to Cayden.

"Ms. James?" Langford pressed. "Are you able to help us or not?"

Cayden despised what the FBI was trying to do. They didn't care about Kate or anyone else. They just wanted a solution to their problem. And now they were bullying her. He didn't want that kind of pressure on her. "It's your decision, Kate."

Kate spoke with reluctance. "Last night, we raised the possibility of Mariana Vasquez being able to help."

Cayden groaned to himself. He didn't expect Kate to involve Mariana Vasquez, especially now that she understood the danger.

"Who's that?" Langford asked.

"She's a graduate student at Caltech. Working on her doctor-ate," Cayden snapped. "And the second you involve her, you put another life in danger."

Kate sank down in her chair, realizing what she'd done.

"Are you saying your friend is better suited for this?" Denbo asked, his tone softening.

"She's not a friend. I mean, not a close one," Kate answered. "My original idea was we should work on it together."

"Why's that?" Langford said.

Kate pointed at the flash drive. "Like I told you, I've never seen anything like this before. If I did the work myself, it would take some time. I'm very good, but Mariana's better. Together we'd cut a lot of time off the process. You know, two heads are better than one."

"Sounds good," Langford said.

Cayden couldn't argue with Kate's logic, but it changed noth-ing. "Don't do this, Kate."

She leaned toward him. "If this thing is connected to terrorists. I mean, if we can help stop a potential terrorist attack, isn't it worth the risk?"

Cayden shared the same train of thought. He fought terrorism throughout his military career. He felt great pride in defending his country, so he identified with Kate's desire to help stop an attack. "It's a big risk."

"Slow down a little," Langford said. "We haven't yet asked Ms. Vasquez for help. She might say no. You willing to reach out for us, Ms. James?"

"Think about it first," Cayden advised.

"They'll be fine, March," Denbo said. "They'll be under FBI protection."

Cayden shook his head. "Gee, that makes it a lot better."

"Ms. James?" Langford asked again.

"I think it's something we have to do, Cay. I can at least call her," Kate said.

"Arrange to meet with her," Langford instructed. "I don't want any of this discussed over a cellular connection."

Kate retrieved her phone, rising from her chair. She dialed while walking to a corner of the room.

Cayden's insides began churning. The FBI was herding Kate into a dangerous position. He couldn't let anything happen to her. He'd hoped he was done with life and death situations, and resisted the idea of being drawn back to it. But if Kate was at risk, as much as he loathed the idea, he'd have to be involved.

Cayden turned toward Langford. "I'm on the protection detail," Cayden said.

"Not a chance," Denbo stated.

Cayden glared at Denbo. "I'm on the detail or I'll make sure neither of them help you."

"The FBI is more than capable of keeping two women safe," Denbo insisted.

"I'm on the detail," Cayden repeated.

"Enough," Langford said. "You'll be there, Mr. March. You'll be a strong asset."

Langford's ruling irked Denbo, but the agent offered no further arguments.

Kate stepped back to the table, the cell phone still at her ear. "Mariana's willing to meet, but isn't available until about seven tonight."

Neither Langford nor Denbo liked hearing this news.

"Why is that?" Langford asked.

"She was at Lake Tahoe, on a ski trip with a friend," Kate said. "They're already on the road, but it's a long drive."

"Ask her if she can meet at nine. Dupont's Bar and Grill on Lake," Cayden said.

She repeated his request into the phone. "She can do it." Kate thanked Mariana and ended the call.

"I want you there," Langford directed Denbo.

"Pick Kate up at my place?" Cayden instructed Denbo. "Say eight-forty."

Denbo's glare made it clear he didn't like getting orders from him.

"I'm not riding with you?" Kate asked.

"It's likely Russo and Craven are still surveilling me. I'm not leading them to this meeting. I'll meet you there."

"That makes sense," Denbo admitted. He handed Kate his business card. "Use the cell number there whenever you need to."

Cayden stood from the table and Kate followed his lead. He held up the flash drive. "Now, what about this?"

Langford began reaching for it.

"We have safes in our evidence locker," Mandala said. "They're secured behind a gated entrance. There's an officer on duty at the locker desk twenty-four-seven."

Langford began to speak, but Denbo beat him to it. "We couldn't secure it any better."

Langford dropped his hand, his gaze moving to Denbo for a moment. Cayden wondered if there was going to be an FBI/police pissing match, but Langford surprised him.

Langford nodded. "Sounds good, thanks."

Cayden passed the flash drive off to Mandala.

"Just let me know when you need it," Mandala told Langford.

"Looks like we're done here for now," Langford said, handing Cayden his business card.

"You've got the rest of the day," Cayden said. "Use the time to find somebody else for the job." He moved toward the door with Kate beside him. She reached it first and pulled it open.

"March," Denbo called to him. "Most special ops guys are just hitting their stride at your age. You're working as a security guard. What happened?"

Cayden paused in the doorway and, without turning around, said, "It wasn't what I expected."

He shut the door behind him.

CHAPTER FOURTEEN

They sat at a comfortable table next to the window in a popular breakfast spot on Walnut Avenue, only a block away from police headquarters. It was still too early for the mainstay breakfast crowd, so the place was quiet and they had a fair amount of privacy. The room was warm and comfortable, and the aroma of frying bacon in the air gave the place a homey atmosphere.

Neither of them had spoken since leaving police headquarters, and Kate had barely looked at him. Once their server had brought mugs of steaming coffee and taken their orders, she leaned toward him.

"I'm so sorry," she said. "I didn't think."

Cayden shrugged. "They were pressuring you."

"I just thought because we'd already talked about reaching out to her." Kate let the sentence trail off.

"That's before we knew what we were dealing with," he explained.

"You really surprised me, handing over the drive." Kate sipped her coffee.

"It was the only reasonable thing to do, considering the terrorist connection."

He wondered now if that was true. Part of him was confident he'd made the right choice in giving the drive to the FBI. But he began wondering if keeping the drive a secret, and then using it as bait, might have been a faster way to the killers. It would have been a high-risk move.

"What have I done to Mariana?" Kate said to herself.

"I gave you the nod to give her up."

"Now I feel a lot better."

"Denbo and Langford shouldn't have strong-armed you. I wanted to put a stop to it. Keeping you and Mariana out of it would have been the better choice. But now we're involved," Cayden reassured her. "I'll be with both of you until it's done."

"So, what's Denbo's problem with you?"

"Not a clue."

"I wish I'd kept my mouth shut about Mariana. I'm so pissed at myself."

"She may not even agree to do it. And if that happens, I want you to tell them you can't do it without her."

Kate leaned back in her chair. "I admit, it won't seem so scary if you're hanging with us. Kind of like having my own Jason Bourne licensed-to-kill bodyguard."

"You're mashing up your fictional spy characters." Cayden shifted his position in the chair. His bruised ribs ached, and a sharp stab of pain struck him when he reached for his coffee. He couldn't help wincing.

"Ribs?" Kate asked.

"Yeah."

"Thank God for your training, your experience. It saved your life."

"According to the FBI, they had something to do with it."

Kate reached for her coffee mug. "You're still all that, March."

She was partially right. He still had the skills, but he was far from being in top shape. After leaving active service, he'd allowed himself to take it easier. His technique had gotten sloppy. If he was going to deal with Alan's killers, Cayden realized he would have to do something about his physical condition. There wasn't much time, but anything would be an improvement. He limited his response to Kate with a simple, "Maybe."

"So, what was it like?" Kate said, her tone serious.

"What was what like?"

"Special ops. I'd ask Rob what he was doing, where he was. But he always just told me he couldn't say."

"That's what he had to say," Cayden responded.

"You left The Unit because of what happened with Rob. I didn't agree, but I understood. But what was it like for you while you were still in?"

He gave a subtle shake of his head. "I can't really say."

Kate scrunched up her face in mock anger.

"I can't talk about what I did, but I enjoyed the life. Our work made a difference. And I have to admit, there was a feeling of power that went along with the gig."

"Well, that was more than Rob ever told me."

"It's not what everybody thinks it is," Cayden said. "It's not like in the movies."

"So what is it?"

"It's a manual labor job, just like any other manual labor job. It just requires a more severe level of training. Instead of clearing dirt with a shovel, you clear it with a gun."

Kate hesitated before speaking again. "So, you've killed people."

Cayden raised an eyebrow. "Doesn't sound like you're asking a question."

"Well?"

He looked at her for a long moment before responding. "If I did, they were bad people who needed to die."

The server approached the table with their orders. They thanked him and dug in.

Cayden bit into a mouthful of omelet and watched Kate as she mowed into her breakfast.

"How many donuts did you eat at the police station?" Cayden asked.

Kate didn't answer as she focused on the food in front of her.

"How many?" he coaxed.

"Two," Kate answered between mouthfuls.

"And now you've got about two pounds of breakfast in front of you."

"Your point?"

"Why don't you weigh three hundred pounds?"

"Healthy metabolism and a hollow leg."

"Unbelievable."

Kate eyed him for a few moments, then between mouthfuls, she said, "I've been wondering about something. Why are you working as a security guard?"

Cayden felt a touch of discomfort. "Where did that come from?"

He didn't want to tell her one of the main reasons he took the job was to be in her general proximity. She wouldn't like it if she knew.

"You're smart. You've got a lot going for you," Kate continued. "I mean, there's nothing wrong with being a security guard."

Cayden said nothing, taking another sip of coffee.

"So, why?" Kate pressed. "Considering your background and everything."

"I like the food in the campus cafeteria."

She frowned at him and turned back to her breakfast.

He swallowed another mouthful of omelet. "You should stay at my place. Just until we're on the other side of this mess."

"You think it's still necessary?"

"They're just moving down the line of anyone who might have come in contact with the drive," he explained. "They assumed I had it, and you were in the house when they broke in."

A little of the color drained from Kate's face.

"Stay at my place," he repeated.

"They'll never get to me there." Kate rolled her eyes.

"At least at my place I'm within calling distance," he said. "Russo and Craven had the nerve to grab the CIA officer from school property. The campus is generally busy, so you should be fine, but don't go anywhere alone."

Kate gave it all some thought. "Okay, I'll pick up some things from home."

Cayden picked up his coffee mug and leaned back in his chair. "Make sure you call me whenever you reach where you're going. And call when you're heading to my place."

"You think Mariana will sign up?" Kate asked, concern in her tone.

He remembered how amused Mariana had been when she learned the school suspended her campus computer access for sixty days. He knew it would be child's play for her getting around the punishment, and she probably considered it a personal challenge to do so. "I don't think she'll be able to resist."

"You know, you told me all this mess was a job for the police. You didn't want to be involved," she said.

"Russo involved me when he broke into my house and tried to kill me."

They both finished their breakfasts, and Cayden signaled for their check. The moment the server put it in front of him, he remembered something that made him flush with a mild embarrassment.

"Kate, my wallet didn't make it to the hospital with me."

"If I had a nickel for every guy who used that line after a meal."

"Sorry."

"No worries; I plan to eat through everything you've got at home."

She pulled cash from her purse and counted it onto the tray with the bill. Without looking up, she asked, "Did it bother you, Cay?"

"What?"

"Killing people."

There wasn't a way to answer her truthfully. He couldn't fathom Kate or anyone else ever understanding. He didn't comprehend the answer himself, and it ate at him. Killing didn't bother him at all.

CHAPTER FIFTEEN

Russo was in a foul mood. His wrist throbbed where March had struck him with something hard and heavy. Cyn taped it up, but he knew from experience the bruises and swelling would annoy him for days. The wrist wasn't the only thing that hurt from the previous night's fight. His chest ached, and he had several nasty bruises covering his abdomen where the man had landed blows. Bruises showed on the left side of his jaw as well. Now he knew for certain March was more than just a security guard.

And beyond that, a call from their contact a few minutes earlier brought unwelcome news. He held off placing the call to Dragović. It was best to put a spin on reporting the recent developments.

Russo's original intention was to kill March and then search the place. The girl, Kate James, was of little concern, but he was prepared to deal with her if she got in the way. He'd been cautious about going into March's house, but he had underestimated the man. That wouldn't happen again.

Then there was the FBI. Their arrival had prevented him from finishing off March. He could have remained in the house and killed the agents, but doing so would have created bigger problems. The greater question was why he had not been alerted to the

FBI's presence that night. The excuse given by their contact was inadequate, but he would handle that later.

He and Cyn had spent the night in the car, taking turns keeping surveillance, first at the hospital where March had been transported, then at the police station. Now March and the James woman were in the little restaurant across the street. Russo had parked far enough down the block from the place, so he was looking at March's back. It was convenient the couple had chosen a seat by the window. Even with the reflections in the glass, he had an unobstructed view of them.

"You think they're a couple?" Cyn asked, bored.

"I don't care."

"We know where the flash drive is now, and this guy doesn't have it," Cyn stated. So, why are we bothering with him?

"Now we know the police have it," Russo said. "I don't consider that an improvement."

She patted his hand. "It's all gonna work out, babe. We always make it work out."

Russo glanced at her, annoyed by her chitchat that had persisted throughout the morning. She looked different from two days earlier. Cyn found a salon near their hotel and her hair was back to being pure blonde, with all the colorful streaks removed. He looked different, too. Cyn cut his long hair to a shorter length and shaved off his beard. It was a good practice to increase the difficulty of being identified.

"How long are we hanging out here?" Cyn asked.

"Until I think we've been here long enough. I want to know more about him," Russo said with brusqueness.

"Geez, why bother?"

"I'm not sure. But I have a bad feeling about this guy," he answered, picking up his phone from the center console. "I've put it off long enough. I need to tell Dragović."

Dragović answered on the second ring. "Yes."

"We have its location, but we can't get to it right now."

"Why not?" Dragović asked, annoyance in his tone.

"I just got off the phone with our friend," Russo said. "The product fell into the possession of a security guard at Caltech. He handed it over to the FBI this morning."

"Where is it now?" Dragović's tone was electric with anger.

"Locked in a vault somewhere inside Pasadena Police headquarters. We already had eyes on the guard. Figured he must have knowledge of the drive's location. But we couldn't confirm he had it, and we didn't know he'd handed the drive over until we got the call."

"Our friend couldn't get possession?"

"He had no opportunity, but it's going to be fine," Russo replied. "The FBI is reaching out to someone at Caltech. A hacker, an accomplished one. They hope she can get past the encryption."

"And who is this?"

"A student at the school named Vasquez," Russo answered. "We'll get the drive when they take it from the vault for her."

"This woman's already agreed?" Dragović asked.

"Uncertain. But if she hasn't yet, she will," Russo said. "The FBI will be persuasive."

"How did this security guard come to have it?"

"No way of telling, but he's no ordinary security guard. I suspected it when I first saw him, but now I'm certain."

"What're you talking about?" Dragović asked, his tone impatient.

"He has training similar to mine," Russo answered.

"If he no longer has the drive, he's irrelevant," Dragović snapped. "Our first concern is this hacker. It's unlikely she can get past the encryption, but we can't afford the chance she might."

"We'll see she doesn't."

"Really? And what will you do about my weapon being in the possession of the authorities? What if they never allow it out of the police facility?"

"The police department doesn't have the computing power necessary on site. They have to move it. I promise you, we'll get it back," Russo said.

"December 31ˢᵗ is not far away." Dragović's voice smoldered with anger.

"We'll get it back."

"If you don't, it will be the last promise you ever break."

For the next few moments, only static was audible through the connection. Russo knew his employer didn't issue empty threats. One always walked a thin line when working with people like Dragović. They didn't handle setbacks or failure well, and could often turn dangerous. But Dragović paid him his immense fees because he always accomplished what he set out to do. No, Dragović didn't believe he would fail. Dragović was afraid of losing the weapon he'd invested so much money in.

When Russo finally spoke, his tone was low, even, and hard as stone. "It's best not to threaten me, Mr. Dragović."

"Do I need to remind you how high the stakes are?"

"You don't have to remind me about anything."

There was a sharp click, and the phone's speaker fell silent.

CHAPTER SIXTEEN

F reshly showered and in clean clothes, Cayden went to what had once been a small servant's quarters on the lower floor of his house and punched in the combination to the twelve hundred pound safe he kept there. The safe contained a variety of shotguns, rifles, and handguns. Most of them were for sport, but several were for professional use.

He pulled his Beretta 92 Elite LLT Compact and a Sig Sauer SRD9 titanium suppressor from the safe, placing them both on the worktable. He had commissioned a friend to fit the Beretta 92 and his Sig P320 XCompact with threaded barrels designed to accept the same suppressor. The lightweight and compact SRD9 also fit his Beretta M9A3 service pistol. He located his supply of 9mm subsonic rounds he loaded himself and removed them from the safe along with extra magazines.

While checking over the equipment, his property tax problem occupied his mind. He mulled over the options for raising the money, but the options were few. With his background and training, he could always get a job with private paramilitary firms like Academi or Triple Canopy. They paid top dollar for men like him. But taking such a job meant he'd be back in the life he was trying to leave behind. The thought made his stomach knot. Besides that, landing one of these high-end paramilitary jobs took time, and time he didn't have.

That left the option Cayden least wanted to consider. The money he needed would be chump change to his father, but asking him for a loan felt like a sizable mountain to climb. Besides, a loan would only be a short-term fix. He was uncertain if his father would help him and he didn't want to revisit the old issues between them. Still, he considered how he might approach the request, playing possible dialogues over and over in his mind. If his father agreed to help, there would be conditions, but would they be reasonable and without strings attached?

After locking up his safe, he headed for Caltech. There were no less than four messages from Raymond in his voicemail, each registering a higher irritation and impatience than the last. It was Cayden's job to keep his boss informed, and he had to admit that, in this case, he'd done a piss-poor job of it. But he figured that getting beaten half to death, spending the night in the hospital, and then being questioned by the FBI should be a good enough excuse.

He accelerated onto the eastbound ramp of the 210 Freeway, and ten minutes later, entered the Holliston Avenue parking structure at Caltech. Building 62, the campus security office, was on the ground level opposite the driveway. Cayden pulled into one of the parking spots reserved for security personnel in front of the office.

Raymond spotted him from his glass-enclosed office the moment he came through the door. He hurried out from behind his desk and waved him in.

"It's about time you dragged your ass in here," Raymond scolded as Cayden reached the doorway. "I don't think I've ever seen such a mess of police on this campus. And what's the FBI doing here?"

"Slow down," Cayden said, sinking into a chair in front of the desk, unable to stop from wincing at the sting from his ribs as the chair took his weight.

Raymond stood at the corner of his desk, glaring down at

Cayden. He was a few inches shorter than Cayden, but tough and muscular despite a slight paunch that was forming with age. "Slow down, my ass. I wanna hear what you know about this crap storm."

Raymond often seemed to have only one volume, loud, and one tone, pissed. But at his core, Cayden thought him to be a decent guy. The man had worked hard in his life to overcome past traumas—joining the Navy to escape an abusive, alcoholic father after his mother passed away, and using his military benefits to get a university education. He'd been in the Los Angeles Police Department for fifteen years, and now he was head of the security force at one of the most prestigious universities in the nation. Cayden knew Ray to be a solid guy dedicated to his staff and the university his job tasked him to protect.

"Pasadena police came by first thing this morning," Raymond said, glancing at a report on his cluttered desk. "Alan Fenland."

"Yeah."

Raymond's voice softened. "I'm sure sorry about that. I know he was a friend of yours."

"Appreciate it." Cayden shifted in his chair and got jabbed with another wave of rib pain.

"You don't look so hot. I heard about the ruckus at your place last night. You okay?"

"A little sore and scratched up."

"Why'd they come after you?" Raymond asked, taking a seat behind his desk.

Cayden filled Raymond in, giving him a thorough report. He explained the police and FBI were convinced the murders took place because the killers were looking for something, but omitted everything pertaining to the flash drive.

When Cayden finished his report, Raymond leaned back in his chair. "The FBI and the police are talking to everybody on campus who even remotely knew Alan Fenland. And they're keeping us out of the bungalow and scheduling office."

"They're doing what they do," Cayden said.

"Well, I'd say you should go home and get some rest," Raymond said.

Cayden couldn't help but laugh.

"What?" Raymond asked.

"You've been yelling at me to get my butt to work for the past sixteen hours."

Raymond looked a little like a boy who got caught with his hand in the cookie jar. "That's before I got a look at you. Geez, I didn't realize you were half dead. You should take tomorrow off, too."

"About that. I've already got vacation time scheduled for the week between Christmas and New Year's Day," Cayden reminded him. "I want to take off these next few days before Christmas, too."

Raymond puffed out a frustrated breath. "With all this police activity going on around here right now? You kidding me?"

"Like you said, the police don't want us involved," Cayden said. "You need me for something, pick up the phone."

"You gonna tell me why you need the time?" Raymond asked.

Cayden couldn't tell Raymond about the FBI involving Kate and Mariana Vasquez in their investigation without revealing information about the flash drive. "Alan was a friend. I need a little time to process."

Raymond mulled it over, looking grumpier by the moment. "All right, take the days. But you better answer the phone if I call," he said.

"You got it," Cayden said, pushing himself out of the chair.

"Hey," Raymond called out to him as he moved toward the door. "You wouldn't be thinking about doing something stupid, would you?"

"Something stupid?"

Raymond's eyes narrowed. "Just leave the man hunting to the police and the FBI. That's what they're paid for."

"No argument here," Cayden replied. "Merry Christmas, boss."

"Merry Christmas, you jackass, and don't go getting yourself killed."

CHAPTER SEVENTEEN

Cayden exited the parking structure, turning north onto Holliston. As he made the turn, he noticed a Jeep Cherokee, dark blue, parked in a delivery loading zone on the opposite side of the street about a hundred feet down the block. The afternoon light reflecting off the windshield made it hard to know for sure, but it looked like the driver might be behind the wheel. He didn't see any campus parking tags on the car, so it had no business being there. If he were on duty, he'd go tell them to move, but he knew one of his patrol guys would get around to it soon enough. He gave the 4Runner some gas and continued on his way.

He had formed a vague plan to make sure no one could tail him when he traveled to the meeting with Mariana Vasquez and decided to make one more stop to see if he could solidify that plan. Halfway to his destination, he glanced in his rearview mirror and noticed a blue Jeep Cherokee several cars back. There were a lot of blue Cherokees on the road, but with all that had taken place in the last twenty-four hours, it was best not to consider this a coincidence.

Cayden made several spur-of-the-moment lane changes and turns; standard evasion tactics. But the only car that kept showing up in his rear-view mirror was the Cherokee. Okay, definitely not a coincidence. His first instinct was to lose the tail. But then he decided it would be better to let the Cherokee know where he was heading.

A couple of right turns headed him back in the right direction. Several minutes later, he pulled to the curb in front of Walker Fighting Arts. Cayden took his time climbing out of the 4Runner. By the time he walked to the entrance, he caught the reflection of the Cherokee cruising down the block in the dojo's plate glass window.

The place wasn't very busy. An instructor worked with a young woman at the back of the room. Closer to the front, two advanced students were sparring, displaying a decent level of skill.

"It's been at least a month, man." The dojo's owner, Seth Walker, greeted him with a handshake moments after he entered the studio.

"Guess I've been a little lazy," Cayden admitted.

"Couldn't have been too lazy." Seth pointed a finger at the bruises on Cayden's face.

"A little roughhousing got out of hand."

"What's the other guy look like?"

"Let's just say I shouldn't have stayed away for a month."

Seth let out a big guffaw. "My next student isn't for another hour, so I'm all yours."

Cayden hadn't planned on working out, but when he thought about the beating he'd taken the night before, a little intense training didn't seem like such a bad idea. "I didn't bring my gear. You have a gi I can borrow?"

"Locker room," Seth answered.

They walked to the back of the room, passing the glass display counter with its selection of martial arts DVDs, gifts, and other supplies, to the locker room entrance beyond. Seth pointed out a rack where Cayden found a clean gi in his size. A few minutes later, he rejoined Seth in the studio.

"A workout wasn't in my plans today, but I'm glad you're available," Cayden said.

Seth grinned. "Nobody else here is much of a match for you."

Cayden knew that was true; Seth Walker was more than a match for him. Born in Osaka, Japan, to a black father and Japanese mother, Seth was just under six feet with a slender but muscular build. He inherited most of his features from his father, a chocolate complexion and a strong, handsome face. But he inherited his mother's eyes, which gave him an exotic look women loved. He'd been studying martial arts since he was four. Now proficient in a variety of styles, he operated this thriving mixed martial arts studio.

"You okay?" Seth studied Cayden as he walked onto the mat. "You're not moving quite right."

"Just do me a favor. Stay away from the ribs today."

Seth nodded. "Broken or bruised?"

"Bruised."

"Whatever you say."

Seth was on him in an instant, launching a lightning fast kick at his right knee. Cayden parried, spinning around in the same motion and launching a kick of his own, and then advancing with a series of rapid punches. Seth blocked most of those punches before countering with his own barrage of strikes. And so it went for the next forty minutes. Despite the constant stabs of pain from his ribs, Cayden felt he held his own well. His instincts were still sharp, and Seth was exercising them to be even sharper.

When they called it quits, Cayden returned to the locker room for a quick shower. After toweling off and getting dressed, he made his way back to the front of the dojo, feeling sore but satisfied.

Seth was waiting for him with curiosity in his eyes. "You said you didn't plan to work out today. So what'd you come by for?"

"I need a little favor," Cayden answered.

"I can handle a little one."

He quickly explained what he had in mind.

A few minutes later, he was back at his 4Runner. He spotted the blue Jeep Cherokee parked in a space down the block on the opposite side of the street. Cayden started the engine and pulled into traffic. He did his best to get the Jeep's plate numbers as he rolled past, but with the angle and the shadows, he could only make out the last one, a nine. He headed home, speculating about what the killers in the blue Cherokee had in mind for him.

CHAPTER EIGHTEEN

Kate arrived at the house a little before 6:00 p.m., a rolling suitcase in tow. A pair of Wrangler jeans tucked into high brown boots and a colorful wool poncho draped over a denim shirt protected her from the chilly night air. With more than an hour and a half before Denbo's scheduled arrival, Cayden suggested they grab a bite to eat in Old Town.

They ended up at the Bicycle Bell and found a table toward the back of the place. It was early for the Bell, so the live music and crowd noise hadn't yet gotten underway. The service was fast and their orders arrived in only a few minutes. Their conversation was casual for a while, but then Kate changed the tone.

"Special Agent Denbo was pissed about you taking control of this meeting with Mariana."

"I took control?" Cayden said.

"Only the when, where, and how parts."

"If he wanted to call the shots, he should have shown me he took the threat more seriously," he said.

As they talked, Cayden couldn't help feeling a nagging discomfort about Kate's participation in the FBI's dangerous plan. He couldn't be everywhere at once, and Kate couldn't be with him all the time. The entire situation kept him in a state of frustration and anxiousness.

"I don't want him taking me to the meeting," Kate said, taking a sip of coffee. "He's been so unpleasant."

"I know, but it's the best way to go," Cayden replied. "I can't risk leading Russo and Craven to you and Mariana. And what if they attacked my truck with you in the car?"

"Still better than riding with Denbo."

Cayden laughed. "Okay, I'm taking the bike. You wouldn't want to freeze, would you? It's not even fifty-five degrees out there."

Kate sighed. "It gives me the creeps they've been following you. Never in a million years did I ever imagine I'd ever be involved with this kind of thing."

"Must be your lucky decade. We need to get going." Cayden got their server's attention and signaled for the check.

They arrived back at the house with ten minutes to spare. Cayden turned on the foyer security monitor so he could keep an eye out for Denbo. The wait wasn't long. The Special Agent turned into the driveway around eight-forty on the dot. Instead of the Black Suburban, he was driving a Chevy sedan.

Cayden walked Kate out to the car, surveying the street on the way. He acknowledged Denbo with a casual wave of his hand as he opened the door for her.

"March." Denbo acknowledged him as Kate slipped into the passenger seat.

He leaned down in order to see the agent, steadying himself with a hand on the open door.

"Right on time," Cayden greeted him.

Denbo responded in his usual charming way. "I want to be clear. This meet is an FBI operation and you're not running anything tonight."

"Good to know."

"I mean it, March."

Cayden gave him a tight-lipped grin. "I got it."

Denbo's frustration increased. "There are no plans that don't get run past me first."

Cayden felt his patience slipping. "You guys dragged Mariana Vasquez and Kate into this mess," he said. "I'll do whatever I think is best to make sure nothing happens to them. This meeting and the way it's going down is me doing just that."

He noticed Kate adjusted her position in the seat, uncomfortable with the conversation.

"I don't know what it is about you, March." Denbo frowned.

"We don't have to go steady. We just have to work together to make sure nobody else gets killed."

Kate issued a fake cough. "We should get going."

"Yeah," Denbo said, his eyes still on Cayden.

"I'll see you there."

As he closed the car door, he heard Kate mutter, "This should be fun."

She nailed him with a glare of annoyance through the car window as Denbo put the car in gear.

Cayden walked behind the sedan, following it to the end of the driveway. When the car turned onto the street and disappeared from view, he kept his eyes on the intersection. After waiting and watching for over a minute, the blue Cherokee did not appear. He hurried back into the house.

Cayden slipped into a fleece-lined denim jacket as he entered his garage from the inside house door. He wore a flannel work shirt under the jacket and a pair of jeans. The Beretta 92 was in a belt holster set back on his hip and well concealed under the jacket.

In a few steps, he reached his bike, a Ducati Diavel Strada. He never tired of looking at it, and it still surprised him a little that he even owned it. His original intention was to find a good sports bike. Something fast and maneuverable, with plenty of power. He first spotted the Ducati in the dealer's service bay. It was the perfect blend of sports bike and cruiser. With its powerful engine, the bike was very close to sports bike maneuverable. The salesperson described it as pre-owned, with less than four thousand miles on the odometer. The former owner's wife gave him an ultimatum: the bike had to go, or she would.

After a test ride lasting more than an hour, he was sold.

Cayden opened up one of the semi-rigid saddlebags. He retrieved three loaded magazines for the Beretta from his jacket pockets, already paired in two belt holsters, and secured them inside. The saddlebags from the factory were not lockable, but he had designed and attached a system to secure them in place on the bike. He also modified each bag so they could be locked shut. It wouldn't stop anybody serious, but it would discourage convenience thieves.

He thumbed the button on the garage door remote and retrieved his helmet where it hung from the right mirror. The Ducati's engine was growling by the time the door was up. He was soon rolling out of the crescent.

Cayden took his time riding the bike around the neighborhood, often checking the rearview mirrors. He slowed when passing side streets, looking to see if the Cherokee might be waiting for him on one of them. If he was being followed, they were doing an outstanding job of staying out of sight. Satisfied he didn't have a tail, he opened the throttle and headed for his destination.

Seth Walker lived in a wooded condo development only a couple of miles from his dojo. By the time Cayden reached the entry gate to the property, there was still no sign he was being tailed. He punched in the code to the gate, rolled onto the property, and parked the bike in front of Seth's condo. After removing his helmet, he hurried up the walk.

Seth answered the door wearing sweatpants and a fleece pullover; clearly an 'in for the night' outfit. He ushered him in, closing the door behind him. "You followed?"

Cayden shook his head. "I'm sure I wasn't. It's a little weird."

"Weird?"

"Yeah, just a feeling."

Seth tossed a BMW key fob to Cayden and led the way through the kitchen to the service porch at the rear of the condo. He opened the door leading into the garage and they stepped through. Cayden punched the fob's unlock button, and the lights on Seth's Z4 flashed. His friend was a fanatic about keeping the roadster clean and waxed, and Cayden could see his image in the black mirror-like finish.

Seth pressed the button beside the doorway, and the garage door rolled open. "Just make a right from the garage, then the next left. It'll take you to the rear gate. The gate card is in the glove compartment for when you get back."

"I appreciate this," Cayden said as he slipped behind the wheel.

"Just bring my baby back in one piece."

"Guaranteed."

A few minutes later, he was heading toward the freeway with still no sign of a tail. He drove past the Lake Avenue exit, taking the next offramp instead. Working his way back with several evasive maneuvers, he arrived at Dupont's Cafe a few minutes after nine.

Cayden parked in the lot behind the café and headed for the rear door. He looked for the Cherokee as he walked, but there was no sign of it. It was possible Russo and Craven had switched cars, but there was still no sign anyone had followed him. It should have registered as a solid positive, but as he entered Dupont's, he couldn't help an uneasy feeling nagging at him.

CHAPTER NINETEEN

The place was busy when Cayden walked in. Rural prints hung on the walls; the booths and tables occupied by several late night diners leaned toward the rustic. The bar was almost full and the sound of conversation filled the place.

Kate, Denbo, and Mariana sat in a roomy horseshoe-shaped booth toward the front of the restaurant, with coffee cups in front of each of them. Kate and Denbo sat at either end of the booth. Mariana, wearing a Caltech hoodie, occupied the center position. Her dark hair looked somewhat unkempt, as if she'd just rolled out of bed. But she was pretty, with bright, mischievous eyes, and the unkempt impression soon faded into the background.

"You're running late," Denbo greeted him.

Cayden ignored the remark. Kate scooted in toward Mariana, and he sat down beside her. A server delivered him his own cup of coffee a minute later.

"Mariana's dying of curiosity here, but I told Agent Denbo we should wait for you," Kate explained.

Cayden extended his hand, and Mariana took it. "Nice to see you again."

"No lingering hard feelings, I hope," she replied.

"About you hacking into the JPL astrophysics server and creating an uproar in the security office?"

"Allegedly," Mariana said with a charming smile.

Cayden couldn't help laughing. She had sass, and he liked who she was even during the JPL fiasco. "Of course not."

"Okay, so what's going on?" Mariana asked as soon as the server left the table.

"Before we go any further," Denbo said. "No matter how this plays out, everything said here doesn't leave this table. Understand?"

"Understood," Mariana agreed. "I feel like I'm in a spy movie or something."

Cayden cringed at the remark. There was no way she could understand the seriousness of the situation. "Before anybody says another word, I want to make it clear we've put you in danger just by asking you to take this meeting."

"Oh, come on," Denbo objected.

The pleasant expression on Mariana's face transformed to wariness.

Ignoring Denbo, Cayden focused on Mariana. "I'm not kidding. If you want us to get up and leave right now, no hard feelings."

Denbo made little effort to mask his annoyance.

"You're serious?" Mariana looked as if she hoped he was joking.

Cayden nodded.

"You're putting the fear of God into her before she even knows what she's here for," Denbo said.

"Should we go on?" Cayden asked Mariana.

She fingered the handle of her coffee mug while giving the matter some thought. "I'm here, I guess. I can at least hear you out."

"Okay," Denbo began. "We have an encrypted flash drive we need you to hack."

"A team of professional assassins wants it. They'll kill to get it," Cayden added.

Mariana paled. "Now you're just screwing with me."

"He's not," Kate said.

"What's on the drive?"

"We don't know," Denbo said. "But we believe it's connected to a terrorist operation. If there is a threat, it's critical we find out what it is so we can take proper steps. Time is critical, or we'd never have involved you."

"I suggested we could work together on it," Kate told Mariana. "We'd get results much faster."

Mariana nodded. "I'd agree with that." She looked across the table at Cayden. "What do you have to do with this?"

"I found the drive on campus."

"On campus?"

"In the computer lab scheduling office," he said. "The same night, one of the killers broke into my place to get it. He didn't."

"They've already killed two people," Kate said.

The statement astonished Mariana. "Two people. Who?"

"I guess you haven't been home long enough to hear about Alan Fenland," Kate said.

Mariana's mouth dropped open. "They killed Alan? Why?"

"We believe the killers thought he had the drive," Denbo answered.

Mariana shook her head in disbelief. "I didn't know him well, but he was such a good guy."

"The other victim was a government official," Denbo added.

Cayden studied Mariana; the news about Alan pierced her. He hoped what she was hearing now would cause her to opt out.

"You're saying whatever's on this flash drive is an actual threat to national security?" Mariana asked Denbo.

"We believe so, yes."

Mariana leaned back in the booth. "Can you keep Kate and me safe? You know, so we don't get whacked?"

"If you decide to help us, I assure you, you'll be safe under FBI protection. A detail of agents will be with you the entire time," Denbo continued.

The agent's arrogance annoyed Cayden. His assurances meant little when dealing with people like Russo and Craven. Mariana looked worried. Good, she should be.

"Cayden will be with us, too," Kate said.

"A member of the Caltech security force," Mariana muttered. "That should really tip the scales."

Kate began objecting to the comment, but Cayden silenced her with a gentle elbow nudge.

Mariana leaned back against the booth, her bright eyes not as bright now. "Alan was such a sweet guy," she said. "I wouldn't mind having a part in catching whoever killed him."

Cayden felt his hopefulness fade. She was considering taking on the job.

After a brief pause, Mariana continued. "Besides, this country's been good to me and my family. I never thought I might get a chance to help defend it. But I want to. Plus, I've been writing a new decryption program. This'll give me a chance to take it out for a spin."

Cayden couldn't help shaking his head in disbelief. Mariana agreed to it.

Mariana turned to Kate. "I've written two other programs that will help, too. They're on my office computer on campus. It'd be best to do the work there."

"Special programs," Kate said. "Now I insist we work on your office computer."

"Please, both of you, reconsider this," Cayden said. "The FBI doesn't have special powers. They can't predict what might happen."

Denbo shot him a disapproving glance. "We'd prefer you begin work on this right away," Denbo said to the women.

Mariana shook her head. "No way I'm doing it tonight; I need to get some sleep. But let's start early tomorrow. Say about seven. Does that work for you, Kate?"

"Sounds good."

"We're booked then. Seven at my office."

"I know this is craziness, Cay," Kate said, before he could object again. "But we have to try it. This is just the kind of challenge I can't resist. I don't think Mariana can either."

"Did anybody launch the drive?" Mariana asked.

"Cayden and I did," Kate said. "There was nothing to see, but the encryption fields were interesting."

"How so?" Mariana asked.

"Sixteen cells around eight cells, around a concentric octagon. It looks 3D, and the octagon rotates."

"Sounds like a sci-fi geek programmed it," Mariana mused.

There was no upside to dwelling on Mariana's and Kate's decision. Cayden changed his focus to planning on how to protect them.

Denbo relaxed for the first time since he sat down at the table. "I'll coordinate with Langford. We'll arrange for the security detail. They'll pick you both up tomorrow, let's say six-thirty."

"That works for Mariana," Cayden said. "I'll see that Kate gets there. She's staying at my place."

Mariana gave Kate a quizzical look. Kate maintained a poker face.

"You should escort Mariana home tonight," Cayden said to Denbo.

"Of course. And I'll put two agents in front of her house for the night."

Mariana cringed. "Is that necessary?"

Cayden nodded. "It is."

"I'll put agents on your house, too, March," Denbo said.

"Knock yourself out."

"I need to get home to bed," Mariana said. "After a stop at the ladies' room."

"I'll go with you," Kate said.

Cayden slid out of the booth, waited until the women were on their way, then sat down again. He rested his gaze on Denbo. He knew the guy didn't like him much. That was fine. He couldn't care less. He wasn't certain just how he felt about Denbo. The guy was probably a decent agent; he seemed dedicated, but Cayden didn't like how the man and his partner were handling such a lethal situation.

Denbo pulled out his phone. "I'll get going on the arrangements."

"You shouldn't have guaranteed those girls the FBI can keep them safe."

"We can."

Cayden shook his head, unable to hide the frustration he felt. "Hold on to that blind self assurance and you're going to get them killed. You might even get yourself killed."

"You're threatening me?" Denbo asked.

Cayden's eyes narrowed and every muscle in his body tensed with anger. This guy just didn't get it. "See, that's the problem. You're worried about me when you should worry about the people who want their flash drive back."

"This work isn't new to me, March," Denbo said. "I've been with the Bureau for over twelve years. I've seen just about everything you can imagine."

"Russo and Craven are well beyond your imagination," Cayden said. "If you had any actual intelligence on them, you'd never have involved Kate and Mariana."

"You just let her and your friend go to the restroom on their own. I mean, if you're so worried." Denbo let the implication trail off.

"Nobody followed me here, and I don't think anyone followed you."

"And how can you be so sure?"

"Experience." And his experience told Cayden he should be worried. Russo and Craven should have followed him, but they didn't. He was missing something, but what?

CHAPTER TWENTY

Daniel Russo studied the Highland Park donut shop across the street from where they'd parked. The shop was in the middle of the block. A sign above its large dirty plate glass window read *HP Donuts and Ice Cream*. The block had seen better days. Most of the buildings were commercial and probably built in the 1920s. Except for an abundance of graffiti, it looked as if they hadn't been touched since then.

Two Latino men in their twenties leaned against the wall next to the shop entrance. Despite the temperature hovering in the low sixties, the taller of the two wore a black T-shirt and faded blue jeans. He sported a clean shaven head and a strip of dark hair ran from just below the center of his lower lip to the end of his chin. Russo nicknamed him *Stretch*. The second man's hair looked as if a tiny lawn mower had mowed it in three strips. The short sleeves of his purple bowling shirt were rolled up even shorter, displaying muscled arms copiously decorated with tattoos. His baggy chinos looked like they were a size too large. The top of his head barely cleared his companion's shoulder. Russo thought *Shorty* was perfect for him.

A few calls to his local contacts revealed that Highland Park, a small city just south of Pasadena, had a strong gang influence. And this territory was under the control of Boulevard 13, a powerful gang reporting directly to La Eme. His contacts had told him exactly who to talk to for what he had in mind.

It was midmorning and occasional customers were still entering the shop for morning donuts and coffee. None of them seemed to stay for long, emerging with paper bags and plastic-lidded cups of coffee. Russo surmised that there were no tables or chairs inside.

Cyn adjusted her position in the passenger seat. "So, they're taking the drive out of the police vault this morning."

"That's what he said," he replied. "They're working on it at Caltech in the Vasquez woman's office."

Russo hoped Cyn would have no more questions. After receiving the call the night before, he'd spent hours reaching out to contacts and garnering intelligence. He hadn't had a lot of sleep, and his patience was short. He opened the Cherokee's door and slid out of the driver's seat. Cyn followed his lead, joining him beside the car. Stretch and Shorty noticed them and watched with curiosity as they approached.

"This could be fun." Cyn smiled, mischief in her eyes.

"Just watch yourself."

Stretch and Shorty studied them as they walked across the sidewalk and entered the shop. The inside was clean, a sharp contrast to the building's exterior. The display cases and the equipment behind them looked new and well maintained. Russo had been right. No tables or chairs. Behind the counter, a Latino man in his late fifties was restocking a rack in the display case with sprinkled cake donuts from a tray. A woman Russo guessed to be the man's wife was wiping down the stainless steel covers that held the three gallon containers of ice cream in neat rows.

The man placed the last donut from his tray in the display case and straightened up to face them. "What can I get you?" he asked with a heavy accent.

"I'm here to see Razor Boy," Russo said.

The donut man's face showed no recognition of the name, but his wife turned from the ice cream counter to see who had spoken.

"Don't know who that is," the donut man answered.

"Sure you do," Russo said.

The counter man and his wife both stood silent, not taking their eyes off him until Stretch and Shorty stepped inside. The two young Latino men no longer looked curious. They looked threatening.

Russo ignored them, but Cyn casually turned toward the men.

"You two cops?" Shorty asked. He made the question sound like a challenge.

Cyn smirked. "Do we look like cops?"

"I dunno," Shorty answered. "These days, cops don't always look like they should."

"We're not," Russo said.

Stretch's eyes covered Cyn from head to toe. "Don't seem like la chica caliente here could be any cop. Don't see how she could hide a piece in those tight jeans."

"Ah, thanks," Cyn purred.

"Let's say there was somebody around here called Razor Boy. Why you wanna be talking with him?" Shorty asked.

"I've got a business deal he'll be interested in," Russo answered.

"Yeah? What kind of business?" Shorty pressed.

"The kind that makes Razor Boy a lot of money."

The two men looked at each other, considering the situation. Shorty shrugged and tilted his head toward the back of the shop. Stretch walked to the back of the store, disappearing through the rear door.

Shorty stepped past them, taking a position in the path his friend had just taken. "You just hang with me a while."

It was ten minutes before Stretch pushed open the back door. "He says bring 'em."

"That way," Shorty gestured.

They headed for the back door, and Shorty fell into step behind them. Russo spotted the semi-automatic pistol in Stretch's hand through the open door. He wouldn't have had much respect for the guy if he hadn't had a gun.

They stepped out the door into an unmarked parking area behind the shop. Several late model cars occupied the lot, most of them near a large old building at the back of the property. Large weather-faded lettering on the aged bricks suggested it had once been an automobile repair business. A variety of BMWs and SUVs made up most of the rolling stock, but there were a couple of Harleys and a few Japanese motorcycles as well.

Shorty produced a pistol of his own from under his shirt before the door slammed shut behind him.

"You guys carrying?" Stretch leveled his gun at them.

Russo responded by opening his jacket, providing an unob-structed view of his own semi-automatic in its belt holster. He wasn't concerned. Even unarmed, if it became necessary to subdue the two Latinos, he and Cyn could manage it with little effort.

Careful to stay clear of Stretch's line of fire, Shorty moved in and pulled the gun from the holster. He shoved it into one of his rear pants pockets and then proceeded with a pat down.

Cyn opened her coat and Shorty repeated the procedure. He was respectful but still thorough patting her down. As he backed away with her gun, she stopped him.

"Uh, sweetie." She reached into her left jacket sleeve and came out with a six-inch blade. She handed it over to him with a coy smile.

"You guys got any more surprises?" Shorty glared at Russo as he tucked Cyn's weapons away.

Russo shook his head. "Not today."

"Move it, then." Shorty pointed at the old building across the lot.

They followed Stretch, weaving between the vehicles until they reached the entrance to the building. He tapped on the formidable metal door, glancing up at a security camera mounted on the side of the building. The sound of a substantial bolt being turned came from within and the door opened from inside.

Stretch stepped into the shadows beyond the threshold. Russo followed Cyn inside, sensing Shorty close behind them. The heavy door slammed shut behind them.

~

The room was large and illuminated by old barn lights hanging from steel cross beams. Smoke drifted through the soft beams of light and the musky, herbal odor of marijuana did battle with the smell of burning cigarettes. Several feet to the side of the door, a grease pit gaped in the concrete floor. Lines of uneven mortar in the wall opposite the pit outlined where a large garage door had been sealed up years ago.

Conversation and occasional laughter echoed off the brick walls. Russo and Cyn drew the curious attention of every man in the room. He counted fourteen of them, all Latino. Most of them looked to be in their twenties or thirties, but there were a few older men who had survived gang life into their fifties. Well-worn jeans or chinos, sweatshirts and hoodies with skull art, or motorcycle jackets over short-sleeved tees appeared to be the fashion trend here. Boulevard 13 boasted over eight hundred members. The men in this room were part of an inner circle; the few men el jefe trusted.

Two of the younger men played a game of pool at a table with a few beer stains spotted across the felt. Three of their friends stood nearby, smoking cigarettes and watching. Beyond the pool table, three more men occupied a wood plank game table, cards and chips spread across its surface. A long kitchen grade countertop and sink occupied the wall near the game table, and at the end of it a refrigerator that had seen better days. The end of the countertop nearest the refrigerator served as a bar, evidenced by the extensive collection of liquor bottles stored there.

Russo picked out Amado Estrada, aka Razor Boy, lounging on

an old, overstuffed leather recliner. He was in his mid-thirties with dark wavy hair. His face was clean shaven but displayed a hardness tempered by gang life. The tattooed wristwatch visible below the cuff of his battered leather jacket testified to the time he'd served in prison.

Beside the chair, a Colt model 1911 with a custom walnut grip rested on a small battered table. Next to the gun was an open pack of Cohiba Club cigarillos and a dirty ashtray. A floor lamp behind the table cast a hazy glow over him. Razor Boy took a draw from the cigarillo in his hand as he watched them approach.

They were still several yards away from Razor Boy when a man slumping in a folding chair near the pool table uncoiled and rose to his feet. He swaggered toward them, his eyes fixed on Cyn.

"Hola hermosa," the man leered at her. "You are *fine*." He took his time with *fine*, drawing out the "i" and ending it with an emphasis on the "n".

Russo watched Cyn appraise the man, sizing him up like a tigress looking at her next meal. He was young, in his mid-twenties, with short cropped hair and strong, handsome features. A single tattooed teardrop trickled below the corner of his right eye. He wore a tight T-shirt revealing muscular, tattooed arms. It was obvious he drew great confidence from his features and physique, and moved with the certainty he was God's gift to all women.

The man stepped up to Cyn and took his time looking her over. "What's your name, baby?"

"Uninterested," Cyn answered.

The man placed his hands on her shoulders. "Me, I'm Stevie." He began sliding his hands up and down her arms.

"Stop touching me *Stevie*."

Russo glanced at Razor Boy. He just took another puff from his Cohiba and watched.

"Don't be that way. How 'bout me and you step into the other room there? We'll relax a little while your friend here conducts his business?" Stevie slid his hands down her arms and slipped them around her waist.

"Best if you back off a little," Russo said, his tone pleasant.

Stevie turned to look at him, his right hand sliding over the grip of the semi-automatic pistol jammed into his waistband. Russo found it amusing.

"You playin' white knight or something? You thinkin' you gonna defend her?" Stevie asked, his tone challenging.

Russo smiled. "I'm offering some friendly advice."

"Keep your advice. We gonna get along just fine." His hands crept down to Cyn's thighs, inching toward her crotch. "Right, baby? It'll be our first date."

Russo saw the sweet little smile form on her lips. He tried to warn Stevie, but the guy still jumped way over the line.

Cyn's right hand streaked across to Stevie's left arm. She gripped his wrist, jamming her thumb hard into the flesh beside the bone. He screamed in pain as she applied pressure to the nerves there, using the leverage to force him down to the ground. Once he was prone, she bent down, yanked the pistol out of his waistband, and released her grip. She tossed the gun to a gang guy standing nearby.

Howls and whistles, and nervous laughter, rose from most of the men in the room. The noise faded away as Stevie pulled himself to his feet. He moved in slow motion, his eyes fierce with anger as he glared at his companions.

Russo hoped the rest of Boulevard 13 was smarter than Stevie. He was about to ask their boss to do something that would require clear thinking from everyone involved.

Stevie turned his attention back to Cyn. "Puta." He spit out the insult.

Cyn treated him to an impish smile.

"Stevie," Razor Boy snapped, the authority in his voice unmistakable.

Stevie looked toward Razor Boy, and then back toward Cyn.

"Go sit," Razor Boy said.

Stevie hesitated, looking around the room, hoping for some kind of support, but not finding any. He turned back and took another step toward Cyn, pointing a finger in her face. "Don't you worry, baby. We ain't done, you and me. We'll be having that date."

Stevie stepped toward the guy to whom Cyn had tossed his gun, extending his hand.

"Hold on to that for now," Razor Boy ordered. "He can have it back after I find out what these two want."

Stevie took another look around the room and retreated to the game table where he slumped into a chair. The three men there soon fell into a hushed conversation with him.

Razor Boy appeared amused as he gazed at Cyn.

"So, you have some business with me?" Razor Boy asked.

"We do," Russo answered.

"And what might that be?"

"I need you to kill someone," Russo said.

"Yeah?"

"I prefer you kill him. If you don't, that's fine, too. As long as you keep him occupied."

Razor Boy's expression hardened. "Who the hell are you, man? You come walking in here out of nowhere and want me to kill somebody. Who the *hell* are you?"

"I'm somebody willing to spend a lot of money for what I need."

Razor Boy picked up his pistol from the side table and considered it thoughtfully. "How'd you find me, anyway?"

"We have mutual acquaintances," Russo answered, pulling his phone from his pants pocket.

Razor Boy smirked. "Kinda hard to believe. Who?"

Russo ignored the question, finding and launching the banking application he needed. As soon as it was running, he accessed the expense account Dragović had established for this kind of situation. Cyn leaned in, looking over his shoulder as he entered a generous dollar amount.

Russo stepped over to Razor Boy and held out the phone. The gang leader set the gun in his lap and took it.

"I've entered an advance," Russo said. "Enter your account and routing numbers. Hit send. No strings."

"I haven't agreed to do a damn thing yet," Razor Boy said.

"I said, no strings. You just need to hear me out."

Across the room, Stevie leaned forward in his chair. "You can't be wantin' to do business with these assholes," he shouted.

Ignoring Stevie, Razor Boy looked back at the phone in his hand. He typed in the required numbers, and with an exaggerated movement, punched the *send* button. "Okay, you got me listening," he said, handing back the phone.

Russo smiled to himself. The information received last night presented a genuine opportunity, and Russo had devised a plan to take advantage of it. But for his plan to work, he had to make certain the FBI and the well trained security guard didn't get in the way. He felt confident that Razor Boy was about to give him what he needed.

Russo brought up a photograph of Cayden March on his phone and showed it to Razor Boy. He described what he wanted, where he wanted it, and how the timeline should work. He held nothing back, explaining that FBI Special Agents would be present.

"You think FBI scares me?" Razor Boy asked with an arrogant tone. "We can handle Feds easy. But the time, man. You're not giving us much time."

"That can't be helped," Russo said.

"The money's gonna have to be a lot better than your little down payment."

"Of course." Russo repeated the banking transfer process and handed the phone over to Razor Boy so he could see the additional payment amount.

"Okay then," Razor Boy said, retrieving the gun from his lap and climbing out of his chair. "I gotta make a call first."

He handed the phone back, but Russo stopped him. "Go ahead. Start the transfer first. Show your people we're serious."

Razor Boy looked surprised, but wasn't about to look a gift

horse in the mouth. He punched the *send* button and handed the phone back. "You chill till I get back."

Razor Boy tucked the gun into his waistband and headed for one of the two doors in the back wall. He tapped twice on the door and it opened from the inside. The rhythmic clacking of a currency counter came from behind the door. Razor Boy stepped into the room, and the door closed behind him.

Cyn strolled over to the wall closest to the pool table and picked a cue from the rack on the wall. Twirling it expertly, she stepped over to the table.

"Quick game while we wait?" she asked the two men who had been playing.

"Sure, lady," one man said. "I'll take you on."

The other player put down his cue and racked the balls.

"Eight ball?" Cyn's opponent asked.

"Fine." Cyn stepped to the side of the table. "You break."

As the game began, Russo noticed Stevie glancing at Cyn as he whispered to the other men at the game table. A minute later, Stevie and the three other men rose. Two of them headed for him, while Stevie headed for Cyn with the third man.

By the time Stevie's friends reached him, they each had their guns out. They took positions behind him, their guns pointed at his back. Russo knew Cyn noticed.

"Stevie wants you to just stand here and watch," one man said.

Russo smiled. "Should be fun."

Stevie came up fast behind Cyn as she took her shot. The cue ball caromed off the side cushion, striking the one ball before rolling into a corner pocket. She dropped her cue on the table, bracing herself as Stevie slammed into her from behind, pinning her against the table. Stevie's backup man stood off to the side, his nervous eyes darting around the room.

"I told you we'd have that date, baby," Steve said as he gripped her wrists, keeping her hands on the felt.

"You made me ruin my shot, *Stevie*," Cyn said.

Cyn's opponent leaned on his cue. "You sure about this, bro? Razor Boy gonna have your cojones."

Ignoring the warning, Stevie adjusted his grip and jerked her around to face him. Russo spotted the pool balls in her hands before anyone else did. But then he was the only one looking for them.

Cyn smashed the balls against Stevie's ears, each landing simultaneously with great precision. He screamed in agony, his hands jerking up to his ears. As he staggered backward, his backup man charged at Cyn. She turned and hurled a ball at him. The Bakelite missile struck the man square in the bridge of his nose. Blood gushed across his mouth and chin as he dropped to the floor, unconscious.

Stevie lunged toward Cyn. She pivoted toward the pool table and retrieved her cue. Fluidly moving into the posture of a major league batter, Cyn swung hard at his right knee. Stevie's scream drowned out the sickening crack. He crumpled to the floor, rolling onto his side, both hands cupped around the shattered kneecap.

Stepping closer, Cyn raised the cue high, taking aim for Stevie's head.

"Cyn," Russo said, his voice loud and firm. "You made your point."

She tossed the cue on the table as the door at the back of the building opened and Razor Boy stepped back into the room. He approached them, his gaze moving from Russo and Cyn, then down to Stevie doubled up on the floor.

"What's this?" he almost shouted.

Her breathing strained, Cyn turned to face him. "We just had a date."

Razor Boy looked down at Stevie in disgust. "Get him out."

Except for the unconscious man, Stevie's backup guys grabbed him under each arm and lifted him up. He groaned miserably as they dragged him to the front of the building and exited to the parking lot.

Shaking his head, Razor Boy approached Russo.

"Okay. We're good at our end," he said.

"Good."

"Let's sit. Go through the details one more time," Razor Boy said.

Russo and Cyn each found plastic folding chairs nearby. They dragged them over to Razor Boy's recliner and sat down. A half hour later, Russo was confident that his plan would be effective.

CHAPTER TWENTY-ONE

Kate wanted a chance to drive the Ducati. Cayden knew her brother had taught her to ride, so it was fine by him. She chauffeured him to the Caltech campus, arriving at the Powell-Booth building by 6:50 a.m. Once Kate parked the bike at the side of the building, he escorted her up to Mariana Vasquez's office on the second floor. The FBI detail was already there. They introduced themselves as Special Agents Bitterhoff, Gutierrez, and Farris. Denbo had briefed them on Cayden, and the agents were expecting him. All of them seemed more accepting of his participation than Denbo. Bitterhoff told him that Langford and Denbo would both be present later in the day.

Mariana's laptop was open in front of her, but she was plugging the flash drive into a tower computer under the desk when they walked in. They greeted each other as Kate pulled a chair over to the desk and pulled her laptop from its carrying bag. She set the laptop on the corner of the desk, and they got to work, soon oblivious to everyone else in the room.

Cayden, Gutierrez, and Bitterhoff stepped into the hallway, leaving Farris with the women. They agreed that, even if Russo and Craven knew the flash drive's location, it was unlikely they'd attempt an attack in the building. With the confined spaces, and the hallway being the only path to Mariana's office, approaching undetected would prove difficult. It made more sense for them to make a move once the drive was in motion, perhaps on its way back to the police vault.

They came up with a plan for the day. One FBI agent would be in the room with Kate and Mariana at all times. Two agents would take positions in the hallway. Cayden agreed to patrol the building and the areas surrounding it. And that is what he'd been doing most of the day, returning to Mariana's office several times to make certain all was secure.

The day passed slowly for him. Everything on the campus appeared status quo. Faculty and students headed to their classes and labs. Campus gardeners scooted down a distant pathway in their electric utility cart loaded with equipment. Students sat on benches and under trees, their faces buried in thick textbooks. It was all business as usual.

There was no good reason to think that Mariana and Kate were in immediate danger, especially here on the Caltech campus. The couple who had killed Alan and the CIA case officer possessed no supernatural powers. They were not all seeing. They could not read minds or sense the thoughts or movements of others. There was no way they could know that the FBI had recruited Kate and Mariana to hack the drive.

But that reality did little to reassure Cayden. His instincts told him that some kind of threat was imminent. Making matters worse, now the operation was underway, he'd begun feeling anxious. He'd made concerted efforts to avoid responsibility for other people's lives after leaving the military. But here he was again, in the middle of life and death circumstances.

He was heading back into Powell-Booth when he spotted Special Agent Denbo approaching from one of the parking areas. Denbo appeared more relaxed than Cayden had ever seen him. The drive was now in the FBI's possession, and hackers were working on it. It was likely Denbo thought there was little reason for concern.

"I thought you'd be up in the office," Denbo greeted him. "Any trouble today?"

"I've been back and forth. It's been quiet so far."

"Good." Denbo glanced at his watch. "Langford's supposed to be here. Must be running late."

The words no sooner left Denbo's lips when Cayden saw Detective Mandala's Charger driving toward them along the walkway. Special Agent Langford rode in the passenger seat. Mandala came to a stop beside them and turned off the engine. The two men emerged from the car.

"Detective. I wasn't expecting you," Cayden greeted Mandala.

"He wanted to make sure the flash drive was safe," Langford said.

Cayden thought he detected a hint of irritation in Langford's tone, but his phone began chiming, drawing his attention.

Mandala shrugged. "It was in my vault. I'll feel responsible for it until you guys cart it out of here."

Cayden accepted the incoming call. "March."

He listened to the caller for several seconds before responding. "They're here now. We're on the way."

"That was Gutierrez," Cayden said, slipping the phone back into his pocket. "They've got it."

Without another word, Cayden, Mandala, and the two Special Agents hurried into the building. Gutierrez stood outside the office door, waving them over.

"They just finished," Gutierrez said the moment they were within earshot.

They hurried into the office. Since the last time Cayden was there, the desk had gained a couple of open cans of Dr. Pepper, a box of vanilla wafers, and a large bag of corn chips.

"We finished up a few minutes ago," Kate said. "What a day."

Cayden made his way around the desk, taking a position behind Kate. Mandala took a chair in front of the desk while Langford and Denbo settled in behind Mariana. The flash drive's octagon rotated on the large display in the center of the desk.

"I thought this would've taken much longer," Langford said.

"Yeah? You really don't understand how long the day was," Mariana said.

"Still, it's remarkable you've accomplished this so fast," Denbo said.

"It's Mariana's program. Brilliant, and much better than the one I wrote," Kate said.

"Ah, shucks," Mariana said. "You ready to see what's on this thing?"

Langford took a deep breath. "Go ahead."

"Okay. When I hit the enter key, the octagon's decryption sequence will run," Mariana said.

A tangible tension filled the room. FBI and CIA intelligence had identified the flash drive as a potential cyber weapon. Cayden knew a weapon was possible, but it was also possible the contents of the drive might contain nothing more than information. It was a roll of the dice. The bottom line was that entering the decryption code might very well unleash something dangerous to the United States, and maybe the world. And everyone in the room knew it.

"Here we go," Mariana said. She tapped the enter key on her tower keyboard.

The octagon's rotation speed increased. One by one, brief flickers of characters, numerals, and symbols occupied the entry fields before rotating out of view. At least two minutes passed before the octagon ceased rotating and disappeared from the display. For a moment, the display remained blank, and then it filled with lines and lines of code.

Kate and Mariana gave each other a high-five, but when they looked back at the display, their faces registered alarm.

"Holy crap," Mariana exclaimed. "It's running."

C ayden leaned in toward the large display. Uncountable lines of code filled the screen, rapidly disappearing as the program scrolled upward. Mariana rushed to turn off the laptop's wi-fi capability while Kate lunged under the desk and pulled the ethernet cable from the tower.

"Stop it. Stop it now," Langford shouted.

Mariana's fingers blurred across the keyboard.

Detective Mandala was out of his seat, moving around the desk so he could see the display.

Cayden felt compelled to help, and helpless at the same time.

Kate crawled out from under the desk.

Every member of the FBI protection detail was now standing inside the office doorway, their eyes locked on Mariana.

"Hurry," Denbo said, almost under his breath.

"Do we risk just yanking the drive out?" Kate asked Mariana.

Mariana shook her head, her fingers a blur on the keyboard. "I almost have it."

Another twenty seconds passed without Mariana being able to interrupt the running program. But her expression suddenly changed. "Yes," she exclaimed as she tapped several keys.

The program ceased scrolling upward, and after a brief pause, returned to the start of the code.

"Lord have mercy," Kate breathed.

"Thank God," Denbo echoed.

"You're sure you've stopped it?" Langford asked. "Did any of that make it to the web?"

"I shut it down," Mariana answered. "But there's no way of telling if it accessed the internet before we cut the feeds."

Mariana leaned down and removed the black weapon drive from her computer. Cayden noticed Kate tap a couple of keys and remove a blue drive from her laptop. He wondered about it, but she was so casual about handing the drive to Mariana, he gave it no more thought.

"Do we have any idea what we avoided?" Cayden asked.

Denbo shifted his attention to the women. "Do we?"

"Not a clue," Kate replied.

Mariana leaned back in her chair. "We don't know what it does. Hacking a file is one thing. Analyzing function is another."

"Can you do that?" Denbo asked. "Tell us what it does?"

"Sure, now that we're inside," Mariana answered. "It'll take some time, and we can't do the work here."

"Why's that?" Langford said.

"My system at home is more powerful than this one, and I've got specialized software there, too." Mariana answered. "I'm willing to see if I can figure this thing out, but we'll have to move this gig to my place."

"How long will it take you?" Denbo said.

Mariana thought about the question before answering. "There's no telling. But if Kate works with me, it'll cut down on the time. We wouldn't have found the decryption code so fast if we hadn't teamed up."

"I'm not stopping now," Kate said.

Cayden felt the familiar tension in his gut. As soon as they transported the flash drive, they were at risk. And anyone around the drive was at risk. But he knew the FBI wouldn't miss an opportunity to discover the purpose of the drive's program.

"Alright," Denbo said. "We need to work out how this is going to go."

Bitterhoff gestured toward Gutierrez and Farris. "We can stay on board. We'll escort the ladies and stay at the house while they work."

"I assume you'll stay on the detail, Mr. March?" Gutierrez asked.

"Count on it."

"Okay," Langford said. "But I want four agents in the house, and four outside. Front and back."

"I'll see to it," Denbo said, glancing at his watch. "It's four-thirty now. It'll take at least an hour to set it up."

Kate's cell phone began chiming. She picked it up from the desk, looking at the screen. "It's my boss. I have to take this."

She rose from the chair and wound her way through the FBI men and into the hallway. Special Agent Farris stepped into the doorway to keep her in sight.

"Aim at six to leave for Ms. Vasquez's house," Langford said. "That'll be ample time for Denbo to set everything up."

Denbo stepped over to the desk beside Mariana. "I'll need your address before I make my call."

"Sure." She found a piece of blank notepaper on the desk, scribbled down her address, and handed it to him. He took the address and headed for the door, letting Kate pass as she returned from the hallway.

"I can send a few patrol cars over there if it'll help," Mandala offered.

"No need for that," Denbo said. "But if you could assign a couple of cars to cruise around the neighborhood, it might serve as a deterrent."

Kate slipped her phone into a pants pocket. "I have to get over to my office. But I'll go to Mariana's as soon as I'm done."

"Why? What's going on?" Cayden asked.

"Dr. May is going crazy because he can't find a budget report he needs for a board presentation tonight. I've got to get over to Moore to help him find it before he reaches the point of no return."

"Who's Dr. May?" Langford asked.

"My boss," Kate answered.

Langford frowned. "Not good timing. You should stay close."

Kate gathered up her things and put her laptop in its case. "Well, I've got to go. The guy signs my checks," she answered.

Special Agent Gutierrez took a step into the room. "I'll go with her."

Cayden wasn't sure how he felt about that. He preferred to stay close to Kate himself. She was looking at him now, knowing what he was thinking.

"It's only a five-minute walk, Cay," she said. "I'll be fine. Anyway, you should be where Mariana and the drive are."

He told himself again there was little possibility that Russo and Craven even knew where they were. "How long will you be?"

"Well, if it's just finding the report, not long at all," Kate answered. "But I can't predict what other stuff he might need."

Langford frowned at her answer. "The plan is to leave at six. Can you be back by then?"

Kate shrugged. "I should be able to, but no guarantees."

"It works fine for me," Mariana said. "I'll have the time to set everything up before Kate arrives."

"If we can't get back here by six, I'll drive her over," Gutierrez said.

"That sounds all right," Langford said.

"You ready, Ms. James?" Gutierrez asked.

"Sure, and call me Kate."

"Kate it is. Let's go." Gutierrez moved aside to let her pass, and fell into step behind her.

"We're going to the Moore Laboratory building," Kate added as she stepped into the hallway.

Langford turned to Mandala. "Detective, if you don't mind driving me back to the police station, I can get my car and head straight over to Ms. Vasquez's house."

"No problem," Mandala answered, heading for the door with Langford falling into step with him.

Once they were gone, Cayden turned to Farris. "I'm going to walk over with Gutierrez and Kate. Make sure everything is okay there. I'll be back."

"It isn't necessary," Farris replied. "Gutierrez will take good care of her."

"I'm sure he will. I'll be back in a few minutes," Cayden said as he left the office.

CHAPTER TWENTY-TWO

Dragović paced back and forth in front of his office's picture window, his cell phone pressed to his ear. It was an overcast day with fluffy gray clouds suspended low over the choppy sea waters. He wasn't certain he liked or agreed with the plan described to him. "You're going to draw much unwanted attention. Are you certain the information is accurate?"

Daniel Russo's voice came through the phone. "I just got off a call with him. I know what they're planning to do. And I know when the drive will be vulnerable."

"You have big balls, a direct confrontation with the FBI."

"But I'm not confronting them."

"Yes, your gang acquaintances. How can you trust them?"

"We can't trust anyone in this business," Russo answered. "But we've paid them a considerable amount. I believe they're smart enough to realize that failing to deliver will bring serious retribution down on them. Besides, I memorized their bank numbers as Estrada entered them. I can recover the money should it be necessary."

Dragović ceased his pacing, standing still as he gazed at the ocean. Russo's skills were remarkable. But hiring outsiders increased the risk. His mind ticked off the ways the plan could go wrong.

The lengthy silence caused Russo to speak up again. "It'll work. It was necessary to adjust the plan, but we now have two opportunities. On the campus, and at the residence, if it becomes necessary."

"I don't like depending on outsiders for this to work," Dragović said.

"Like it or not, this may be the last opportunity we have to recover the drive. We're running out of time, so I need an answer."

"Alright, move forward, but make certain you keep me informed."

"Of course. And I've already sent Cynthia on ahead."

CHAPTER TWENTY-THREE

After leaving the gangbangers in Highland Park, Cyn relaxed as Danny drove them back to their boutique hotel in Pasadena. As soon as they were in their room, the first thing she did was take a hot shower. Her encounter with the gang boys had been fun, but she felt soiled, as if she'd picked up a thin coating of slime from the troublemakers. Soap and hot water took care of all that, and the forty-minute nap that followed recharged her. She and Danny then found a secluded corner in the hotel's bar and grill for lunch. Danny reviewed his plan for the upcoming evening with her while they ate.

Cyn was well rested, well fed, and ready for just about anything by the time she steered the stolen Chevy onto the block that included Mariana Vasquez's family home. Danny provided her with the house address, but he also did some internet work to gather more detail about the girl. The hack into the Caltech student and personnel databases did the trick. Vasquez was a graduate student working on her doctorate while paying the bills as a Caltech employee. She did research and coding work in the same computer science building where they had caught up to the CIA guy. But most entertaining was the little black mark Danny discovered in her school records. Caltech had busted Miss Mariana twice for hacking into systems that were verboten.

The Vasquez girl's propensity for hacking clarified why she popped into the security guard's mind once he decided to find out what was on the flash drive. Their client made it clear the drive's content was nobody's business, so she and Danny would make sure they got the damn thing back before Vasquez and the James girl could do any harm.

Cyn reconnoitered the entire neighborhood, familiarizing herself with a four block area. Soon she was confident that she could navigate the neighborhood blindfolded. She pulled over to the curb on the block behind the Vasquez girl's house and checked to make sure everything she needed was where it should be. Satisfied, she climbed out of the car, throwing the keys on the seat. She wouldn't be needing the Chevy again. Cyn raised the hood of her jacket over her head and began walking.

She strolled down the sidewalk, trusting that if anyone noticed her black attire, they would just think she was a Goth or something. Most homes on the street were decorated for Christmas. It wasn't quite dark yet, so none of the Christmas lights were lit. And the giant inflatable snowmen, Santas, and Peanuts characters lay sadly crumpled on the ground in the front yards, their air pumps silent.

An anger rose in her as she looked at all of it. Her family had been so screwed up that doing normal things like decorating the house for Christmas never happened. Cyn didn't mind Christmas itself and getting gifts was always a kick, but she didn't get the whole celebration of Christ's birth thing. If Christ existed, He had never done a thing for her.

A couple of neighbors were chatting in a front yard across the street. They noticed her and went back to their conversation. Cyn just kept walking; it didn't matter if they'd seen her or not.

It took her only a few minutes to locate the house directly behind the Vasquez property. There were no cars parked in front of the house or in the driveway. There was no sign of any activity at all. She casually looked around to make sure she wasn't observed and hurried up the driveway. The backyard gate was unlocked, and she hurried through it.

Cyn moved past a small swimming pool to the rear of the yard where a six-foot high cedar plank fence divided the neighboring properties. She used the lower branches of an old elm tree to gain a little elevation and dropped over the fence into Mariana Vasquez's back yard.

There was no sign of an alarm system on or around the house. Three steps led up to the door of a service porch. Glass panes were set in the top half of the door; any of them could easily be broken. But Cyn opened her jacket and removed the lock pick kit from the leather pouch on her belt. Twenty-seconds later, the lock was open. She slipped on a pair of thin black leather gloves and stepped inside, locking the door behind her.

It occurred to Cyn that Danny had assigned her a bummer of a job. The odds of the flash drive making its way to this house were slim to none. Her evening was sizing up to be a real snooze.

But she sucked it up and explored the house. She looked into every room, acquainting herself with the layout. The place was neat, clean, and decorated with a young, funky sense of style. It was sort of how she imagined a house being if you grew up in a normal family. But that was just imagination; she had grown up with a monster in her house.

Toward the end of the hall, near the living room, an open archway led to a small dining room. On the opposite side of the hallway, a doorway opened to a room that caught her interest. It was a spare bedroom converted to an office.

Cyn didn't know as much about computer technology as Danny, but she knew a lot, and this room was impressive. Two long utility tables with wood laminate tops were positioned end-to-side in an L formation. Two keyboards and a few cable hub units occupied the table tops. On the end of one table sat a high-speed internet modem and separate router. Behind each table, adjustable racks supported four 36 inch flat screen displays.

Another rack set against the wall housed a bank of external storage drives. Four powerful CPU towers secured under the monitors provided the main computing power.

A small master bedroom with an adjoining bathroom, a second smaller bedroom, and a half-bath occupied the second floor. Satisfied she had a solid knowledge of the home's layout, Cyn entered the half-bath where she accessed the hatchway into the attic. Yeah, she was just going to be sitting around, waiting for nothing. But what if she was lucky enough for the women and the flash drive to show up here? The night just might turn into tons of fun.

CHAPTER TWENTY-FOUR

After escorting Kate and Special Agent Gutierrez to Dr. May's office, Cayden patrolled the Moore building's perimeter. He broadened his search pattern as he worked his way back to Powell-Booth, but found nothing out of the usual.

By the time he got back to Powell-Booth, winter darkness had closed over the property. Pools of glowing amber from the path lights spilled across campus walkways. He took a quick survey of the surrounding area, then entered the building.

Farris was leaning against the hallway wall when Cayden reached the second floor. In the office, he found Mariana still at her desk, sipping from a can of Dr. Pepper. Denbo had pushed the chair Kate occupied earlier to the front of the desk. He rested in it, checking his phone, while Bitterhoff sprawled out in the remaining chair.

"I was hoping Kate and Gutierrez would get back here before I did," Cayden said.

"You haven't been gone all that long," Denbo said.

Cayden shrugged. "Yeah, well."

Denbo checked his watch. "We will have to get going soon."

Cayden glanced up at the clock on the wall behind Mariana. Denbo was right, it was five-forty. Even though he had left her less than an hour earlier, he couldn't help worrying about Kate, and fought the urge to hustle back to May's office. But he knew his responsibility now was to stay close to Mariana and the flash drive. They waited through the next fifteen minutes with a minimum of conversation.

Denbo consulted his watch again. "Okay, time to get going."

"Finally," Bitterhoff sighed, standing up from the chair.

Cayden looked into the hallway, hoping to see Kate coming toward him. But the hallway was empty.

"Give Gutierrez a call," Denbo instructed Bitterhoff. "Tell him we're moving out."

Bitterhoff pulled out his phone and stepped past Cayden into the hallway.

Cayden made his way to Mariana. "All set?"

"Just about," she said, placing her laptop into its case. "What about this?" She held up the flash drive.

"Put it in your case. It's safe enough there," Denbo answered.

"Roger that."

They all joined Bitterhoff and Farris in the hallway.

Bitterhoff was just putting away his phone. "Okay, Gutierrez says they're about fifteen, maybe twenty minutes from wrapping up. They'll head for the Vasquez house as soon as Ms. James is done."

"Good," Denbo said.

Cayden and Denbo took the lead, with Bitterhoff and Farris falling in behind Mariana. They took the stairs down to the lobby where Denbo intercepted them.

"You stay put," he told his agents. "March and I will have a look outside. We'll wave you out once we know it's all clear. You know this building's back exits?"

"We scoped it all out as soon as we got here this morning," Farris answered.

"You guys hear or see anything out of the ordinary, head for the back and get Ms. Vasquez out. Drive her to the Pasadena Police headquarters and stay put."

Bitterhoff nodded. "Understood."

"And be careful," Cayden added. "They could have all sides of the building covered."

Cayden and Denbo made their way to the doors. They waited a few moments and then stepped outside. Pausing at the top of the stairs, they surveyed the area. The sound of an engine revving drew Cayden's attention. A dark gray Suburban, its headlights glaring, was bearing down on the front of the building. Cayden instinctively moved his hand toward his gun.

"Whoa, hang on," Denbo said. "That's our transportation."

Cayden relaxed as Denbo directed the Suburban to park in front of the building's entrance. Four agents climbed from the SUV, all in the standard FBI attire of suits and ties. As Denbo stepped forward, they all stepped forward to meet him.

"Right on time," Denbo greeted them.

The detail lead responded, "Always."

Denbo gestured toward Cayden. "This is Cayden March. Consider him part of this detail until I say differently."

The agent nodded to him. "Special Agent Jameson. Glad to have you."

"Thanks," Cayden responded.

Denbo walked back up the steps to the lobby doors and waved his agents forward. A minute later, they gathered next to the Suburban. Special Agent Bitterhoff opened the door to the back seat, helped Mariana inside, and closed the door.

"March and I will meet you at Ms. Vasquez's house," Denbo said to Jameson.

Jameson and his detail climbed back into the car. The driver turned over the engine and put the SUV into gear.

Cayden, Denbo, Bitterhoff, and Farris stepped back as the driver started the big car rolling. They all watched as the SUV followed Mandala's car toward the exit.

Cayden turned to Denbo. "Where's your car?"

"The structure on Holliston," Denbo answered.

"You could've just driven up the walkway here."

"Now you tell me," Denbo said.

"We're on the street," Bitterhoff said.

Cayden began walking toward the Ducati. "I'll see you over there."

He hadn't taken five steps when the loud crack of a rifle shot echoed off the buildings.

CHAPTER TWENTY-FIVE

Adrenaline coursed through Cayden as he drew his gun and dropped low. He ran toward the closest cover, a four-foot high concrete sign wall identifying the Powell-Booth Laboratory. More shots rang out as the FBI agents, guns drawn, scrambled to join him. They were just short of the wall when Special Agent Bitterhoff cried out and crumbled to the ground. Denbo and Farris grabbed his arms and dragged him behind the wall.

Cayden heard alarmed shouts and screams, and glimpsed several students scattering for cover. None of this would be happening if he hadn't lifted the flash drive from Alan's office. He felt angry toward himself, and even more angry at whoever was shooting at him.

The gunfire was loud and sporadic. Chips of concrete flew into the air as more bullets struck the wall. Special Agent Farris positioned himself next to the unconscious Bitterhoff and applied pressure against the wound.

Denbo fished his phone from his pocket with his free hand. He thumbed a pre-programmed number and put the phone to his ear. "Langford. We're still on campus. Under fire. Multiple shooters." Denbo ended the call, then punched in another number. "Gutierrez, we're under fire. Get Ms. James off campus now."

Cayden agreed there were multiple shooters, but where were they? He slipped out of his jacket and rolled it up tight. "Stay low."

"No problem," Denbo said as he and Farris hunched down.

He took aim and hurled the balled up jacket across the wall toward the building entrance. The jacket caught the light from the entrance lamps and several more shots rang out. A loud crack sounded as several bullets punched through the building's front glass wall.

Cayden spotted two groupings of muzzle flashes. "At least four shooters," he called out. "Two in the dumpster enclosure next to the student center building on the left. The rest of them are across the path behind the steps leading up to the engineering laboratory's side entrance."

"Distance?" Denbo asked as another volley of bullets smashed into the wall and the building behind them.

"About a hundred-and-fifty feet."

The shooters had the advantage; longer range weapons and better concealment. If they decided to advance, all they had to do was lay down consistent fire as they moved forward. They'd come at them from both sides of the wall, and there would be little he and the FBI men could do.

More shots rang through the night and slammed into the wall. Cayden knew the best course of action was to become the aggressor. "We can't stay here, but there's no cover if we move," Cayden addressed Denbo. "How are you for ammo?"

"Mag in the gun only has a couple of rounds," Denbo answered. "Two more full mags on my belt. Same with Farris, and we've got Bitterhoff's gun and mags."

Chips of concrete flew off the top of the wall as more bullets plowed into it. Cayden peered around the end of the wall to get his bearings. Two low hills of landscaping decorated both sides of the Powell-Booth walkway. Three redwood trees rose upward from one hill offering some cover, but the rest of the area contained only low bushes and plants.

He turned back to the FBI agents. "On my signal, you and Farris open fire on the dumpster enclosure to the left. I'll handle the other side of the walkway. Just keep their heads down until I reach the trees on that little hill."

"You're going out there?" Denbo's eyes opened wide in disbelief.

"If they advance, we won't stand a chance. I'm going to get behind them."

Denbo shook his head. "You need to stay put."

"It's our best move. Once I reach the hill, alternate your fire to both sides of the path."

Denbo looked doubtful, but moved into position.

"Set?" Cayden said.

"Set."

Cayden waited until the next salvo of bullets stopped chipping away at the wall.

"Now," Cayden shouted.

Denbo and Farris raised themselves up and opened fire.

Cayden bolted around the end of the wall, raising his pistol to a two-handed grip. He ran hard for the hillock, his Beretta cracking as he squeezed off one round after another. Behind him, the FBI gunfire was reassuring.

He reached the hillock and dropped flat on the ground behind the closest Redwood. Adrenaline fueled excitement mixed rushed through him, familiar feelings from his days in The Unit. Cayden sprinted from cover, heading for the northwest corner of the engineering laboratory building. If the FBI agents' barrage of gunfire had kept the shooters' heads low, there was a chance they hadn't spotted him.

He reached the corner of the engineering building and took a cautious look down the pathway. It was empty. He continued forward along the south side of the building. Behind him, gunfire from the FBI pistols ceased, and an immediate flurry of explosions from the rifles erupted.

Cayden was about to round the corner that would head him

east toward the shooters when he heard a soft rustle of fabric and the faint clinking of metal. He moved close to the building. Dropping low behind a line of tall bushes lining, he peered around the corner.

Diffused light from the lamp posts silhouetted a dark figure moving toward him, hugging the side of the path close to the bushes. The man was less than twenty feet away. Lamplight illuminated the assault rifle held at the ready.

The shooters had either spotted him or they were executing the same tactic he was using. Cayden didn't want to alert this guy's friends. He holstered his Beretta and moved around the corner of the building, staying under the cover of the bushes. The man was close now, only a few feet away, his dark gray hoodie casting a shadow across his face.

Cayden launched himself through the bushes toward the shooter. The man heard him and turned, leveling his rifle at his chest. Cayden struck the rifle barrel aside with his left palm, locking his grip on the barrel as he launched two brutal elbow strikes to the side of the shooter's head. A violent upward twist on the rifle jarred it from the man's hands. The movement broke the shooter's finger, shoving it against the trigger. The rifle blast sent a shot into the night sky. So much for stealth. He followed through, slamming the rifle stock into the shooter's temple.

As the shooter crumpled to the ground, Cayden spotted the second man less than ten feet away. He also wore dark clothing, his head covered with a black baseball cap, and his torso protected by a Kevlar vest. He was already raising the pistol gripped in his right hand. There was no time. Cayden fired the assault rifle from waist level, then fired again. The two bullets knocked the shooter off balance, giving Cayden time to aim. The third round struck the man in the head. He dropped to the ground, dead, a dark stain of blood pooling around his shoulders.

Gunfire exchanged between the FBI agents and the unidentified shooters continued reverberating against the buildings. Cayden felt relieved to see students and campus personnel running from the gunfire. There were longer gaps now between the FBI's pistol shots. The agents were trying to conserve their ammunition. He had to hurry, but he couldn't risk leaving the unconscious man behind him.

He took hold of the breathing man's arm and dragged him over beside the body of his companion. Both men were Hispanic, and judging from the tattoos on them, both had done prison time. Gangbangers? If they were, what were they doing on the Caltech campus? The shooters were in position, waiting, when he and the FBI detail exited Powell-Booth. It couldn't be a coincidence. Instinct told him Russo and Craven somehow connected to the ambush, but he couldn't see a plausible link.

Cayden pulled the tie cords from both men's hoodies. In less than a minute, he also had the shoelaces from their expensive basketball shoes. It took little time to tie them together. He looped the makeshift rope through the dead man's belt several times, and then tied the unconscious man's hands, pulling them tight against the corpse. It wasn't perfect, but it would keep the guy from going anywhere should he awaken.

The sound of distant sirens cut through the night. Cayden gathered up the assault rifle and the dead man's handgun. After tossing the handgun into the bushes, he checked the rifle's high capacity magazine, finding it half full. More than enough. The weapon would give him a distance advantage.

The rifle fire was loud and jarring as Cayden continued along the back of the engineering building. This wasn't the first time he'd been in the middle of something like this. He slowed as he reached the corner closest to the shooters.

Cayden had an unobscured view of the dumpster enclosure across the walkway and the backs of the two shooters there. The iron gate, normally padlocked, was open. One shooter squatted in the opening, leaning out from the wall to take his shots. His companion stood on the opposite side of the opening, doing the same. Cayden could see only the man's rifle barrel protruding from the wall. The second man he encountered had been wearing Kevlar. It was prudent to assume the rest of them were, too.

The would-be assassins shooting from the side steps of the engineering building were out of his field of view, but Cayden knew there would be nothing between them and him once he broke cover. He'd have to be fast. The sound of sirens grew louder.

Cayden moved fast, advancing on the dumpster enclosure, the rifle pressed against his shoulder. He squeezed off two rounds. The first struck the squatting shooter in the neck, the second round bored through the top of his head. The dead man collapsed on his knees against the edge of the wall. His companion moved into the open for a clear shot at Cayden. Cayden was counting on it. He fired three rounds. The first round struck the shooter's thigh. As the man went down, the next two rounds smashed into his gun arm.

Cayden advanced toward the side of the engineering building. The remaining two men kneeling on the steps had already turned to face him. Both looked surprised, but one of them took aim at him. Cayden fired first, sending two bullets into the shooter's skull. The man had barely hit the ground when his pal threw down his rifle and raised his hands, crying out for mercy in Spanish. Cayden kept the rifle trained on him.

"Denbo, it's March," he yelled at the top of his lungs. "Hold fire."

Cayden gestured with the rifle barrel and yelled in Spanish, "Move to the middle of the pathway."

The gunman, his hands held high, did as he was told.

"Face down on the ground."

The man obeyed as several police vehicles sped up the wide walkway to the Powell-Booth building. Cayden held the rifle ready as he moved in on the dumpster enclosure. He kicked the wounded man's rifle out of reach, then confirmed the other man was dead. He was heading to do the same at the engineering building when the police cruisers, their sirens cutting out, their emergency vehicle lights flashing bright blue and red in the darkness, screeched to a stop.

Several police vehicle headlamps covered Cayden in intense light. He placed the rifle on the pathway as voices yelled orders to flatten himself on the pavement.

CHAPTER TWENTY-SIX

The number of police cruisers had doubled since the first responders arrived, and four ambulances soon joined them. The windows in the surrounding buildings reflected the blue and red flashing emergency lights, creating a surreal carnival atmosphere. Curious students and school employees congregated behind the police lines, straining their necks for a better view and sharing theories about what might have gone down at their peaceful school.

The crime scene investigation unit had cordoned off the area and had teams working at each body site. The frequent strobe flashes from their digital cameras illuminated the activity around the dead men. Denbo stood at the side of the walkway, reporting the details to Langford.

As Cayden watched the proceedings, he began feeling like himself again. His attack on the shooters didn't bother him. He felt some of his old confidence returning, and even a sense of satisfaction.

Mandala approached him, staring down at the bodies next to the dumpster enclosure. "You took out all of them."

"Some of them are still alive." Cayden stuck his hands into his jacket pockets. One of the police officers had retrieved the jacket from the front steps of the Powell-Booth building after they had determined he was not a threat.

"My guys give you your gun back?" Mandala asked.

"Yeah, thanks." Cayden tapped the butt of the Beretta under the fabric of his jacket.

"We were close to the station when we heard the dispatch call over the car radio." Gesturing toward the two bodies, Mandala said, "You move fast."

Cayden wasn't sure how to respond to the comment, so he remained silent.

Ray Chalmers, advised at home of "shots fired" by one of the security guards on duty, had almost broken the land speed record getting back to the campus. Ray was eyeing him with suspicion, mixed with a solid amount of disbelief. "I know you're former military. But six guys."

"Asking a question, Ray?" Cayden asked.

Frustrated, Ray pointed toward the bodies. "There are dead folks on my campus."

"They were shooting at us."

Raymond frowned at Cayden. "You had to kill them?"

"It was a better alternative to them killing me."

Special Agent Denbo joined them. "We're glad he did kill them. We've got one student with a bullet in her leg and the owner of a backpack with three holes in it. The textbooks in the pack stopped the bullets. It could have been a lot worse if the shooters remained in play any longer."

"What about the wounded girl?" Ray asked.

"The bullet passed through the fleshy part of her thigh," Denbo answered. "No broken bones. She lost some blood, but she's going to be okay."

"Thank God," Ray said.

Denbo extended his hand to Cayden. "I've never seen anything like that. Thank you. I mean it."

It was the first time the guy had looked at him with respect since they'd met. Cayden shook the agent's hand. "How's your agent doing?"

"He's in a world of hurt, but the paramedics say he's going to be okay."

"Good."

Special Agent Langford joined them from the direction of the engineering laboratory building. "They're all Hispanic. Four of them have prison tattoos. All of them have gang tattoos."

"Gang activity? On this campus?" Ray said, the doubt in his voice unmistakable.

"Boulevard 13 according to the body art," Langford said.

"If they're Boulevard 13 guys, then they're way out of their neighborhood," Mandala said. "They control Highland Park, Eagle Rock, Glassell Park, Cypress Park. I've never heard of them coming over here."

"The guy March hogtied to his dead buddy is conscious, but he won't say a word," Langford said.

"Not now, maybe," Denbo said. "Once we get him in an interview room, things might be different."

"So nobody recognizes any of these men?" Langford gestured toward the bodies on the steps of the engineering building.

"Never seen them before tonight," Cayden answered.

"You didn't piss somebody off?" Denbo asked, humor in his voice.

"Sure," Cayden answered. "Just nobody running in gang circles."

"We'll pay a visit to Boulevard 13's big *jefe*," Mandala said. "Guy named Amado Estrada. Goes by Razor Boy."

Denbo's eyebrows arched upward. "Razor Boy?"

"He's going to be just as tight-lipped as his man with the broken nose. But you never know. We might get something out of it," Mandala said.

"Get in touch once you've talked with him," Langford told Mandala.

"No problem."

"It makes no sense," Ray said.

"What's that?" Langford asked.

"Gang activity like this, here. It makes no sense," Ray repeated.

Cayden had to agree with his boss. None of it made any sense. What reason could six members of a powerful Los Angeles gang have to start a firefight on a university campus in Pasadena? The attack had begun soon after the FBI detail had driven Mariana Vasquez off the campus. That couldn't be a coincidence.

An icy chill rushed through his body as the most plausible explanation suddenly hit him. The words came out of his mouth more loudly than he intended. "Diversion. It's a diversion."

CHAPTER TWENTY-SEVEN

Cyn laid on her back in the musty blackness of Mariana Vasquez's attic. She didn't mind the darkness. It was soothing and quiet. It enabled her to think through the possibilities for the evening. There was still a little ambient light in the attic when she first climbed up through the ceiling hatch in the hallway bathroom. Dim ribbons of light filtered in from the two gable vents, but that light soon faded as the sun dropped in the late afternoon sky.

The familiar soft beep sounded in Cyn's earpiece. She checked her digital watch. 6:11. "Razor Boy's idiots waited too long," Danny's voice came through her earpiece. "The FBI drove Vasquez out of there before they started shooting."

"Where is she is now?"

"They left the campus before the shooting started. If they don't know about it yet, they're most likely heading toward you right now."

"Super duper," she responded, the excitement making her skin tingle.

"I'm already on my way," Danny said. "I'll contact you once I'm in position. Don't move till then."

"Understood. Love you, babe."

She savored the spike of adrenaline Danny's report kindled. The rush and the excitement never got old. She repositioned herself so she could move quickly when the time came. Then she was still again, staring at the blackness, waiting, listening. It wasn't long before the sound of a car approaching reached her. It slowed, and the sound of the engine changed as the car turned into the driveway. Cyn heard the car doors open and close, and only moments later, the metallic scraping of a key in the front door lock. Then the muffled voices, impossible to understand, wafting up from the first floor.

She'd wait. It wouldn't be long now.

CHAPTER TWENTY-EIGHT

Cayden pushed the Ducati hard, weaving through the traffic, all of it moving slower than his bike. Denbo, in the saddle behind him, clung tight, and his grip grew tighter every time Cayden made a quick lane change or took a corner too fast.

He turned onto Mariana Vasquez's block, easing up on the throttle as he approached the house. A soft light glowed through the closed curtains covering the front window. There was no porch light visible, a bad sign.

The FBI's Suburban sat parked in the driveway, but there was no sign of any agents. Cayden pulled over to the curb just short of the driveway. Except for Burl Ives singing "A Holly Jolly Christmas" escaping from a nearby house, the neighborhood was quiet.

"At least one of your guys should be out front," Cayden said as they climbed off the bike.

"One in front, one in back, two inside," Denbo said, removing Cayden's helmet and dropping it on the ground beside the bike.

They drew their weapons and, spreading several feet apart, advanced onto the property. From the moment he realized the shooting incident at Caltech was choreographed as a distraction, Cayden feared he would find Mariana dead in her home. The thought sickened him. He chastised himself for not seeing the ambush for what it was earlier.

As he approached the house, he knew it was possible at least one killer was still inside. Or they might have already left the house with the flash drive in their position. Glass from the shattered porch light bulb spread across the doormat. The second discovery was the body of one of Jameson's team, dead, his throat cut, rolled under a hedge at the corner of the house. More people dead because of the flash drive. Cayden whistled softly, attracting Denbo's attention.

Denbo looked anguished as he examined the body. At that moment, a muffled thump sounded from inside the house and an undistinguishable shadow moved across the front window curtains.

"I'm going around back. I'll get inside from there," Cayden whispered. "You okay covering the front?"

Denbo nodded. They made their way to the driveway. Denbo concealed himself behind the Suburban, his gun ready. Cayden left him, hurrying up the shadowy driveway.

The body of a second FBI agent beside the back porch steps added to his tension. Blood from the gash in the man's throat had pooled into the grass around his head, appearing black in the dim, ambient light. He surveyed the shadows in the yard, but there was nobody else present.

Cayden moved up the steps and tried the door. Locked. The only light he saw through the door's glass panes came from the front of the house. Picking the lock would take time. Besides, if one or both of the killers was inside, they would already know of his presence, and Denbo's. He used his elbow to shatter one of the lower panes, reached inside, and felt for the deadbolt handle. Finding it, he turned the latch and eased the door open. His gun ready, Cayden stepped inside.

A shadowy hallway stretched from the kitchen to the front of the house. From Cayden's vantage point, he had only a limited view of the living room. A rustling sound came from somewhere ahead of him. Slow and watchful, he continued forward.

A soft glow of light spilled into the hall from an open door in the center of the hallway. With much caution, his gun ready, he peered inside. The space was full of computer equipment. The undulating screensavers on several displays created a ghostly pattern of moving shadows across the walls. Cayden pivoted into the room. Slumped backward across a small sofa on the back wall, his face shattered by a bullet, was Special Agent Jameson.

A sickening gnarl swelled inside him. If three of the FBI agents were dead, it was likely the fourth agent was as well. That made it more likely Mariana was already dead. He stepped back into the hallway and, with another four steps, reached the archway opening to the living room.

He stopped dead in shock. Mariana Vasquez stood in the middle of the room, her eyes staring wide at him. Holding her from behind was the girl from the surveillance photos, Cynthia Craven, her left arm locked across Mariana's throat. Her right hand gripped a semi-automatic pistol, the barrel of its suppressor pressed against Mariana's temple. Mariana's face was taut with fear, but she appeared unharmed. The fourth FBI agent lay dead in front of the hearth, a bullet hole in the back of his head.

Cayden was relieved at finding Mariana alive, but the situation was still grave. Craven used Mariana as a shield, but her head was exposed enough for a head shot. He'd taken such shots several times in his former job, never missing. It was still risky, but if he did nothing, Mariana's death was a certainty. Cayden was on the verge of firing when Craven seemed to read his mind.

Moving directly behind Mariana, she made herself a harder target. "Bad idea," she said, her tone playful. "I'll kill her right now."

Cayden lowered his pistol.

"Put it on the floor," Craven ordered.

Cayden lowered his gun a bit more, but he knew the odds of Mariana and his surviving dropped considerably if the weapon left his hand.

"You or her," Craven said with a hardness in her tone, her eyes narrowing.

He had little choice, and he saw no immediate way of getting the upper hand. Kneeling, Cayden dropped his gun on the carpeted floor, then straightened up.

"Give it a little kick."

Cayden kicked the pistol away. It slid across the carpet, coming to a stop beside the hall doorway.

"Wow. You didn't get shot tonight. At least not yet. And you got here way sooner than you should have." She mocked a frown. "Impressive, but I already got what I came for."

A wicked smile replaced the frown as she opened the fingers of her left hand. The flash drive rested against her palm, secured by her thumb. With his gun on the floor, Craven must have assumed he was no longer a threat. She kept a tight grip on Mariana as she stepped to her side.

Her body was lean and athletic. She had what many men would consider a beautiful face, but there was a hint of hardness in her features, despite the smile on her lips. Besides being a cold-blooded killer, there was something off about her. Her eyes were bright and glinting with excitement—she was getting a big kick out of taunting him—but there was a dark emptiness behind it all. A brief glance into those eyes sent a chill snaking down his spine.

"You've got the drive. Let her go," Cayden said.

Craven giggled. "Don't think so."

She removed the gun barrel from Mariana's head and leveled it at him. The empty eyes narrowed again as she took aim and her finger squeezed the trigger.

It happened in an instant. Mariana twisted hard toward Craven's gun hand and pushed back with her legs. The gun fired as both women stumbled backward, the bullet plowing into the wall above the fireplace. Mariana's legs struck the corner of the coffee table. She went down, pivoting around the edge of the table and landing on her knees. Craven's legs connected with the table behind her knees. She tumbled backward, holding on to her gun, but dropping the flash drive onto the tabletop. Craven placed her hand on the table for balance, corrected in midair, and landed on her feet.

Cayden was already charging forward when Mariana scooped the flash drive into her hand. She bolted toward the front door, but Craven launched a kick at Mariana's legs. Mariana fell hard, striking her head against the corner of the foyer wall. She lay still, stunned.

Cayden grabbed Craven's gun arm with both hands as he slammed into her. She yelped in pain as he twisted the arm and the gun fell to the floor. With her free hand, Craven landed a solid kidney punch, hurting him and causing him to release his grip.

He spotted the gleaming knife blade just in time to pivot to the side. She came at him fast, but he rushed in close, pinning the knife hand to her side. He delivered two swift strikes to her stomach before she kneed him in the groin and twisted away.

Cayden straightened up as she came at him again, moving with a kind of manic grace, wielding the knife with expert skill and forcing him to leap away to avoid the blade. He gave her credit for tenacity, coming at someone who outweighed her and whose skill set she couldn't know. She showed impressive speed, but he countered her attack, pinning her knife hand each time while landing several blows in fast succession.

His ribs were on fire, the pain intense, slowing him down. And Craven saw it. The little smile widened to a grin as she escalated her assault. The risk was inconsequential to her. He could see it in her eyes. It turned her on. The violence turned her on.

Cayden saw Mariana stir and knew he had to end the struggle fast. He moved in close, parrying another knife thrust and again pinning her knife hand against Craven's side. She gasped as he slammed her back against the wall.

He tightened his fingers around her wrist and forced the blade upward. With her free hand, Craven gripped his arm, fighting hard to control the knife's upward movement. But the blade still moved toward her throat. She launched a desperate knee strike. It missed his groin but jarred him enough that the knife blade moved off target. It slashed across her face, carving a gash from the corner of her lip to just beneath her ear.

With the cry of a wounded animal, Craven kneed him again, twisting away and leaping into the center of the room. A flash of panic showed in her eyes as her hand shot up to her cheek. The blood oozed out between her fingers, and her panic turned to fury. She adjusted her grip on the knife and threw it. Cayden leaped to the side as the blade whooshed through the air, missing him by mere inches. The hilt slammed into the back wall and clattered to the floor.

Craven rushed toward her gun. In the same moment, Cayden dived across the floor to retrieve his pistol. He took hold of it and rolled onto his side to take aim. But by the time his eyes were on the killer again, he couldn't fire.

Mariana was on her knees with Craven, gripping her pistol, squatted down behind her. The suppressor barrel pressed against the side of Mariana's head. The flash drive lay on the floor, next to Mariana's left foot.

"Get the drive," Craven ordered Mariana.

Craven smacked the gun against the side of Mariana's head when she didn't immediately do what she was told. Mariana winced and reluctantly ran her hand over the carpet until her fingers found the drive.

"Up up up," Craven said to Mariana, her voice playful.

The tension in the room was tangible as the two women got to their feet. Craven's face dripped with blood. Her eyes flashed with rage and hatred. She had the drive. She had a hostage, and Cayden knew she was eager to kill.

His eyes flicked to Mariana. She swayed unsteadily and blood oozed through her hair where the gun struck her.

"Time to go," Craven said.

Cayden realized she wasn't speaking to anyone in the room. She had to be using an in-ear com system. Time was running out. He had to do something, but his position on the floor was awkward, with no unobstructed line of sight to Craven.

Mariana's eyes, wide with terror, began tearing, and her mouth quivered.

The sound of an approaching car grew louder from outside the house. A moment later, the sound of automatic weapon fire came from the street.

Craven suddenly lowered her gun out of sight below Mariana's shoulders. Two shots in quick succession rang out. Mariana managed a half-strangled scream before she hit the floor.

Horror and guilt hit Cayden in the gut. Craven raced toward the front door. He fired at her and missed as he got back on his feet and took cover behind the dining room wall. He barely reached cover as Craven fired a quick succession of shots. The bullets ripped through the old walls, splattering him with plaster dust and debris.

Mariana, crumpled on the floor next to the dead FBI agent, distracted him. If she was still alive, she had to be his priority.

Multiple shots sounded from outside the house as Craven yanked the door open and bolted outside. Cayden took aim and fired. His bullet struck her upper back. She cried out, but she only lurched forward, almost falling but quickly getting her footing again. A vest; she had to be wearing a vest.

The gunfire outside intensified as Cayden rushed to Mariana. She was lying face down, a pool of blood forming beneath her. When he saw the entry location of the bullet, Cayden knew she was gone. Craven had shot her through the heart. Another person in his charge, dead.

He rushed through the open door in time to see Denbo diving behind the Suburban as a barrage of bullets clanged into the truck's chassis. Russo stood behind the driver's side of a late model black Mustang, an automatic pistol in his hand. The moment

Craven reached the car, they both jumped inside. Cayden opened fire as the Mustang sped away, tires screeching. On the second shot, the slide on his Beretta jumped back and locked in place. The gun was empty. Denbo broke cover, squeezing off a few more rounds before the Mustang disappeared into the night.

The Ducati was only yards away. Cayden could chase them down. Instead, he turned back to the house. Even though Mariana was gone, he couldn't leave her.

CHAPTER TWENTY-NINE

His call to Kate was both a relief and painful. Special Agent Gutierrez had rushed her to his car, driving her to Pasadena Police headquarters. Kate was safe, but breaking the news about Mariana's death was horrible. She burst into tears and nothing he said consoled her.

He stood on the front lawn, gazing at the open front door. FBI and Pasadena police crime scene investigators worked side by side within. The bright glow from their work lights poured through the doorway. He turned his attention to the driveway where two paramedics loaded Mariana Vasquez's bagged body into a city ambulance. Cayden felt numb inside. He promised he'd protect her. He'd failed. Turning his back on the ambulance, he walked inside the house, pausing in the foyer. He wasn't there long when Mandala and Denbo emerged from the hallway.

"There's no copy of the drive on her computer system," Denbo reported. "At least if there is, we can't find it."

"Well, we instructed her not to make a copy." Langford sighed.

"We need to find Dragović's people before they can use that thing," Denbo said.

"I want every agent available on it," Langford said. "Handle it now."

Denbo pulled out his smartphone and stepped out to the front yard.

Cayden watched him go. He'd been angry at Denbo for not entering the house when the gunfire began, but Denbo explained. At the first gunshot, he rushed to the front door but found it locked. His attempts to kick it in failed. He was heading for the back of the house when Daniel Russo arrived and opened fire on him. Pinned down, all Denbo could do was take cover and return fire. Cayden didn't question Denbo's explanation; the proof was in the Suburban, speckled with uncountable bullet holes.

Cayden couldn't direct anger at anyone but himself. He gazed at the bloodstained carpet where Mariana had fallen. Death was nothing new to him, and his training mandated he should be impervious to it. But this was different. This was an innocent woman he knew, liked, and respected. And it could have been Kate as well.

"Mariana had no business being anywhere near this mess." It surprised Cayden that he spoke the words aloud.

Standing nearby, Langford muttered, "It's a tragedy."

Denbo returned from the front yard. "We're all set."

Langford ignored him, his attention on Cayden.

"She was a civilian who had no business being involved here," Cayden said, his tone angry.

"Agents died tonight, too. All good men. Three of them with wives and children," Denbo said.

"And I'm sorry for it," Cayden said. "But none of this should've ever happened."

"You've no reason to feel guilty," Langford said.

He turned on the special agent. "Is that so?"

"You can't blame yourself is all I mean," Langford said.

Cayden bristled, his body rigid with anger. "I blame you. You should've never asked her, and I told you that the second her name came up."

Mandala interrupted. "How about we focus on something more productive?"

The only sound in the house came from the investigators performing their work. Cayden lost himself, staring into the living room. He did his best to reconstruct the order of events that evening, trying to determine if he might have done something differently. The room became stifling to him, and a question that had been vague and formless solidified.

Cayden made his way to the front door and stepped outside. He wandered onto the lawn, looking at the small police convention taking place on the street. The block had been closed off the moment the police arrived. But residents on either side of the Vasquez house, and on the opposite side of the street, had gathered to watch the real life drama unfold. They crowded the barricades, leaning to one side and then the other to get a better look, holding their phones high, hoping to snap a photo that might reveal something they weren't already seeing with their own eyes.

Detective Mandala quietly appeared beside him. "For what it's worth, I'm sorry," Mandala said.

"Yeah."

"She shouldn't have ever been near this disaster. Ms. James, too."

"I should have made sure they weren't involved," Cayden said.

"Our FBI friends in there pushed pretty hard for it," Mandala said.

They had pushed hard. And he had objected hard, but not hard enough. Cayden shook his head, trying to push his feelings aside so he could concentrate. Something wasn't right.

Cayden faced Mandala. "How did they know where to find her? How did they even know who she was?"

Mandala frowned. "Good question."

"The Craven girl was waiting for her here."

"Surveillance," Mandala suggested. "They'd been watching you. It's possible they might have connected you and Ms. Vasquez."

"I expected them to be on me this morning when I drove to the meeting," Cayden said. "They weren't on me then, and they weren't on me when I went to Caltech after our meeting."

"You're sure of that?" Mandala asked.

"I'm sure. Besides, let's say they surveilled our meeting and figured out what Mariana's involvement was. They wouldn't have had time to pull all this off. It took time to arrange it all. The gang shooting on campus to keep us busy; the time to get into this house."

"Tapped phones then," Mandala offered. "I mean, not our department phones. They're checked regularly."

"Cell phones are vulnerable," Cayden agreed. "There's plenty of spyware and electronic hacking techniques."

"Then we have our phones checked. All of us. The FBI guys, too." Mandala said.

"You're suggesting a lot of solid possibilities." Cayden met Mandala's gaze and held it. When he spoke again, he lowered his voice. "Makes me wonder if you're dancing around the possibility I'm considering."

"A mole," Mandala said, matching his volume.

Cayden nodded.

"It's a small group that knew about Mariana's involvement," Mandala said. "You, me, Langford and Denbo in there. Your friend, Kate. Who else?"

"We know the CIA is in the loop," Cayden said. "And Langford was holding a folder marked with a Secret Service stamp the first time I met him at the hospital."

"Yeah. I remember seeing it," Mandala said.

Cayden took a step closer to Mandala. "FBI, CIA, Secret Service; that's a lot of possibilities."

They both considered the problem and the ramifications that came with it.

After a minute of silence, Mandala shuffled, uncomfortable. "Seems like you're taking a big chance discussing this with me. How do you know I'm not the mole?"

"Anything's possible," Cayden responded. "But I've known

you for three years. I don't believe you knew anything about that dead CIA officer until you showed up at the crime scene. You don't run in the same circles as black ops guys or international arms dealers. A look into your past will prove it."

"I'm pretty dull when it comes right down to it." Mandala sighed. "What about your lady friend?"

"The same goes for her," Cayden said. "Kate's a grad student working at Caltech and that's all she is. She's familiar with special ops, but only because her brother served with me. The only thing that pulled her into this was her friendship with Alan Fenland."

Mandala's eyebrows rose. "Her brother served with you?"

Cayden looked away. "A story for another time, maybe."

Special Agents Langford and Denbo strolled through the front door onto the porch, engaged in conversation. With all the noise from the police activity, their voices were audible, but not their words.

Cayden gave a subtle nod toward the special agents. "From this point on, we need to be less forthcoming with our friends over there."

"Uh huh," Mandala agreed. "We've got a new question to answer."

Cayden nodded. "Yeah. Who?"

CHAPTER THIRTY

Russo watched in silence as the doctor worked on Cyn's face. To his credit, the doctor's anxiety did not hamper the skill he applied to suturing the long gash that ran across her cheek.

Cyn lay on the treatment table, her head turned to the side, not uttering a sound as the doctor worked. Her face was void of expression, her wide open eyes staring unblinking at nothing.

A rotund nurse stood behind the doctor with her back against the wall, her eyes fixed on the gun Russo had trained on them, particularly the suppressor he'd screwed onto the barrel just before entering the place.

Once Russo was certain no one was on their tail, he'd pulled the car over and examined Cyn's face. He concluded the wound was too serious for him to treat himself. After urging Cyn out of the Mustang, they stole a beat up Honda Accord he'd found parked on the street.

This clinic was the fourth on a list compiled by his phone's map application. The first two were in busy sections of the city, well-lit areas with too much walk-in traffic. The third clinic had been more isolated, but the parking lot was full. This East Pasadena location was a small facility with only two cars in the parking lot.

Russo had circled the area and parked the car a block away.

Neither of them had said a word as they walked to the clinic, Cyn pressing the handkerchief he'd provided against her cheek.

He knew Cyn well enough to know she was furious to the point of hatred that March had cut her with her own knife. He was certain, too, that a depression descended on her at the realization there was going to be a lifelong scar.

But Cyn wasn't the only one angry. Engaging the security guard hand-to-hand was unforgivable. He'd warned her March was more than he appeared, and she was now experiencing the consequences of having ignored him. He was also pissed that Cyn failed to kill March. Even though he could hear the anger in his voice, he was keeping it under control.

"How much longer?" Russo glanced at his watch, his gun never wavering.

The doctor glanced up, his forehead damp with a thin beading of sweat. "We're almost there."

The doctor knotted the sutures and trimmed off the excess. He then picked up a tube of Mupirocin ointment from the instrument table, and using a cotton swab, applied a generous layer along the sutured wound. The doctor cut a strip of surgical gauze from its roll. He folded it into a thick bandage and taped it in place.

"That it?" Russo asked.

The doctor nodded. "You can sit up now."

Cyn sat up, moving slowly as she rotated her legs off the table. She sat there, her eyes fixed on the floor.

"I think I have a sample supply of hydrocodone here." The doctor reached for a cabinet door handle.

"Stop." Russo raised the gun barrel.

The doctor stopped, lowering his arms to his side. "The local I gave her will wear off soon. I've got hydrocodone to help with the pain, and help her get some sleep."

"No. I want her to feel it," Russo said. "It'll help her remember."

Cyn's eyes moved to him, but she remained silent.

The doctor shrugged, and Russo cared little for the look of

disapproval on his face. He waved the gun barrel toward the back corner of the room.

"If you'll all just move over there, please."

The nurse could barely move in her fear.

"Come on. Let's do as he says." The doctor managed a smile for her.

With some reluctance, they moved into the corner.

"Cyn," Russo snapped her name.

She slipped off the table, taking a position next to him, her expression still as pale and blank as a new canvas.

"We did as you asked," the doctor said. "There'll be a scar, but if she sees a good plastic surgeon as soon as possible, they can minimize it."

"We appreciate your help," Russo replied. "We'll just be on our way; leave you both in peace."

He put a bullet in each of their hearts before they could react. Even with the suppressor, the shots sounded loud in the small room. Once the bodies had dropped to the floor, he shot each of them one more time in the head. No good thing ever came from leaving witnesses.

Russo donned a pair of latex gloves pulled from a dispenser on the counter. He found supplies in the examination room's cabinets and spent the next five minutes sanitizing the room, meticulously wiping down any surface that might have picked up their finger-prints. Completing the task, he opened a new plastic trash bag and placed all the supplies he had used in the bag.

He carried the bag with him as he took Cyn by the arm and ushered her into the hallway. After a last look around the room to make sure he had missed nothing, he closed the door behind them.

CHAPTER THIRTY-ONE

After suffering a restless night, Cayden awoke the morning of December 23rd to see the alarm clock on his nightstand reading 8:30 a.m. That was late for him. He was wide awake by the time he showered and dressed.

The sound of a door followed by footsteps reached him from the floor below. He hurried from the bedroom, pausing at the top of the stairs. Kate stood in the entryway, fishing for something in her large, baggy purse. Her travel bag rested on the floor beside her. When she turned toward him, her red, puffy eyes told him how her night had been.

"I think I'll go home now."

It troubled Cayden to see her in such pain. But he didn't know what to say. He ended up with the most banal of responses. "Oh, okay."

"They got what they came for," Kate said, her voice strained. "I mean, I'm not in danger anymore, right?"

"Well, they're still out there, but I don't believe so. It'd be better if you stay here, though." He didn't want her to go. He hoped it would all be a little easier if they hung out together.

Kate gazed up at him, considering his words.

He ran a hand over his head, unsure of what to say. "What I

mean is, maybe this isn't the time to be alone."

"I don't know."

"Christmas Eve is tomorrow. Why don't you hang out for Christmas?"

"I just want to go home." Kate opened the front door, then turned back and picked up her bag.

He descended the stairs and took the bag from her hand. "I'll never be able to say I'm sorry enough."

"I should have never mentioned her name. You tried to tell me." She looked as if she was about to cry again.

"Kate, this wasn't your fault. They're killers. They're going to do what they do. That's who you blame." He felt like a liar just speaking the words.

Kate gazed down at the floor for several seconds. "I think I'll go home."

Cayden walked out the door with her, following her along the entryway to the driveway. As they made their way to her Nissan Rogue, Mandala's Charger drove in. He killed the engine, climbed from the driver's seat, and joined them. Kate acknowledged the detective, unlocking her car and waiting as Cayden placed her travel bag on the rear seat.

"Morning," Mandala greeted them.

Cayden returned the greeting, but Kate remained silent.

"How you doing, Ms. James?" Mandala asked.

"I've been better."

"Understandable. I'm very sorry." Turning to Cayden, he said, "We didn't catch up to them last night."

At the mention of *them*, Kate became more eager to leave. Mandala noticed. "The FBI and my department are coordinating the manhunt. We've already got that FBI photo of them at airports, train stations, the seaports. We'll get them."

That was enough for Kate. She pulled the driver's side door open and dropped into the seat. She started the engine and lowered her window.

"Since they have the drive, we want to make sure they don't

have time to use it," Mandala said to Cayden.

"They can't use it," Kate said.

"Sorry?" Mandala said, turning to Kate.

"They can't access the software on the drive."

"How's that?" Cayden asked.

Kate looked like answering the question was almost too much for her. "Once Mariana and I hacked the original decryption code, the first thing we did was to replace it with a new code. I used a program I wrote to generate it. Not as complex as the original, but still time consuming to crack."

A sense of relief surged through Cayden. "That's a huge game changer, Kate. Do you have it with you?"

She shook her head. "I copied it to a flash drive before we wiped it from Mariana's computer. I gave it to Mariana before I left to help Dr. May."

"The drive in the blue casing?" Cayden asked.

"Yeah," Kate nodded.

Mandala's brow creased with concern. "If it was at the Vasquez house along with the drive you found in Fenland's office, what if Russo and Craven took them both?"

"Possible," Cayden said. "But why would they even look for another drive? They couldn't have known about the new decryption code. They'd be thinking all they needed was the drive with their software on it."

Mandala pulled his phone from a jacket pocket. "Give me a couple of minutes."

The detective walked away with the phone to his ear, and Cayden turned his attention back to Kate.

"If they did get hold of your blue drive, what would they need to use it?"

Kate didn't hesitate. "Just a dual USB to USB-C conversion cable to connect the drive to a phone or computer, something with access to the internet."

"Nobody'd look twice at a phone, and they could carry it anywhere," Cayden said to himself.

Kate's face grew more unhappy at the comment.

"Don't stress over this, Kate. It's unlikely they have your code." He hoped he sounded reassuring.

"Like you said, why would they even think to look for it?" she said.

A sinking feeling began pulling at Cayden. Once Russo and Craven discovered the drive in their possession was useless, they'd begin searching for a solution. If they knew Kate was working with Mariana, they might conclude she was a good place to start. They were desperate. There was a strong possibility they'd go looking for Kate.

Cayden placed his hand on her window frame. "You should stay a few more days. Please."

Mandala joined them again, pocketing his phone. "One of our investigators at the crime scene found your blue flash drive in the office trash bin. The lab analyzed it once they got it back to the station. There wasn't a thing on it, just wiped clean."

Cayden turned back to Kate. "What do you think?

Kate looked at him with anguished eyes. "I don't know, Cayden. I just want to go home."

"Please, stay here with me," Cayden pleaded.

Kate put the Nissan in gear.

"I need to go," she said, easing the car down the driveway.

He and Mandala stepped away from the Nissan, watching until Kate reached the street and disappeared from view.

"She's a potential target again, isn't she?" Mandala asked.

Cayden shrugged. "She could be if Russo figures it all out."

"I was thinking the same thing," Mandala said. "You have a few more minutes?"

Cayden gestured toward the front door as he started back to the house. "Sure. Come on in."

O nce inside, Cayden headed for the stairs. "Coffee?"
       "Sounds good."

Mandala followed him down to the kitchen. "So, this new decryption code. You think Mariana Vasquez made a copy before she wiped Kate's flash drive?" he asked.

"It's hard to believe she'd destroy something like that," Cayden responded.

"I was thinking the same," the detective said.

"I'll tell you one thing, though," Cayden said, pulling two mugs from the cupboard and placing them on the counter. "If she did make a copy, she hid it, and hid it good. Mariana was a smart woman, and she understood what was at stake."

Mandala began exploring the kitchen. "I'm gonna be optimistic, and believe Russo and Craven don't have the new code."

Cayden made sure the hopper of his burr grinder was full, then punched the start button. The machine growled rhythmically while he measured water into the coffeemaker.

"No K-cups around here, I guess," Mandala said.

"Nope." Cayden turned to face Mandala, leaning back against the counter. "So, what did you stop by for?"

"I didn't want to get into details while Ms. James was still here," Mandala said. "We reviewed traffic cam footage last night. The Vasquez house is in a residential area, so there are no traffic cams there at all. But a camera in a commercial zone picked the Mustang up, moving east. We lost them about thirty seconds later."

"That's disappointing."

"Not so much," Mandala said. "One of our cruisers found it about five this morning. They dumped it on the east side of Pasadena, near Rosemead."

"But you got nothing from it."

The detective shook his head. "They're thorough. There wasn't a shred of anything that would put them in that car. They stole it from the driveway of a house near the Huntington Library, but that doesn't help us."

"They steal a car each time they have to travel. That's what you do if you want to be hard to track." Cayden poured the fresh ground coffee into the paper filter lining the brew basket, slid the basket into place, and punched the start button.

"Makes sense," Mandala said, his voice uneasy.

Cayden saw something in the detective's expression. "There's something else."

"Yeah. There's a twenty-four-hour clinic near where our cruiser found the Mustang. A university student stopped in with a cut hand from a broken beer bottle. Found the staff dead."

"How many?"

"The doctor on duty and a nurse."

Cayden couldn't help wincing. Two more people were dead because he cut the Craven girl's face.

"There's no solid proof it was them," Mandala said.

"But no evidence, no witnesses."

"No." Mandala shrugged.

"You believe in coincidences like that?" Cayden asked.

"I believe it was Russo. Right after the doctor patched up his girlfriend's face."

The aroma of freshly brewed coffee permeated the room.

"Take anything in it?" he asked.

"Just black."

Cayden poured the coffee and handed one of the steaming mugs to Mandala. The detective took a sip as Cayden led him to the dining room where they settled in at the table.

"Great coffee," Mandala said.

Cayden acknowledged the compliment with a sip of his own. "So, what's the FBI saying about the clinic murders?"

"They've got agents there working alongside my team. And Langford offered me the resources at Quantico," the detective said, shaking his head.

"Well, that'll lead us to them, especially with no evidence to process."

"I've got officers watching the metro stations, and we alerted LAX and just about every other airport in California. LAPD is working with the port authority in case they try to board any kind of ship. Langford has agents looking, too, and they're coordinating with the government offices," Mandala said.

Cayden leaned back in his chair. "I've got to admit, I'm not sure what the next move is here. Russo and Craven are very good at disappearing."

Mandala nodded. "There's an understatement."

"I want to know who gave up Mariana Vasquez. Figure that out and it could be the first step to getting to her killers," Cayden muttered.

"For what it's worth, I've already got my people looking into that angle," Mandala said.

Cayden didn't respond, distracted by the myriad of thoughts running through his head.

"You're worried about Kate," the detective said.

Cayden leaned his elbows on the table, his hands clasped in front of him. "It was smart what they did, making sure the original decryption code wouldn't work. But even if Kate's new code was permanently wiped, Russo and Craven still might come for her. Russo's the kind of man who's going to cover all the bases."

"She really didn't want to stay here," Mandala said.

"No, but I'm going to keep at her. I'll carry her back here over my shoulder if I have to."

Mandala nodded. "In the meantime, a couple of FBI agents keeping an eye on her isn't a bad idea. If we can find any we trust."

"I'd feel better if your men could do it.

"We don't have that kind of staff right now," Mandala answered. "But I'll call Denbo about it."

They sipped at their coffee for a while, content with the quiet.

Mandala broke the silence. "I've got one more thing you should know. The only surviving member of Ms. Vasquez's family turned out to be an older sister."

"A sister," Cayden repeated.

"I spoke to her. She's flying out today."

"From?"

"Ithaca, New York. Works at Cornell University," Mandala explained. "Looks like she and her sister had big brains in common."

The silence returned as they finished their coffee. Mandala pushed his chair back and carried his empty mug back into the kitchen. Cayden stayed put until he returned.

"I've gotta get going. Just thought you'd want the update," Mandala said. "Thanks for the coffee."

"Anytime," Cayden answered, getting up from his chair and leading Mandala up the stairs.

Mandala headed for his car, but paused, turning back toward Cayden. "You're not planning on going after Russo and Craven yourself, are you?"

The truth was, he'd look for any opportunity to catch up with Mariana's and Alan's killers. He wanted justice, and he had little faith that regular law enforcement could get it. But he wasn't about to voice his opinion or intentions. "I haven't done enough already?" Cayden answered, a hint of bitterness in his tone.

"I just wouldn't want to come over here with an arrest warrant."

Cayden kept a steady gaze on the detective. "I wanted nothing to do with any of this from the beginning."

Mandala nodded. "I'm sorry it didn't work out that way."

Cayden turned and walked back down the walkway.

"I'd feel better if I heard it from you," Mandala called out behind him. "Tell me you won't go after them."

"Whatever you say." Cayden kept walking.

Behind him he heard Mandala say, "Promise?"

CHAPTER THIRTY-TWO

After Mandala drove away, Cayden wasn't sure what to do with himself. Thinking about Mariana Vasquez and the people at the clinic numbed him. He felt like doing nothing, but focused his mind to mull over ways to locate Russo and Craven. And what would he do once he caught up to them? He felt a loathing for the killers, and harboring those types of personal feelings could prove lethal to an operator. But he found the feelings impossible to shed.

Kate was also very much on his mind. He knew she'd had plenty of time to get to her apartment. After glancing at his watch several times, he tapped her number on his "favorites" list. It rang several times before going to voicemail.

"It's Cayden. Please call me when you get this."

He felt anxious for a quick response.

With some effort, he forced himself to go down to the studio. He felt restless, and he found music uplifting and healing. Cayden needed the music to work its magic now. There was a song he and Alan had been working on that needed a better rhythm guitar track than the one he'd first recorded. He switched on the equipment and tuned his Martin acoustic.

Cayden recorded several tracks, one after the other. Playing each one back, he determined if it was working for the song. Hearing nothing in his playing he liked, he continued refining his performance to get what he wanted. But his concern about Kate, and her failure to respond, distracted him. An hour-and-a-half after making his initial call to her, he tried again. The call again went to voicemail.

With the phone still in his hand, he remembered another call he needed to make. His father was still the best chance of his resolving the property tax problem. He already felt like crap, so what did he have to lose by calling his father? His phone's favorite list did not include his father's number, but he still remembered it. Taking a deep breath, he made the call.

"Thomas March's residence," a pleasant female voice emerged from the phone's speaker.

Why was he surprised to get his father's assistant? What did he expect? "This is Cayden March, his son. If my father's in, I'd like to speak with him."

"Oh, of course," the assistant sounded surprised. "Let me see if he's available."

She put him on hold where he remained for a full two minutes.

"Your father would like to know what this is about," the assistant said when she got back on the line.

Cayden began wondering if he'd made a mistake. Why did it have to be so hard? "I'd like to see him about an important matter. I won't take much of his time."

"Just give me another moment."

This time, the wait was shorter. "Mr. March would like to know if December 26th works for you," the assistant said. "Four o'clock at his residence."

There was no turning back now. "I'll be there. Thanks."

The way the call went wasn't a surprise. What did surprise him was the hurt he felt over his father not bothering to take his call. This is what they'd become, and he didn't like it.

After entering the meeting date in his phone's calendar, Cayden hoped returning to the music would diminish the conflicting feelings. He laid down another track but didn't like it. He couldn't seem to focus, so he put the guitar back on its rack. The call to his father ate at him. And Kate's refusal to pick up his calls triggered him into thinking about the reason behind it— Russo and Craven.

The deep, cold desire for revenge inside was growing. He had never hesitated to kill when it was necessary, but killing had always been part of war or a special assignment in the service of his government. He'd never felt a desire to kill.

This time, it was different. There would be a great satisfaction in seeing Russo and Craven die for what they'd done.

Not only did he think Russo and Craven were still in the country, it was probable they were still in the city. Considering the injury he'd inflicted on the woman, he felt confident he'd derailed the killers. It was necessary to attend to Craven's wound, and that cost them time. Cleaning up evidence after they murdered the clinic staff ate up more time. They knew they were the focus of a major manhunt. It was likely they had little time to do anything but go to ground.

After powering down the gear and locking up, he considered going to Seth Walker's for some sparring, but his aching ribs argued for staying home. If he needed a workout he could use the gym he'd set up on one side of his garage. It wasn't much, just a heavyweight punching bag hanging from a rafter and a multipurpose exercise machine, but it provided a thorough workout.

Cayden began working through his normal routine on the multipurpose machine. But for no conscious reason, he stopped what he was doing and walked over to the bag. He stared at it for several seconds and then threw a powerful punch into the leather. A moment later, another punch. And then he unloaded on the bag, throwing one brutal strike after another. Each punch landed harder than the last. Beads of sweat covered his face as his fists began stinging and his arms ached with pain. He delivered the punches faster and faster. He kept at it until exhaustion overtook him and he lowered himself to the floor.

Sitting there, arms folded across his heaving chest, Cayden fought to catch his breath. He did not know how long he sat there before his breathing became normal again. With much effort, he walked back into the house and headed upstairs to clean up.

~

Street parking was always a challenge in Old Town, so Cayden left the 4Runner on the second level of a convenient parking structure. On the way down the stairs, he pulled out his phone and tried Kate again. By the time he reached the ground level, he connected to her voicemail. "Kate, it's me again. It's important. Call me as soon as you can."

His next call was to Special Agent Denbo. "Denbo, it's Cayden March."

"Hey, March. What can I do for you?"

"You put a detail on Kate James, yes?" Cayden asked.

"Yeah, they've been with her about three hours so far," Denbo answered. "Is there a problem?"

"Probably not, but I haven't been able to get Kate on the phone. Is everything okay over there?"

"I touched base with her detail when they landed at her place. She was still in her apartment. If you can hang on a couple of minutes, I'll get them on the phone right now."

"Please," Cayden answered.

It was a full five minutes before Denbo got back on the call. "The Special Agents on duty said she hasn't set foot outside her apartment since they escorted her in. I sent one of them to knock on her door. He spoke to her, so she's still in there."

"Thanks," Cayden said. "I appreciate it."

"No problem. I'll let you know if anything changes over there."

"Thanks."

"Hey, before you go," Denbo said. "Detective Mandala told us about a new decryption code. Ms. James wrote it, but it was wiped from her flash drive?"

"That's what it looks like," Cayden answered.

"The detective doesn't believe the bad guys have it. What about you?

"It's hard to say, but I'm leaning toward the positive. Like I told Mandala, if Mariana made a copy and secured it, it's going to be hard to find, very hard. And Russo and Craven had no reason to believe their original code wouldn't work. Why would they even look?"

"I hope you're right," Denbo said. "Okay, thanks. I'll keep you in the loop on Kate."

"I appreciate it. Have a good evening."

They ended the call. Cayden slipped the phone back into his pocket and headed out for something to eat. He felt less isolated as he made his way toward the Bicycle Bell. The sidewalk was crowded with Christmas shoppers, diners leaving or entering restaurants, and the teenaged couples holding hands and smiling blissfully at one another.

It was just past 7:00 p.m. when he entered the Bell, early for the saloon, but it was almost three-quarters full with after work drinkers in no hurry to head home. The patrons' conversations converged in a boisterous cacophony, but the sixties cover band on the stage didn't seem to mind. Cayden gave his server his order and listened to the music while he waited for his food.

He took his time with the French dip, house salad, and the bottle of Negra Modelo to wash it all down. His intention was to stay and listen to the band for a while, but after paying his check, a restlessness settled over him.

Once back on the sidewalk, Cayden began walking again, the thought of returning to an empty house unappealing. After a few minutes, he'd put the bustle of Old Town behind him.

He didn't know how far he'd walked when the sound of live music reached him from somewhere up ahead. He recognized the

Christmas tune as "Angels We Have Heard on High." It was coming from an odd-shaped building at the end of the block.

Whoever was playing gave the old hymn a new life, with a contemporary groove filled with guitars and drums that gave the tune a refreshing power. Drawn to the music, Cayden headed toward the sound.

CHAPTER THIRTY-THREE

A sign mounted next to the open side door read *Faith Road Church.* The room was round, which explained the building's odd shape. Several tiered seating levels descended to the main floor. The seating surrounded the front, and two sides of a low platform that served as a stage. The entire place was decorated for Christmas.

A tall, slender man in his early thirties, and wearing a headset mic, stood at the front of the stage, playing a guitar solo with professional skill. A band of bass, drums, piano, percussion, and rhythm guitar backed him. There was even a Hammond B3 in the mix. Behind the band was a row of seven microphones, manned by four women and three men. Behind them, standing on risers, was a small choir. Cayden counted twenty-two voices, a diverse group with ages ranging from late teens to seniors.

He leaned against the door frame and listened as the guitarist completed his solo and cued the vocalists and choir. They sounded great as they followed the guitarist's lead vocal into the hymn's refrain.

Gloria, in excelsis Deo
Gloria, in excelsis Deo
Cayden found himself caught up in the sound and spirit of it

all, and for the first time in two days he felt something other than guilt or rage. As always, music proved healing, rescuing him from his dark mood.

After repeating the chorus three times, the leader of the band used the neck of his guitar to conduct the finish. "Sounds great, everybody. Think we've got it. Last run through and sound check tomorrow at three-thirty. Everybody, please, be on time."

The group dispersed, retrieving coats and purses from nearby chairs, and chatting with a genial familiarity as they made their way toward the exits. A few of them passed Cayden, greeting him as they exited. He wasn't sure why, but instead of leaving, he stepped into the room to clear the doorway. The band leader noticed and acknowledged him with a friendly smile.

"You guys sounded great." Cayden took another couple of steps into the room.

"Thanks. Were you listening long?" The band leader placed his guitar on its stand and stepped off the stage toward him.

"Just your last song."

"Come back tomorrow. We're having our Christmas Eve candlelight service. You can hear it again and plenty more."

"I'll have to do that."

The band leader chuckled. "Your words say you will, but your expression says probably not." He walked toward Cayden, extending a hand. "Jake Matthews."

Cayden descended to the main floor, offering his own hand. "Cayden March. Was it that obvious?"

Jake shrugged, but his face held a genial grin. "You get to where you can tell."

"Nothing personal."

"Didn't think so. What brings you here tonight?" Jake asked.

"Just heard the music while I was passing by. Couldn't help but stop in."

Jake nodded in understanding. "You play?"

"Not like you do. That's a nice Tyler." Cayden pointed to the guitar.

Retrieving it from the rack, Jake held it out. "You're welcome to try it."

"I've got one at home, but thanks."

"You up for playing something now?" Jake slipped the guitar strap over his head. "I've got another guitar right here."

Cayden's eyes went to the guitar. A part of him wanted to stay, but another part rationalized he should leave and go home. "I don't think so."

Jake kept his eyes on Cayden, his genial smile still in place. "Most people, if they're not regular churchgoers, they don't always feel comfortable when they stop in for a visit."

"I'd have to say that's probably true," Cayden said.

"Come on," Jake coaxed. "A guy who owns a Tyler must know what he's doing."

Cayden hesitated. "You're wrapping up for the night."

Jake shrugged. "I'm always up for another tune."

"Okay, how about I play keys?" Cayden stepped onto the stage next to the piano.

"Guitar and piano, too? Now I feel threatened," Jake laughed.

"You might want to wait until you hear me play." Cayden sat down and adjusted the bench.

"You pick one," Jake said.

Cayden gave it some thought. Sticking to the Christmas theme seemed the way to go. "Do you know 'Mary's Boy Child'?"

"The old Harry Belafonte song? That's going back some." Jake laughed. "How old did you say you were?"

"My grandparents used to play it every year. We can do something else."

"No, it's fine. I'm just surprised somebody else close to my age knows it," Jake said. "We've done it here a few times."

"You do the singing," Cayden said. "I don't think I can remember all the lyrics."

"Key of E okay?" Jake began playing an intro.

Cayden came in after four bars and Jake began singing the 1956 tune. He had a strong, pleasant voice and sang with just the right measure of emotion. Their playing styles blended well, and they both knew it. As Jake reached the song's first chorus, Cayden surprised himself by joining in, singing the tenor harmony.

For whatever inexplicable reason, he'd wandered into this place, and it was exactly what he needed. He could feel the music further soothing him as they played. For a few moments, the troubles that had been consuming him seemed to fade into the background.

Jake played a solo that complemented the old ballad, and then they sang the final chorus.

"Nice," Jake said. "You've got some chops there."

"Pretty good, considering it's the first time we've played together," Cayden agreed. It felt good during the music. But now the room was quiet again, and less desirable feelings began returning.

Jake must have noticed the change in him. "What brought you in tonight?"

"Like I said, the music." Cayden slid out from behind the piano.

Jake's knowing gaze stayed steady on him. "Any other reason?"

"No."

"In some kind of trouble?"

"Most of the time." Cayden tried to make it a self-deprecating joke, but it just sounded sad.

Pulling the guitar strap over his head, Jake put the instrument back on its stand. He sat down on a nearby stool, still gazing at Cayden. "You know, you didn't look all that happy when you first got here."

Cayden managed a thin smile. "You're observant."

"This is a good place to talk."

Cayden studied this man he'd known for only a few minutes. He saw no idle curiosity, no hidden agenda.

"Let's just say I screwed up," Cayden said.

"Who doesn't?"

"My screw-up cost someone their life." It was the first time he'd said it aloud, and he heard the heaviness in his own voice.

The smile faded from Jake's face. "But you didn't take their life?"

"No."

Jake studied him for several seconds, swiveling back and forth on the stool. "What is it you want right now?"

Cayden gave the question some thought. "I guess I want to put at least some of it right."

"Ah, redemption." Jake smiled again.

"Redemption?"

"We all want redemption for the bad things we've done, whether we know it or not."

"My list of bad things is pretty long."

"Hope is one of God's specialties." Jake slid off of the stool. *"But those who hope in the Lord will renew their strength. They will soar on wings like eagles; they will run and not grow weary, they will walk and not grow faint."*

"The Bible, I assume."

"Isaiah 40:31."

It surprised Cayden that he felt some comfort in the words. But he felt awkwardness as well and wasn't certain how to respond. He decided a simple retreat was best and extended his hand. "I need to get going. Thanks for the song."

Jake shook his hand. "I hope we can do this again. Come back anytime."

Cayden started up the steps to the exit.

"Hey," Jake called out behind him.

He paused, turning back toward the worship leader.

"Our Christmas service, tomorrow night. Six o'clock."

"I just might be there," Cayden told him.

Jake's smile broadened. "Your words say maybe, but your expression says probably not."

Cayden managed a smile of his own and then hurried out into the night.

CHAPTER THIRTY-FOUR

Slumped in her seat, Cyn gazed out the passenger side window at the lights blurring by in the darkness. For the hundredth time that day, she caught herself stroking her wounded cheek. It was sore, but she didn't mind. The sensation was a constant reminder of what the over-trained security guard had done to her. The pain stimulated her mind with plots she might employ to get to him. And thoughts of methods she might use to kill him slowly.

They both knew they had to get off the streets as soon as possible. So, after Danny got her face treated, he found a small dumpy motel on the north edge of Pasadena. They dropped onto the bed the moment they got into the room, sleeping until midmorning. Well, Danny slept. She spent the night on her back, staring at the ceiling, her mind replaying the scene in the Vasquez living room.

Except for Danny venturing out to get fast food for them, they stayed in the depressing room until nightfall. Remaining in the motel was too risky. But getting out of town without being detected was unlikely with the authorities watching the airports, train and bus stations, and the ports. The situation created the inconvenient necessity to disappear, and Danny concluded they needed a place to disappear for at least a few days more.

So, here they were, driving up a two-lane road called the Angeles Crest Highway toward a place called the Angeles National Forest. Danny was counting on the isolation of the local mountains to make being invisible a little easier. They had spoken little since the clinic visit, and now he was on the phone with that well-paying butthole, Dragović. She hadn't been listening much, but she sensed the conversation was ending.

"Understood." Danny's voice reached her. "We'll see to it."

She watched Danny listen, his expression passive.

"I'll confirm once I have it." Danny ended the call and removed his earbuds.

"Everything okay, hon?" Cyn knew speaking to him was risky when he was displeased with her.

"Dragović's sending a courier with the programmed smartphone and adaptor."

"He expects us to launch it?"

"Yes, and that means we're stuck here until it's done."

"Why do we have to do it?" Cyn whined.

"Time is running out, and he's determined to stay on schedule."

The lights became fewer and fewer as the incline increased. By the time they reached the winding mountain road, there were no lights at all.

"It's dark as hell up here and I have to focus on the road," Daniel said. "Look for a place we can use."

Cyn sat up straight in the seat, hoping she could find the perfect place. If she did, it might calm him down a little.

They encountered no traffic heading in their direction and passed only two cars coming down the road. Since the mountains were federal land, privately owned properties on the Angeles Crest Highway were few, but Cyn spotted a place that would work about fifteen minutes into their trek up the mountain.

Just off the road was a long abandoned café with two old gas pumps in front. The place had probably done a lot of business in the fifties and sixties, but now rust covered the pumps and rotting boards hid the decaying café's windows and doors. It was the light on the hillside behind the café that had caught Cyn's attention. It came from the windows of a small cabin, perhaps once the home of whoever had owned the café.

A short driveway opened to a small parking lot with space for about twenty-five vehicles. Daniel guided the Honda into the driveway and around the back of the café. He parked out of sight from the highway between a weather-worn shed and an old Ford pickup truck. They climbed the stairs leading to the cabin's front porch where Daniel took a position out of sight to the side of the door. Cyn knocked on the door, prepared to perform her little girl lost act. After a minute, she heard movement behind the door, and a nice old man soon opened it.

"Hi," she beamed at him. "Merry Christmas."

CHAPTER THIRTY-FIVE

It rained on the morning of December 24th. After finishing breakfast, Cayden got only a little wet retrieving two days' worth of mail from his mailbox. Locking the door behind him, he stood in the entry and began sorting.

After leaving yet another message for Kate, he found himself unmotivated to do much of anything else. Aside from going for a run, he accomplished little throughout the rest of the day. By 4:00 p.m., the rain had dwindled away, leaving a sky of dark clouds. He merged his desire to get out of the house with the decision to drive to Kate's apartment. He'd been trying to contact her for almost two days; it was time to press the issue.

He put on fresh clothes and was gathering up his wallet and car keys when the front doorbell chimed. The sound triggered caution in him. He didn't think Russo and Craven had the stones to return to his house, but he pulled the Beretta from its holster as he walked to the door.

Cayden activated the security display mounted on the wall next to the door. The camera feed surprised him. Kate stood on his doorstep with two bags of groceries cradled in her arms. The wide-brimmed floppy hat covering her head still glistened with moisture from the earlier rain. Cayden holstered the gun and opened the door.

"Is it okay? That I came over?" She sounded down and uncertain.

"Don't be crazy. Of course." Relief at seeing her safe poured over him. "Come on in."

"I brought some food if you're not doing anything."

Cayden took the groceries from her. She removed her hat and long coat as she stepped inside. As relieved as he was to see her, Kate's presence created a certain heaviness. But he knew it wasn't her. She reminded him he'd let her down, and that he'd failed Mariana Vasquez.

"There are FBI agents in my lobby and my hallway," Kate said. "What's that about?

"They're just keeping an eye on you until we get Russo and Craven. Where are they now?"

"They followed me over. They're parked on the street," she said. "Since it's you I was visiting, they didn't follow me in here."

"Ah, okay."

Kate's eyes narrowed. "I thought I wasn't at risk anymore."

"We should talk about that, but let's square away these groceries first."

Kate followed him downstairs to the kitchen. He put the bags on the counter and she started unpacking them. Her shoulders slumped and her head was held low. He wanted to lift the burden of Mariana's loss from her, but he didn't know how to do it. And then a thought occurred to him; something he found helpful.

Cayden touched her shoulder. "You up for going out for an hour or so?"

"What about dinner?" Kate asked, puzzled. "You don't want to eat?"

"We'll take care of dinner when we get back."

"Okay, I guess. Where are we going?"

Kate's expression went from puzzlement to mild surprise when Cayden led her into the Faith Road Church. They were thirty minutes early, but the place was already packed. He saw a few sports coats and even one or two ties, but most of the congregation was in casual attire. They found seats near the back and to the side of the stage.

Jake Matthews, the band, and choir took their places on the stage. At six on the dot, Jake greeted the assembly with a warm, enthusiastic welcome, and then started the service with the arrangement of "Angels We Have Heard on High" Cayden had heard the previous evening.

The congregation engaged with the music from the beginning, singing with enthusiasm and following the lyrics projected onto two large LED screens on each side of the stage. Music occupied the next thirty minutes with the band and choir performing powerful, contemporary arrangements of traditional carols, and a couple of Christmas tunes Cayden didn't recognize. He wondered if Jake had written them.

During the first five minutes, Cayden could see that Kate was uncomfortable, but soon she was singing along with everyone else, soothed by the atmosphere and the spirit created by the music. He sang as well and again found himself grateful to be occupied by something other than the world outside the walls of this church.

The band and choir left the stage as a man in his mid-forties introduced himself as the senior pastor at the church. His message centered on the story of Christmas, the birth of Christ, and the meaning behind it all. The pastor closed the service with a prayer of thanks, and then a prayer of invitation for anyone present who might want to know Christ.

Jake took the stage again, directing everyone to retrieve the small battery-powered candles stored beneath each chair. The lights dimmed and the electric candle flames flickered to life throughout the room. The band began a moving rendition of "O Holy Night," with the choir entering through the doors at the back of the room, carrying their own candles down the tiered aisles and taking their places on the risers at the rear of the stage.

On the last note of the old hymn, the congregation again erupted in enthusiastic applause. Jake concluded the service with a "goodnight and merry Christmas."

Cayden realized he was more at peace as the service ended. The music, the hymns, proved reliable. He hoped Kate felt the same as they drove back to his house in silence.

CHAPTER THIRTY-SIX

Once back at the house, they pitched in together to fix dinner, with Kate ordering him around the kitchen. He fetched utensils, pots and pans, and answered questions about what he had or didn't have in the way of supplies.

"Mariana has a sister." Kate said it without looking up from the mushrooms she was slicing.

"Detective Mandala told me."

"She's been handling arrangements long distance. There's a funeral scheduled for the 27th at Forest Lawn."

Cayden just nodded.

"She arranged for the school to send out a department-wide email, so I got one," Kate continued.

"That was the funeral announcement?"

"Yes, with an invitation for friends and associates to attend." Kate sliced harder and faster. "You want to get the steaks out of the fridge?"

Cayden moved over to the refrigerator and pulled open the door. "I want to be there."

"Just put a little salt and pepper on them," Kate instructed.

Cayden unpackaged the steaks and did as he was told.

"You think we'll be welcome?" Kate leaned on the counter, staring down at nothing.

It was a good question. Cayden had to admit he was concerned about how Mariana's sister might view his presence at the service. But he couldn't conceive of not going. There was a more important consideration. "We'll be there to honor her."

Kate responded with a quiet nod and then continued with the food prep. It appeared she was done talking for the time being, so he climbed the stairs to the main floor and busied himself making a fire in the living room hearth. As soon as the logs were burning, he got some Christmas music playing through the room's stereo system.

By the time Cayden returned to the kitchen, Kate's spirits had improved, and she announced her plan to broil the steaks in the oven. He volunteered to grill them instead, and she liked that idea better. A light rain began after he started cooking, but the gas grill was under a covered section of the patio, so the weather was of no consequence.

They carried their plates and glasses up the stairs to the living room, laying the dinner out on the coffee table in front of the fireplace. Sitting cross-legged on the floor, the warming fire crackling before them, they dug in.

"I'm glad you came over tonight. Especially with Christmas dinner," Cayden said.

"It's a Christmas Eve dinner, and it's not exactly traditional." Kate took a sip of wine, a French Cabernet Sauvignon he found in a kitchen cabinet.

"Steak with sautéed mushrooms and onions, salad, buttered rolls; nothing to complain about here," Cayden reassured her.

"I didn't want to spend the holiday alone."

"I felt the same."

"Did you ever reach out to your dad about the property tax thing?" She took another bite of steak.

"I've got a meeting scheduled with him on the 26th."

Kate's jaw dropped open. "You have a meeting? You can't just drop in?"

Cayden smiled thinly, not wanting to get into the strained dynamics between him and his father. "I guess not."

"I'm sure he'll help," Kate encouraged.

"We'll see."

Cayden poured a healthy glass of his Old Forester. There was still a trace of melancholy in Kate, but the profound sadness appeared to have lifted. They finished dinner in silence, watching the flames and listening to the holiday music.

Kate put down her fork, gazing at him. "Why did we go to that church service tonight?"

"Did you forget about the hell of the last few days while you were there? At least for a while?" Cayden asked.

She sat in silence for several seconds, just watching him. "Yeah, for a while."

"That's why."

"How did you even know about the place?"

Cayden explained how he stumbled on the church the previous night, and his experience there.

Kate nodded when he had finished. "It had a good vibe."

"So you liked it?" Cayden asked.

"I did, a lot."

Kate's shoulders drooped and he could see the guilt on her face. He realized Mariana Vasquez's death devastated her, but there was something more going on, and he knew what it was.

Cayden took another fortifying sip of bourbon. "I told you this before, and nothing's changed. What happened to Mariana, that's on me. I'm the only one responsible."

She stared at the fire. "But I'm the one with the big mouth."

"You did what the FBI pressured you to do," Cayden interrupted. "I underestimated the people who killed her. There's no blame on you."

The look in her eyes told him that little he could say would make a difference. At least not tonight. The room grew silent and remained that way for a while. The evening had proven to be pleasant, and Cayden hated to bring up the killers again. But Kate's safety was the priority. She had to understand the situation.

"Kate, it's important you move back in here right away," he said, breaking the silence.

Kate didn't seem surprised. "Why?"

Doing his best to make it sound like it was no big deal, he explained how changing the flash drive's decryption put her at risk.

She listened in silence, and when he'd finished said, "You think they'll really come for me?"

"I hope not, but we have to prepare for the possibility. You're better off here until it's all settled."

Kate picked up her wineglass and took a sip. "My bag is in the car. You can bring it in before we turn in."

A sense of relief touched him. He was expecting much more resistance from her.

She stood from the table and gathered their plates. "I brought pie. Blackberry."

"Sounds great."

"You sit, I'll get it." Kate headed toward the kitchen. Pausing at the head of the stairs, she looked back at him, the sadness in her eyes transforming to anger. "They killed our friends. I want them to pay. I want them dead."

She disappeared down the stairs before he could respond. He knew he should tell her that a revenge killing was not right, not a solution. But he wanted Russo and Craven dead too.

CHAPTER THIRTY-SEVEN

The cabin above the boarded-up café proved to be a more than adequate place to stay under the radar. As for the old man who answered the door, it took little effort for Russo to break his neck. He and Cyn dragged the body down the stairs and dumped it in the shed behind the café.

A search of the cabin revealed that the man lived alone. It was unlikely anyone would miss him anytime soon. The only phone in the place was an old olive green push-button model mounted on a wall beside the kitchen door. It didn't appear the old man owned a cell phone, and they soon discovered why. Both their smartphones displayed signals that fluctuated between weak and zero.

Despite Cyn's choice of a hiding place being close to perfect, Russo could still not fathom the depth of manure she had sunk them into. The Vasquez woman had to die, of course, but Cyn should have handled it quickly and left with the flash drive before March and the authorities reached the house. Killing Vasquez in front of the security guard was another mistake, especially since she'd left him alive. March's witnessing the kill made him more dangerous. Russo knew March's type; he was certain the man took Vasquez's death personally. Russo would want revenge if he were in the same position. He was certain March would want the same.

And there was the icing on the cake. Russo rendezvoused with Dragović's courier late on Christmas Day. After getting the smartphone containing the decryption sequence, he returned to the cabin. Per Dragović's instructions, the first thing he did was attach the USB conversion cable connecting the phone with the flash drive. And nothing happened. He'd been told what to expect from the pairing; he'd been told how to stop the weapon software once it began running. But the software never launched. He had spent most of the day trying to get the system to work. Now, most of the 26th was gone with no success.

Russo knew he had to report this development to Dragović, but anticipating the unpleasantness of such a call, he planned to put it off as long as he could. Perhaps he'd find his own solution in the meantime. He had to.

Cyn strolled in from the kitchen, a quart of strawberry ice cream in one hand, a spoon in the other. "How's it going, hon?"

She moved along as if everything were cool. It pissed him off, and combined with his frustration over the phone problem, he found himself in a slow burn. "I've tried everything I know, but I can't get this thing to do what it's supposed to do. There's only one reason I can think of; those women had to have switched out the original decryption code. Nothing else makes any sense."

"If there's a new code, how do we get it?" Cyn asked.

He knew her well. She was frustrated at this new fly in the ointment, but excited at the prospect of formulating another plan to meet the challenge as well. Especially if the plan jacked somebody up.

"Whatever we do, we can't risk creating more problems." He could hear the smoldering anger in his voice.

"There's a bunch of food in the kitchen," she said. "The old guy must have just made a grocery run."

Russo remained silent as she headed for a makeshift media cabinet where an old Dual turntable sat. She placed her ice cream on the cabinet and kneeled down to leaf through a stack of vinyl record albums resting against the wall. She found something she liked and pulled it from the album sleeve. Several seconds later she had the LP on the platter and "Fire On The Mountain" came blasting through a pair of old, but great sounding JBL speakers.

"Check it out," Cyn said, picking up her ice cream. "The old guy was into the Marshall Tucker Band."

"Turn it down."

Frowning at him, she lowered the volume on the Pioneer receiver that was at least as old as the turntable. After waiting a few moments to see if he had any more objections, she made herself comfortable on the well-worn sofa. Her hand moved up to the bandage on her cheek, stroking it. The cheek had swollen enough to make her face look lopsided.

Russo understood her appearance was a constant reminder of how she'd screwed up and gotten them into this bottomless sucking hole. Cyn noticed him looking at her and attempted a smile, and then raised the first spoon of ice cream to her mouth.

"You think you've got something to smile about?" He stood up from the table, looking for a fight.

"I said how sorry I am," Cyn replied, her voice pouty. "How many times can I say it?"

"Yeah, you're sorry." Russo vented his own frustrations at her.

Cyn finished her carton of ice cream and uncurled from the sofa. She disappeared into the kitchen. He heard her drop the spoon into the sink before reentering the room, wearing a contemptuous expression on her face.

"You know, hanging around longer works for me," Cyn said. "I've got unfinished business."

Russo understood her meaning immediately. "Are you out of your mind?" he shouted.

Cyn crossed her arms. "I want him dead for what he did."

"Have you learned nothing?" This time, his shout was louder.

"I'm going to kill him," Cyn shouted back.

"He could've put a bullet in your forehead and you'd never have seen him move. The only reason he didn't was because Vasquez was there."

"That's why I killed her, to distract him. It worked," Cyn argued.

He backhanded her so fast and hard she had no time to block him. She stumbled backward, tripping on the corner of the coffee table and landed sprawled across the sofa. Her face registered genuine surprise, and then a flush of anger. He followed her onto the sofa, pinning her down with one hand locked around her neck, the other pushing her shoulder down into the cushion.

"Did you even take the right drive?"

"I'm sure of it."

"But it doesn't work, does it?" Russo hissed.

Cyn glared at him, silent and stubborn.

"Does it work?" he bellowed.

She shook her head, the color fading from her complexion.

His breathing, deep and heavy, began easing with the dissipation of his anger. Still straddling her, he loosened his hold. She launched a right punch. He blocked it, but her left came through with a solid blow to his cheek.

"You ever hit me again, I'll kill you." Cyn's eyes glittered with fury.

She tried to land another strike, but he pinned her arms again. She twisted to the side, attempting to bring a knee into his groin, but he shifted his weight, thwarting the attempt. He used his advantage to push her knees apart, positioning his knees between her legs.

She twisted violently, still trying to strike out at him. He lowered his body, resting more of his weight on her. Her movements were more hampered now, but the anger in her eyes was transforming to excitement. She was so predictable.

Cyn raised her head. Her lips parted to kiss him. He hesitated, taking a measure of his anger, then pressed his lips against hers. He kept her pinned down during the kiss, and it only excited her more. The moment he let her go, she began tearing at his clothes.

CHAPTER THIRTY-EIGHT

Five minutes before four o'clock in the afternoon, Cayden turned the Ducati onto San Rafael Avenue. The wooded street ran through one of Pasadena's most exclusive neighborhoods. Beautiful homes faced the street across landscaped yards, though many of them were hidden behind old brick walls and ornate iron gates.

The gates to his father's home were open. Thank God for that; he wouldn't have to go through the paces of talking his way in through an intercom. He drove past the large brick gatehouse and guided the Ducati along the long driveway, up the incline toward the manor house. The imposing home rested on the top of the hill, an 18,000 square foot Tudor revival built in 1929 on almost four acres. It was the house where Cayden grew up and he felt a twinge of nostalgia returning here.

He parked the bike in the driveway and walked to the porch leading up to the massive oak door. The clang of the doorbell echoed from inside the house. About a minute later, a woman in her mid-forties pulled open the door.

"You have to be Cayden," she greeted him, businesslike but pleasant. "So nice to meet you. I'm Kimber Ross, your father's assistant."

"Good to meet you," Cayden said as she ushered him through the door.

The woman was just the type of person his father preferred in his employ. Attractive, well put together, and all business. She led him along the fifty-foot foyer toward a gothic doorway at the end of the marble floor. After passing the large portal opening to the main living room, they arrived at the library. Ms. Ross paused in front of the door, holding up a single finger to signal he should wait. She tapped her knuckles twice against the wood, then went inside.

Seconds later, she was back. "Your father can see you now."

Cayden stepped into the library, a spacious room of mahogany paneling and built-in, hand carved bookshelves. Most of the books occupying the shelf appeared well read. His father had used the room as an office as long as he could remember.

Thomas March sat behind his large mahogany desk topped with dark green leather and trimmed with nailheads. An open legal folder lay open before him. Additional folders, stacked high, occupied the side of the desk. He had changed little since Cayden last saw him. His strong, chiseled features were intact, and his eyes were still cold. The gray hair, streaked with white, contributed to his distinguished appearance. As always, he wore an expensive suit with the jacket unbuttoned.

The moment Cayden saw his father, the many differences between them seeped back into his memory. His reaction was not of discomfort, but a stressful anticipation of his father's inevitable disapproval.

Thomas stood, extending his hand across the desk.

"Hi Dad. Good to see you," Cayden greeted him, taking his hand.

Thomas didn't bother with a reply as he waved Cayden toward one of the maroon leather chairs in front of the desk.

"How's your firm doing?" Cayden asked, hoping to ease into a safe conversation.

His father gazed at him as he sank back into his chair. "Corporate tax law is always good. You may not remember, but I told you that years ago."

And so it began. Cayden refrained from commenting.

"March and Bellows has grown steadily over the past six years," Thomas continued. "Annual revenues have increased with the growth."

Cayden looked around the library. "Are you working from home these days?"

"Now and then. I was in the office this morning. I'm home now for this meeting."

Cayden got the impression his father believed being home now was an inconvenience.

Thomas scrutinized him for a long moment. "When were you here last? How long has it been?"

"Five, maybe six years."

"And why are you here today?"

The small talk was over. True to form, his father pushed through to the business at hand.

"I could use a favor," Cayden replied.

"A favor. Let's hear it."

Cayden explained his predicament with the property taxes, providing as much detail as possible. His father listened in silence, his face expressionless.

Thomas swiveled his chair back and forth. "Your grandfather provided a trust to help you with expenses at the house. That included easing the way with property taxes. I assume that money is still in place."

"Some of it, yes. But the house required maintenance projects that couldn't be put off. They've all been expensive. The costs put a real dent in the cash. More than I expected." Cayden began feeling like a young boy being raked over the coals for not completing a school project.

"I see," Thomas said, his face unchanging.

"I have half of it. A loan for the balance is all I need," Cayden continued. "You'll have it all back before the end of next year."

Thomas shook his head. "I still think you should sell the place. Get into something more affordable you can handle. But I know the house has meaning for you."

"I won't let it go if I can help it."

His father watched him in silence for a long while, and then said, "This isn't surprising. You should've listened to me, pursued a better career path. The military would never pay you enough. And instead of doing something to establish yourself afterwards, you took a job as a security guard."

There it was, the dependable disappointment. His father couldn't help himself, peppering him with the old differences of opinions, the old disapprovals. Cayden fought to hold his tongue. He needed the money if he was to keep the house, and arguing with his father wouldn't help his cause. But he knew silence was far from a guarantee.

"I'm sorry I've disappointed you. I've chosen what I thought was best for me," Cayden said, his voice weak.

"Yes, to this result."

"A short-term loan, Dad. That's all." Cayden hoped there was no hint of begging in his voice.

His father watched him across the desk for what seemed like an inordinate amount of time, the poker face still in place. After a few moments, he sat up straighter in his chair. "I'll consider it and get back to you."

"I appreciate it."

With the main event behind them, Thomas relaxed somewhat. "Now, unless there's something else?"

"No." Cayden rose from the chair and started for the door.

"Cayden."

He paused, turning to face his father. The man's face had softened, and his eyes didn't appear so cold.

"There is one thing I think I need to say," Thomas continued. "I followed your Army career somewhat."

The statement caught Cayden off guard. His father smiled, just a little, at the dubious look plastered on his face.

"I have extensive contacts through the firm, through the work we do. Colleagues at the Pentagon were kind enough to fill me in from time to time. They couldn't tell me much, of course, that top secret file of yours. But I got an adequate overview."

Cayden kept his stunned silence.

"I understand you distinguished yourself." Thomas paused, choosing his next words with care. "That's nothing for anyone to be disappointed about."

His father sounded almost proud. It was a tone he'd rarely heard from the man before—not in a long while. Cayden could do nothing more than nod his head in acknowledgement. He turned and headed for the door.

"Nice seeing you, Cayden. I'll be in touch."

CHAPTER THIRTY-NINE

Mariana Vasquez's funeral took place at ten in the morning on one of the manicured rolling hills of the sprawling Forest Lawn Cemetery in Glendale. Rays of sunlight pierced through the overcast sky, assuaging any threat of rain.

Cayden and Kate arrived early after making the drive from his house in silence.

He estimated about forty people in attendance and recognized several faces from Caltech, most of them students, but several faculty members as well. Mariana had been well liked on campus.

Jodi Vasquez was taller than Mariana. Where Mariana had been slender in build, her sister was more full figured, with a strikingly lovely face. She sat in the front row, facing the simple coffin suspended at ground level above the open grave. Her face showed no expression, as if she occupied a chair in a high stakes poker game.

Just before the service began, Cayden noticed Mandala's Charger pull into a parking spot. The service itself lasted only twenty minutes. Each word pricked at him, and Kate as well, he noticed. Everyone waited in silence as a groundskeeper lowered the coffin into the ground.

Cayden wanted to be present to honor Mariana, but there was a sense of relief when the service ended. The moment the guests dispersed, he started back toward the car, forcing Kate to hustle in order to catch up.

"We should pay our respects to her sister," Kate said as they walked. "But I'm afraid."

"Might be best to look her up later, after she's had time to process." It sounded lame and cowardly even as he spoke the words.

"You're worse than I am."

"Cayden March." A voice called out from somewhere behind them.

Cayden and Kate turned at the same time. Mariana's sister walked toward them, her lovely face drawn in a wary frown.

"You're Cayden March?" The woman pointed a finger at him.

"I am." He nodded, steeling himself for whatever was to come.

"I'm Jodi Vasquez, Mariana's—"

"You're Mariana's sister," Kate interrupted. "I'm so sorry for your loss, for what happened."

"We both are," Cayden added.

Jodi Vasquez's brown eyes glared with anger. "The police told me about you, about what happened."

Cayden remained silent, uncertain how he should respond.

"I want to hear it from you," she continued. "Are you responsible for what happened to my sister?"

The direct confrontation caught him off guard, but he held her gaze. It weighed on him seeing Jodi Vasquez's unhappy face looking up at him, and his mind struggled to find the right response. "I'm responsible for failing to keep her safe."

The anger in her eyes broke for a moment, and he recognized the grief it masked. He wanted this to be over. She looked at him, her eyes brimming with grief.

When Jodi Vasquez spoke, her voice cracked. "She was all the family I had."

Again, Cayden couldn't find a response. There wasn't anything he might say that would take away her grief. Still, he shook his head in remorse and said, "I couldn't be more sorry."

The response caused her anger to rise again. "*Sorry* doesn't give me my sister back."

The truth in the statement stung him, and the guilt and regret he felt amplified times ten.

Kate looked as if she wanted to die right there, and Cayden could see she was holding back tears.

"In case the police didn't already tell you, your sister was a hero," he said. "I know it doesn't make anything better, but it's true. She was helping the government prevent an act of terrorism."

Jodi's forehead creased in confusion. "What are you talking about?"

"So, the police didn't tell you?" Cayden asked.

"They told me my sister died during a robbery at the house. That she was doing some kind of work for the FBI," Jodi Vasquez answered. "They brought you up when they tried to convince me they'd taken precautions to protect her."

"Robbery is one way to describe it," Cayden said. "The killer was after an encrypted flash drive. The FBI enlisted Mariana and Kate here to get past the encryption, and figure out what was on it."

"Why?"

Cayden realized he was walking a fine line here. If he said too much, it might violate national security acts. Not saying enough would only add to this woman's frustration and pain.

"The authorities had reason to believe the flash drive contained a cyber weapon. A weapon intended for use against our country."

"Why would the FBI even think of my sister for that? How'd they even get her name?" Jodi's tone contained anger and pain.

Kate released a sob and looked down at her shoes. "It was—"

"I found the drive," Cayden interrupted. "I wanted to know what was on it, and I knew about Mariana's hacking skills. She was a logical choice to try getting past the encryption. That was before I turned it over to the authorities."

"You got her involved with the FBI?" Jodi's inflection inferred more accusation than question.

Cayden hesitated, choosing his words with care. "Her name came up during an interview with FBI agents."

"You had no right," Jodi snapped.

Cayden nodded his agreement. "I'll regret it the rest of my life."

Jodi Vasquez's anger withered away to frustration and grief. She lowered her gaze to the ground, and then, after a long moment, looked up again, her moist eyes moving between him and Kate. Without another word, she turned and walked back toward her sister's grave.

Cayden watched her go. As she put distance between them, he heard her repeat, "She was all the family I had."

CHAPTER FORTY

Cyn sat, legs crossed, on the wooden floor in front of the old man's stereo rig. She glanced at Danny across the small room. He leaned back against the old couch, staring balefully at Dragović's phone and flash drive resting on the little coffee table. It was just 8:30 a.m. and he'd already been messing with it for two hours. She knew his failure to get the software doing what it should do was darkening his mood.

She placed the vinyl of Lynyrd Skynyrd's *Second Helping* on the turntable and switched it on. With music streaming being the technology of the day, she got a kick out of watching the needle arm raise, position itself over the first track, and lower onto the record. After a second or two of a vintage scratching noise, "Don't Ask Me No Questions" whispered through the old JBL speakers. Cyn was reaching for the volume knob on the Pioneer receiver to crank it up when Danny's phone began chiming. She left the volume low, pulling her hand back from the knob even before he shot her his *don't even think about it* look.

Danny looked at the caller ID and she could see he was instantly pissed off. He tapped the "accept" button.

"You better have a damn good reason," he barked into the phone.

Danny listened for a few moments, then said, "You're breaking up. Say again."

After another pause while he listened, he suddenly signaled her to pay attention. He switched the call to speaker and said, "Repeat that."

"There's—new decrypt—code for—software." The cellular connection was terrible and the informant geek sounded stressed.

"What're you talking about?" Danny asked.

"Vasquez replaced—drive—original decryption with—code of her own."

No wonder Danny'd been pissed when the phone rang. The fool on the phone knew he wasn't supposed to call unless the frickin' world was ending.

"You're just telling me this now?" Danny snapped.

"I just found—about it myself, not fifteen min—ago," the informant replied. "—called—soon as—could get away."

"Explain," Danny said.

"Vasquez's sister, she found the original—ware and the new—code hidden on—sister's computer," the informant said. "She's been analyzing it for hours."

"You're saying she knows what it does?"

"No,—don't know. We're leaving for her place—find out what she has."

"Get me a copy of the new code," Danny said, his tone acidic.

Now the conversation was getting interesting, Cyn thought.

"Are you crazy? There—no way," the informant whined. "There's—team of agents on their way—the Vasquez house. I'd never stand a chance."

"I'm just crazy enough," Danny said. "Think about what a crazy guy like me will do if you don't do as I say."

"I'm telling you I can't," the informant said, fear and desperation overwhelming his voice. "I'll end—in prison—rest of my life."

Probably true, Cyn smiled to herself.

"Find a way," Danny ordered. "Once you have it, call this number again, and not until. We'll arrange a meet. Or I'll text you my location, so you bring it to me if that becomes necessary."

"I'm telling you—"

"Find a way," Danny interrupted, ending the call.

"Wow. Your guess about those women screwing with the decryption was right," Cyn said, turning the volume up on Lynyrd Skynyrd, but stopping at a conversational level.

Danny ignored her, standing and pacing in front of the couch.

Cyn wrinkled her brow. "You really think our little friend can get it for us? I mean, the guy's not a total idiot, but come on."

"His chances of getting it on his own stink. But I'm covering every base."

"Oooh, you've got something else in mind, too." Cyn smiled like a kid anticipating a birthday present.

Danny frowned. "As I said, cover every base."

"A contingency plan." Cyn's face lit up even more. "Let's see. Vasquez has gone to a happier place, but what about the other one?"

"Kate James, yes," Danny replied. "She could be helpful."

"But Vasquez was the heavy hitter, right?"

"Maybe, but they were working together. James may have worked on the new decryption with her."

Cyn gave the matter some thought. "She'd never have her own copy of it, or access, for that matter. The FBI wouldn't let her."

"But she might be a good bargaining chip," Danny snapped with impatience. "I'll give it thought."

"This is getting fun again. Any friend of the security guard is a friend of mine," Cyn said. "I'd be happy to spend a little time with her."

Danny covered the distance to her in three steps, glaring down at her. "Listen to me, and I won't say it again. Get that crap out of your head. I'll handle the girl and March. Understand?"

Cyn presented her best pout and nodded. Danny could warn her all he wanted. It changed nothing. The security guard would pay, and the woman, too.

"I want to hear it."

"I get it."

Danny returned to the coffee table, staring at the phone and flash drive again.

Cyn raised the music volume to a listenable level. She didn't know exactly what Danny was planning, but she had a good idea. Things were sizing up to be quite satisfying.

CHAPTER FORTY-ONE

The morning of December 30th was just another lousy day. Mariana's burial was two days in the past, and Cayden felt no better now than he had at the funeral. He rose early and went for a run. His ribs were healing well, but still tender. With every step, they gave him a sharp reminder of Daniel Russo and his psychopathic girlfriend. The image of Jodi Vasquez was fresh in his mind, and the words she spoke to him replayed over and over. He hadn't just gotten Mariana killed; he had destroyed her sister's life as well.

New Year's Eve was a day away. From what Denbo told him, the FBI believed it was the scheduled day for the alleged terrorist attack. With the flash drive missing, there was a reason for concern. Daniel Russo and Cynthia Craven were still out there. And they had the weapon drive, but not the decryption code. Cayden intended to get them before they could cause more havoc. The only obstacle in his way, nobody had any idea where they might be.

He took his time eating breakfast and was almost finished cleaning up when his doorbell jarred him from his thoughts. He glanced at the wall clock. It was just shy of 10:00. He picked up his

Beretta from the dining room table and tucked it into his waist-band as he hurried up the stairs to the main floor.

With one hand resting on the gun, he checked the surveillance monitor. Cayden unlocked the door and pulled it open. Mandala stood in the entryway, looking harried.

"Detective," Cayden greeted Mandala, surprised to see him. "Come on in."

Mandala shook his head. "You need to come with me. Now."

"What's up?"

"Jodi Vasquez called the FBI about an hour ago. She found a copy of the original flash drive contents stashed away on her sister's computer system."

The news stunned Cayden. "Mariana made another copy? When did she do that?"

"Who knows? The FBI told her not to, but her sister found the new decryption code, too. She says she knows what the program does."

"Give me a minute to get my stuff." Cayden hurried back inside and gathered his coat and gun. In less than a minute he joined Mandala in the entryway.

"Denbo called me from the car. He and Langford are already on their way to the Vasquez house," Mandala said. "They might be there already."

"Jodi's first call was to the FBI." Cayden closed the door behind him and locked it.

"You're thinking about the mole possibility."

Cayden nodded as he opened the garage door with his remote. "Yeah. I'll follow you over there."

"The FBI was the logical choice from her perspective," Mandala said, heading to his car. "Besides, we don't have proof that it's someone in the FBI."

"I know," Cayden answered. He mounted the Ducati, put on his helmet, and turned on the engine. As he rolled out of the garage, he wondered just what Jodi had found.

Special Agent Denbo pulled open Jodi Vasquez's front door before the doorbell chime could fade away. His normal all business face looked more relaxed, and he appeared to be in a good mood when he greeted them. He led them through the living room and down the hall to the office.

Jodi Vasquez stood in front of the computer desk wearing sweatpants and a well-worn sweatshirt displaying MIT in faded lettering. She appeared tired, and her hair looked like she'd pushed it back with her fingers to make herself presentable. She also looked excited.

Beside her stood Special Agent Langford. He also appeared more at ease than usual.

Cayden noticed the sofa cushion splattered with Special Agent Jameson's blood had been removed and replaced with a mismatch.

"Gentlemen," Langford welcomed them.

"Jodi," Cayden greeted her.

She acknowledged him cooly.

"Ms. Vasquez believes she knows what the software's function is," Langford explained.

"I *do* know," Jodi said.

"We told Mariana not to copy the drive, but her sister found a copy on this system," Langford said, gesturing toward Jodi.

"Yeah, she flipped you the middle finger there," Jodi replied. "It was her work process. She started every project by making a copy of the file she'd be working on. In case she had to start over. So, I went looking for it. Found it on one of the encrypted external drives here."

"I'm curious why you even bothered with a search," Cayden said.

"I was told my sister was trying to determine the software's function before her death. I wanted to know what she died for."

"Show us, please," Denbo said, trying to suppress his impatience.

Jodi dropped herself into the desk chair and pulled a battle-scarred laptop resting on the desk closer to her. She tapped a command across the keys, and the displays came to life, their luminescent surfaces adding a soft glow to the dim room. Seconds later, the now familiar octagon appeared on Jodi's laptop display.

Jodi ignored them. "I'm ready if you are."

"Hold on," Denbo said. "The last time that thing was opened, it started running."

"It did the same to me, but I found a way to prevent it. Once it's decrypted, the only way to run this copy is with a key command," Jodi explained.

She tapped another key and the octagon's rotation speed increased. One by one, brief flickers of typographical characters occupied the entry fields before disappearing, rotating out of view.

Cayden remembered seeing this same thing in Mariana Vasquez's office only days before. Some time passed before the octagon ceased rotating and disappeared from the display. For a moment, the screen remained blank, and then the lines of code filled the screen.

"One minute, twenty-nine seconds. That's how complex it is," Jodi said.

"So, what does it do?" Cayden asked.

"It's kind of like a siphon."

Jodi placed the computer mouse, positioning the cursor at the edge of a block of code. "It's multi-function, very complex. It operates in four distinct stages. This first block of code runs a kick-ass security buster. It can overcome multiple firewalls. The second block runs decryption algorithms. The third gathers information and creates a series of pathways. Last but not least, the fourth block, it starts the transfers."

"Transfers?" Mandala looked puzzled.

"This thing is an aggregator," Jodi continued. "It defeats any security measures that might be in place, mines the account numbers, and transfers the funds."

Langford frowned at the screen. "You're talking bank accounts?"

Jodi nodded. "Bank account numbers. Bank online transfers."

"So, this thing is just for a bank robbery?" Cayden asked.

"There are five different commercial bank ID numbers in the code, or routing numbers, if you like. So, it'll be a pretty big bank robbery if anybody gets the chance to trigger this thing," Jodi explained.

Langford and Denbo exchanged troubled glances.

Denbo spoke first. "The day Ms. Vasquez and Ms. James decrypted the drive, early that same evening our liaisons at the Secret Service reached out. They advised there was an attempted online security breach at the Federal Reserve branch in Chicago at the same time the program was running."

"That can't be a coincidence," Mandala said.

"At first, we thought it might be," Langford said. "But now."

"I get it cracks the accounts, but where does the money go?" Mandala asked.

"Private banks, secret banks," Cayden replied.

"By private bank, I assume you mean like an offshore account in the Cayman Islands," Mandala said.

"The Caymans, or Switzerland, Singapore, Luxembourg," Cayden said. "There are plenty of them. And these days, they're not always physical locations. Private banking has become virtual. It's often portable, and sometimes nothing more than a temporary network of legal arrangements. The cash becomes near impossible to trace."

Jodi turned toward her laptop. "I'm running the five ID numbers. They may all be Federal Reserve banks."

They waited in silence as Jodi navigated the keyboard, entering the nine-digit numbers one by one. She scribbled down information on a worn piece of notepad paper whenever she got results. After several minutes, Jodi snatched up the paper and swiveled her chair to face them.

"Federal Reserve banks. All of them," Jodi reported. "Chicago, New York, Boston, Atlanta, and Philadelphia."

Cayden took the paper from Jodi and examined the list. There was no question the flash drive was linked to a terrorist attack. "If Dragović or his assassins launch this thing, the damage to the United States economy could be catastrophic."

Both Langford and Denbo appeared shaken by his words.

"At least you can notify those branches so they can beef up their online security," Mandala said.

"Sure, but it won't do any good," Jodi said. "This thing will just adjust to the changes and keep on plowing."

"We'll notify them anyway," Denbo said.

"How much could this thing transfer from Fedline?" Cayden asked Jodi.

She didn't hesitate. "Billions, maybe trillions. I don't think it has limits, and it will do it fast."

"What are we looking at if terrorists use the software?" Mandala asked.

Langford looked stressed as he gave the question much thought. "Well, investors will panic and try to withdraw billions from money market accounts. Businesses keep cash in those accounts to fund day-to-day operations. So, trucks will stop rolling and grocery stores will run out of food. Businesses will shut down. Investors will lose their life savings. After the stock market collapse of 1929, the Dow didn't recover for twenty-five years." Langford frowned. "This could be worse."

"How do you know this stuff?" Denbo asked his partner.

"An economics degree in my undergraduate years. Unemployment will reach unprecedented numbers. It could easily exceed fifty percent. When the economy collapses, you lose access to credit. Banks will close and demand will exceed food supplies, gas, and all the other necessities of life. People are going to panic, and when they do, they'll revert to survival and self-defense modes. It won't be pleasant, or safe." Langford looked a little ill at the realization of how grave it would be if these events took place.

"I'd think there'd be global panic, too," Jodi said.

"It'd be inevitable," Langford replied. "As demand for the dollar and US Treasury Bonds plummets, interest rates will skyrocket. Investors will rush to other currencies. The yuan, euro, or even gold. It'll create not just inflation, but hyperinflation because the dollar will become dirt cheap."

"So, Dragović, and whoever's in this with him, they'd have to be converting cash to gold in order to survive something like this," Mandala said.

"That's exactly what they'd have to do," Langford said.

"In a worst-case scenario, those circumstances have the potential to make us vulnerable to military invasion," Cayden added. "The currency system degraded to the level you're describing would make it difficult to maintain the military and military operations."

"That alone translates to an invasion?" Mandala said.

"No, there'd be other factors," Cayden continued. "You can expect civil unrest because people don't have what they need. Normal, peaceful, reasonable people begin killing each other just to get the basics. The nation divides even more than it's divided now. The U.N. offers and then insists on sending in peacekeeping troops. So you have foreign military on US ground. It could start that way."

"Wow," Jodi said. "It's like our butts are sitting on the biggest time bomb ever."

Cayden knew it wasn't a bomb. A bomb wouldn't cause as much damage as the siphon.

CHAPTER FORTY-TWO

As far as Dragović was concerned, the telephone call was a gross source of irritation for more than one reason. The signal was weak and noisy, but at least it wasn't cutting out this time. "You tell me it won't function at all," he said into the phone, his voice full of rage.

"Not without the new decryption code," Russo answered.

"I must tell you how displeased I am," Dragović said. "I find myself losing faith in your abilities. None of this has run as it should."

"My abilities haven't diminished in the least," Russo said, his anger unmistakable. "Not every operation runs a straight line. This is one of them."

"You can't believe that fool will be able to take this new code from the FBI. He's barely been adequate as an information source."

"Whether he does or doesn't, there's more than one way," Russo said.

"We've only a few days left," Dragović snapped. "Whatever you plan to do, do it soon."

"You've no reason to worry."

"I think I do. I'll give you twenty-four hours. Then I take a different path," Dragović shouted.

Dragović ended the call, his mind racing, and his anger so intense he found it difficult to speak. Russo had always delivered before, but his operation was not going as it should. All he could do was stare at Bojan standing across the room from him.

Bojan waited, patient and curious.

He dropped the phone onto the desk, leaning back in his chair. "The smartphone decryption isn't working." His voice trembled with rage.

"How's that?" Bojan asked.

"The two women recruited by the FBI replaced it with their own code," Dragović shouted.

Bojan looked at him with an uneasy gaze.

Dragović put a renewed effort into calming himself. "Russo and his girl have never failed me before. But there have been an unusual amount of difficulties in this operation."

Bojan stepped over to the desk. "The fault may not be all theirs. From what I see, this security guard, what's his name? March? He's gotten in their way more than once."

"He's a security guard. A school security guard," Dragović scoffed.

"Perhaps, but they've gone at him twice and he's still alive. What are the odds of that, considering Russo's track record?"

Dragović gave the question serious thought. "You make a strong point."

"If you're unsatisfied with how Russo's handled the operation, I can see to him and his woman. But from what I overheard, he's already taken steps to secure this new code."

"You're right, of course. For the time being, I need them where they are," Dragović said. "Besides, there are greater concerns. Kazimi is a vengeful man. If we can't launch the weapon, there will be consequences."

"You can always return the payment."

"Oh, he'll take the money and his revenge, too," he said. "I'd do the same thing in his position."

"Melina and Elissa should go on holiday." Bojan's meaning was clear.

"The sooner the better," Dragović agreed.

"We have some time. Kazimi can't know anything yet," Bojan said.

"And I won't be telling him before it becomes necessary," Dragović said.

"His organization is resourceful. They could learn of the situation on their own," Bojan pointed out.

"It's likely they will. But as you say, we have some time," Dragović said.

Bojan began pacing again. "I'll bring more men in to strengthen security."

"Start by choosing four men you'd trust with Melina and Elissa."

"I already have men in mind," Bojan said. "You've no need to worry."

Dragović tapped his fingers on the desktop. "Melina has friends on Kefalonia Island. They've no connection to me."

"Greece," Bojan acknowledged, stepping over to the door. "I'll see to the rest."

"If you were Kazimi and intended me harm, I assume you have an idea of how you'd go about it."

Bojan paused in the doorway. "I do."

"Return as soon as you can. We'll compare notes and discuss tactics."

"The man's a cobra," Bojan said. "We mustn't underestimate him."

Dragović stood from his chair, turning toward the picture window behind the desk. The boats bobbed like colorful corks in the quaint harbor far below. "A cobra, perhaps. I prefer the mongoose. While the cobra coils and hisses, preparing to strike, the mongoose circles it, waiting for the right moment. The mongoose is agile. It charges the cobra before it can strike, sinking its teeth into the snake's body just below the head. Those jaws hold on until the cobra's dead." Dragović turned back toward Bojan. "And then the mongoose eats the snake for supper."

CHAPTER FORTY-THREE

Denbo took a position beside Jodi. "Okay, Ms. Vasquez, copy the new code and the weapon software to separate flash drives. Once you've done that, delete any copies that are on your sister's system here. And I mean every copy. No hidden surprises this time."

Jodi gave him a smile, heavy with sweetness. "Of course not."

Langford pulled his phone from his jacket pocket and walked toward the door. "I need to report in. I'm sure the Director will have some thoughts on this."

While Langford was out of the room, Special Agent Denbo supervised Jodi as she copied the decryption code to one flash drive and the siphon software to another. After she put the drives into his hand, he was especially vigilant in making certain she deleted the copies on her computer.

Cayden watched, amused. No one could say Denbo wasn't diligent. As for Jodi, she looked exhausted, and he wondered how much longer she could stay on her feet.

Langford walked back into the room, pocketing his phone. "The Director is speaking with the Secretary of the Treasury and POTUS now," he reported. "In the meantime, we're to send the flash drives to Quantico for analysis."

"When?" Denbo asked.

"First thing in the morning."

"You want to figure out how it works so you can build a defense against it. Just in case somebody else comes up with the same idea," Jodi said.

"That's the plan," Langford said.

"I'll assign four agents for transport to Virginia," Denbo said.

Langford nodded. "Good, and give them the background on this situation. If Russo and Craven go after our people, I want them to be ready."

They better be ready, Cayden thought. Russo and Craven had been consistent in knowing their plans in advance.

Mandala sat down on the arm of the sofa. "Can we be sure there aren't more copies of this *siphon*, as Ms. Vasquez called it, aside from the copy Russo and Craven stole?"

"They took extreme measures to get hold of the original drive," Cayden said. "That makes me think this copy Jodi just made is the only other. It needs to be secured, and the decryption drive, too, at least until your agents pick them up."

"I can lock them in our department safe, just like the original drive," Mandala said.

Langford looked like he was going to respond, but Denbo beat him to it.

"That's a solid idea. The drives won't be in the open long, and they'll be safe until our agents claim them for transport," Denbo said.

Langford hesitated, as if considering the idea. "I think that would be best. An FBI jet will be waiting at the Burbank Airport for the agents. Again, less distance to travel, less exposure."

Cayden listened as Langford agreed with his partner and then began discussing options in tracking down Russo and Craven. Their options sounded reasonable, but he questioned if they'd work.

Denbo turned back to Jodi. "I'm going to assign a couple of agents for your security. Just until we clean up this mess."

Jodi gazed at Langford with tired eyes. "I hope they do a better job than they did with my sister."

Before anyone could respond, Jodi rose from her chair and headed for the door.

"I need to get some sleep," she said without looking back. "Lock up when you leave."

Cayden watched her go. The FBI detail for Jodi was necessary. He silently prayed that this time the protection would be effective. The only way to really guarantee her safety was to get Russo and Craven. He was tired of sitting on his thumbs, and he resolved to move against them before they made another move. All he had to do was figure out how to find them.

CHAPTER FORTY-FOUR

Kate James' TA position to one of Caltech's tenured computer science professors came with a perk or two. Thus, she enjoyed a small second floor office in the Moore Laboratory building. She had the qualifications and credentials to teach her own class, but she found more time to work on her doctorate and conduct her own research projects working as an assistant.

Except for a quick break to pick up a grilled chicken salad for lunch, she spent most of her time in her office working through assignments. Dr. May expected them graded by the first day of classes following the Christmas break.

By the time her wall clock read 3:15 p.m., Kate was done. Not that there weren't more papers to grade, there were. But she didn't have another paper left in her. There were only a half dozen of them on the desk, and they'd wait until tomorrow morning. It occurred to her that tomorrow was the last day of the year. All the Rose Parade chaos had already begun, but it was three long blocks north. The campus would be quiet, and she'd get the remaining work done in no time.

Kate put the finishing touches on the last paper of the day, scribbling a note advising the student to review two chapters in one of the class textbooks. She rose from her chair, dropping her red pen on the desk.

Her daytime FBI guy, Special Agent Brenner, stood when she did. "Done for the day?"

"Yep," she answered, slipping into her long pecan brown coat that fell just below her knees. "We're heading home."

Kate led her very own Special Agent to one of the stairways descending to ground level. The sky was full of stratocumulus clouds visible over the tops of the campus buildings. There was some gray in the clouds, giving them an appearance of lumpy rows of dark cotton. All the crazy people camping out on Colorado Boulevard to see the Rose Parade just might get a little wet.

She led the way along Moore Walk, a wide concrete path lined with trees and benches, with Special Agent Brenner following her a few steps behind. Her TA job entitled her to a campus parking pass, allowing her to park in one of the convenient lots on Michigan Avenue, only a couple of hundred feet from her office.

The lot was almost empty, with only about a dozen cars occupying spaces. Special Agent Brenner had been chauffeuring her everywhere, so they headed for his FBI sedan parked at the edge of the lot. She noted the space next to the driver's side of the sedan was vacant, but in the next space over was an older model, beat up Honda Accord.

They were five feet from the FBI car when Kate heard a scuffle behind her. She spun around in time to see Special Agent Brenner dropping to the asphalt unconscious. Beside his crumpled body stood Cynthia Craven, a syringe in her latex gloved hand.

An overwhelming wave of shock and fear overtook Kate. Craven smiled, and Kate realized she was smiling at someone else. She turned and was sorry she did. Daniel Russo stood at the back of the sedan, his face passive, his eyes dark. She was in real danger, and there was only one option. Without another glance at the two killers, Kate bolted.

She ran as fast as she could toward the street, hoping to find someone there who might help her. But it was a useless effort. She hadn't gone ten feet when both killers were on her.

Russo's arm circled around her. Her training with Cayden kicked in, and she spun around before he could tighten his grip, landing a solid blow to Russo's chin. Unlike the guys at the bar several days ago, Russo didn't react at all. Kate's fear spiked as his eyes darkened further, his grip only tightening on her. She yelped in pain as he twisted her arm behind her. His other hand came around to cover her mouth while he dragged her back toward the FBI sedan.

Russo stopped beside the Honda, and Craven approached them, a fresh syringe at the ready.

Craven giggled. "This is going to hurt."

Eyes wide with terror, Kate struggled against Russo's grip, but he held her still.

Craven stepped in close, and Kate felt a stinging sensation in her neck. Russo relaxed his grip on her, dragging her to the rear door of the old Honda. Craven studied her as if she was a lab rat, but it soon became a struggle to keep Craven's face in focus. Terror clawed its way up Kate's throat, but she couldn't scream. Before she could even blink, everything became a blurry blob floating in front of her. She felt a tired heaviness sweep over her and had a vague awareness of being loaded into the back seat of the Honda. The blurry world grew darker and darker until soon there was nothing but blackness.

CHAPTER FORTY-FIVE

I t was late morning before he could slip away from his colleagues. But he was alone now, and he knew he had to make the call. He hated having to do it. He hated everything about what they forced him to do over the past few years. And now he realized he hated himself. There was no way around it. There was no one to blame but himself for the crappy position he was in. He had been greedy and stupid.

He stared at the burner phone in his hand, remembering the massive mistake he'd made almost four years earlier. It began at a dockside warehouse in Baltimore. He was part of the FBI task force conducting a raid there. The assignment was to find and confiscate an illegal armaments shipment. The raid proceeded like clockwork, and they met no resistance. Only two men were on site guarding the weapons, and they never had time to reach for their guns.

During a subsequent search of the warehouse, it was he alone who stumbled on a gym bag packed full of cash. Someone had concealed it under a canvas cover in a small skiff stored at the back of the building. He'd never seen that much money before. It surprised him when he caught himself thinking about his bills, the expensive home projects his wife was nagging him about, the cost of education for his kids. His job would never pay him what he deserved. In fact, his job had been a source of frustration for some time. It wasn't only the money. Promotion was a slow process, and he'd been passed over more than once.

The sound of his colleagues echoed in the large space, but none of them were within sight. He'd stolen nothing substantial in his life, but in no time at all, he convinced himself he deserved the cash. He pulled the bag from the boat and carried it out of the warehouse through a rear door. A chain link fence, rusted and worn, ran along the back of the property. On the other side of the fence was a strip of vacant land, overgrown with weeds and littered with junk. Beyond that ran an access road. Making sure no eyes were on him, he headed for the fence.

Someone had cut the chain link with wire cutters; likely the midnight work of someone bent on no good. He tugged the fence apart, ducked through, and followed it. Ahead of him was just what he needed: a bunch of discarded mattresses and box springs. There must have been a dozen of them in a dirty, careless pile. He began thinking this windfall was meant to be. He lifted two box springs apart and forced the gym bag down into the lower one through its torn fabric. It was too bulky to fit inside, but lowering the other box spring onto it solved that problem. He pulled a brown-stained mattress into place, leaning it against the box springs, enveloping the gym bag.

Moving fast, he retraced his steps to the warehouse. When he stepped inside, two members of his team were approaching. His heart hammered in his chest, but he handled it, reporting that there was nothing of interest outside the building. They believed him.

Late the same night, after a nerve-racking afternoon at the office, he drove back to the warehouse. It took only a few minutes to retrieve the gym bag.

Once in the privacy of his hotel room, he counted the money to find he'd stolen $300,000. He couldn't believe how easy it had been, and was riding high until two nights later when he returned to his hotel room to find Miroslav Dragović and his man, Bojan, waiting for him.

He still remembered the first thing Dragović said to him: "I had to see the guy with the balls to steal from me in person." The confiscated weapons were part of a deal Dragović brokered. The task force knew only about the weapons shipment, not of Miroslav Dragović's involvement. Of course, the money in the gym bag was also Dragović's, and he wanted it back. The tiny GPS transmitter sewn into the bag's lining led right to the money, and him.

Bojan stepped behind him and pressed the gun's suppressor against the back of his skull. The man was about to put a bullet in his head when he blurted out he was an FBI agent. Dragović held up a hand, and he felt the suppressor move away from his head. The arms dealer considered this new revelation for several seconds and then presented an option. Dragović could kill him and take back his money. Or he could take all but $20,000 of it—a retainer for future information about FBI activities and operations. And there was a promise to pay a substantial amount of cash for every piece of useful information. Living and keeping some of the money was the only reasonable choice.

It hadn't been so terrible at first. He never spoke to Dragović after their initial meeting, and the calls from Bojan were infrequent. The calls came with a question or two about a specific FBI investigation. Sometimes Dragović was interested in the whereabouts or political position of some prominent person in government. The information he provided was what the FBI knew or didn't know, and it didn't seem that it caused much harm, if any.

But his relationship with Dragović turned into nothing less than a nightmare with his assignment to investigate the CIA case officer's murder. He was involved now, no longer feeding harmless information, and just as responsible as the people who did the killing. It wasn't what he signed on for.

Months earlier, Bojan had strongly advised that he buy as much gold as he could. Now that he understood why, he was shocked.

He knew Bojan would not have offered the advice without Dragović's permission, and it dumbfounded him that they even considered him enough to throw such a life preserver. Of course, he'd taken the advice, converting his cash to gold at every opportunity. He calculated he'd have enough to survive the economic crash, and might even come out ahead in the end.

He held the phone closer to him, his finger hovering over the call button. An overwhelming feeling pushed him to tell Russo the FBI had again locked the new decryption code in the police department's safe. The information would support his claim that there was no way to get to it. But he knew the assassin wouldn't care, not one bit.

Russo, or whoever he was, had always unnerved him. The man was void of feeling, and speaking with him was always a tension-filled experience. He had no direct contact with the Craven woman, but he knew Russo wouldn't hesitate to kill him at the slightest provocation.

No, calling Russo now was a bad idea. Taking a shaky breath, he placed the phone back in his pocket. From the desperation to escape the nightmarish life he'd been living, an idea began forming. What if he could find a way to get a copy of the new decryption code and use it as leverage? After all, Russo needed it to avoid serious repercussions from Dragović.

If he could make his demands directly to Bojan, he'd be assured Dragović would hear them. But that wasn't possible. Bojan had always called him from a blocked number, and they had never offered him that number. As frightening as it was, he'd have to negotiate with Russo. If he could slip from Dragović's iron grasp, it would be worth the risk.

He'd have to confront Russo in person. Russo had told him the location where he and Craven were hiding out would be provided once he confirmed he'd stolen the new code. He could present his terms to Russo in person. As long as the decryption code wasn't on him, he'd be safe. He'd compel Russo to call Dragović on the spot, delivering the message that he would hand over the drive only if Dragović released him from his obligations.

Getting into the police department's evidence room and safe without detection was almost impossible. Almost. But he felt a new hope in him, and a powerful drive. He'd find a way if there was one.

CHAPTER FORTY-SIX

I t was after 4:30 p.m. and already dark. Cayden was on the Caltech campus when his phone rang. He pulled the phone from his pocket and looked at the screen. It was an incoming Face-Time call. "Unknown caller," he said, declining the call and returning it to his pocket.

"I never answer blind calls," Jodi Vasquez said.

Cayden felt an infinitesimal touch of redemption when Jodi called earlier, asking him if he'd mind acting as a Caltech campus guide, and to help her clear out her sister's cubicle. She interacted with him with civility, but there was still a noticeable coolness and distance throughout the afternoon. "It was a FaceTime call," he said. "I've never used it."

"I was a little surprised you agreed to help me when I called." Jodi handed him another box packed with her sister's things.

"Why wouldn't I?"

"I haven't exactly tried to hide how I feel about you."

"You have good reason."

Jodi crossed her arms. "I didn't have anyone else to call."

"I'm glad you called. I'm glad I can help." He pushed the second box of Mariana's personal items into the back of his 4Runner until it pushed against the first one.

"I guess that's it," Jodi said.

Cayden was about to reply when his ringtone sounded again. He closed the 4Runner hatch with one hand and pulled out his phone with the other. Again, a FaceTime call by the same unknown caller. He thumbed the decline button.

"Same caller?" Jodi asked.

"Another FaceTime, yeah."

The phone began ringing again before he could put it back in his pocket. He stared at the unknown caller tag on the screen.

"Could be some friend of yours," Jodi said.

"My friends know enough not to FaceTime me. I'm going to answer just to put a stop to it." Cayden tapped the accept call button.

The incoming call screen morphed into a live image, and that image chilled him. Jodi must have seen the swift change of his expression, because she stepped over so she could see the screen.

"Holy crap," Jodi murmured.

Illuminated in the beam of a tack light, the form of a woman hung against a dark wooden wall. A rope tied around her wrists and secured from something above her head held her upright. Her head hung down, her long disheveled hair falling forward, covering her face. Another person, indistinguishable in the darkness, stood close to the hanging body. The illumination created harsh, horrific shadows.

"Cayden March," a man's voice sounded through the speaker, the sound quality poor.

"Yes."

"I assume you hear me."

"Just barely." Cayden realized he was speaking to Daniel Russo.

"We paid a visit to Caltech today. Not many people there this week, but we ran into a friend of yours."

Moving closer to the woman, Russo adjusted the phone, centering her better in the frame. The video became stilted, freezing for a moment and then resuming. The hanging woman sensed the closeness of her captor and raised her head. A sickening sensation filled Cayden's gut. It was Kate. Her eyes appeared glazed and sleepy, and full of terror.

Jodi gasped, and Cayden held up a warning hand.

Russo continued. "Your friend's well-being depends on you doing everything you're told to do."

"So talk," Cayden said.

"You're going to get me a copy of the decryption code Vasquez's sister found this morning."

Cayden wasn't surprised Russo knew about the code. He knew there had to be an information leak, and this call was proof of it. "Not possible," Cayden said. "It's locked in a safe I have no access to."

"You'll bring me the code, copied on a standard USB flash drive," Russo said, his tone passive. "You'll bring it to Oak Grove Park, the last entrance at the northern end of the parking lot."

The sound faded, and Cayden barely caught the last few words. "How do you suggest I do that?" Cayden asked.

"You're a resourceful man. You'll figure something out. Make sure you're at the park with the flash drive tomorrow night, New Year's Eve, seven-thirty sharp."

"At least you're giving me some time."

"You'll need it. Seven-thirty sharp. If you aren't there, Ms. James here will die badly."

A hand gripping a wicked looking combat knife entered the frame. The poor signal displayed the movement as jerky and uneven. And then the person holding the knife appeared, darkly clothed, blending into the shadows. Russo did his best to keep her face out of frame, but there was little doubt it was Cynthia Craven.

"Hey, handsome, remember me?" she greeted him. "Looking forward to seeing you again. So excited. I'm all goose-bumpy."

Cayden didn't like the knife in such close proximity to Kate, and he liked it even less when Craven moved the blade to Kate's cheek. If he attempted to tell this killer to stop, it would only delight and encourage her. The helplessness he felt kindled a fury within him.

Craven used the blade to push Kate's hair back over her shoulder. "She's so pretty."

It wasn't a compliment, it was a taunt. Cayden remained silent as she moved the tip of the knife to Kate's neck, just below her ear.

Craven chuckled. "It sort of makes me jealous. It'll be a real kick in the pants, leveling the playing field."

She applied pressure to the blade and drew the tip downward across Kate's throat. Kate cried out and twitched a little, but held still. The thin line of blood that appeared told Cayden the cut had not been deep. But the closeness to the carotid artery made him grit his teeth.

Jodi murmured, "Oh, God."

"Enough," Daniel Russo snapped from behind the lens.

Craven's knife pulled away from Kate and disappeared from view. "More cutting happens if you don't show up on time with the goods," she said.

Cayden knew that wasn't true. Craven would kill Kate the first chance she got.

"Seven-thirty, New Year's Eve. The driveway at the northern end of Oak Grove Park," Russo repeated. "You bring the code. You bring it by yourself, and you bring it on time, or my friend cuts your friend into ribbons. Repeat it."

Clenching his jaw, Cayden repeated the words back to Russo. Hatred for the man overwhelmed him, but he tamped it down. He'd been on the defensive from the moment he was attacked in his home, his past influencing his decisions. He shoved it behind him; now it was time to go on the offensive. Kate's life depended on him.

"If you tell the FBI, I'll know. If you tell the police, I'll know. Involve anyone else, and your girl here dies."

"Understood." His mind raced. There had to be a way to get to Kate before the killers decided she was no longer useful.

"You're already running out of time," Russo said. "And March, don't even think about screwing with me."

The image on the phone fluttered and went black.

CHAPTER FORTY-SEVEN

"Those are the people who murdered my sister?" Jodi asked, her voice trembling.

"Yes," Cayden answered, his knuckles white against the wheel of the 4Runner.

"What was wrong with her, Kate? Did they hurt her?"

"They drugged her." Cayden was certain of it, judging from Kate's cloudy eyes and dulled response to the cut from Cynthia Craven's knife.

"We need to call the police," Jodi said.

"No. He meant what he said. Killing Kate won't even put a wrinkle in his day. I can handle this better on my own."

He drove into the parking structure too fast and came to a jolting stop in his reserved space outside the security office. Cutting the engine, he climbed from the 4Runner, with Jodi right behind him.

There were only two security staff in the office. One guard manned the radio and phone while another sat at a desk, eating his dinner out of a battered lunch box. Both of them greeted Cayden with a wave.

"Ray gone for the day?" he asked.

"Yeah, you just missed him," the guard on the radio answered.

Cayden made his way to the extensive bank of displays fed by the many security cameras strategically placed around campus. He sat down at the desk and slid the keyboard controller closer to him. Jodi rolled another chair to the desk and sat down beside him.

"Kate works in the Moore Laboratory building," Cayden murmured to himself.

He typed the building name into the computer. Within seconds, several of the displays filled with interior and exterior shots of the building.

"Daily archives?" Jodi asked.

Cayden nodded his reply as he found the camera covering Moore's front entrance. Built in a Spanish style, the three-story building comprised east and west wings. The camera perspective was above the wide brick pathway running between the two wings to the main building entrance. The view included the two second floor exterior stairways that ran down the face of the building, one on each side of the main entrance.

"We just heard from them, so they probably grabbed her sometime this afternoon. I'll start looking from noon on. If we don't see anything, then I'll go back to the morning footage."

The timestamp on the display's corner raced forward as he advanced the footage. They watched as people entered and exited the building with the jerkiness of an old silent movie. Since it was a holiday week, there were very few people on campus, let alone visiting the Moore Laboratory building.

"Is there another exit she might have used?" Jodi asked.

"Several. I started with the most likely, but we'll look at all of them if we have to."

The timestamp completed the 1:00 p.m. hour and moved swiftly into the 2:00 p.m. hour. Cayden focused on the display, closely studying every person who passed through the frame. He'd know Kate when he saw her.

The footage moved into the 3:00 p.m. hour. The later into the afternoon the footage advanced, the fewer people appeared on camera. At the 3:17 mark, Cayden glimpsed two people descending the left stairway. They then moved up the brick walkway, disappearing from view in the blink of an eye.

Cayden tapped the keyboard, reversing the footage. Another tap and the two people moved backward, back into the frame. He froze the image. It was Kate and one of the FBI agents assigned to her.

"Three-twenty-two," Cayden read the timestamp on the display.

"But where'd they go next?" Jodi asked.

"She always parks in Lot 11. It's closest to Moore."

A moment later he had the camera view looking down on the parking lot. He selected the camera viewing the parking lot entrance from Moore Walk, advanced the footage to 3:22 p.m., and then let it play at regular speed. A short time later, Kate and the FBI agent entered the shot. They walked west across the lot and then disappeared from the frame.

Cayden switched to the camera with a westward view across the lot. Kate entered at the bottom of the frame, walking away from the camera. A short time later, the FBI agent came into view.

Cayden spotted the FBI sedan parked toward the top of the frame. The space beyond it was empty. An older, beat up car occupied the next space over. A third person suddenly appeared behind the FBI agent. They were at the edge of the display, so he couldn't tell who it was. The FBI agent appeared to struggle for a moment, but then collapsed, falling from view. His attacker made a short step forward. Even though her back was to the camera, Cayden recognized Cynthia Craven.

Jodi gasped at the attack.

Kate turned back, facing the camera. As soon as she did so, Daniel Russo appeared from behind the FBI sedan, and both he and Craven moved toward her. Kate took off like a rabbit, with Russo and Craven following. They disappeared from camera view. A short time later, they re-entered the frame, dragging Kate toward the old, beat up car. Russo held her up against the car as Craven, a syringe in her hand, stabbed the needle into Kate's neck. Kate soon stopped struggling and went limp. They opened the rear door of the car and wrestled her inside. Moments later, Russo backed the car out of the parking space, then put it in drive.

Cayden got a better look at the car when it changed position. It looked as if the original paint job was brown or copper, but the body was so dinged up it made it hard to tell. He was certain it was a Honda Accord. The car sped forward, exiting the frame.

Cayden's fingers typed frantically until he had the picture from the camera facing the Michigan Avenue driveway.

The Honda entered the frame, pausing at the driveway and providing a clear view of the license plate. Cayden froze the footage.

"There, you can see the plate number," Jodi said.

"They stole the car and switched out the plates. It won't help us." Cayden tapped the keyboard, and the old Honda disappeared from the display. "That's as far as our cameras go. I need to know where they're headed."

Jodi perked up. "No problem," she said.

Hearing the excitement in her tone, he turned to face her. "What?"

"No problem, but we need to get back to the house for my laptop."

CHAPTER FORTY-EIGHT

A curt knock sounded at his office door, and Bojan hurried in. Dragović recognized urgency in his friend's movements. "You look flushed. Sit."

Bojan sank into a chair in front of the desk. "One of your accounts was hacked two hours ago. The bank's cyber security people contacted us as soon as they detected it."

"Which bank?" It was unnecessary to ask *who* was behind the hack. What concerned him was how Assad Kazimi got one of his account numbers..

"The Crédit Agricole Group in Paris," Bojan answered. "They shut it down, but not before forty-five million dollars disappeared."

Dragović considered the irony; one of his accounts being plundered by software. "Quite a coincidence. That's the exact amount Mr. Kazimi advanced for the weapon and our services."

Bojan nodded. "Our people traced the transfer to the Bank of Alexandria, Egypt. We zeroed in on an account held by a shell corporation. With a little digging we found Kazimi sits on the board."

"Since he still owed me the forty-five million balance, now I've received nothing for my efforts," Dragović thought aloud. "No matter. I will deal with it."

"There's something else, more pressing. Our man on Kazimi's security force reports a great deal of activity. They're preparing for an assault. Considering your forty-five million going missing, it's no coincidence. He's coming for you."

Dragović held up his hands in a gesture of futility. "A disappointing show of his lack of confidence in our abilities. Kazimi is more concerned with his money than the plan he helped conceive. It's rather hurtful."

Bojan leaned forward in his chair. "We need to prepare."

It was dispiriting. He hoped Kazimi would be reasonable and show some understanding of the complexities of the operation. But it was not to be. Now violence would be inevitable, and he'd make certain the violence did not happen to him or his family. "Put extra men on Melina and Elissa's detail in Greece, just as a precaution."

Bojan rose from his chair. "Of course, and I'll double the men on duty here. I'll come back as soon as I've seen it done. We'll discuss what comes next."

"Your second in command. Is he capable of overseeing an operation against a man such as Kazimi?"

"Hamada? Without question. He's been with me for fifteen years; I trust him with my life," Bojan assured him.

"Bring him along when you return."

"As you wish, but I don't understand," Bojan said.

"All of us will collaborate on a plan," Dragović answered. "You work with Hamada on the logistics. He'll command the operation."

Bojan frowned. "I've done something you find fault in?" Bojan asked with great concern.

"No, no. I have something more important for you," Dragović answered with a wave of his hand.

Bojan looked relieved.

"I've grown more uncertain of Russo. Too many things have

gone wrong. I need you to fly to California. Take control of the operation; make certain the weapon is launched on schedule."

"Understood. And I have all confidence Hamada will make certain things go as planned here."

"Good."

"What about Russo and the girl?" Bojan asked. "Do I dispose of them?"

"Only if they get in your way."

"Understood."

"Go fetch Hamada," Dragović said, picking up his phone. "I'll see to the jet for you."

Bojan nodded and headed for the door, but paused and turned when Dragović called his name.

"About Russo and his girl. Don't be too hasty. They've been more than effective in the past. I'd hate having to kill them."

CHAPTER FORTY-NINE

Back at the Vasquez house, March watched Jodi work her magic. Using her decryption program, it took Jodi a brief minute to hack the City of Pasadena's traffic engineering site. "It's going to take me a little time to figure out their camera system," she reported.

Cayden nodded, feeling as if he couldn't wait a second more for anything. Traffic cam images began appearing one by one on the rack of monitors. A directory window opened, and Jodi positioned it on her laptop screen.

"When the Honda left the parking lot, what street did it exit to?" Jodi asked.

"Michigan. Try searching Michigan and Del Mar. Del Mar is the closest major street. If it were me, I'd head for it."

"Here we go." Jodi studied the directory, found what she was looking for, and tapped a command into the keyboard. The traffic cam image for the intersection appeared on one of the large screens.

"There's the timestamp. We need to jump forward," Cayden said.

Jodi typed in a command, and the image on the monitor began speeding forward. Vehicular and pedestrian traffic moved through the frame in a blur. The timestamp moved into the three o'clock hour, and Jodi slowed down the video.

Cayden pointed at the screen. "There."

Traveling north, the beat up Honda appeared on the screen. It had the green light as it turned west onto Del Mar Avenue, soon disappearing from the frame.

"The next signal controlled intersection is Wilson," Cayden said. "It should have cameras."

Jodi brought the footage from the Wilson cameras up and advanced it to the correct time frame, then let the footage play at normal speed. After a brief wait, the Honda appeared again, continuing west.

"The next street west isn't signal controlled," Jodi reported, peering at the directory. "The street after that has signals, but no cameras. Next camera is at Lake and Del Mar."

Cayden prayed the Honda didn't take one of the streets not covered by traffic cams. Jodi's fingers rapidly typed in another keyboard command, and the Lake Avenue intersection footage appeared on the screen. Again, she advanced the footage to the proper time frame and then allowed it to play at normal speed. They watched as traffic passed through the busy junction. Several Hondas entered and exited the frame, but none of them were the car carrying Kate. The timestamp on the screen showed six minutes of footage had played.

"We should have seen them by now," Cayden said.

Jodi consulted the traffic cam directory. "Crap. They must have turned on either Catalina or Mentor. But which one? And what direction?"

Cayden thought for a second, then said, "They want the siphon delivered to Oak Grove Park. That's north, La Cañada."

"You don't think they're just hanging out in the park until tomorrow?"

He shook his head. "They'll be holding Kate somewhere close to the park."

"So, north?" Jodi typed another command.

"Best guess is they're heading for the freeway," Cayden said. "There's an on-ramp at Lake, a block north of Walnut. Check all the streets with cameras that feed into Lake."

For the next twenty minutes Jodi pulled up camera views at the Lake Avenue intersections, working her way north. Each one took time, with both of them staring hard at the screen to make sure the Honda didn't slip past them. Cayden felt more edgy with each passing minute, and he noticed the same in Jodi.

The first three intersections yielded no results. Nor did the fourth one, and Cayden began wondering if his deductions were accurate. It was possible that Russo and Craven hadn't headed north at all.

Then, about two minutes after they began viewing the Union Avenue intersection footage, Jodi gave an excited cry. "There. There they are."

The old Honda slowed to a stop at the signal, paused for several seconds as cross traffic passed, and then turned north onto Lake Avenue.

"The freeway on-ramp is at Lake and Maple," Cayden said.

Jodi quickly brought the traffic cam footage up and forwarded to the correct time. After waiting only about twenty seconds, the Honda stopped for the red light in the left turn only lanes. The light turned green, and it turned onto the freeway ramp.

"What's the name of this state's transportation agency?" Jodi asked.

"Caltrans."

Jodi immediately began typing again. "We're gonna need their cameras."

It took just a few minutes for her to find the Caltrans site, hack into it, and then locate the freeway camera system.

"You've been right so far," Jodi said. "If they're going to keep heading north, which freeway?"

"The 210." Cayden was certain they were heading toward La Cañada. For the first time since seeing Kate in the killers' hands, he began feeling some hope.

Jodi entered more commands into the system. They pulled up each file for every camera on the northbound side of the freeway. There was more traffic, making spotting the Honda more difficult, but with each camera view they were rewarded. After another twenty minutes, the Honda took a ramp leading off the freeway.

"Angeles Crest Highway," Jodi said, reading the directory.

"Is there a camera at the top of the ramp?" Cayden asked.

Jodi's fingers tapped rapidly across the keyboard. "Yes. Got it."

They watched the battered Honda turn right onto the Angeles Crest Highway, heading north into the San Gabriel Mountains and Angeles National Forest. She began looking for the next file, checking the directory.

"Don't bother," Cayden told her. "There are only a few side streets off the highway. They all lead into a residential development. No traffic cams."

Jodi frowned. "What's beyond the developments?"

"The mountains. That's where they're heading."

"Crap." Jodi leaned back in her chair.

"There isn't much up there. Not that many places they can hole up." Cayden sank down onto the sofa at the back of the room, staring at the frozen image of the Honda on the monitor. *Not much up there*, the words replayed in his head. *Not many places to hole up.* A course of action began forming in his mind.

"That looks like a big mountain," Jodi said. "So, how do we get Kate's decryption code out of the police safe before tomorrow night?"

"The FBI will never give it up, not even for Kate." He stood up, stepping over to the computer desk. "Can you duplicate the decryption software? Not so it's functional. It just has to look like the real thing."

Jodi nodded. "You mean make it look like it's working, but it isn't?"

"Exactly. Something convincing enough so they're compelled to spend time making sure it's authentic."

"I can program it so the lines of code look like decryption is in progress, but all it'll do is keep recycling," Jodi replied. "But even if you show up with the real thing, won't they just kill you and Kate the second they get hold of it?"

"Oh, they plan on killing us. But if I was Russo, I'd want to make sure I had the real thing first," Cayden answered. "If the code keeps recycling, it'll be a while before they realize they've been screwed. Any time I gain might help."

"Okay," she said. "I'll get started on it."

Cayden's eyes drifted back to the displays and the old Honda. Jodi said it earlier. It was a big mountain. But he didn't think it likely Russo and Craven would travel up very high, especially if they planned to trigger the software. The farther they climbed, the less cell signal they'd have. "I just might have a chance," he muttered.

Jodi looked at him with raised eyebrows. "What are you talking about?"

"Just thinking out loud."

Jodi sized him up for another moment, then said, "I hate thinking about Kate alone with those animals all night. Is there anything you can do now?"

He felt the same way. It agonized him, thinking about Kate's life in such serious jeopardy. "It's already dark, even darker in those mountains. Not much I can do until morning."

"Will they hurt her?"

"I don't think so, at least not until I show up."

"Super," Jodi replied, sounding glum.

"So, can you have the fake drive ready by tomorrow morning?"

Confusion wrinkled Jodi's face. "Tomorrow morning? You don't need it until tomorrow night. I could really use the extra time."

Cayden shook his head. "You can't have it. I want to be early for this meeting."

CHAPTER FIFTY

He had to get a copy of the decryption code, and fast. Russo might kill him if he didn't. Special Agents would pick up the new code along with the weapon copy from the police station at ten o'clock the following morning. Once in their possession, there would be no further opportunities.

He came up with a rough plan to get to the new decryption code. Russo and Craven had the original drive, but to play it safe, he'd make sure he got the weapon software as well. There'd be a significant risk, but he was certain Mandala would buy it. Once the drives were in his hands, there was no guarantee he'd be left alone with them. But the more important question was how to duplicate them. He'd look suspicious carrying his laptop with him, and just might cause Mandala to keep a closer eye on him. What he needed was a device small enough to conceal in a pocket. He wondered if there was such a thing.

An internet search revealed a device perfect for his needs did exist. A USB duplicator. He found one that was battery powered, rectangular, thin and had four USB ports. According to the product specifications, the device was small enough to fit into a coat pocket. A quick phone call confirmed an electronics store only five miles from him had one in stock. He got there in fifteen minutes.

The thing cost him over a hundred bucks, but if it got Russo off his back, it was worth every penny. The next step was to contact Mandala.

He called the station and gave his name. A short time later, the detective answered the call.

"What can I do for you, Special Agent?" Mandala asked.

"The Director wants me to take another look at the flash drives before we transport them," he began. "I'd like to come over now if that works for you."

"What on earth does he want you to look at?" Mandala sounded incredulous.

"Sorry, I didn't phrase that well." He hoped his nervousness wasn't apparent in his voice. "He wants me to photograph the drives and write a report describing how we secured them. I'm supposed to send my notes and the photos to him as soon as possible." The words sounded ridiculous as he spoke them. He feared Mandala's reaction.

"Didn't you already submit a report?" the detective asked.

"Only a preliminary. I think part of this is the Director's got a lot of pressure on him over this mess. I'm just guessing, but I think he may be trying to cover his ass."

"Yeah, I'm sorry, but I'm not even in the office," Mandala replied. "I've got a burglary-assault that came up late last night. I'm at the victim's home."

"Could you tell someone at the station I'm coming in, or perhaps we can do it later this evening when you're back?"

"Look, I want to accommodate you, but I can't make it work today," Mandala replied with some impatience. "How about tomorrow morning? Say nine-thirty. You'll be done before your guys show up to take them off my hands."

Tomorrow was the last day of the year. He'd be cutting it close. With a buffer so he didn't encounter the FBI detail, nine-thirty would give him only twenty minutes at best. He was certain he could complete the copy process within the time frame if nothing went wrong. But what if something did go wrong?

"Would nine work for you?"

"That works fine," Mandala answered. "See you then."

"Good luck on your investigation," he said, and ended the call.

An hour would be more than enough to pull it off. But after his call to Mandala, the stress and anxiety began eating away at him again. The internalizing made the feelings more acute, and worse still was the mounting guilt. Tomorrow morning he'd commit another act of treason. If all went according to plan, it'd be his last.

In less than twenty-four hours he'd have the leverage he needed to break Dragović's grip on him. If his plan didn't work, he feared he'd put a bullet in his own brain.

CHAPTER FIFTY-ONE

After a sleepless night, he arrived at Pasadena police headquarters ten minutes early. The front desk officer picked up the phone to tell Detective Mandala he had a guest waiting. Seconds later, the officer placed the phone back in its cradle.

"He's in an interview now," the officer reported. "He'll be out as soon as he can."

His anxiety swelled at that news. An interview meant an interrogation. If Mandala was making any headway, he wouldn't leave the interrogation until he had what he needed. Any delay would eat up his margin of safety. He glanced at his watch as he walked to the nearby waiting area and sank down on a chair.

Ten minutes passed and still no Mandala. Another ten minutes flew by, and then another. His watch displayed nine-twenty. Rising from his seat, he began pacing, his tension intensifying with every minute that passed. He was about to pester the desk officer when, thank God, he heard Mandala's voice call to him.

"Good morning," Mandala said. "Sorry for keeping you waiting, but you know how these things go."

"Did you get what you were after?"

"Let's just say I'm giving the guy a little time to think about it. Follow me."

Mandala led him down the hall and through a door with a slip-in sign plate reading EVIDENCE. The room was large with a heavy duty chain-link barrier separating three-quarters of the room. A heavy gate with an electronic combo lock was the only entrance, and before the gate sat a metal desk. The officer stationed there acknowledged them as they entered.

"Morning, Bill," Mandala greeted the gatekeeper. "I need access to the safe."

"Sure," Bill answered, climbing from his chair. He stepped in front of the door and, careful to block the keypad from view, entered a combination code. A buzz sounded, and Bill pulled the gate open.

"Thanks," Mandala said. "You can leave it open. We'll only be a few minutes."

Mandala escorted him to a large safe in the back corner of the locker, entered the combination, and pulled open the heavy door. He located the small box containing the flash drive and removed it from the safe.

"Here you go," Mandala said, handing the box to him.

"Thanks."

The two drives lay side by side within the box, each with a tag stuck on its plastic casing, identifying one as the weapon software, the other as the decryption code. Mandala moved to a worktable next to the safe and leaned back on it. Damn his luck, Mandala intended to stay with him.

He stared into the box, trying not to panic as he looked for a way to handle the detective. With nothing clever presenting itself, he withdrew his phone from his jacket pocket. He placed the open box on the table and, feeling like a fool, began snapping pictures of the drives. With so few photo options, he put aside the phone, pulled out his pocket notebook and pen, then began jotting down a log of the pictures.

"You know, Detective, there's no need for you to wait," he said. "I still have a few notes I need to make. I may be another ten minutes with this. There's no need to wait if you have more important things to do."

The explanation sounded ridiculous, even to him.

"I can't leave if the safe's open," Mandala replied.

"So, lock it up. As soon as I finish, I'll get Bill out there to put the drive back in."

Mandala gave the proposal some thought. "I do have to get back. I'll tell Bill on my way out."

"Thanks for the help."

Mandala gave him a nod, took a step over to the safe, and swung the door closed. With a casual wave, he made his way between the shelving to the exit.

He listened as Mandala spoke to Bill and waited until the detective's footsteps faded away. Stepping to a spot with a better view, he looked down the aisle to the gate. Mandala was gone, and he could see Bill's right shoulder above the back of the desk chair.

He returned to the table beside the safe, pulling the duplicator and empty flash drive from his coat pocket. The moment he did so, his heart began pounding. He couldn't afford to lose it now. He checked his watch: 9:32.

Placing the duplicator on the table, he inserted two blank drives into the copy ports of the device. He then placed the drive containing the decryption code in the first source port, and the drive with Dragović's weapon in the second. His intention was to work fast, but his fingers fumbled with the drives. Tiny orange indicator lights began glowing above each blank drive. The instructions stated the orange lights would turn to green once the copy was complete.

He waited long enough to make certain the device was copying, then returned to the spot where he could see the front gate. His heart almost stopped beating as Bill rose from his chair and turned toward the open gate. He moved behind the aisle shelving. His head pounded with the realization that he was only seconds away from discovery and spending the rest of his life in a federal prison. After a deep breath, he stepped into the aisle, hoping he didn't look the way he felt. Bill was only ten feet away.

"I thought I heard something," he greeted Bill.

"Just wanted to check on you," Bill said, still approaching. "You need anything?"

"No, I'm good. I'll finish up in about two minutes."

Bill stopped about seven feet short of him. "No hurry. Just let me know when you're finished."

"Will do."

The sense of relief when Bill turned around and headed back to the gate was tangible. He hurried back to the table. The orange lights on the duplicator still glowed. Another glance at his watch told him it was 9:43. He tried forcing himself to calm down with little result. After what seemed like an interminable wait, the orange lights disappeared and the green lights sparked to life. He removed the drives from the device, immediately returning the duplicator and the flash drive copy to his coat pocket. After double-checking the area, he carried the original drive to the front of the locker.

Bill looked up from his work on the desk. "All done?"

"I am," he said, handing the box flash drives to Bill.

"I'll get these back in the safe, then."

"I appreciate the help."

Bill smiled. "All I did was unlock the gate."

"Just the same."

"Have a good day." Bill stepped into the locker and headed for the safe.

Eager to get clear of police headquarters, his heart continued pounding as he hurried out of the room and headed for the lobby. It was 9:52 as he exited the building.

Once back in his car, he called Russo. The phone rang feebly before the connection dropped. He tried twice more, each time getting the same result. There was no more time for this. He'd have to try placing the call later. If he had any chance of slipping

Dragović's noose, he had to let Russo know he'd gotten hold of the new decryption code. Then he could make his deal for freedom.

His cell phone began ringing as he started the car. He pulled it from his pocket, checking the screen. His partner was calling in.

"Yeah," he answered the call.

"How soon can you get over to the Wilshire office?" his partner asked.

"The plan was to meet in Pasadena. What's up?"

"The Director's scheduled a series of conference calls. He wants all the agencies involved with this mess to be on the same page. It's all being coordinated from Wilshire."

The day was already turning to crap.

"Give me forty-five minutes."

"Brace yourself. It's looking like a long day."

The connection went dead. He stared at the phone in his hand for several seconds, a fretful pressure building in his chest. He tossed the phone on the passenger seat, then started the engine. No sooner had he put the car in gear, his phone sounded with a text alert. Dear God, what now? All he wanted to do was get as far away from the police station as possible. He picked up the phone. The notification bar displayed "unknown" as the sender.

The message contained directions, nothing more. The text had to be from Russo, and the directions had to be to his current location. But what prompted the assassin to send them now? The only reasonable answer he could think of was the calls he'd made to Russo a few minutes earlier. Russo had warned him not to call unless he had the decryption code. Even though his calls had not connected, Russo's phone had probably captured the incoming number. Since he'd had the guts to call, it was likely Russo assumed the code had been secured.

His mind turned to driving to the Wilshire office, and how the conference call might eat up his day. His gut felt as if he'd swallowed a boulder. He muttered a curse to himself. Getting the drive to Russo was going to be difficult.

CHAPTER FIFTY-TWO

The ten-man kill team reached the top of the wall, dividing Dragović's home from the rest of the world. They stayed there long enough to reposition their grappling hooks from the inside of the wall to the outside. In unison, each dropped their ropes down the wall and slithered to the ground.

The light from the lamps lining the driveway and some of the landscape lighting made its way through the foliage, casting a dim glow around their position. They stayed put until their tech man cut power to the property. The moment the ambient light disappeared, they advanced through the trees.

They reached the front lawn, but curtains drawn across the windows prevented any sight inside the house. To their surprise, lights burning inside the house penetrated the curtains with a soft luminescence. A backup generator. Moving closer, they heard music from inside the dwelling, barely audible. Soft jazz. The team reached the sprawling front porch. Voices from inside sounded over the music.

"You left it in here." Dragović's muffled voice came through the walls.

"I found it," his daughter's voice answered.

"How about you put it away now and pick up the rest of your toys?"

"Tomorrow," the child's voice answered.

"Now is better, little mouse. I'll help you. We need all this back in your room before you go to bed."

Dragović swelled with pride hearing Elissa's sweet voice coming from the recording playing in their living room. She proved to be a fine little actress and was very convincing. He marveled, too, at the hi-resolution camera feeds on the bank of security displays in front of him. There he was, Kazimi's security chief, standing in front of his front porch. He could almost make out the color of the man's eyes.

Dragović sat comfortably in the security center concealed among the trees at the east border of his property. He took a sip from his coffee mug and placed it on the console in front of him. He'd observed the little gang of thugs from the moment they threw their lines and hooks over his wall.

Now they stood facing his front door, fooled by the recording inside the house. The security chief motioned to five of his men. Another gesture sent those around to the back of the house. The rest of them followed their chief onto the porch.

One man stepped forward and attached an explosive device around the front door's latch and lock. The team flattened themselves against the wall on either side of the door and waited.

Dragović slammed his hand down on the console and glanced up at Bojan's second, Mr. Hamada, standing next to him. "I designed that door myself; handmade and hand carvings. Now I'll have to have a replacement made."

Hamada acknowledged the complaint with a slight tilt of his head.

Kazimi's security chief issued the order and his explosives man punched a button on his wireless transmitter. The fire and smoke of a contained explosion burst inward, blowing the lock and latch from the door and leaving a jagged hole in the wood. One of the men gave the door a powerful kick. The door swung open and they moved inside, their pistols held ready.

Dragović smiled as the cameras concealed in the house captured the men in his backyard charging inside through the French doors. They moved forward, clearing each room until meeting the front door team in the living room.

He looked forward to this moment. Every one of them looked perplexed. Not one of their designated targets was in the house. They turned their ears to the disembodied voices coming from the stereo, and in unison, each face registered they were in trouble.

The team took defensive positions, guns ready, each man choosing a doorway to cover. Dragović couldn't help chuckling. The fools couldn't figure out why no one was coming at them. Of course, he had no intention of allowing his home to be shot full of holes. The damaged door was all he'd tolerate. Besides, he didn't want the game to end too early. Not when he could increase the intruders' anxiety just a bit more.

The security chief gestured toward the front of the house, and the team hurried out through the open doorway. Dragović moved his eyes to the outdoor camera feeds. They crossed the driveway and sprinted across the lawn, reaching the tree line without opposition. Without slowing, they disappeared into the trees.

Dragović leaned forward, his eyes moving to the monitor showing the perimeter wall and the surrounding area. He could make out the intruders' black lines of ropes, creating a row of stripes along the white face of the wall. Kazimi's killers came into view through the trees. They rushed to the foot of the wall, slipping their guns back into the holsters. They were reaching for their ropes when they all froze. A moment later, they raised their arms high.

He clapped his hands together in delight. The trap was sprung. A contingent of twenty of his men emerged from the trees, their faces smeared with dark camouflage paint, each of them dressed in black. They leveled Heckler and Koch MP5-SD 9mm machine pistols with suppressers at the intruders. The killers turned, their hands still in the air.

It appeared Kazimi's security chief refused to die without a fight. His hand darted to his holstered pistol, and his men did the same. At the same moment, Dragović's men opened fire. Bright white muzzle flashes sparked from the suppressors, like bursts of little firecrackers in the dark night.

It was done. There was only one more thing to do, and Dragović would see to it himself.

CHAPTER FIFTY-THREE

Just after nine the next morning, Cayden pulled the Ducati up to the Vasquez house. He had removed the saddlebags from the bike. Everything he needed he was carrying on him. The air was damp and chilly, and the sky was overcast. He pulled the zipper of his leather jacket down a few inches to get a little ventilation. Between his undershirt and his fleece pullover, he was wearing covert body armor. All his gear and clothing were black. When he moved against Russo and Craven, he intended it to be at night for the advantage of darkness.

He'd holstered the Beretta 92 beneath the jacket, along with four full magazines paired in two belt holsters. Each of them contained subsonic rounds he'd loaded himself. The suppressor was in one of the jacket's deep inner pockets.

Jodi was still in pajamas covered by a plush fleece robe when she answered the door. Looking like she'd been up all night, she ushered him inside.

She reached into the robe pocket, her hand reappearing with a flash drive. "Here you go. It looks like the real thing and will run code like the real thing when they connect to the companion device."

"How long will this keep them busy if they're trying to confirm authenticity?" Cayden asked.

"Depends. The code is non-functioning and runs in a long cycle. It'll move too fast for them to tell if the same alphanumeric sequences are repeating. It might buy you ten minutes, maybe thirty, before they realize they got a booby prize. Just depends on how impatient they are."

"I hope I won't need to get close enough to them to use this. If I do, well, it'll help."

"You sure you won't at least call your detective friend?" Jodi asked, her hands worrying the belt of her robe.

The last thing he wanted was any help from the authorities. The police and FBI often made their presence known when they converged on a suspect. Russo and Craven would see them coming. They would kill Kate and disappear. But if Cayden found them, they'd never see him coming. Besides, he didn't trust the authorities to get justice for Alan or Mariana. They had to play by a different set of rules. Cayden had no such restrictions. And he planned on making things right—as right as they could be after so much senseless murder. If that meant killing Russo and Craven before they could hurt anyone else, it was fine by him.

"I'll do better on my own," Cayden reassured her, depositing the flash drive in an inside jacket pocket and zipping it shut. He turned and pulled the door open.

"Wait," Jodi called to him, her voice wavering. "I don't know if I can ever forgive you for getting my sister involved in this crap storm. But now I'm seeing firsthand what those people are capable of and why it happened the way it did."

Cayden kept his eyes on Jodi, focused on her every word. She was rocking from foot to foot as she spoke, nervous and anxious.

"I mean, I'm saying I can see that not all of it's on you."

Her words provided some relief, but his guilt remained strong. "And now I've gotten you involved, too. I'm sorry for it."

"Don't be," Jodi said. "I never thought I'd get any kind of

justice for Mariana. If I can help you end those bastards, well, you know."

He reached out and gave her shoulder a brief squeeze before dropping his hand back to his side. "You have helped."

"I don't want to see anything happen to your friend," Jodi said, her tone anxious.

"I'll find her," Cayden said. He sounded more confident than he felt, and Jodi wasn't fooled at all.

"It's a big mountain," she said, sounding doubtful.

She was right, and he knew it would take an act of providence to find Kate. To be honest, the odds troubled him, but he wasn't about to reveal his doubt to Jodi.

"I've got a few ideas."

"What else can I do?"

"Just stay close to your phone."

"When will I hear from you?" Jodi asked.

Stepping outside, he looked over his shoulder. "When they're dead."

If everything went the way Cayden intended, the meeting Russo had ordered would never happen. If the meeting did take place, he intended to be familiar with every square foot of the area around the designated meeting location.

He guided the Ducati onto Oak Grove Drive, opening the throttle and reaching the northernmost driveway entrance in a matter of seconds. After parking the bike, he stood in the parking lot, taking in his surroundings.

There was nothing distinguishable about the parking area itself. It was long and narrow, shaded by a canopy of mature oak trees along the entire length of the lot. A two-lane road, its asphalt faded and rough, ran along the border of the park. Small boulders formed three-sided, rectangular parking areas. Each of these dirt areas provided space for six cars. The Jet Propulsion Laboratory campus was visible above the trees on the foothills overlooking the park.

Cayden removed his helmet and walked some fifty feet into the park. Concrete picnic tables claimed their spots below many of the oaks, all of them damp with morning dew. Rusted trash cans sat among the tables along with much used, blackened charcoal grills mounted in concrete on steel poles.

He turned to face the parking lot. There were plenty of trees between him and the driveway entrance. A shooter could conceal themselves in the trees while maintaining an open view of the parking lot. Perhaps Russo intended to keep Kate concealed in the trees. He could produce her to prove she was still alive, but keep her too far away for Cayden to reach her with any speed.

Staying among the trees, Cayden walked the length of the park. The asphalt road made a turn and descended into the Arroyo Seco. The park continued below, spreading out across the valley floor. He felt certain that Russo and Craven would stay on the upper level. The old road was the only way in or out of the lower section. They wouldn't want to be trapped down there. After committing the area to memory, he started back.

Cayden knew Russo chose this place as a rendezvous point for its isolation. No one would be here at night, especially on New Year's Eve. Russo and Craven would take the flash drive and kill him, and then Kate, leaving their bodies among the trees. It was unlikely anyone would be near enough to hear suppressed gunfire.

Cayden had his helmet back on by the time he reached the Ducati. A few minutes later, he was on the freeway, heading north-west. It didn't take long to reach the Angeles Crest Highway exit. He turned right at the end of the ramp, heading toward the mountains.

It wasn't long before he passed the residential housing developments and the highway became a true winding mountain road. A small park came into view and Cayden slowed the bike for a better look. The only structure on the property was a large open gazebo. There were no other buildings, no place for three people to hide. He opened the throttle again and began winding up the mountain.

He took his time riding upward through the Angeles National Forest. Since it was federal land, there were very few private buildings on the mountain, at least not until the 7,000 foot elevation where the ski areas were located. The scarcity of buildings along the route made the search less of a "needle in the haystack" endeavor. That was what Cayden was banking on.

He was banking on a lot of things. First, that the killers hadn't moved Kate from the location where she appeared on the FaceTime call. If Russo and Craven spotted a guy on a motorcycle riding near their hiding place, he was banking they wouldn't recognize the Ducati or him, especially with his face covered by a helmet. They had no reason to think he'd be up here. He was betting he'd be able to handle both of the killers on his own. The Craven girl had proven herself dangerous. Cayden knew Daniel Russo would be even more to contend with. In each of his encounters with them, he'd almost died. He would make sure that didn't happen again.

The air became colder the higher he climbed, and the drop-off on his side of the highway became steeper and more severe. He passed a small, vacant camping area but could see the entire facility from the road. There were no buildings, only a few camping plots with picnic tables.

Another two miles up he spotted a turnout on the road. Passing it, he saw it was a wide, short driveway leading to a small shed. There were no signs of any vehicles, but he wasn't about to assume anything. He rounded the next curve, found a suitable place to leave the Ducati, and pulled over. With a modicum of effort, he pushed the bike behind a growth of foliage and hung his helmet on the left mirror before climbing the hill back toward the shed.

Cayden didn't have to climb very high or far. The ground was moist but not muddy, and it took only ten minutes to make his way through the trees to a slope descending to the rear of the shed. He hunched down behind a tree, watching and listening. Aside from a few bird calls and a single car that passed heading up the mountain, the area was quiet. He pulled his Beretta from its holster and headed down the slope.

The FaceTime image had shown Kate being held in a long wide structure that was older and in ill repair. Once he reached the back of the shed, Cayden realized this building wasn't large enough, and it was in good a condition. He slipped the pistol into his coat pocket but kept his hand on the grip while he made his way around to the front of the building.

A redwood sign next to the padlocked shed door, not visible from the highway, displayed the green and yellow emblem of the US Forestry Service. This was nothing more than a tool storage facility for the park rangers. Cayden hurried back toward the road.

As he walked along the shoulder toward his bike, he wondered just how many buildings like this one he might encounter. He couldn't afford to doubt himself now, but he couldn't help wondering if he had enough time.

CHAPTER FIFTY-FOUR

Kate James felt unprecedentedly horrible. Even though she still wore her coat, the wood plank walls of her makeshift prison did little to stop the frosty night air from chilling her to the bone. She was exhausted. Her stomach churned with hunger, and her mouth was dry with thirst. Kate's feet were on the rotting wood floor and her legs supported her weight, but the zip cuffs binding her wrists dug into her skin. Her captors had knotted a length of nylon rope around the restraints and then pulled her arms up over her head, securing the rope to some kind of industrial-sized eyebolt screwed into the stud above her head decades ago. The throbbing numbness in her hands and arms had to be from loss of circulation.

Mostly, Kate felt terrified. She knew her captors never left witnesses. After regaining consciousness, she couldn't help the paralyzing fear from taking her over. It was almost as debilitating as whatever they'd drugged her with. Then, following her captors' FaceTime connection with Cayden, hopelessness set in. In the glow from their flashlight, she glimpsed the body of an elderly man, his open eyes staring into nothingness, and his head cocked at an unnatural angle. They had dumped him at the end of the workbench, near the shed's entrance.

There was no doubt the man was dead, and seeing the body, she resigned herself to the idea she would soon join him. She was going to be murdered. Once her captors left her alone, despite being hung from a wall, her tears gradually led to a semiconscious, uneasy sleep.

The sun was up when she awoke, and with it came a slight element of hope. The sleep revived not only her physical strength, but her desire to live. If she was going to end up dead, she decided it wouldn't happen with her just sitting around waiting for it. She'd put up a fight.

Sunshine forced its way through the many gaps in the wall planks, and dust floated in the thin ribbons of light that spread across the shed. She was bound to the back wall, facing the only way in or out of the building, two double doors constructed from the same rotting wood as the rest of the structure. The room was about twenty feet long by twelve feet wide. It looked like it had been a workshop at one time.

There was a slight odor of decay coming from the old man's body, but it wasn't overwhelming. The cold temperatures were slowing the decomposition process. She did her best not to look at it while she surveyed the rest of the shed. The workbench ran along three-quarters of the wall to her left, covered by a heavy layer of dust, debris, and a few old, rusted tools. An ancient vise was mounted on the end of the bench farthest from her. Close to the vise was a small short-handled axe, its blade covered with the same reddish-brown patina as the rest of the tools. If she could get loose—when she got loose—it would make a decent weapon.

Kate also noted a heavy wooden handle leaning against the wall opposite the workbench. It looked like something that might attach to a pick or ax head. An assortment of rusted table saw blades hung on rusted brackets above the handle. There wasn't a single thing in the shed that was within her reach. She looked downward, surveying the flooring and wall near her. Aside from a big nail pounded into one of the 2 x 4 framing studs just above floor level, only dust occupied the area around her feet.

She looked upward and found some encouragement. Somebody had hammered a railroad spike into a cross stud only a few inches away from the eyebolt holding her rope in place.

With a little effort, the spike was within reach. It was four-sided and had edges. The edges wouldn't be razor sharp, but they were still edges, and might provide enough cutting surface to wear down the rope. Better still, the spike jutted from the wood at a slight upward angle. That would help prevent her from sliding the rope off the end.

Kate leaned back against the wall for balance and then stood on her toes. Stretching upward, she worked to get the nylon rope over the top of the spike. The first try was a wash when she lost her balance. She tried again and failed again. Positioning her feet together, she bent her knees as much as the rope would allow. It wasn't much, but it might be enough. Her eyes fixed on the spike, she jumped upward while moving her arms back toward the spike. It was enough. The rope cleared the top of the spike and held fast.

Kate rested a couple of minutes while she got used to the uncomfortable pressure on her arms created by the rope being held off to the side. She pulled down on the rope to create more friction, then began sliding it back and forth along the length of the spike. It soon became obvious she could only keep up her efforts for a couple of minutes at a time before needing to rest. There was no way of telling if the spike's edge was biting through the threads of the rope. But if it was cutting, it was going to take quite a while to get all the way through.

She had been working on the rope for about twenty minutes when she heard footsteps approaching outside the shed. No sooner had she frozen her movements to listen than the sound of a chain rattling against the wood of the double doors reached her.

Kate jumped up and attempted to clear the rope off the spike. The rope hung up, remaining where it was. The sound of the chains sliding against the wood drew her gaze to the doors. One of them was moving outward. Kate jumped again, jerking her arms as far forward as her binds would allow. The rope just made it off the end of the spike. She desperately willed her breathing to slow as sunlight poured into the shed, silhouetting a human form in the door frame.

It was the woman. Cynthia Craven. Unhurried, she approached Kate. The backlighting made it difficult to make out any details, but as Kate's eyes adjusted, she could see that Craven wore an amused smile. There was a thick bandage across her left cheek, making the smile seem more perverse than it already was.

"You look terrible," Craven greeted her.

Kate thought it best to remain silent. Craven wore a medium weight, dark purple parka, open over a dull white work shirt tucked into loose fitting, brown cargo pants. A wave of panic rushed over Kate when she saw the pistol held casually in the woman's hand. The psychopath was here to kill her.

Craven's smile widened at her reaction. She raised the pistol, pointing it at the center of Kate's face. "What, this?"

The woman slid the barrel of the pistol along Kate's cheek. It moved downward, across her chin, and then under the collar of her coat.

Craven took a step back, her eyes roaming over Kate. "I just love your coat. Gotta make sure we don't get any blood on it."

"Stop it." The man's voice sounded sharply from the doorway.

The other one, Daniel Russo, entered the shed, a cell phone in his hand.

"Such a buzzkill," Craven pouted, lowering the gun.

"You kill her now, March has no reason to hand it over."

"We don't know if he can get it," Craven responded.

"I won't warn you again. Stay away from her."

Kate began breathing easier. At least for the time being, she would continue living.

Figuring she had nothing to lose, Kate worked up her courage. "Can I get some water? Maybe some food?"

The killers only gazed at her, their eyes dark and empty.

"At least some hot coffee or tea. I'm freezing."

"You won't need anything," Daniel Russo said, his voice void of emotion.

The woman giggled as they turned away from her and left the shed. The door slamming shut snuffed out the sunlight. Kate waited until she heard the padlock snapping onto the chain, then executed another jump, looping her rope over the railroad spike on the first try. With a renewed, desperate energy, she returned to her task.

❧

Russo watched Cyn as she positioned the chain and locked the shed. She had never been moody before. Cyn had always been rather phlegmatic in her work, satisfied by the violence she did, but never being consumed by it. But she had changed since March cut her face. On the surface, she appeared the same, but he knew her well enough to sense a constant, smoldering anger in her. It didn't take a rocket scientist to know she needed revenge against March. She would have inflicted some torture or even killed the James woman if he hadn't intervened. Cyn knew James was close to March, and that was enough for her.

Cyn turned from the door, catching him watching her. "What?"

"I'm just waiting for you."

Avoiding his gaze, she headed for the stairs. He followed her up to the cabin and then inside.

Russo returned his phone to his pocket as Cyn went to the album stack and began leafing through them. She found one she liked; he recognized the artwork. *Sticky Fingers* by The Stones in the original album cover with the working zipper.

"I was on the phone with Dragović," Russo told her. "He's sent Bojan to us."

"Bojan, why? We don't need him." She sounded pissed.

Russo felt angry resentment as well. Bojan was a skilled, capable man, but along with Bojan, Dragović was also signaling a lack of confidence. It tarnished his reputation. His skill had given him dependable success throughout his career. His jobs always proceeded smoothly and with no one's help. But this time there had been several unexpected obstacles, and a good many of them because of Cayden March. But he didn't need Bojan to remedy the March problem.

"I told him that," Russo groused. "He's concerned things haven't gone as planned. Bojan is taking control of the operation to make certain the weapon is launched on schedule."

Cyn slipped the LP out of its sleeve and placed it on the turntable platter. "When is he supposed to be here?"

"Sometime this evening. Dragović told him where to find us."

"That's cutting it close," Cyn glanced at him with some impatience.

"His jet had to put down at a regional airport in Monterey, about three hundred miles north. Something to do with an electrical problem. Bojan told Dragović the mechanic found the problem, and it's being fixed now. He'll be back in the air as soon as they're done."

"So, we're just supposed to wait for him?"

Russo leaned back in the sofa cushions. "If Bojan's here in time for the meet with March, fine. If not, we move without him."

"What about our geeky friend?" Cyn asked.

"There were those dropped calls this morning. We never spoke, but if he had the balls to call, there's a possibility he actually did what I told him to do," Russo said. "It's almost laughable, but in the off chance he actually got the code, I texted him this location."

"Cover all the bases," Cyn said. "That's what we're doing.

He nodded. "Between James and our puppet, we've a solid chance.

"Well, March can't get the drive," Cynthia sneered.

"He doesn't want James to die. Even if he can't get it, he'll come. He'll make it more convenient to kill him."

Cyn glanced at him with a hint of impatience and switched on the stereo receiver. "What if Bojan doesn't make it?"

"Like I said, we continue without him."

His answer pleased her. She switched on the turntable and "Brown Sugar" came rocking through the speakers.

Cyn turned toward him. "We don't need Bojan."

"Turn it down, please."

She hesitated, glaring at him.

"I won't tell you again."

Biting her lip, Cyn leaned down over the receiver and lowered the volume. She glanced down at her feet, absentmindedly running her fingers across her bandaged cheek. "I'm just looking forward to the part where March dies. And that bitch of his, too."

He didn't like that kind of talk, and it concerned him she was more and more focused on revenge. Vengeance always put an operation at risk; there was no place for it in his kind of work. She had always been somewhat unstable, but he worried the knife wound from March may have pushed her over the edge. Now, more than ever, he needed her to hold up her end of things.

"Cynthia," he said, his voice hard and sharp.

She returned her attention to him.

"Our timetable is shrinking fast. We can't afford mistakes."

"I know."

The obstinance in her voice was hard to miss. He stepped in closer, gripping her arm. "Just in case you don't, let me lay it out for you. Dragović isn't a forgiving man. We are both dead unless we get that decryption software."

"I said, I get it." She pushed away his hand. "I wouldn't have killed March's bimbo tonight, if that's what you're thinking."

"That's exactly what I'm thinking," he snapped. "If we don't pull this off, Dragović and Kazimi will flip a coin to see who gets to kill us. And we need to be careful around Bojan."

She stared down at her feet again.

He stepped in closer and lifted her chin. "Don't let your emotions drive you to do something stupid. You stay away from the girl. She's already dead. So is March. But when I call it."

CHAPTER FIFTY-FIVE

The office was not so much to his taste, but it was comfortable enough. Some of the artwork on the walls was to his liking. The lights were off, so he was viewing the room in shadow. That had to be influencing his opinions. The leather on the desk chair was luxurious and warm. The desk itself was opulent, hand carved and spacious. Illuminated by the glow from the computer display, Dragović marveled at the tidiness of it. He had always viewed Assad Kazimi as a chaotic man, but his desk was immaculate.

The office building, a single-story structure of perhaps fourteen-hundred square feet, sat near the back of the property a hundred yards behind the main house. A flagstone walkway led from the building to the main house, originating at the courtyard and circumventing the pool.

Getting past the perimeter security proved to be easier than Dragović could ever imagine. He had heard rumors for years about a hidden tunnel Kazimi built; an escape route should one of his many enemies get past the small army guarding his compound. The man Bojan placed on Assad's security team confirmed the tunnel's existence; he provided the entrance location as well. And most important, Bojan's man identified a susceptible guard on Kazimi's security force. A substantial sum paid to the guard guaranteed them safe access to the rear of the property where the tunnel entrance was located.

Assad would come directly to his office the moment he arrived home, no matter what the hour. A fraudulent text sent from his wife's account notified him a package had arrived for him. The courier told her it was urgent her husband open it right away. It was waiting for him in his office. Assad's curiosity would assure his presence.

Dragović's impatience made the wait longer than it was. The sound of the main entrance door being unlocked made its way to the office, and then there were footsteps. Assad Kazimi stepped into the room and switched on the light. He turned and froze. Dragović felt some satisfaction as Assad's eyes fixed on the suppressed pistol pointed at him. He took notice of the gun Mr. Hamada pointed at him as well.

"Move your hand anywhere near the gun under your coat and you die," Dragović said.

Hamada moved around the desk and pulled Assad's pistol from its shoulder holster. He tucked the gun into his waistband and conducted a thorough pat down for any additional weapons. Finding none, Hamada took position in front of the door leading to Assad's private bathroom.

Dragović rose from the chair, moving beyond the side of the desk. He motioned with his gun. "Sit."

With great reluctance, Assad walked to his chair. And with the same reluctance, lowered himself into the leather seat. Once settled, he moved his hand along the edge of the desk as if brushing off specks of dust.

Dragović shook his head, his face lined with disappointment. "The first thing Mr. Hamada did once we arrived was disable your panic alarm. Press the button all you like if it makes you feel better."

Assad glowered with fury. "How did you get in here?"

"You should pay your security people better." Dragović

shrugged. "Now, let's discuss the forty-five million dollars you stole from my bank account."

"I stole nothing. You can't deliver what I paid for. I took my deposit back."

"You were premature. The operation is ongoing, progressing as we speak."

"So you claim."

Dragović studied Assad across the desk, proud and defiant. He did not enjoy this kind of thing, these types of confrontations. And he did not like what had to be done. They had worked well together over the years whenever the need arose. It was a mystery to him how the man could lose confidence in him to this degree. And steal from a friend. A past friend.

"Log into your computer. You'll see I've already turned it on for you."

"I'll *not* log in. I'm giving you nothing," Assad answered, his voice overflowing with contempt.

Dragović tilted his head toward the bathroom door. Hamada pulled it open and stepped inside, reappearing seconds later, carrying the client's oldest son. The boy wore American made superhero pajamas. A length of tape gagged his mouth; his wrists and ankles were bound with zip cuffs. His eyes were moist with tears and wide with fear. Hamada lowered him to the floor so he was facing his father.

The arrogance and determination in Assad's demeanor disappeared. For the first time since walking into the trap, fear showed in his eyes.

Dragović reached into his pocket, removed a small sheet of paper, and placed it on the desk. "You'll need the information here to complete the transfer."

Hamada raised his gun to the back of the boy's head. The child couldn't see it, but his father could. The last small bit of color drained from Assad's face.

"He's only twelve," the client said, his voice uneven.

"A fine looking boy. You must be proud," Dragović said. "My

daughter's only nine. Did you know that when you sent men to my house to kill her and my wife? And me?"

Assad tore his eyes away from his son and looked up at him. "Your word that he lives after I make the transfer."

"So, we agree," Dragović continued. "Forty-five million dollars. Ah, wait. I almost forgot the balance owed. So, ninety million."

"Please." Assad sounded lost now, desperate.

"We'll make certain the transfer is completed." Dragović's gaze flicked to the boy before looking back to Kazimi. "I know you understand what happens if it isn't."

Assad pulled the piece of paper closer to him and began tapping commands across the keyboard. Hamada kept his eyes on the computer screen.

"I'm curious," Dragović said. "What's the balance?"

Hamada leaned down to see the screen better. "Two-hundred million and change."

"Impressive." Dragović smiled without humor.

Assad typed in the transfer amount. He scanned the paper Dragović had given him and entered the account's routing number he found there.

"Ninety million," Hamada confirmed.

After staring at the keyboard for several seconds, Assad punched the send key.

"Done," Hamada reported.

His gun never wavering from Assad, Dragović retrieved his cell phone from his coat pocket and placed the call. Thirty seconds later, he had confirmation the money was in his account. "Mr. Hamada, take the young man to the reception room, please. I'll join you in a moment."

Hamada picked the boy up under one arm and headed out the office door, closing it behind him.

"Don't harm him," Assad raised his voice. "So help me, I'll kill you."

Dragović had to give the man credit; he revived his defiance at the end. "So, our business is concluded." He raised his gun and pulled the trigger twice. Two loud pops sounded in the room.

Assad Kazimi slumped back in his chair, dead.

Dragović lowered the gun, walked to the door and opened it. He switched off the lights, closed the door, and walked to the front of the building. The reception room was dark. Hamada had turned off the lights when he first brought the boy from the house.

"He'll need to walk," Dragović said.

Hamada reached down and pulled a small combat knife from the sheath strapped to his shin. Kneeling beside the boy, he sliced through the zip cuffs around the child's ankles.

Dragović kneeled down so he could look the boy in the eye. "You go back to your house now. Go there and don't speak with any of the guards on the way. You understand?"

The boy just stared at him, his eyes round and full of fear.

"Understand?" Dragović repeated.

The boy nodded.

"Good."

Hamada opened the door just wide enough for the child to slip through. The boy eased through the doorway and began running toward the main house. Hamada closed the door and turned the deadbolt.

"Please excuse me, but letting the child live is dangerous," Hamada said as they hurried toward the back of the building and the entrance to the escape tunnel. "Once grown, he might seek revenge for his father's death. His brother, too."

"His father might have been willing to kill a child, but I have no such inclination," Dragović answered. "I'm a businessman, not a monster."

CHAPTER FIFTY-SIX

The old, beat up Honda wasn't visible from Cayden's current position across the highway. He'd concealed himself among a stand of pines, watching and waiting for over two hours. His view of the long abandoned café and gas station was good, but not great. He hadn't spotted it at all on his ride up the mountain. But once he doubled back for a closer look, the higher elevation coming down the mountain afforded him a better view. Moving at twenty-five miles per hour, he caught just a glimpse of the old car parked next to an even older pickup truck through the narrow gap between the boarded up café and the hillside. A second building, perhaps a storage or work shed, rested behind the café. He could hug Jodi Vasquez for her skill in tracking the killer's stolen Honda the day before.

Cayden continued past the property and found a place to conceal his bike just around the curve. He hid the key fob on the bike. He didn't want to chance it being taken from him, stranding him on the mountain. Crossing the road, he hiked the short distance through the trees to his current vantage point.

Except for a hawk swooping down to rest on one of the rusted gas pumps, he had seen no movement at all. He had no way of knowing just where Russo and Craven were. His best guess was the cabin on the hillside, but he wouldn't bank on that unless he saw them there. And not being able to track their movements made Kate's location a total guessing game. He could see only a small section of the shed and only the top portion of the rickety stairway climbing to the cabin's front porch was visible. Kate could be in any of the three buildings. He'd check them all.

As the sun dropped lower in the sky, so did the temperature. Cayden felt grateful for the extra layer provided by the body armor. He blackened his face with a military paint kit as he watched the darkness envelop the café property. The sun disappeared around four-fifteen, and a dim light appeared behind the heavy curtains in one of the cabin's windows. Aside from that, nothing changed. There had been no movement of any kind. He hadn't seen or heard anyone.

The drive back to Oak Grove Park would take only twenty minutes. It was unlikely the killers would plan their trip to arrive on time. They'd want to be there early, long before he had been told to arrive. He had to locate Kate and get her out before they went to fetch her. Fifteen minutes later, when night fell across the mountains, he moved.

Cayden stayed in the trees beside the highway as he headed up the mountain. The only light came from the quarter moon, still low in the sky, and very little of it cut through the forest canopy. He wouldn't chance using his tack light within sight of the cabin, and within a few steps he wished he had night vision gear.

Cayden hadn't advanced twenty-five feet when the toe of his boot snagged something on the forest floor. He fell down hard and began tumbling. Grabbing out in the blackness, he got lucky with a gnarled tree root jutting out of the ground. He jerked to an abrupt stop and sat up. It took a moment to catch his breath and get his bearings. The slope steepened beyond where he sat. If he hadn't stopped where he did, he would have kept rolling, picking up speed and possibly breaking his neck.

He picked himself up and climbed back along the slope, proceeding with more caution. Once the café property disappeared from his line of sight, he switched on his tack light, leaving it on its lowest brightness setting. He continued upward, now making better time. It didn't take long to spot what he was looking for. Across the highway was a small bluff. The café would be on the opposite side of it.

The sound of an approaching engine reached him through the still, icy mountain air. He switched off the tack light and waited. Several seconds later, the headlights of a small pickup truck moving down the mountain flashed through the trees. Once the truck sped past and disappeared around the curve, Cayden broke cover from the trees. He ran across the highway, reached the bluff and began climbing the slope.

Making the climb in the black of night was slow going. It took just under ten minutes to cover the fifty feet to the top. The north end of the café and shed was almost directly below him. From this vantage point, he could see the light behind the curtained windows. There was a clear line of sight from the cabin to the bluff; the risk of being spotted during the climb down was high. Cayden peered down the slope, plotting his route. The hillside wasn't heavy with trees, but there were enough of them to provide at least some cover.

He drew the Beretta from its holster, attached the suppressor, and pushed the weapon into his waistband. After studying the terrain below him, he took a last, thorough look at each of the buildings. It was time to go get Kate.

M oving from tree to tree, Cayden made his way cautiously down the slope. Without light, the descent took a frustrating amount of time. When he finally reached the rear of the café, he retrieved the pistol from his belt, attached the suppressor, and hurried to the end of the building. Pressed against the wall, he peered around the corner.

The shed was some twenty feet beyond the café. The Honda

and the pickup truck were parked between the shed and the café building. He looked along the long side of the shed. There were no windows in the wall facing him. The entrance would be at the narrow end of the building, facing the cabin.

He'd start his search with the café, then work back. Edging his way along the café wall, he saw two window openings, both boarded over. He spent several seconds beside each of them, listening for any sign that someone might be inside, then made his way around to the front of the building. All the windows, along with the main doorway, had been nailed shut long ago with wooden planks. There was no way in from the front. Again he listened, and again he heard nothing to make him think someone might be inside.

Cayden retraced his steps, and staying low, worked his way along the back of the café. Just as in the front, he found more boarded windows. He assumed he'd find it the same with the fourth side of the building. It would be chancy checking it out. He would be in clear view of the cabin. Deciding to play it safe, he headed for the shed.

He maneuvered around to the Honda and pulled out his tack knife. After stabbing the blade into the right front tire, he repeated the procedure on the left front tire. The old pickup truck got the same treatment. Cayden closed the knife blade, placed it back in his pocket, and headed for the side of the shed. As he drew closer to the old building, the faint sound of music reached him, drifting down from the cabin; Rod Stewart rasping out "The First Cut Is The Deepest."

He paused next to the rotted board wall to listen. There was nothing to hear but the music. He moved around to the back of the shed. Again, there were no windows or doors. He continued forward to the opposite side wall. The cabin had an unobstructed view of this side of the shed, so he restricted himself to brief glances around the corner. There were no openings. That meant his original guess was right. The entrance was on the narrow side of the building facing the cabin.

Cayden went back the way he came, moving along the shed wall. He reached the front corner and leaned forward to get a look along the front of the shed. He couldn't make out the outline of the doorway in the darkness, but a new chain and padlock caught the pale moonlight. This had to be it. His gut told him Kate was inside. But to open the lock, he'd have to move into the open.

He checked his watch. It was after six and he was running out of time. Reaching into his jacket pocket, he retrieved his lock pick set and opened the snap on the leather case. He looked around the corner, just enough to see the cabin. There was no sound, no movement. He waited and watched, then moved forward, keeping low and close to the shed wall. When he got to the chain and padlock, he dropped to his knees in front of the chain and padlock.

Cayden placed his pistol on the ground next to him and chose the appropriate lock picks from the set. The padlock was not much of a challenge and opened quickly. He slid the lock shank out of the stainless steel chain, gripping the chain to prevent it from rattling or swinging against the door. Setting the padlock on the ground, he threaded the chain through the staple. Once it was out, he placed it next to the padlock and pulled the hasp free.

Cayden looked back at the cabin. There was still no sign of movement. He picked up the Beretta and eased the door open. The door moved only seven inches when the rusted hinges issued a horrific squeak. He froze, his eyes locking on the cabin door for several long moments. There was no sign the killers had heard the noise. He gritted his teeth and continued pulling the door open. The hinges continued squeaking, sounding to Cayden as if it were being amplified through a mega-amp sound system. There was no getting past the old hinges, so he kept pulling until he had enough of an opening to fit through. He offered a silent *thank you* to Rod Stewart for covering the sound of the hinges, and after a final check back at the cabin door, slipped inside the shed.

The shed interior was void of light. Cayden preferred to close the door behind him, but didn't want to risk the additional noise from the hinges. As he paused, giving his eyes time to adjust to the darkness, the odor of decay reached his nose. In the small amount of ambient light making its way through the doorway opening, he saw a body. An old man crumpled on the ground against the end of a workbench.

A soft shuffling sound came from the blackness at the back of the shed. He readied his gun and headed for it.

"Who are you?" The whisper came from the back of the shed.

"Kate, quiet," he whispered back.

"Cayden?"

"Quiet."

As he moved into the shed, Kate gradually came into view through the shadows. Her hair was disheveled and her arms tied above her head, held fast to something on the wall he couldn't make out in the darkness. A few more steps and he was standing in front of her. Kate's eyes were puffy from crying.

"Thank God," she said, keeping her voice low.

"Are they in the cabin?" Cayden asked.

"I don't know any cabin. This is all I've seen."

Cayden tucked the Beretta into his belt. His eyes adjusting to the dark, he examined Kate's bonds. He found the knot in the rope and examined it. It was tight as it could be. He pulled his knife and began sawing away at the section of rope next to the knot.

"They're going to kill us," Kate said, her voice trembling. "They're going to kill us as soon as they get the flash drive from you."

"How about we just get out of here? Save them all that trouble."

The high angle made the work awkward, but the knife soon cut through the last strands of the rope. No longer supported by her binds, Kate dropped downward. Cayden caught her before she could fall.

"I'm okay. I'm okay," she assured him. Standing on her own, she took a short step forward.

He was reaching to support her when he sensed movement behind him. His hand moved to his gun, and he began turning.

Daniel Russo's impassive voice came from behind him. "Move another inch and I'll kill her."

Cayden froze. Jodi's suggestion that he tell Mandala his plans now sounded like a good idea. But Mandala wasn't responsible for Kate. He was. He'd feared being responsible for another human life, but now he felt nothing but a determination to get Kate out of this disastrous situation. There was no way he would fail her the way he'd failed Mariana.

"You're early, March," Russo said, his voice closer.

A blast of pain shot through his head. He heard Kate cry out before the blackness overwhelmed him and he dropped to the floor.

CHAPTER FIFTY-SEVEN

Cayden became aware of someone's hands poking and prodding him. As his eyes fluttered open, the throbbing pain in the back of his head quickly displaced all other sensations. His vision was blurry at first, but soon cleared. Daniel Russo, leaning over him, was going through his pockets. Cynthia Craven stood next to him, holding Cayden's cell phone in her left hand, and pointing his own gun at him with the right.

He was on his back next to the workbench, the worn and splintered floorboards rough beneath him. His arms extended around one of the bench's corner legs, his wrists secured with zip cuffs. The old man's body lay to his left, the head near his knees, the sightless eyes staring upward. The last few notes of Rod Stewart's "Reason To Believe" drifted down the hill from the cabin and faded into silence.

Russo tugged at his jacket, unzipping a pocket. There was more tugging, and Russo straightened up with Jodi's spurious flash drive gripped between his fingers.

"I thought you'd never have this on you," Russo said. "But here it is."

"He's nothing special," Craven said, her voice full of rancor.

Cayden knew he'd blown it. He hadn't given himself enough

time; he'd cut it too close. Now he and Kate were in serious trouble. But he wasn't dead yet.

Russo kicked him in the side. There wasn't a lot of force behind it, but the toe of Russo's shoe landed next to his ribs. Cayden gasped, jerking his knees upward.

"Now I'm wondering why he has it on him." Russo nudged Cayden with his foot. "Why?"

"Who cares why," Craven said.

It took Cayden a moment to catch his breath. "I want Kate back."

Russo stared down at him, his expression blank, his eyes dark and thoughtful.

Craven stepped around her partner. "We've got it. He's done." She raised the gun, pointing it at his crotch. "But I'm gonna take a few minutes."

"Stop," Russo ordered.

"Nobody does this to me." She touched her bandaged cheek with her free hand.

Her finger tightened on the trigger, and Cayden braced himself.

"I said stop." Russo stepped in front of the gun.

Craven froze, and Russo pushed her gun arm down.

"You can kill them both. But not until we test this drive," Russo said. "If he's screwing with me, we may need him alive."

"But Bojan isn't here yet," Craven whined.

"He will be," Russo said. "I can start testing without him. In the meantime, nothing happens to these two."

Cayden didn't care who Bojan might be. The only thing that mattered was he had more time now to free himself and Kate.

Russo kneeled down beside Cayden, checking to make sure the restraints were secure. He straightened up and looked at Kate, again tied against the wall. Without another word, he ushered Craven out of the shed. As the doors closed, Cayden heard a phone ring. He focused on the doorway, listening.

"Yes." Russo's voice filtered in through the old wood. "You're in Los Angeles?"

There was nothing but silence for several seconds. Then Russo spoke again. "Good. We'll see you soon."

Over the sounds of the chain and padlock being secured, Cayden heard Russo tell Craven, "He's on the way up here."

Cayden remained still until the footsteps outside the shed faded away and then adjusted his position so he could see Kate. "You okay?"

"Aside from being strung up like a ham and knowing I'm going to be murdered, I'm super."

"Seriously," Cayden pushed.

"I'm starving and need some water."

"We'll take care of that."

"What're we gonna do?" Kate asked, worry in her voice.

Just the question he was asking himself. He surveyed the area, ticking off possible ways of escape. He was a special operator again, pushing the fear behind him and focusing on the task at hand. The rush energized him.

Cayden adjusted his position. "I'm working on it."

"You really gave them the siphon decryption code?" It was a question, but Kate made it sound like an accusation.

"Kind of." He wedged his shoulder under the workbench and pushed upward. The bench didn't budge. He slid his hand down the bench leg. The feel of cold metal greeted his fingertips; a steel bracket bolted the bench leg to the floor. The rest of the legs would be the same.

"What's that mean?" Kate pushed.

He replied with a brief explanation of what Jodi had done as he pulled the zip cuffs against the bench leg, exerting more and more force to break it. The plastic cut into his skin, forcing him to give it up. He took a moment to catch his breath again. "Whatever we do, we have to do it before whoever they're waiting for gets here."

"So start doing it," Kate said.

He had to hand it to her. Kate was holding on to her wry wit. The throbbing in his head lessened while he looked for something that might help him. His eyes came to rest upon the old man's body. It was a long shot, but maybe something was there.

Cayden adjusted his position and edged toward the body as far as his wrist restraints would allow. Angling his right leg, he worked his right foot under the old man's arm and lodged it under the armpit. Drawing back his leg, he began pulling the corpse toward him.

"What on earth are you doing?" Kate whispered, a hint of disgust in her voice.

He ignored the question, focusing on the task at hand. It was slow going, but inch by inch he made progress. Once the body was close enough, Cayden used both legs to angle it so the old man's chest was near the bench leg where his wrists were secured.

He rolled onto his side and pivoted around until his body was almost parallel with the workbench, then edged forward until his shoulder pressed against the bench leg. Reaching the right side of the body was impossible, but he could work with the side nearest him. Stretching out his arms, Cayden reached the old man's left buttoned shirt pocket and began working to unfasten it.

"This is so nasty," Kate's voice sounded from the shadows.

"Shush," he hissed at her.

The button came free. Cayden pulled the pocket flap back. The pocket was empty. The left trouser pocket was worth checking, but it was out of reach. He got a grip on the old man's arm and began pulling. In a few moments, the body was close enough.

The zip cuffs made it difficult, but with some effort, Cayden managed to get his right hand inside the pocket. At first he thought the pocket was empty, but then the tip of his index finger contacted a hard, narrow object. Cayden worked his fingers deeper down into the pocket and soon realized he'd found a pocket knife. He locked his fingers around the knife and pulled.

Easing himself into a more comfortable position, he examined his find. It was an old canoe knife with well-worn stag handles, probably manufactured in the sixties. He unfolded one of the two blades from the case. The metal had darkened with age, but he didn't detect any rust.

"What is it?" Kate asked.

Cayden worked the knife in his right hand until the sharp edge of the blade was facing him. "A pocketknife."

He angled his body back to where it had been when Russo and Craven left the shed, pushing the old man's body out of the way as he moved. Turning on his side, he lowered the blade under the zip cuffs.

There was no way to keep a firm hold on the knife and apply enough pressure while sawing at the restraints. Instead, he began moving his left arm up and back in quick strokes, sliding the cuff against the stationary blade. Due to his restraints, the strokes were short. After a couple of minutes, he checked his progress. The knife blade proved itself to be dull, and the cut mark he felt with his fingertip didn't seem deep. But at least it was something. He started again, this time exerting as much downward force against the blade as he could.

"Cayden?" Kate's voice came out of the shadows.

"Working on it."

He rested just long enough to get the circulation back in his wrists and hands and then started sawing again.

More rock 'n' roll sounded once again from the cabin. Cayden recognized the Allman Brothers, but he couldn't place the song.

He moved the knife to the beat of the music, wondering if there would be enough time.

CHAPTER FIFTY-EIGHT

Cayden heard an approaching car engine and tires rolling over gravel. He checked his watch; the radial dial showed eight-fifteen. He'd been working on his restraints for less than an hour.

"Cay." Kate's whisper sounded desperate.

He adjusted his grip on the pocket knife and vigorously returned to the cutting. "Almost there." He hoped he sounded reassuring.

The car engine shut off and music from the Allman Brothers record that'd been playing for the last five minutes became audible again. The car door slammed shut, and there was the sound of muffled voices, and then footsteps crunching across the gravel. March couldn't make out the conversation, but it didn't matter. What mattered was the voices and footsteps were diminishing; they were heading up to the cabin. He exerted all the pressure he could, pushing the knife blade against the ties.

"It's the guy they've been waiting for." Kate's voice trembled.

"We'll be okay," he answered. "It'll take time for them to brief him. And they're probably still messing with the flash drive. It'll be a while before they figure out they've been screwed."

"Even if you get free, how do we get out of here?"

"These walls are nothing but rotting old planks. It won't take much to pry a couple of them loose. You see anything that might help? Old tools, a crowbar or something."

"During the day, I saw some stuff."

"Yeah?"

"I think there's an old hatchet on the bench above you," Kate said.

"That should do it," Cayden said.

He could tell he was making progress on the zip cuffs, but after several minutes of sawing, he still couldn't tell how much. His hands were cramping, and he found it tougher to keep a firm grip on the knife.

The unmistakable, unwelcome sound of the chain clinking came from the other side of the door, followed by the metallic scraping of it being drawn through the staple. Cayden made a few more desperate strokes against the blade and then closed his hand over the pocketknife, concealing it in his palm. The hinges creaked and the volume of the music increased as the door opened.

The Craven girl slipped through the door. Cayden glimpsed a gun in her hand, silhouetted in the dim light seeping through the open door. She paused for a moment, just inside the doorway. He hoped she hadn't noticed the old man's body wasn't where it had been. She made a half turn and pushed the door shut behind her, once again muffling the driving bass line of "Saturday Night Special." A pale light suddenly glowed in her left hand as she stepped around Cayden to the far end of the workbench. She placed whatever the source was on the bench top and the light began fluttering softly, the sign of a failing bulb or weak batteries.

Craven turned, leaning back against the bench, alternating her gaze between them. She kept her voice low. "So, why do you think that decryption code is taking so long to work?"

Cayden thought it likely Russo didn't know she was down here. He looked over at Kate, finally able to see her more clearly in the dim light. She was frightened, on edge.

"Danny's getting really frustrated with it. You didn't do something you shouldn't have, did you?"

"A decryption sequence can take a lot of time to run," Kate said.

Craven glared down at Cayden. "Yeah? Well, I think this little scamp gave us junk."

"I brought you what you asked for," he replied. "Your boyfriend hasn't finished running the code, has he?

"Nah. He and our babysitter are working on it now." Her eyes glittered with hate and madness. "I figured they'd barely notice I'm gone, and I was right," she giggled.

Cayden knew she was ready to snap. He didn't know how far he'd cut through his restraints, and she'd know it if he continued his work with the pocketknife. That alone would be enough to push her over the edge.

"Pretty sure he told you to hold off," Cayden said.

Craven shrugged. "I've never been great at waiting." She held up his Beretta, running her fingers sensually up and down the suppressor barrel. "This is gonna be very satisfying."

Craven placed the pistol on the corner of the bench, and the next thing Cayden saw in her hand was a tactical knife. Unhurried, she strolled toward Kate.

"Let's start with Katie," she taunted. "Bad news. You get to watch while I cut her like you did me. The good news, she won't have to live with it as long as I will."

Craven's back was to him, and she was only a step away from Kate. Cayden let the pocketknife drop from his hand, hoping he'd hacked through the restraints enough, then yanked them back hard against the bench leg. The plastic cut into his wrists, stinging and holding fast. At the sound of his movement, Craven turned back toward him, straining to see him better in the dim flickering light. She moved toward him.

Cayden wound up and again drew back with all the force he could muster. The plastic tie struck hard against the bench leg and snapped apart. He rolled away from the table as Craven rushed for his gun.

He leaped forward from the floor and struck at her knees, knocking her off balance and away from the gun. She stumbled and went down just in front of Kate, but rolled back to her feet.

They both rushed for the gun, but Craven was just ahead of him. Cayden realized he wouldn't get to the Beretta in time. Instead, he lowered his shoulder and slammed into her, shoving her away from the gun again. Even as she fought to regain her balance, Craven slashed at him with her knife. He retreated, avoiding the blade by only inches.

The moment he regained his footing, he closed the distance between them, making it hard for Craven to maneuver with the knife. He grabbed her knife arm, and body-slammed her to the opposite side of the shed. Her back hit the wall hard, and he used the momentum to smash her wrist into a wall stud, jarring the knife from her hand. He prayed the rock 'n' roll coming from the cabin was drowning out the noise of the fight.

The moment she lost the knife, Craven jammed her knee into his crotch, the unexpected blow causing him to lose his grip on her arms. She followed through, driving both fists into his chest. His already aching ribs exploded with pain as he stumbled away from her.

As Craven rushed back toward the gun, he saw Kate grip the ropes running through her zip cuffs. In a single fluid motion, Kate drew her knees up above her waist and kicked outward. Her boot heels connected high on Craven's shoulder at the base of her neck. With a cry of pain, Craven hurtled sideways, losing her footing and hitting the ground hard.

Cayden fought through the pain as he watched her recover, leaping back to her feet. She moved fast, and he realized this time she was going to reach the gun. As he straightened up, he glimpsed the rusted hatchet Kate had mentioned lying on the workbench. It was only two steps away, and he lunged for it, taking hold of the handle.

Craven raised the gun, and he recognized the same look in her eyes he'd seen days before at the Vasquez house. A glint of insane excitement suspended in a pool of dark emptiness.

She began squeezing the trigger, but Cayden's arm was already in motion.

"Hatchet at a gunfight," was all she had time to giggle before the hatchet blade cut deep into the base of her neck.

She swayed unsteadily on her feet for a moment, her free hand reaching up to the hatchet, as if she intended to pull it free. Then a gurgling sound bubbled from her gaping mouth as she crumpled to the floor.

Cayden felt a sense of satisfaction as he leaned over her, removing his Beretta from her fingers. But it didn't make him feel any better. Craven's death wouldn't bring Alan or any of the people she'd murdered back to life. He kept his eyes on the dying killer. Her breathing was shallow, her eyes blinked sporadically, and the pool of blood spread around her shoulders and head. A moment later, she was dead.

The faint beat of rock from the cabin above them was the only sound in the shed. Craven was gone. The music was their only hope Russo and the other man had not heard the fight.

"Cayden?" Kate's voice came from behind him.

"Hang on." Cayden set his pistol on the bench next to the flickering sixties era Teledyne lantern flashlight Craven had brought with her. He began searching for Craven's tactical knife. A few seconds later, he'd found it and was cutting through the rope binding Kate to the shed wall.

"Is she dead?" Kate's voice trembled.

"Yes. And thanks for the help."

The knife sliced through the rope and then through the zip cuffs around her wrists. The moment Kate was free she threw her arms around him, clenching him tightly. He gently pulled away from her and looked toward the door.

"We have to go," he told her.

CHAPTER FIFTY-NINE

Kate was a little unsteady on her feet. It didn't surprise him; she'd been roughed up, deprived of food and water, and was numb with fright. He supported her as they walked to the shed's open door.

"We have to move fast once we get outside," he told her.

She let him go, but grabbed his arm again, her legs still a little wobbly. After several seconds, she seemed more steady and let go of his arm. Cayden waited a moment to make sure she was okay, then retrieved his pistol. He ejected the magazine; it was still full, and Russo had left the extra mags in place on his belt. He slid the mag back into the Beretta.

Kate's eyes locked on the body, and she began hyperventilating. He returned to her side. "Slow, deep breaths, and keep your eyes on me."

"Okay."

Cayden leaned over and switched off the Teledyne light, then took Kate by the hand. "Quiet as you can. Do what I tell you."

She nodded.

His gun ready, he led Kate around the two bodies and stopped at the shed door. He eased the door open wide enough to slip through, wincing at every groan the hinges made. Peering through the opening, he looked up at the cabin. He watched for several seconds, motionless, listening. Another Lynyrd Skynyrd tune drifted down from the cabin. An occasional shadow moved across one of the lighted windows, but there was no sign that the two men in the cabin had heard his fight with Craven. He wondered if Russo had even realized his girlfriend was no longer inside.

Cayden guided Kate through the doorway. They kept low as they moved around the building to the parking spot for the old pickup truck and the stolen Honda. Kneeling between the two vehicles, he surveyed the open stretch of parking lot. He preferred to retreat the way he'd come, over the hill and across the highway to the tree cover. But Kate wasn't up to it, especially without the benefit of a light.

He settled on a second best route, making their way through the parking lot. They'd be exposed for thirty feet, crossing the area at the base of the cabin stairway. But they'd minimize the risk by moving across the open area fast.

"You okay to run?" he asked her.

"Pretty sure, yeah."

With a last look up at the cabin, Cayden took them into the open, moving at an easy run. He expected to hear a shout or a gunshot at any moment, but soon they were in the shadows at the base of the hill. They stumbled a few times on small rocks along the way, but stayed on their feet, and a short time later reached the highway.

Cayden led the way down the mountain, staying on the road shoulder. He conducted a personal search as they walked, taking inventory. His tack light was in a jacket pocket, but Russo had taken his cell phone and knife.

They were now well out of sight from the café property, and he switched on the tack light. With the advantage of seeing where they were stepping, it took only a few minutes to reach the spot where he'd hidden the Ducati.

A wave of relief washed over Cayden once they entered the

cover of the trees. "Any chance they left you with your phone?" he asked, half serious.

"If only."

He retrieved his helmet from the bike and handed it to her. "Get down the hill and get to a phone. Call Mandala; he'll call the FBI."

"No," Kate objected. "You're coming. You're driving."

Cayden was shaking his head before she even finished. "Russo's still up in that cabin, and he still has the siphon. I have to make sure he doesn't get to use it."

"Come with me. Let the FBI handle it," Kate pleaded.

"Russo's going to find his girlfriend soon. When he does, he'll come looking for us. Get as far away from here as you can."

"Geez, Cayden. He's got that other guy up there with him. That's two against one."

He pulled the Ducati's key fob from where he'd hidden it and pushed it into her hand.

"Please come with me," Kate pleaded, as he rolled the bike out of the trees to the edge of the highway.

Ignoring her, he said, "You need to get down the hill and make that call."

He helped her with the helmet and watched as she started the bike, the engine growling to life. Kate found first gear and eased the throttle open. The bike lurched a little, but she got it under control, rolling onto the asphalt. She switched on the headlight and accelerated. The moment she was on her way, Cayden turned and started back up the mountain.

CHAPTER SIXTY

Cayden felt his way through the darkness. If Russo had already discovered their escape, he wouldn't expect a return visit. He'd switched off his tack light, but he was more familiar with the terrain now and made decent time back. Just north of the café property, he crossed the highway to the base of the bluff and began the climb upward. An unintelligible shout reached him as he reached the top. He hunched down and peered out from behind the trees.

Light poured from the cabin's open door. The silhouetted figures of Russo and the other man were halfway down the stairway. Within seconds, Russo would find his girlfriend dead. Cayden hoped it would put him off his game, at least a little. He'd be angry, and with any luck, not thinking straight. And the element of surprise gave Cayden an extra advantage.

The roof of the shed blocked the two men from view. A short time later, they reappeared. Both of them were facing away from him. Russo, agitated, paced back and forth. Cayden heard them talking but couldn't make out the words. Russo spoke in a normal tone of voice, but with fury in each word. Both men hurried to the cabin stairway and began climbing, taking the stairs two and three at a time.

Cayden started his descent, moving fast from tree to tree. He reached the bottom of the slope and stayed low, running for the rear corner of the café. He made it to cover mere seconds before Russo and his friend reappeared in the cabin doorway. They slammed the door shut and hurried down the stairs. Russo was now wearing a hunter green parka. The other man wore a dark leather jacket and a tweed Irish flat cap. They were moving out.

Cayden raised the Beretta. They didn't know he was there. He'd get them both before either of them could reach a gun. As he prepared to fire, the glow of moving headlights washed over the two men. Guns appeared in their hands as if by magic. The sound of tires rolling across the gravel slowed and stopped. A car door opened. Footsteps sounded on the gravel, but the car door never shut, and the engine kept idling. Whoever it was stopped outside his field of view.

"What's this?" Russo asked the new arrival, lowering his gun.

Taking his lead from Russo, the other man lowered his gun as well.

"Just listen to me," a man's familiar voice came from the opposite side of the café.

"What are you doing here?" Russo said, his tone unpleasant.

"I have the new decryption code."

"What are you talking about? We took the new code off March when he came to get the woman."

Special Agent Langford walked into view, stopping several feet short of Russo and the other man. He held a gun in his right hand, its muzzle pointing downward. "Impossible. March never had access to it."

Cayden felt little surprise at Langford showing up. He'd suspected an FBI leak.

Now Russo looked flustered. "You claimed you couldn't get to it."

"I came up with a way, and I got lucky," Langford answered, pride in his voice.

"You don't have it," Russo snapped.

The man with Russo stepped forward. "You can't be sure we have it. The drive you took from March never unlocked the weapon."

Cayden thought he heard Serbian in the accent.

Russo shook his head. "We probably didn't give it enough time."

"You should listen to Bojan," Langford said. "I don't know what March fed you, but it isn't the real thing."

Cayden focused on the man next to Russo. Now he had a name.

"Come, give me what you have," Bojan ordered.

"I need something first," Langford said.

"Don't play games with us," Russo snarled.

"You think I'd be stupid enough to have it on me?" Langford said. "No. First, you're going to call Dragović. Tell him I give you the drive only if he guarantees my debt is paid in full. I hand it over and we're even. We're done. I owe him nothing ever again. Call him now."

The moment Langford finished speaking, Russo raised his gun and fired two rounds into his forehead. The echoes of the gunfire were still fading away as Langford crumpled to the ground. Russo and Bojan put away their weapons. Bojan kneeled beside Langford's body and rifled through his pockets.

If Langford had been stupid enough to have the code on him, then Cayden had to get hold of it. He'd wait to see if Russo and Bojan found anything before making a move. The surrounding trees began rustling as a breeze blew down the mountainside.

"Anything?" Russo asked.

"No," Bojan answered. "He couldn't be so stupid as to have it with him."

"Maybe not on him, but he brought it," Russo said. "He'd be too afraid not to, after waving his ultimatum in front of us. Search his car."

The men disappeared from sight as they hurried toward Langford's car. Cayden made his way around the shed, maneuvering past the open doors to the corner of the structure. He risked a look. Russo sat behind the wheel of Langford's sedan, the driver's door open, while Bojan searched the trunk.

The breeze grew stronger as Bojan slammed the trunk closed and walked around to the passenger door, a Remington semi-automatic shotgun in his hand. "He had this back there. Nothing else."

Taking the shotgun with him, Bojan began searching the car's back seat.

Five minutes had passed when Cayden heard liquid spilling onto the ground.

"I've got it." Russo climbed from the driver's seat holding a paper coffee cup in his hand. He tossed the plastic lid on the ground and poured out what was left in the cup.

Bojan joined him. "Show me."

Russo reached his fingers inside and pulled out a small plastic bag. "He put it inside the cup and covered it with coffee. Held it down with these fishing weights in the bag."

Bojan tucked the shotgun under his arm and took the bag from Russo. He unzipped the seal and removed the flash drive.

Russo said, "We can't launch it up here. Cell signal is too weak."

"My instructions are midnight, not before. There's time to find a location with an adequate signal," Bojan said.

"Waiting's a big risk."

Bojan pushed the flash drive into Russo's hand. "The hour matters to Mr. Dragović. Keep this safe until we're ready."

Cayden couldn't allow them any more headway. He raised the Beretta, giving up some cover as he positioned himself for a clear shot. At that same moment, the wind gusted, catching one of the shed doors. The hinges screeched in protest.

Russo and Bojan turned toward the sound and spotted him. Cayden cursed himself for hesitating as a pistol appeared in Russo's hand. Bojan brought up the shotgun with impressive speed. Cayden jumped back and dropped low as the shotgun boomed. The steel pellets blew a chunk out of the corner of the shed where his head had been a moment earlier. Sharp cracks from Russo's pistol sounded as slugs drilled through the rotted wooden planks.

Cayden leaped back around the shed in time to see Russo and Bojan taking cover behind Langford's sedan. He fired three quick rounds before he spotted the shotgun muzzle rising from behind the car. Cayden dove behind the shed as the shotgun discharged several successive rounds and sizable chunks of wood splintered off the building.

If he stayed where he was and they advanced on him, he'd be dead. He fired off two more quick shots as he moved back along the front of the shed. He'd make his way around the other side and use the parked vehicles as cover. If he moved fast, they wouldn't know he'd changed position.

He was nearing the opposite corner of the shed when Russo yelled, "Get in."

Russo didn't have time to kill him now. They were going to run. All they had to do was lose him, and Bojan would have time to launch the weapon.

Car doors slammed shut. The sedan was backing up as Cayden rounded the side of the shed. Russo was behind the wheel. Gravel and dirt flew up from beneath the tires as Russo cut the wheel, threw the car into drive, and punched down hard on the gas.

Cursing, Cayden rushed into the open, emptying his magazine at the car as he ran. At least three of his bullets bore through the rear windshield, but the car kept moving. The car skidded from the parking lot gravel and onto the highway, the tires screeching as they gained traction and sped forward.

Cayden watched with frustration as the sedan disappeared around the curve. He'd slashed both the Honda and truck tires. He had no way to get off the mountain with any speed. Cursing to himself, he unscrewed the suppressor from the pistol barrel and returned it to his jacket pocket. There was no need for it now.

The unexpected whine of an approaching engine pierced through the night. Cayden whirled around toward the parking lot entrance as Kate steered the Ducati into the parking lot, heading straight for him. He ejected the spent magazine from the Beretta, replacing it with one from his belt as he hurried forward to meet her.

"I couldn't just leave you here," Kate shouted over the engine.

"Slide back," Cayden yelled as he holstered his pistol.

He steadied the bike as she shifted her position and then swung himself into the driver's saddle. Kate's arms tightened around his waist as he shifted into first and opened the throttle. The moment the Ducati reached the highway he opened it up, and they sped down the mountain road. There was still a chance.

CHAPTER SIXTY-ONE

Cayden gave the Ducati more gas as they hurtled down the mountain road. The sedan was nowhere in sight, and the snaking curves of the Angeles Crest Highway made it difficult to estimate just how far ahead Russo and Bojan might be.

The engine noise fused with the wind created a screeching wail. He felt Kate's firm grasp around his waist as they navigated curve after curve, speeding down the narrow road. Not until he reached the base of the mountain did he catch sight of the sedan. Not more than a quarter mile ahead, a set of taillights became visible, moving down the straight expanse of highway toward La Cañada. Cayden opened the throttle, and the quarter mile gap shrank to an eighth mile. He was sure of it now; the sedan ahead carried Russo and Bojan.

Russo ran the red light at the intersection to speed onto the freeway ramp. The light was still red when Cayden reached the intersection. He ran it, speeding down the ramp onto the freeway leading toward Pasadena.

Cayden maneuvered through the heavy New Year's Eve traffic, having no trouble keeping the sedan in view. Russo couldn't lose him; the Ducati gave Cayden the advantage.

The traffic slowed at the northwest border of Pasadena. He and

Russo both had to reduce speed. Cayden muttered a curse, easing off on the gas.

"New Year's Eve backup," Kate shouted in his ear.

Russo veered onto the shoulder, speeding up the next off-ramp. Cayden stayed with him, following him through another intersection, and making the turn onto Linda Vista Avenue. The avenue ran through an affluent neighborhood along the edge of the Arroyo Seco. There was little traffic on this straight stretch of road, and Russo gave the sedan more gas, broadening the distance between them.

Cayden had no desire to kill himself or Kate, but he pushed the Ducati to a dangerous speed, determined to catch Russo.

Linda Vista ended at the junction of the 210 and 134 freeways. Russo ignored the freeway ramps, skidding onto a street leading to San Rafael Avenue. Cayden followed the sedan onto the long street. It was crowded with people walking to the Colorado Street bridge, a short one mile hike to the parade route. Russo kept his speed up, ignoring the speed bumps and forcing pedestrians to jump out of its path.

When the congestion of pedestrians thinned, Russo hit the gas hard. Cayden pursued him onto La Loma Road, and across the bridge crossing the Arroyo. The sedan turned north on Grand Avenue, disappearing from sight.

Cayden drifted the bike onto Grand in time to see Russo smash through a wooden barricade at the north side of California Boulevard. The two white-suited tournament officials manning the intersection leaped out of the way as the barricade splintered into pieces. Cayden maneuvered around the debris. The sedan was about a hundred feet in front of him.

Russo headed toward the Rose Parade staging area in front of the Wrigley Mansion, headquarters of the Tournament of Roses Association. That area always drew the biggest crowds, and Russo probably didn't know he wouldn't be able to drive through them. Cayden realized that he didn't have to. Russo and Bojan only had to ditch the car and then disappear into the endless sea of people.

He couldn't let that happen.

The crowd of pedestrians thickened, but Russo kept moving, forcing people out of his way. Cayden watched the sedan turn onto Arbor, a short block leading to Orange Grove Boulevard. Like all the other streets in the area, it was packed with people. He made the turn. The empty sedan was parked twenty feet ahead in the middle of the street, its driver and passenger doors open.

Cayden pulled to the curb and killed the engine. He and Kate hurried off the bike. Kate removed the helmet while he surveyed the crowd. There was Russo, looking over his shoulder at him as he disappeared into the throng.

"Find a phone. Tell Mandala what's going on. Tell him Langford's the mole, and he's dead."

Kate's eyes widened in shock hearing Langford's name, but she nodded and hurried into the crowd. Cayden looked at the spot where he had last seen Russo and took off at a full run.

CHAPTER SIXTY-TWO

A full out run proved to be impossible in the throng of celebrators. Cayden pushed through the crowd, clearing his own path. By the time he reached Orange Grove Boulevard, there was no sign of Russo and Bojan.

Wrigley Mansion and the surrounding area were bustling with television news crews, videographers, and a variety of other media personnel. The chilly night air carried the cacophonous sound of noisemakers and party air horns over the joyful shouts and laughter of the crowd.

Police presence was sizable as well, and Cayden considered enlisting their help. But as quickly as the idea entered his head, he dismissed it. Police procedure being what it was, they'd question him before taking any action. It meant losing valuable time he didn't have.

Cayden reached a pair of Tournament of Roses Association mobile office trailers parked near the corner of Orange Grove. He made his way toward the trailer closest to the intersection. Reaching it, he jumped up the steps to the landing and then climbed onto the guard railing. Grabbing on to a light stanchion beside the door to steady himself, looked out over the boulevard.

Orange Grove was a slow moving river of humanity. Heavy

vehicular and foot traffic moved sluggishly along the pavement in both directions. Celebrators walked alongside the moving cars or weaved among them as they crossed the street. After several long seconds, Cayden got lucky.

There was Russo, his green parka visible some two hundred feet away, shoving his way north toward Colorado Boulevard. Just ahead of him was Bojan, his tweed flat cap standing out among the baseball and knit ski caps. As if sensing Cayden's presence, Russo looked back and soon spotted him.

Cayden jumped to the ground and pushed into the crowd.

"Hey, watch it," a twenty-something drunk yelled at him as he shoved past.

Cayden moved forward, but he'd already lost sight of them again. He needed another vantage point over the top of the crowd. Empty bleachers, waiting for the morning's parade audience, rose upward from the sidewalks. Cayden pushed hard for the nearest one. A new, stronger determination overshadowed his desire for vengeance.

He jumped the chain strung across the entrance to the bleachers, and in seconds climbed a solid eight feet above the crowded street. He sprinted along the benches, searching the crowd ahead. With his new vantage point, it didn't take long to locate the green parka. Russo and Bojan were well ahead of him. Russo was looking back over his shoulder, but he was looking along the street, his line of sight angled away from Cayden.

He could see Russo, but Russo couldn't see him, and the bleachers enabled him to travel fast. The advantage energized him. By the time he reached the end of the bleachers, he'd narrowed Russo's lead by half. Cayden paused at the railing just long enough to scan the ground below. He vaulted over the rail, landing on his feet.

He reached the next bleacher and used it the same way as the first. When he got to the far end of the rows, he paused. Forty feet of ground stretched from the end of the bleachers to the television equipment scaffolding extending from Green Street and around the corner onto Colorado. A temporary chain-link fence spanned the gap to prevent anyone from getting under the scaffold structure. Russo and Bojan were dropping to the ground on the opposite side of the fence. Seconds later, they disappeared under the scaffolding.

Cayden jumped over the railing and dropped to the ground. He ran hard for the fence, jumped onto it, and pulled himself over. The scaffolding ran a good eighty feet along the edge of the Elks Club parking lot, rising fifty feet above the street. The standards, vertical metal poles bearing the load of the structure, created a narrow corridor.

He peered into the shadowy opening under the scaffold. Russo and Bojan may have kept running. Or they might be waiting for him in there. Cayden pulled his Beretta and checked the mag again. He would avoid using it if he could; there were too many innocent people in the area. Once he replaced the gun with his tack knife, he moved into the shadows.

CHAPTER SIXTY-THREE

The noise of the crowd was just as loud beneath the scaffolding. Some ambient light found its way through the structure, but not enough to cut through the shadows. Cayden listened for any sounds that might signal Russo and Bojan's presence. He was aware of his fear, but it was a good fear—the senses sharpening kind of fear.

Fifteen feet into the corridor, a scuffling sound reached him from ahead. Straining to see through the darkness, he glimpsed the dark silhouette of a man exiting the scaffold toward the Elks Club parking lot. He continued forward, watching for a second man to follow, but none appeared. Both men may have already moved through the scaffolding, opting to outrun him, but he wasn't going to bank on it.

Cayden advanced, scanning the shadows. As he neared the far end of the corridor, he sensed movement behind him. He turned in time to see Bojan drop out of the darkness from the cross pieces above, a knife in his hand.

Cayden sidestepped, moving in close to block the knife thrust, but Bojan's weight still hit him full on. The impact knocked his gun from his hand as he staggered backward with Bojan leaning into him like an NFL tackle. His back collided with scaffolding cross pieces, but he maintained his footing. Bojan wore a deep frown of rock-hard determination as they struggled, but Cayden managed to get a grip on his wrist, pushing the knife blade away. It wasn't easy; the man was built like a bull elephant, and just as strong.

Bojan countered, hurling Cayden down the corridor. He lost his footing and fell, landing next to the edge of the scaffold frame. Almost within reach, a pile of debris lay just under a section of cross pieces. Among it was a length of pipe, he estimated about three feet long. His gun was nearby, but the pipe was closer.

With Bojan bearing down on him, Cayden rolled within reach and got the pipe in his grasp. He swung it hard just as Bojan came at him with the knife. The big man roared with pain and anger as the pipe connected with his knife wrist, but held on to the weapon. Cayden used the moment to get back on his feet.

Over the next several seconds, they traded blows one for one; Bojan using combat knife techniques and Cayden deflecting each attack with the pipe. And then Bojan slipped up with a misstep that compromised his balance. Cayden moved in, smashing the pipe against Bojan's knife hand with all the force he could summon. The man howled with pain as the knife flew from his grip. Cayden repositioned, then slammed the pipe just below Bojan's windpipe.

Bojan staggered backward with the force of the blow, one hand going to his throat, the other slipping beneath his coat. The moment Cayden glimpsed Bojan's hand close around the pistol in his belt, he dove for his own gun. With the gun in his grasp, he rolled to the side. Bojan squeezed off a shot. The bullet slammed into the asphalt next to Cayden as he jumped back on his feet.

Bojan was about to fire again, but Cayden was faster, squeezing off three rounds in quick succession. The bullets plowed into the big man's chest, hurtling him backward. Bojan crashed into the scaffolding and fell hard to the asphalt, landing on his side, his arms twisted under him.

Cayden moved closer, keeping his gun aimed at the body.

Bojan still had a pulse, but he wasn't going anywhere with three slugs in him. Cayden retrieved the big man's gun, pushed it under his waistband, and rushed toward the far end of the scaffolding corridor. The entire battle had lasted less than thirty seconds; there was still time to catch up to Russo. Cayden couldn't, wouldn't allow him to use the siphon weapon. And he'd make certain the killer paid for what he had done to his friends.

CHAPTER SIXTY-FOUR

Cayden emerged from beneath the scaffolding, finding himself in the northwest corner of the Elks Club parking lot. Television production trucks and vans crowded the lot, along with several tented food service areas for the crews. Busy men and women hurried between the vehicles, some carrying equipment, others delivering food to crew members. Bleachers blocked access to Colorado Boulevard. The only logical route for Russo would be through the parking lot, south to Green Street.

Stressed but determined, he broke into a run, skirting past the food tents, and weaving through the production vehicles. His body ached with a heavy weariness. He was running on pure adrenaline now.

Cayden slipped between the parking lot barriers, emerging onto Green where the street ran downhill for almost two hundred yards before leveling out. Orange Grove Avenue and the throng of celebrators were to his right. There was no sign of Russo. The view from the hill gave him an advantage. There were fewer people on the street and he could see a substantial distance. In seconds, he spotted the back of Russo's green parka. The killer was moving fast, shoving through the people on the street, heading toward Old Town.

Charged with fresh hope, Cayden sprinted down the hill. He reached the bottom and stepped into the street, where there were fewer people. He began closing the gap. Russo glanced back and spotted him. He looked shocked to find Cayden still in pursuit. Good, Cayden wanted him shocked and afraid.

Cayden put on more speed, confident he could overtake the killer. A plan must have been in place to launch the siphon; a predetermined location and procedure. But he knew he'd ruined those plans. He was certain Russo had no definite destination. Now he had to ditch Cayden long enough to launch the weapon.

He watched Russo turn north at the next intersection, heading toward the parade route. Cayden rounded the corner in time to spot the killer rush past the barricades at Colorado, ignoring the two police officers directing traffic as he ran across the street. The traffic and abundance of people made following Russo a challenge. Russo was about a hundred yards ahead of him when he dodged into an alley. Allowing Russo out of his sight was dangerous; he pushed harder through the throng of people.

He reached the mouth of the alley almost a full minute behind Russo. The street wasn't as crowded as the main parade route, but there were still plenty of people. Cayden pulled Bojan's pistol from his waistband, and several of them cried out and scattered when they spotted the gun in his hand.

He kneeled down and chanced a look around the corner. Aside from several dumpsters pressed up against the brick walls, the alley was empty. No sign of Russo. The buildings were old, all of them brick, many of them built toward the end of the nineteenth century. The only light came from a single lamp hanging above one building's rear entrance, and it wasn't much. Cayden thought it unlikely Russo would wait for him behind a dumpster. He'd keep moving, looking for an opportunity to launch the siphon with no interference. Hugging the wall, Cayden entered the alley.

CHAPTER SIXTY-FIVE

Cayden moved down the alley as fast as he could while still exercising caution. As his eyes adjusted to the darkness, he made out several fifty-five gallon metal storage barrels against the wall to his right. Above the barrels, an access ladder extended to the rooftop three stories above. The bottom of the ladder stopped seven feet short of the ground with an extension that would drop to ground level with the weight of a person. The far end of the alley was a dead end, blocked by the back wall of another building. There was only one direction Russo could have gone. Up.

Cayden tucked the pistol into his waistband and climbed up on the barrel closest to the ladder. The wail of approaching sirens sounded in the distance. Somebody had reported him; a man with a gun. That was fine; he might need some help in a few minutes.

He took hold of the ladder, keeping his eyes on the roofline as he pulled himself up and got a foothold on one of the lower rungs. As long as he was on the ladder, he was a sitting duck. If Russo opened fire from the rooftop, there'd be no cover. If Russo was waiting for him to show his head at the top of the roof, that scenario was only marginally better.

Cayden reached the top of the ladder, keeping his head below the roof ledge and pulling the pistol from his waistband. Feeling a sense of urgency, he risked pulling himself up to peer over the roof ledge. The roof was flat, spotted with several ventilator turbines, most of them rotating lazily from the ambient heat left in the building. Two large commercial grade air conditioning units also occupied the roof. The nearest to him was about fifteen feet away. The other was at the opposite end of the roof, partially blocking a clear view of Russo. He was still alive because Russo's attention was fixed on the cell phone in his hand. There was no more time.

He launched himself over the roof ledge and sprinted to the air conditioning unit nearest him. Russo spotted him. Two shots rang out, the bullets ripping through the corner of the AC unit's sheet metal cowling, narrowly missing Cayden. The shots renewed his determination; he wasn't giving Russo the slightest chance. He'd end him and do it quickly.

Before Russo could get off another shot, Cayden leveled the pistol and opened fire. He advanced steadily toward the AC unit concealing Russo, squeezing off round after round to prevent the killer from breaking cover to fire back. Each round exploded with a sharp crack, reverberating into the night. He fired the last round from Bojan's gun, dropped it on the rooftop, and swiftly replaced it with his Beretta. Without missing a beat, Cayden resumed firing.

Four rounds fired from his gun, and he was now only about five feet from Russo. His bullets ripped into the corner of the air conditioning unit where he'd last seen the man. Five, six, seven more rounds. By the time he fired the eighth round, he was at the corner of the unit with two rounds remaining. He leaped around the corner of the AC unit, ready to fire, but Russo had crouched low next to the corner of the housing. Cayden was right on top of him, almost tripping over him.

With no room to raise his gun, Russo lunged upward, throwing his entire weight into a tackle as Cayden fired. The shot went high, the bullet grazing across the top of Russo's shoulder. Cayden hit the rooftop hard, Russo on top of him. The killer hammered his gun against Cayden's wrist until he lost the grip on the Beretta. As they struggled for control, Russo brought the muzzle of his gun up against the side of Cayden's head. Adrenaline surging, Cayden grabbed hold of the gun, twisting it away from him.

He felt himself sweat. His ribs were killing him, and he was tiring. But Russo's face reflected fatigue and even desperation. It worried him he hadn't seen the cell phone since first glimpsing it in Russo's hand. What if Russo had time to start the decryption sequence?

He sent two brutal punches to Russo's chin. The blows stunned the killer long enough for Cayden to break free and roll to his feet. He brought his boot down hard on Russo's gun wrist, causing the man to scream out. Russo's grip automatically opened on the gun, and Cayden kicked the weapon so hard it clattered across the roof, coming to rest just short of the access ladder.

Russo launched himself upward, slamming into Cayden. He kept his footing this time, but the killer feigned to the side, pivoting to deliver three quick elbow strikes to the side of his head. Cayden felt his knees go weak as Russo followed through with two more quick blows. He staggered backward, lost his footing, and crashed to the ground.

Russo bolted for his gun. His heart pounding, Cayden scrambled toward the Beretta some six feet away. A shot rang out and he felt a stinging sensation as the bullet grazed his arm. Cayden grabbed his pistol, dropping to his knees. Russo stood across the rooftop, taking careful aim. Cayden was at least thirty feet away with a single round left in the gun. He took a millisecond to aim and fired.

Russo lurched backward, blood spurting from a bullet hole just below his sternum. His legs hit the roof ledge next to the access ladder. He kicked wildly, attempting to catch himself. His boot caught hold of the railing, but it wasn't enough, and he toppled backward over the ledge.

Cayden heard a wrenching crack, ran to the edge of the roof, and looked over. Russo dangled upside down, the back of his skull crushed where his head slammed into the brick wall. His boot came loose from the railing. Cayden watched the body fall the three stories, bouncing off the storage barrels, and landing on the concrete.

He holstered his gun as he ran back to the air conditioning unit where he had first seen Russo. He circled around the unit, his eyes scanning the rooftop. With no sign of the phone on the roof's surface, he began moving along the ledge. Nothing. He turned back to the unit, this time looking upwards. He spotted it almost immediately, resting on top of the cowling about a foot from the edge.

Cayden retrieved the phone. The flash drive jutted from a USB adaptor, its cable hooked into the phone. The phone screen displayed the running decryption sequence. He yanked the cable from the phone, and the display went dark. A moment later, he'd turned off the wireless connection. He was working on removing the battery when he sank down to the rooftop, his back against the air conditioning unit. Just before losing consciousness, he sensed he'd conquered an old demon.

CHAPTER SIXTY-SIX

Cayden watched the cadre of uniformed officers and crime scene investigators busily going about their duties in the narrow space under the scaffolding. Once again, his eyes returned to the spot where Bojan had gone down. "There was no body when you got here?"

Detective Mandala shook his head. "There's a small pool of blood there, so you hit him. He may have been wearing a vest. One of your shots hit an unprotected area."

Cayden reprimanded himself for not following a basic rule of training. "I knew he was still breathing; I should have killed."

"You were in a hurry," Mandala said.

"Yeah."

Kate, her hands deep in her coat pockets, moved closer to Cayden. "If he's alive, will he come for you? More to the point, will he come after me?"

"Unlikely," Cayden replied. "If he's still alive, he'll be putting all his energy into getting out of the country."

She frowned at him. "You're saying that to make me feel better."

"Is it working?"

Special Agent Denbo approached, weaving his way through

the gaggle of police officers, his cell phone in his hand. "Our guys up at the café described how they found the Craven girl. Really March, an axe?"

Mandala's eyes widened. "An axe?"

Cayden shrugged. "It was handy. What about Langford?"

"They confirmed it's him. What he was doing up there, I don't get it. But we'll find out."

"It had to be about money," Mandala said.

"Not that this hasn't been a swell day, but if you guys don't need me anymore, I'd appreciate it if somebody could drive Kate and me to the hospital," Cayden said.

"I'll take you over," Mandala said.

"I'm okay," Kate said.

"You're going," Mandala ordered.

Kate fixed the detective with a steady glare.

Mandala continued in a more gentle tone. "You've been through a lot. It's a good idea to get checked out."

Kate sighed. "We're going to the hospital, I guess."

"March." Denbo stepped forward, extending his hand. "Thank you."

Nodding, Cayden accepted the hand.

"We'll need to talk with you again, but it can wait until tomorrow," Denbo said.

"Understood."

"Hospital, friends." Mandala began walking.

The detective escorted Cayden and Kate out from under the scaffolding. The New Year's Eve crowd was thriving, and a strong contingency of officers lined the bleachers' perimeter to keep back the curious onlookers.

As soon as they began walking, weariness penetrated down to Cayden's bones. The adrenaline was wearing off and his entire body hurt. It was possible that Dragović would retaliate for his interference in the siphon plot. Or perhaps it would be Bojan. Both men were something to be concerned about, but he put it in the "cross that bridge when you come to it" compartment. All the same, he'd be watchful.

"Well, thanks for saving the country," Mandala said.

"Not sure I did that," Cayden replied. "But maybe next time you guys can throw the rope around somebody else."

After a night and one day in the hospital, Cayden headed home with a doctor's advice to do nothing but rest. Rest was fine with him. His torso was bruised, and his face didn't look much better. His entire body ached and throbbed.

The moment he stepped into the hospital lobby, Special Agent Denbo hurried him along to an FBI debriefing. Once the FBI finished with him, Detective Mandala took over. Cayden had killed people within the detective's jurisdiction. The detective made it clear no charges would be filed against him considering the circumstances. But there were still formalities, and Mandala made sure there were no loose ends dangling. It was early evening by the time the detective chauffeured him home. He went straight to bed.

When he got up the next day, Cayden discovered he'd slept for over fourteen hours. The bedside clock displayed 11:10 a.m. by the time he rolled out of bed. It soon became clear his body had discovered a new level of soreness. And the bruised, swollen face he saw in his mirror was a new level of achievement. A hot shower proved to be soothing.

He had finished dressing when his doorbell sounded. The police had kept his Beretta 92 for ballistics testing, so he pulled the M9A3 from the holster behind the nightstand and headed downstairs. The gun was probably unnecessary, but he was still edgy from the recent events.

Thomas March appeared on the surveillance display wearing a tailored charcoal suit. Cayden couldn't remember the last time his father had visited the house.

He tucked the gun into his waistband at the small of his back, put on a pleasant smile, and opened the door. "Dad, come in." He hoped the surprise washing over him wasn't apparent in his tone.

As he stepped through the doorway, his father's brow furrowed at seeing his son's battered face. "Good Lord. How does that feel?"

"Pretty much the way it looks."

"Word reached me this morning you'd been injured. Something about you helping the police and FBI, but no other details. I was concerned."

It felt strange. Over the years, his father had rarely shown concern of any kind. But Cayden sensed his visit was a positive thing. "I'm doing okay. Not at my best now, but I'm going to live."

His father's gaze raked over him slowly before he said, "I'd like to hear what happened."

Cayden shrugged. "I got knocked around a little by some people the FBI was looking for."

A moment of impatience flashed across Thomas March's face. "That's all you'll tell me?"

"Not much more I can say. The reason your source had no details is national security is involved. The FBI wouldn't appreciate me sharing."

For the first time since his arrival, his father smiled. "Ah, national security. I have a contact who can help me with that."

It surprised Cayden to hear himself laugh. "I was about to make some coffee. Join me?"

"Thanks, but no. The rest of my day is quite full, but I wanted to drop this off myself," his father said, pulling a blank envelope from his coat pocket and handing it to him.

Cayden pulled open the envelope flap. Inside was a check for $15,000. A deep sense of relief washed over him. "I *will* get this back to you."

"Damn right you will," his father answered, all business. But then the edge left his tone. "At your convenience."

"You know I appreciate this," Cayden said.

Thomas March acknowledged the comment with a thin smile. "I'll be on my way."

Cayden watched his father turn and walked toward the driveway. Something between them seemed different to him. It was hard to pinpoint what it was, but something had changed. Whatever it was, he was at peace with it.

Closing the door, he headed down to the kitchen. He'd no sooner reached the ground floor when the doorbell chimed again. With an about-face, he trudged back upstairs. Kate and Jodi appeared on the monitor, their arms full of grocery and takeout bags.

The moment he opened the door, Jodi's mouth dropped open at the sight of his face. "Oh my God."

"It looks worse than it is," Cayden lied.

Kate pointed. "Who was that guy in the Tesla?"

"My father."

Kate's eyes opened wider in hope. "Property taxes?"

"Yes."

"That's so great," Kate said, and then spotted the pistol. "You told me there was nothing to worry about."

He glanced at the gun. "Just habit."

"So convincing." Kate said with an eye roll. "We figured you'd be hungry," she said, leading them downstairs. "It's a tad early for lunch, but we brought Chinese from Dragon Pearl."

"And groceries, just to hold you over until you're up to shopping," Jodi added. "Just sit. We'll take care of everything."

He put the gun down on the dining able, sat down and angled his chair so he faced the kitchen. Kate put away the groceries while Jodi unpacked the takeout food. They soon joined him at the table with the takeout, plates, and utensils. The first bite of food made Cayden realize just how hungry he was.

After several minutes of nonstop eating, Jodi put down her fork. "I never thanked you for getting that woman who murdered Mariana."

Cayden shook his head, feeling odd about receiving thanks.

Mariana should never have been murdered in the first place. He swallowed the guilt that still lingered. "We would've never had a clue where they were without you hacking the traffic cam system. And Kate doing what she did saved my life."

"Both our lives, thank you."

"So, what now?" Jodi asked.

"Once I stop hurting all over?" Cayden chuckled when he said it, resulting in a stab of pain in his ribs. Both women winced along with him.

Kate leaned toward him, her elbows on the table. "So?"

It was a good question. He'd overcome the fear haunting him since Rob's death. He'd succeeded in protecting Kate, and for the most part, overcome the dread of being responsible for her life. And there was new confidence in running an operation again, as improvised as it was. The biggest plus, his friends were no longer in danger.

"My plan is to settle back into my dull life," he answered.

Kate smiled. "Not near as exciting."

Cayden leaned back in his chair. "Fine by me."

EPILOGUE

Major Steven Dorn walked as quickly as he could along the pathway through a light drizzle of rain. Dorn didn't mind the tiny droplets accumulating on his cap and overcoat. A heavy shower had washed over Fort Bragg during the past two days, and this was the lightest rain he'd seen since it began. His right hand gripped a dark brown manila folder, the front of it pressed against his heavy winter coat. It wasn't a natural way to carry a folder, but it hid the muted red block letters spelling CONFIDENTIAL below the United States Army insignia and the coded file number on the tab.

Dorn waited for a supply truck to pass and then crossed the road to the walkway leading up to a nondescript two-story brick building. The sign beside the walkway identified the building as Fort Bragg Waste Management Operations. He entered through the double glass doors into a large room of cubicles. The sounds typical of a busy office filled the space as uniformed personnel went about the business of keeping the base waste free. Dorn pulled the gloves from his hands as he hurried down the aisle to the elevator flanked by two armed sentries. He returned their salutes, then waved his ID card in front of the elevator's magnetic reader. The doors slid open, and he stepped inside.

The atmosphere on the top floor was more subdued than on the ground floor. There were fewer cubicles and more enclosed offices. Anti-eavesdropping technology built into the second floor and integrated into the building design operated around the clock.

Every person in the Army knew that Delta Force existed, but nobody spoke of it much. And no one but a handful of executive officers knew of Dorn's special group within The Unit. Formed eighteen years earlier to deal with only the most sensitive and difficult of missions, his men employed methods that no government ever admitted condoning. He'd handpicked every man for the group and they underwent specialized training, even beyond the standard vigorous training employed by Delta.

Dorn exited the elevator and made his way to the small office suite on the opposite side of the building. The nameplate beside the door read Lieutenant Colonel Ernest Vindman. A sergeant stood from behind his desk and saluted the moment Dorn entered the outer office.

"You're expected, sir," the sergeant greeted him.

"Thank you, Sergeant." Dorn stopped in front of the inner office door, removed his cap, and tapped his knuckles twice against the heavy wood.

"Come," the muffled voice came from the other side of the door.

Dorn opened the door and stepped through.

Colonel Vindman, slumped in his tilted back desk chair, looked up from the report in his hand as Dorn closed the door behind him.

"Morning, Major," Vindman greeted him.

"Good morning, sir." Dorn leaned across the desk and placed the folder he carried in front of the Colonel. "Have you seen this yet, sir?"

Vindman flipped open the folder and scanned it. "Uh huh, First Sergeant March. I got the Secret Service report first thing this morning. Sit if it suits you."

"He saved the FBI's bacon, no question," Dorn commented, sitting down in one of the two chairs facing the Colonel's desk.

"I never imagined they'd allow him that level of involvement."

Dorn uttered a short laugh. "Doubt he gave them much choice once he got started."

"When the FBI came sniffing around about March a few weeks ago, you wanted to test the waters," Vindman said. "So I gave the okay. So what now?"

"Sir?"

Vindman's lips pursed into a thin smile. "You want him back."

"We were far from done with him when he chose not to re-up. I'm still pissed at myself," Dorn said.

"That you couldn't convince him to stay?"

Dorn frowned. "He's too damn valuable to lose."

"March didn't just assist the FBI. He took point and eliminated the threat," Vindman said. "Could be he misses the action."

"March only got involved because a friend of his ended up a murder victim," Dorn answered with a touch of admiration in his tone.

"So he's got a vengeful streak."

"It's more about justice than vengeance," Dorn said. "He didn't believe there was much justice in what we do here. That was one of his issues."

Vindman turned thoughtful. "Maybe, but it was the death of his friend."

"Robert James, Sergeant," Dorn prompted.

"Yes, Sergeant James' death. That's what sent him packing."

Dorn leaned back in his chair, as if surrendering to the circumstances. "At any rate, his leaving left a big hole. We had operations well suited to March's set of skills. We have situations developing now I'd assign him to in a heartbeat."

"If you think getting him back here is that important, move on it."

"Sir?"

"Once an operator, always an operator," Vindman said. "He needs to be reminded of that."

Dorn gave it considerable thought before answering. "I'll plan on paying First Sergeant March a visit."

GET YOUR FREE GIFT

Why Did Cayden March Leave Delta Force?
Find out in the Sergeant March Inquiry Transcript

Receive your FREE copy of the Sergeant March Inquiry Transcript and become a member of my Readers Group.

- Be among the first to know about upcoming book releases, cover reveals, and exciting announcements!
- Get exclusive glimpses into my writing process, deleted scenes, and entertaining and informative content.
- Limited-time Offers: Enjoy special discounts, signed copies, and exclusive merchandise available only to Readers Group members.

It's easy - just enter this URL address in your browser:
https://www.pgkassel.com/cm-transcript

Don't wait! Do it now!

DID YOU LIKE THIS BOOK?

Reviews are the most powerful tool I have when it comes to getting attention for my books. Honest reviews of my books help bring them to the attention of other readers.

If you've enjoyed this book, I would be very grateful if you could spend just a few minutes leaving an honest review (it can be as short as you like).

Simply visit the *Siphon* book page where you made your purchase (Amazon, iBooks, Barnes & Noble, or Kobo) and look for the "leave a customer review" link.

Sincere thanks in advance,

P.G. Kassel

ABOUT THE AUTHOR

P.G. Kassel (Phil to his readers) is a former film and television writer-director turned novelist. With over 30 years working in the entertainment industry his teleplays have been produced for television, and his feature length screenplays optioned by major studios and production companies.

Phil is married to an amazing and beautiful woman who puts up with all his artistic moodiness. They make their home in Los Angeles, California.

If you have any questions or comments for Phil connect with him online:

~

phil@pgkassel.com
www.pgkassel.com